BY ARTISTS
KAREN CAMPBELL
& LUCY BRYDON

How to Draw & Paint Magical Mythical Creatures

A STEP-BY-STEP FANTASY ART FAN'S GUIDE TO DRAWING AND PAINTING MYTHICAL CREATURES IN A VARIETY OF FUN ART MEDIUMS!

How to Draw & Paint Magical Mythical Creatures!

with Karen Campbell and Lucy Brydon

This book is a carefully curated collection of easy-to-follow and super cool Celtic, Fairy, and Fantasy-themed art lessons created specifically for those who are as obsessed as we are with all of this fun stuff!

For more information about our virtual monthly Celtic Collective Art Club (where projects like these are all we create!) and our Scottish Folkore Podcast visit us at **1scot1not.com.**

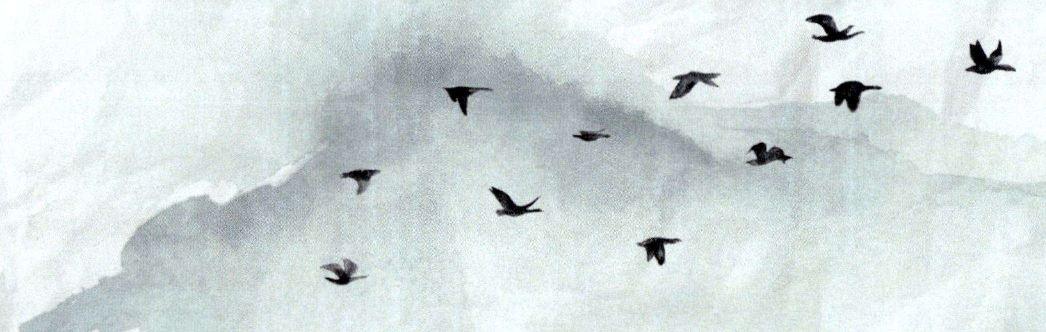

Author, Illustrators: Karen Campbell & Lucy Brydon
Publisher: Karen Campbell, Artist, LLC **karencampbellartist.com**
Cover Design: KT Design, LLC **ktdesignllc.com**
Editor: Linda Duvel

MAGICAL CREATIONS

From Karen Campbell

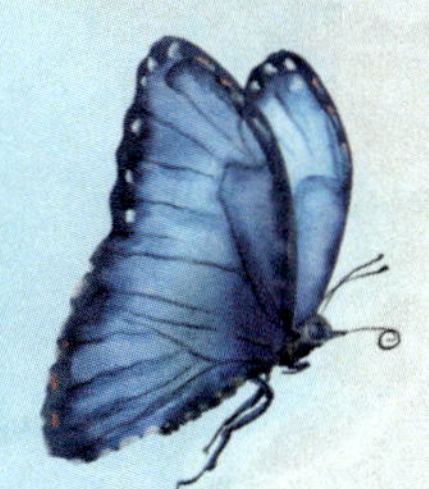

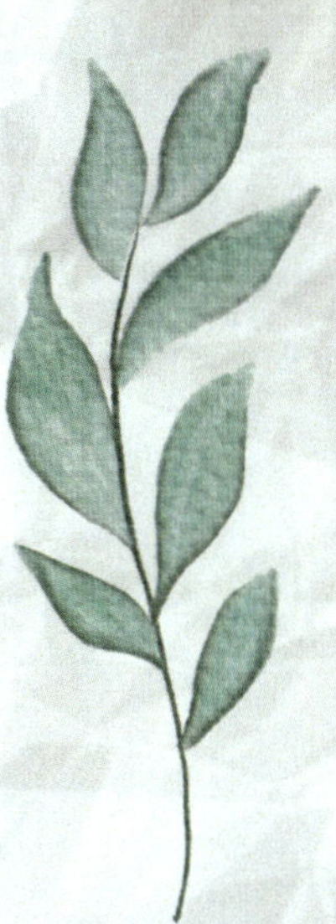

Who I am...

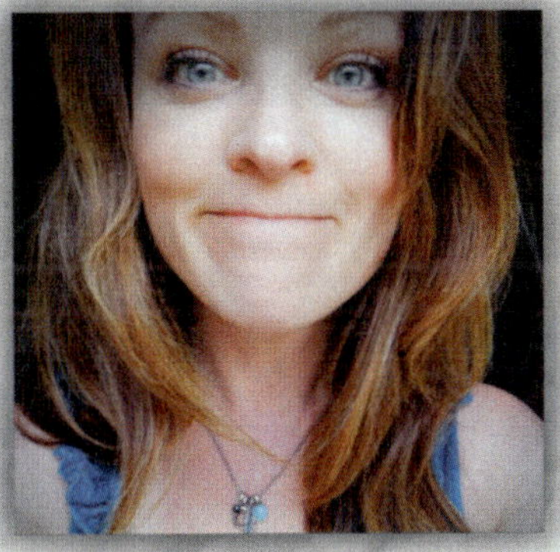

Lovely to meet you! I'm a professional artist, owner of AwesomeArtSchool.com and author of a slew of fun art books. My passion is igniting (and re-igniting) excitement in people who WANT to learn how to draw and paint but who may be too scared or too insecure to try! I also love creating YouTube videos so that I can reach more people than I ever could through books alone! Plus, YouTube is free and who doesn't love free?

My favorite way of getting people of all ages and abilities started is to make art as EASY and as FUN as possible! I'm also obsessed with fairy folklore and all things mythical so this book is a tribute to pretty much all of my favorite things, and doing it with my bestie art pal, Lucy, just makes it all that much more fun! We do lots of art activities together and we really hope you enjoy learning from us both in this book.

karencampbellartist.com

Mythical Creatures

From Lucy Brydon

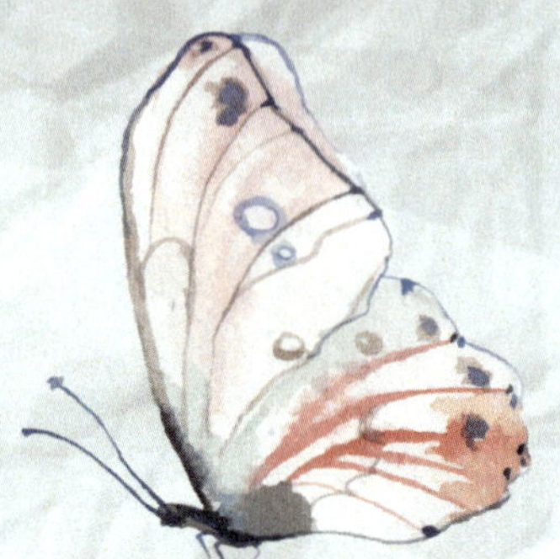

Who I am...

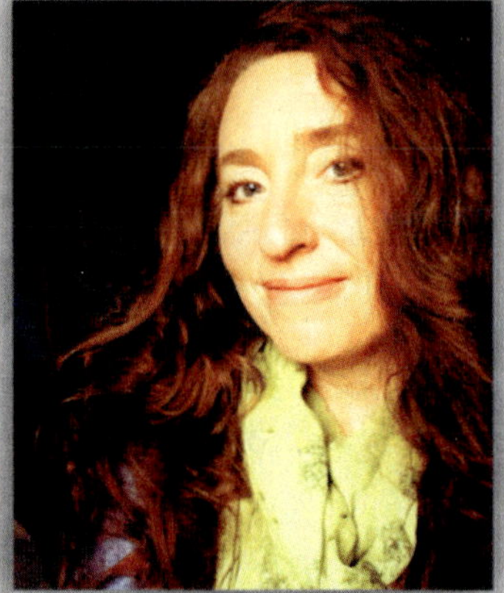

Hello there! My name is Lucy and I am a professional artist and art instructor living in Scotland! I worked as a primary school art teacher for nearly 15 years before deciding to make the leap into self-employment about 4 years ago! I love how I can take the teaching methods I learned teaching children and apply them to my adult students to help them achieve their art goals!!

As well as working on lots of projects with my bestie Karen, I also have my own online art school (lucysartlab.com) and sometimes teach in person too! It is so fulfilling for me to see my students enjoy learning new skills and having fun creating!! I can't wait to share my watercolor and gouache techniques with you!

lucybrydonart.com

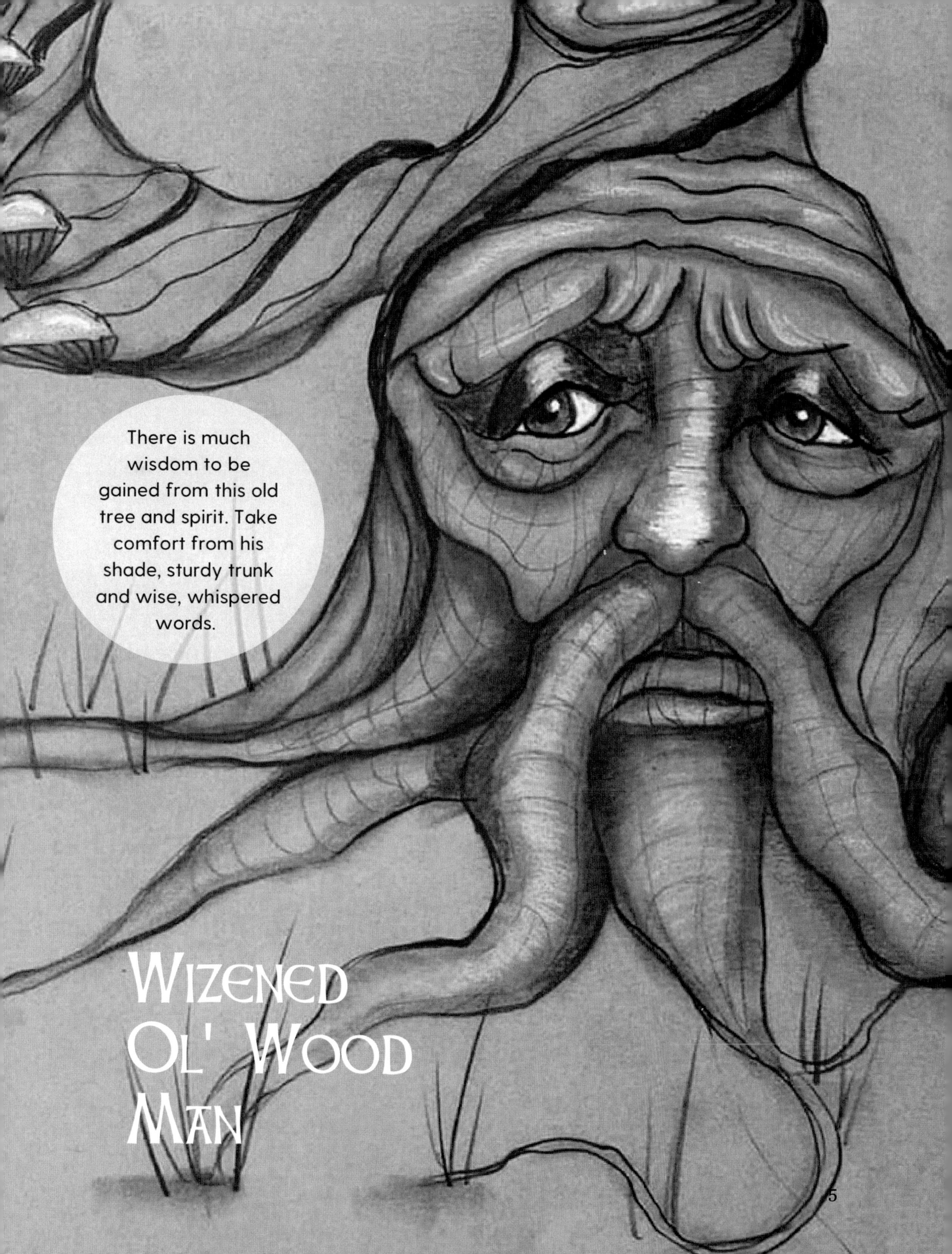
There is much wisdom to be gained from this old tree and spirit. Take comfort from his shade, sturdy trunk and wise, whispered words.
Wizened Ol' Wood Man

SUPPLIES

The true scale of this drawing is 30" x 18" - feel free to work at any size you are comfortable with.

A large sheet of toned paper.
This is actually a huge sheet of toned watercolor paper by Stonehenge that I ripped down both sides to make it look weathered a bit.

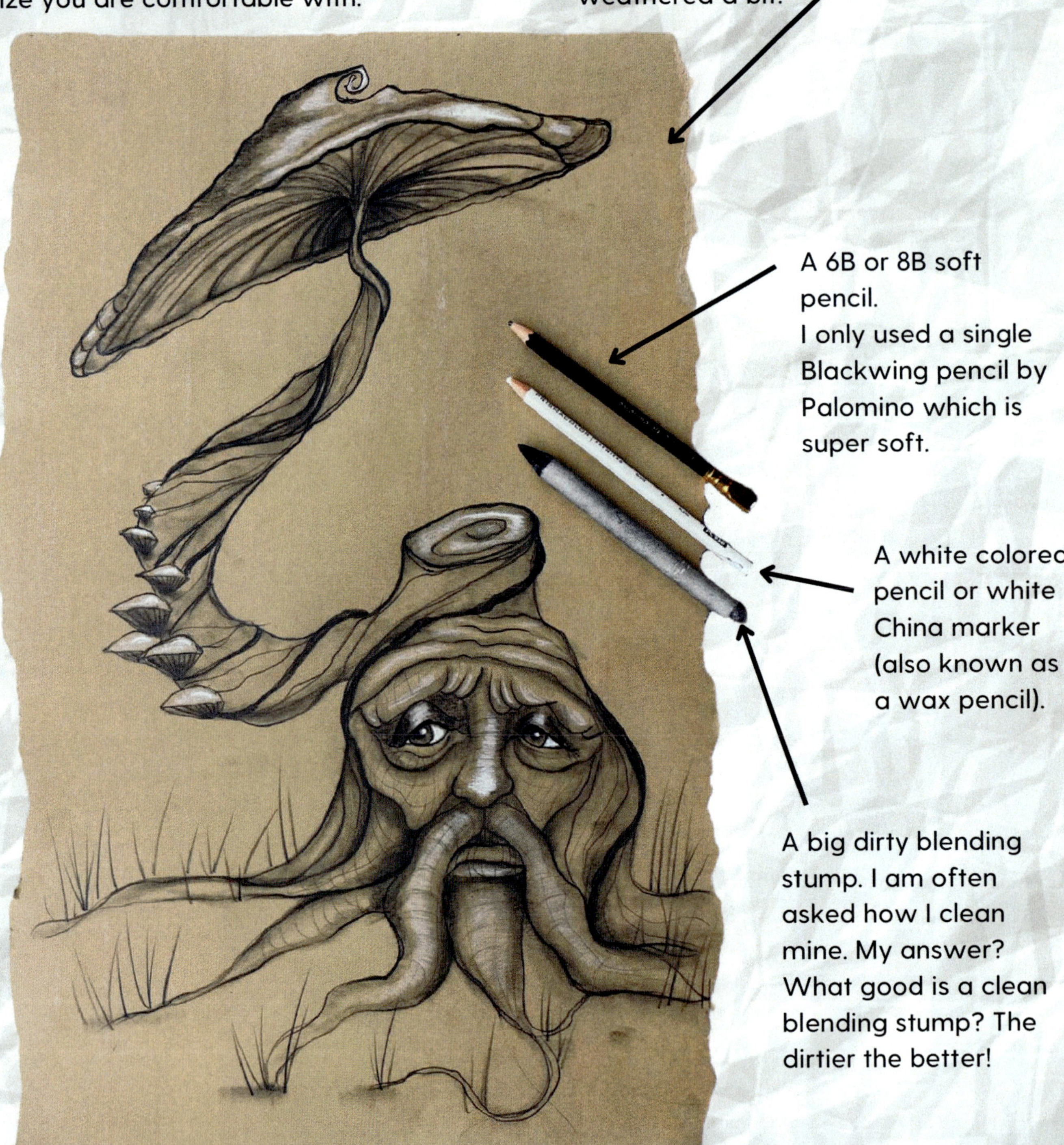

A 6B or 8B soft pencil.
I only used a single Blackwing pencil by Palomino which is super soft.

A white colored pencil or white China marker (also known as a wax pencil).

A big dirty blending stump. I am often asked how I clean mine. My answer? What good is a clean blending stump? The dirtier the better!

This is quite a large-scale drawing! I encourage you to use this image as your reference and guide throughout each step. To come up with this final drawing I mashed together concepts from 3 different sketches (by 3 other artists) to make this uniquely my own!

Start out by drawing a light and slightly slanted triangle shape like this first.

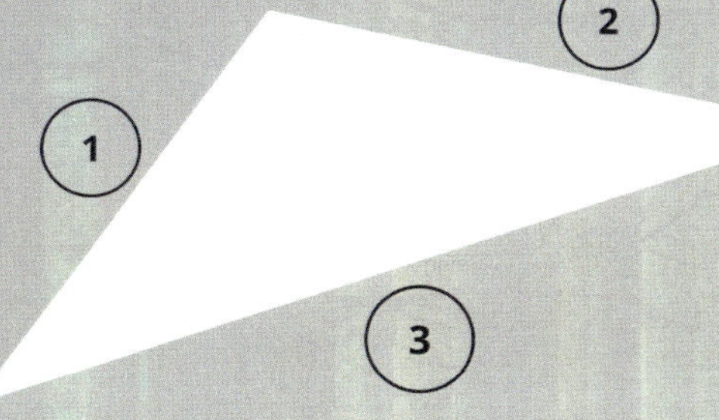

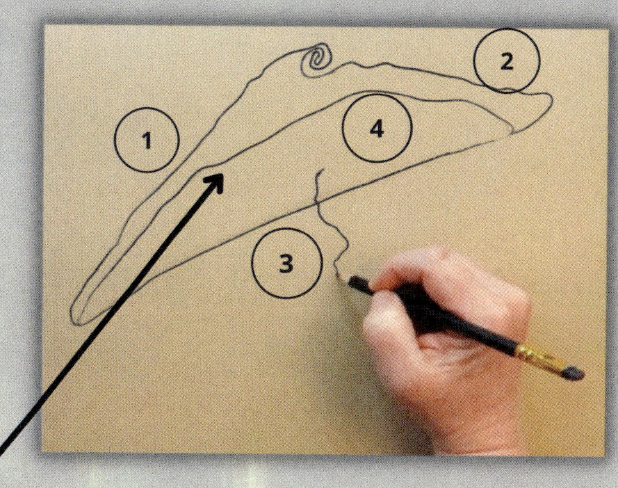

Then go back with your pencil and trace the top lines again. This time make them darker and a bit more wobbly. Then add the fourth line in. You can make that wobbly too! Fun!

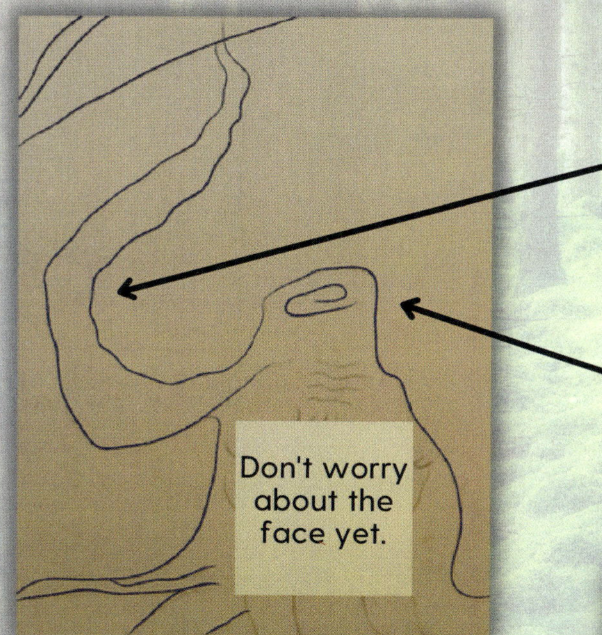

Now make a squiggly path out of two lines that go from the bottom of the mushroom top all the way and back up to the side of the stump (as shown).

Add a swirl in the center of the stump top.

We will worry about drawing the face a little later. Let's do the outline of the stump first.

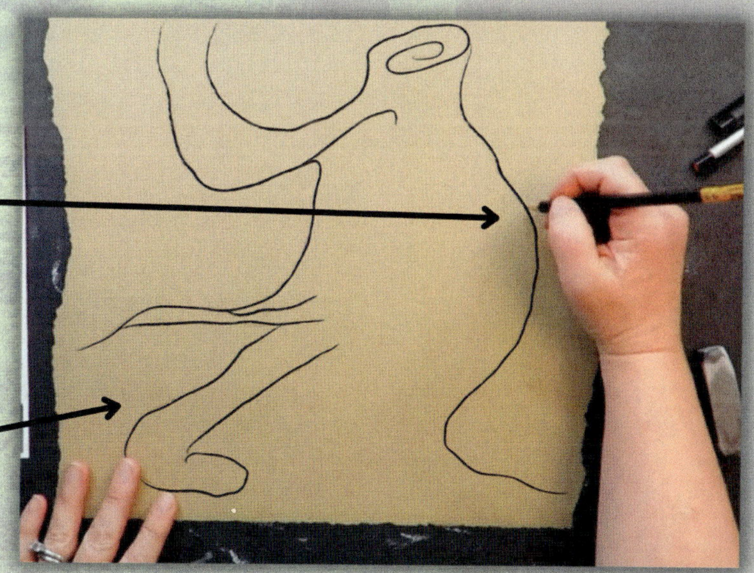

Make the right side of the stump curve outwards. This will be the wider side of the face.

At the bottom create more "legs" out of squiggly parallel lines like so. They should look like fat worms!

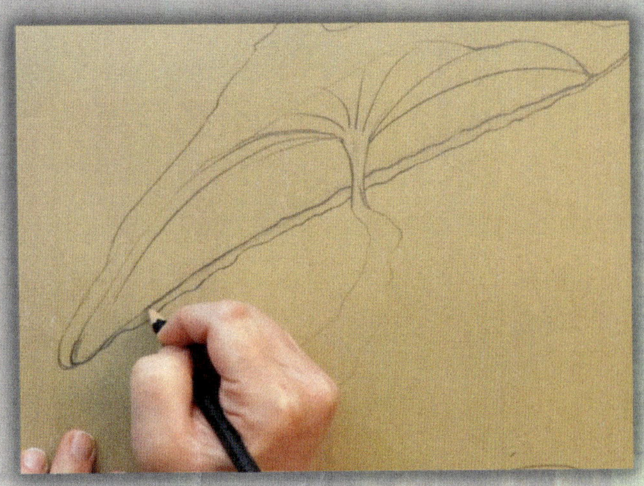

Now add a "lip" to the bottom of the mushroom (or line 3 of the original triangle). Make all mushroom lines nice and wavy and bumpy. It's nature!

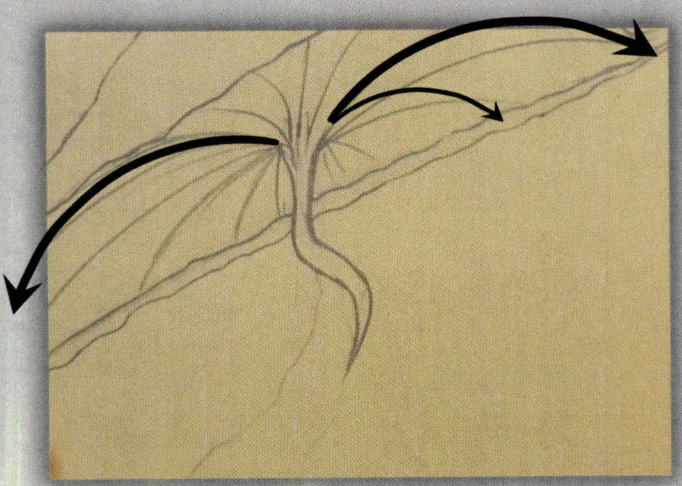

Then add swooping lines from the middle of the stem top, splaying out towards the sides. Continue until the lines go all around the underside of the mushroom cap.

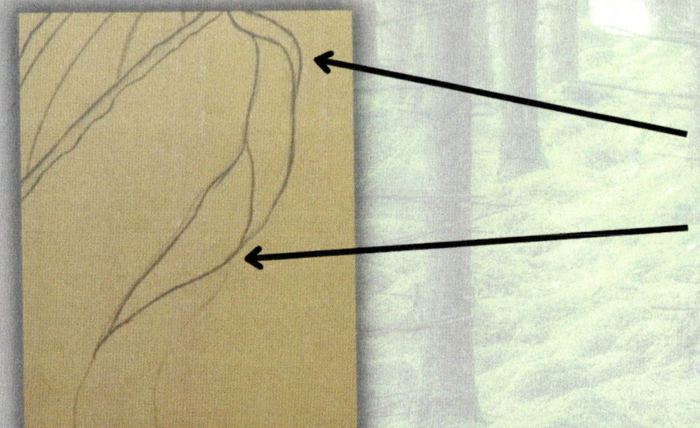

Using a darker pencil (or applying more pressure to the one you're using), outline the long stem and add a few loose lines twisting around it like so.

This is how it should look so far.

Next stop? The face!

Sharpen those pencils one more time and meet me on the next page!

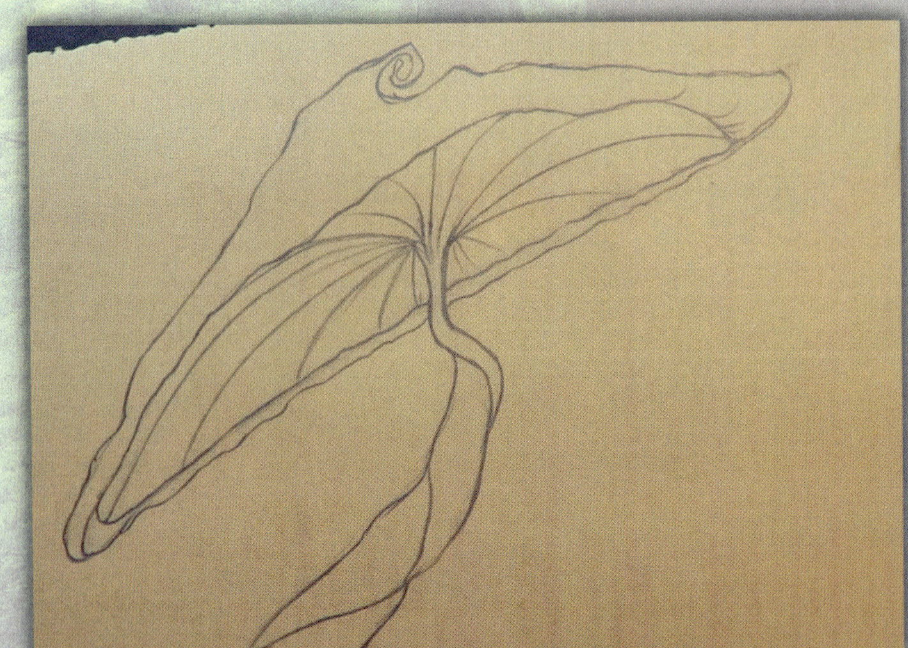

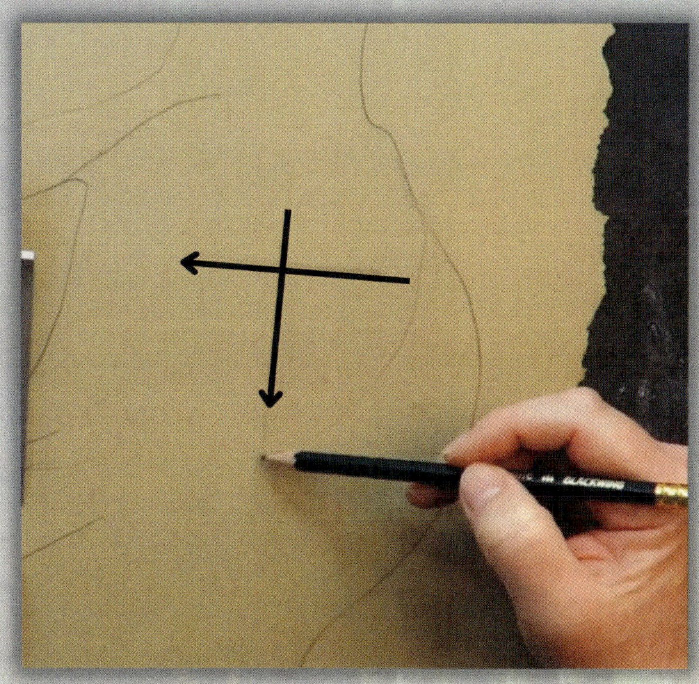

Crazily enough, it's still a good idea to draw in the same horizontal and vertical face guidelines for our tree man in the same fashion we'd do for drawing a realistic portrait!

The vertical keeps us centered and the horizontal line here is the eye line.

Go ahead and draw them in lightly, even if it feels funny to do it on a tree trunk!

Just like in realistic portraits, in this drawing, I still draw 3 ovals across to make sure that my eye spacing looks proportionate! When all 3 ovals look the same you can go ahead and begin to refine the eyes more.

Add an iris (circle) and a pupil.

A large curved line on top makes for a wonderful and real looking eye lid!

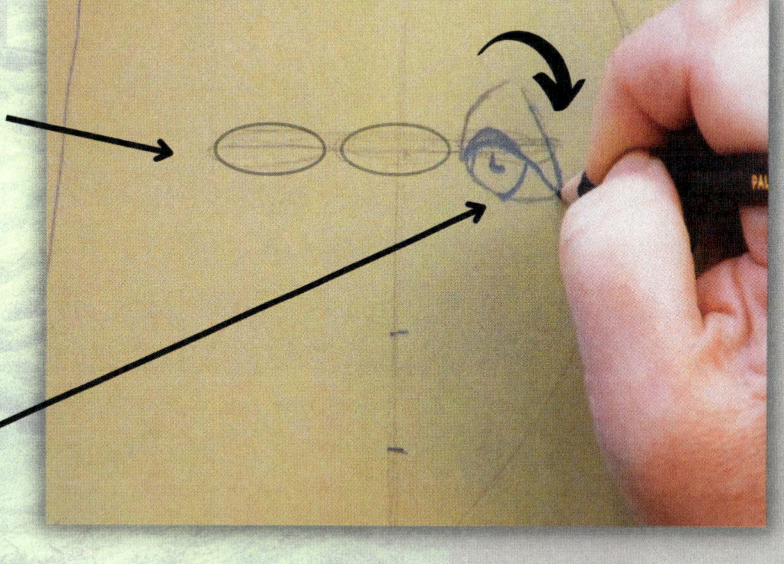

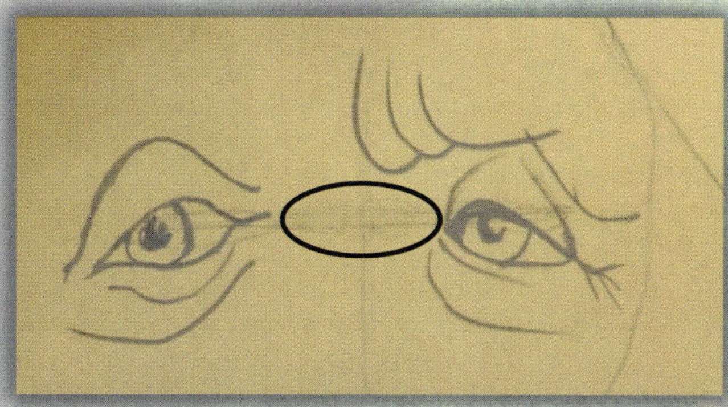

Draw 2 additional lines underneath the right eye and some wrinkles going off from the eye crease on the right.

When you're finished with the right eye, repeat the same process to draw the left one. Be sure to keep that middle oval in place and only erase AFTER you've completed both eyes.

He's a wonky tree dude so it's okay if his eyes are wonky too! That's all part of the fun!

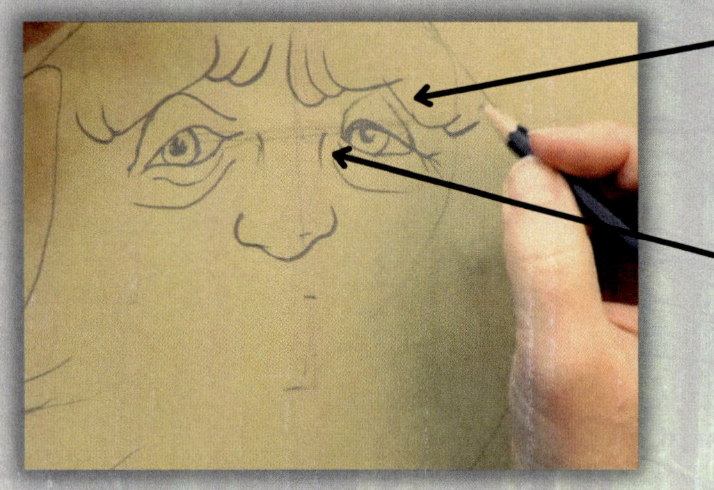

Add a series of curved lines over the eyes. These give the appearance of hair and/or eyebrows.

Then you can add a very simply nose shape. The bridge of the nose is indicated by two small lines at each side of the eye (on either side - right where that middle oval used to be).

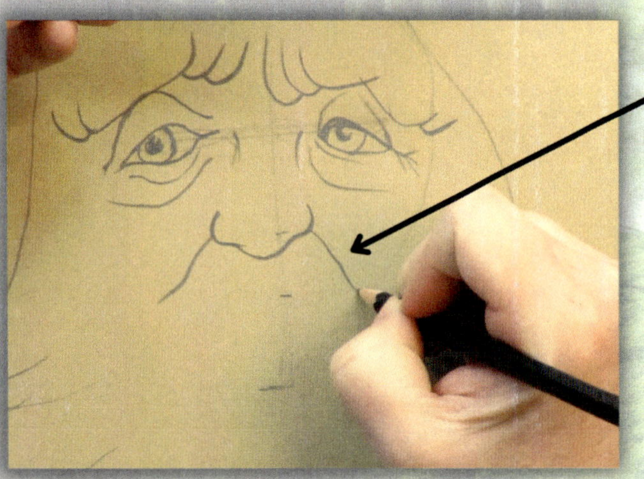

Then draw 2 lines coming out from each corner of both nostrils.

These lines then curve and swoop back up to create the appearance of cheeks on each side of his face!

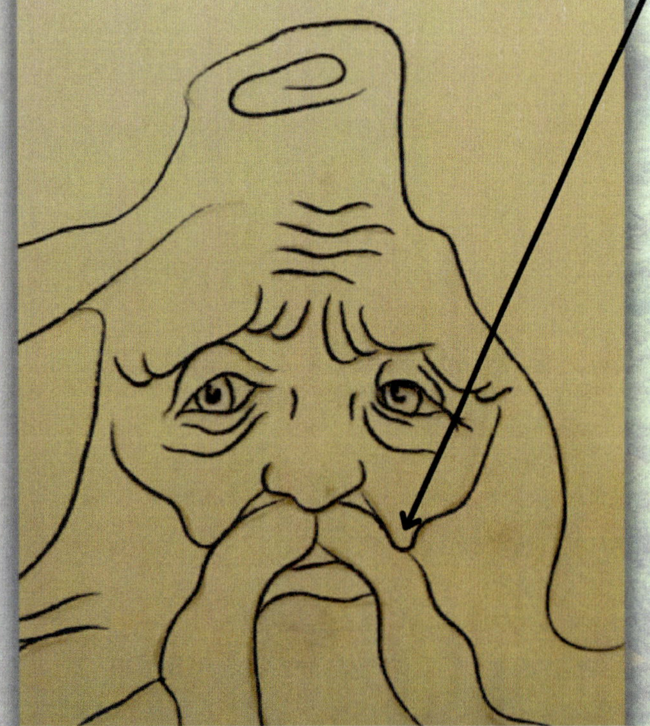

Under his nose begins his mighty mustache! The mustache is simply more of those large wavy tube shapes! Easy!

Add 4 wavy forehead wrinkles over his brow area. You can absolutely add more if you want to!

His lips are just two lines drawn under his mighty mustache! I made a super dark version so you could see the lines really well.

Doesn't he look almost human?

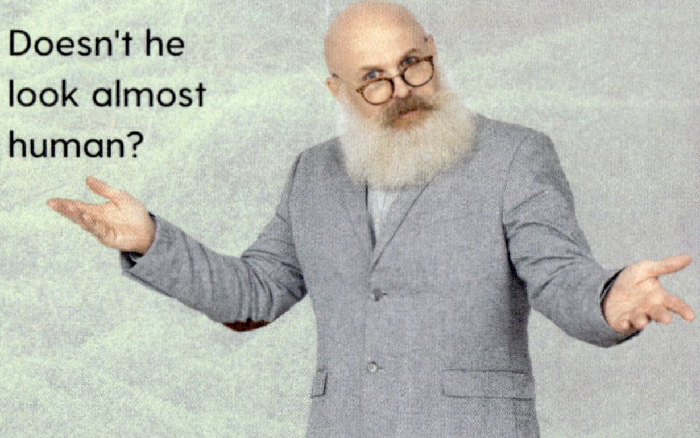

Now we'll get going on the details.

First let's add a series of adorable mushrooms, climbing up the side of the windy mushroom stalk!

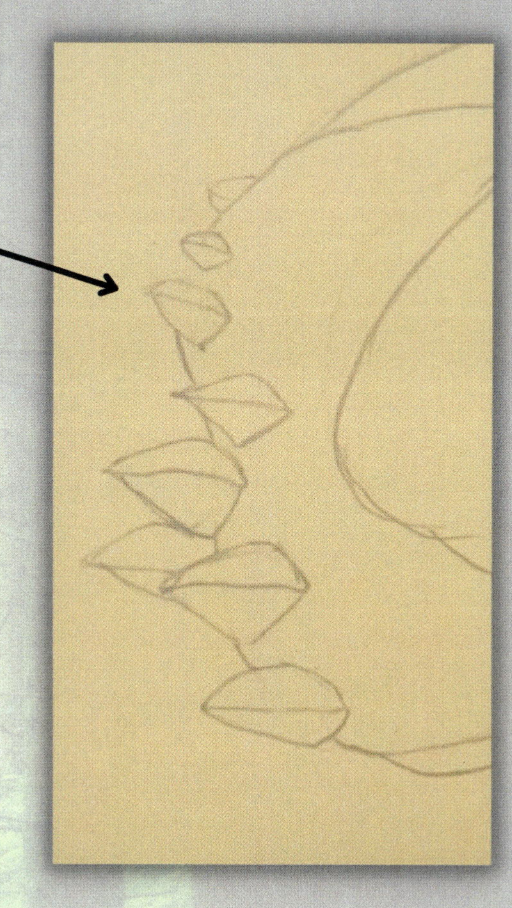

To make one like these, draw a curved line at the top and add it to a triangle at the bottom with a line in between!

Voila! Baby lichen! Or mushroom thingy!

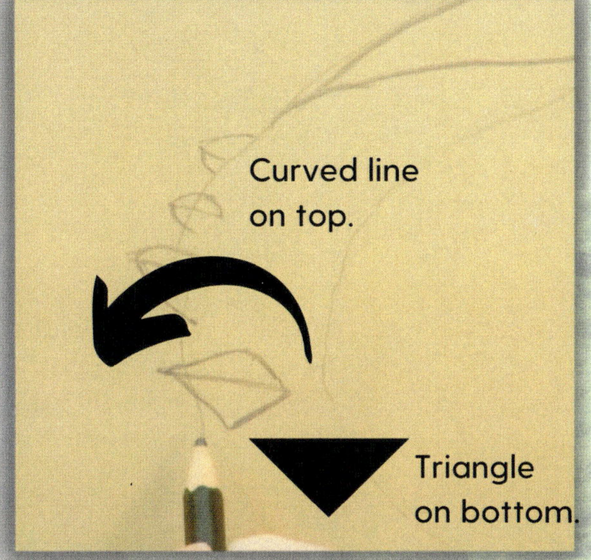

Once your series of baby lichen growths have all been added (and you've erased the stalk lines that were at first running through them), draw straight lines on the bottom (triangle) part of all of them.

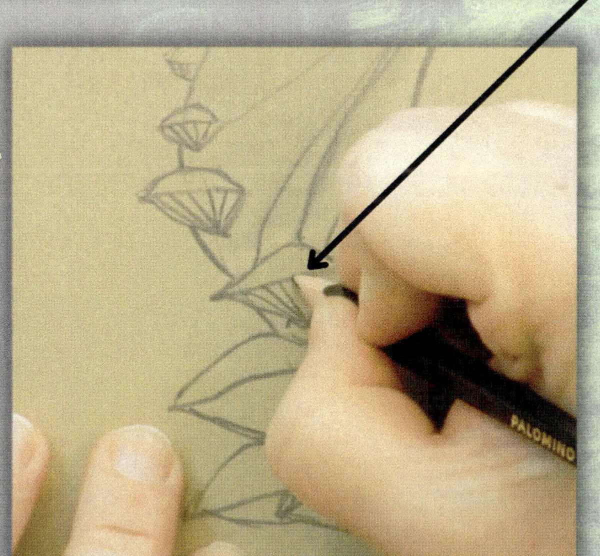

We'll soon be using our blending stump to add a TON of depth and drama to this piece!

But first we'll get those details in like adding curved lines to the mushroom top!

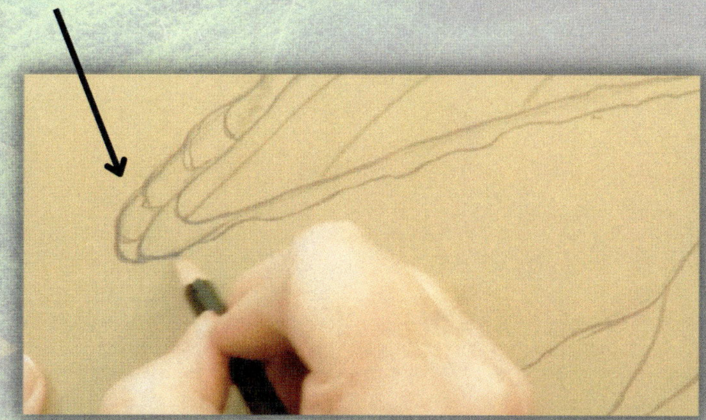

Sounds weird but now we're going to go around with our soft pencil and scribble in the areas that we want to eventually be darker (because they're in shade). I'll show you just where to go so don't worry!! After we "lay down" a nice layer of graphite with our scribble scrabble, we'll cruise around with our blending stump. The blending stump transforms those scribble areas into lovely shaded regions. Couldn't be easier!

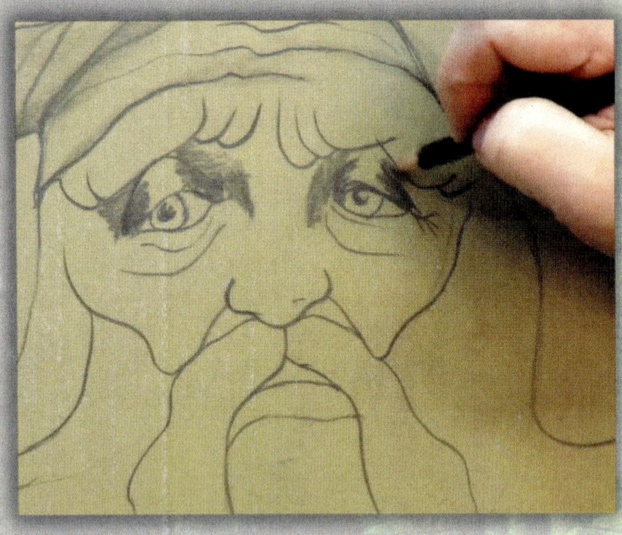

For small areas, use the TIP of your pencil to add scribbles OR to darken outlines. Like this:

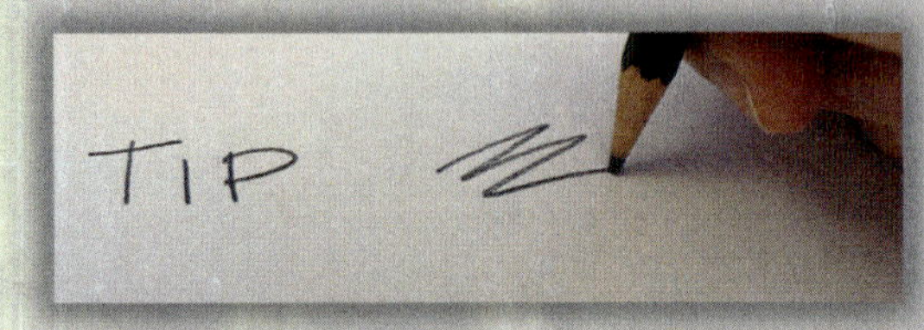

For larger areas, use the SIDE of your pencil to add scribbles. Like this:

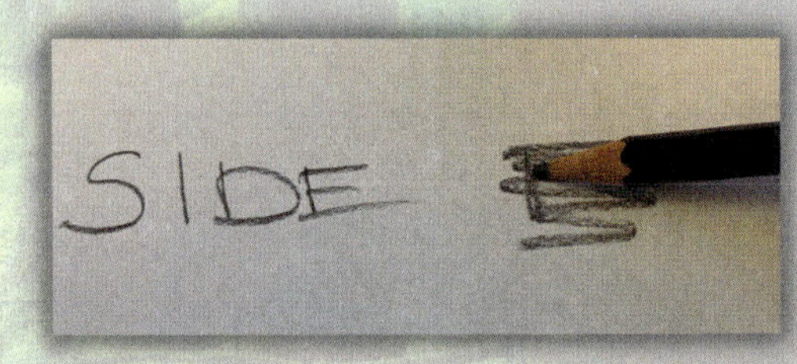

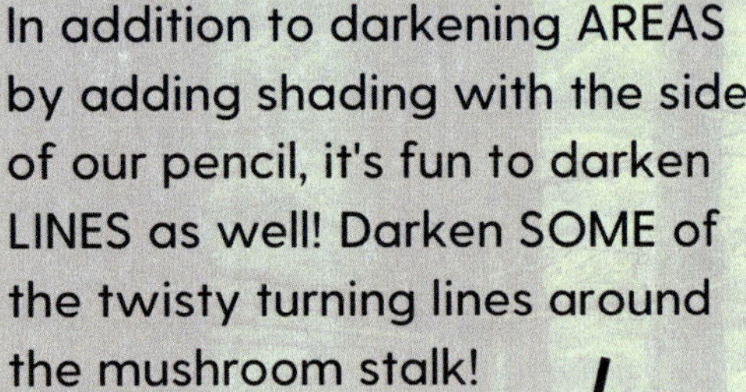

In addition to darkening AREAS by adding shading with the side of our pencil, it's fun to darken LINES as well! Darken SOME of the twisty turning lines around the mushroom stalk!

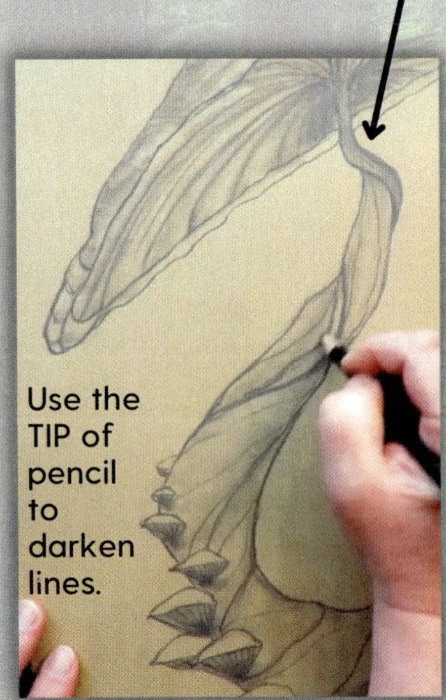

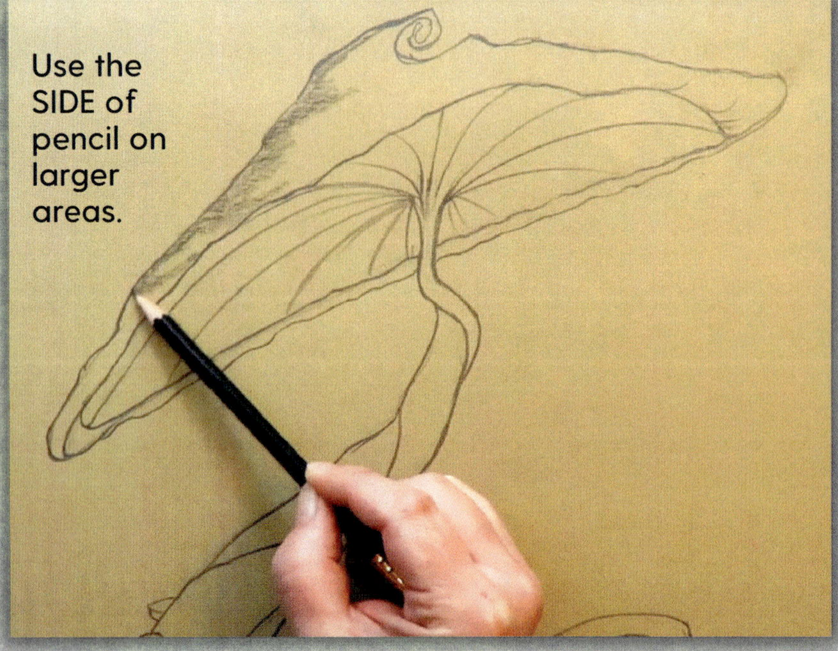

When all of the areas have been darkened with the graphite, you can now blend it all together using a blending stump. The exact same method applies for blending as it does for darkening and shading with a pencil.

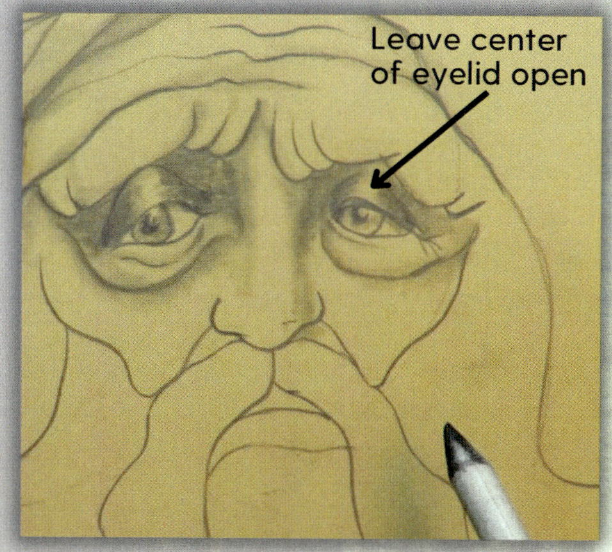

For small areas, use the TIP of your blending stump. You can also use a smaller blending stump as they come in various sizes.

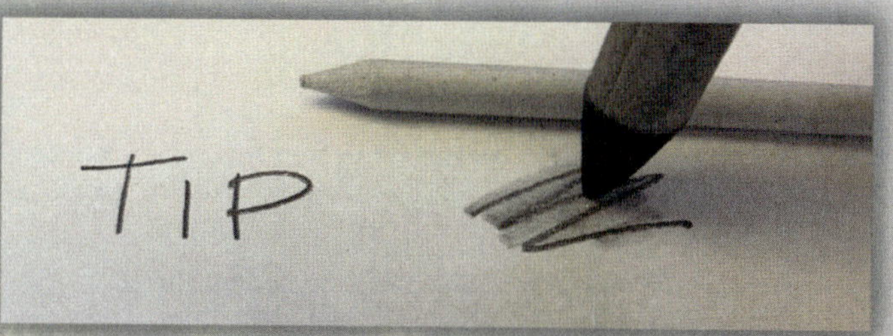

For larger areas, use the SIDE of your blending stump to smooth. Like this:

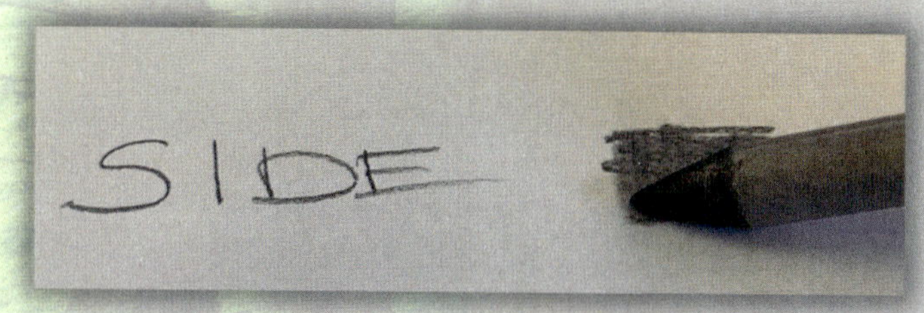

A good rule of thumb for shading is to make every object darker on the UNDERSIDE, since the sun can't penetrate to that area. So, top is light, underside is dark. Apply to all areas and you're good!

Work systematically around your drawing to darken lines with your pencil and to add shade in dark areas with your blending stump. Use my finished drawing as your guide.

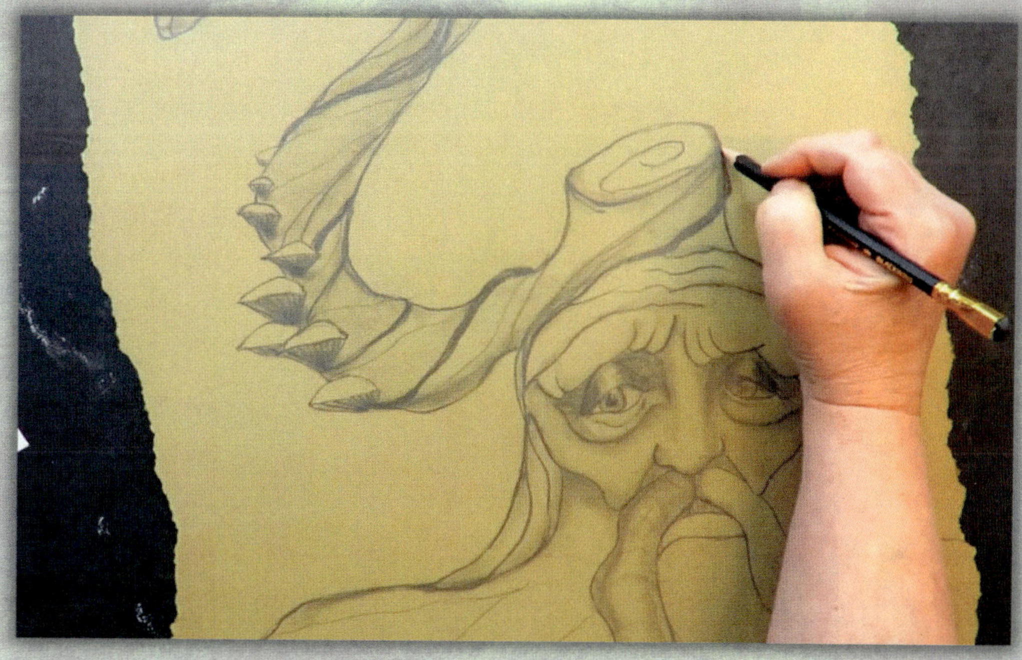

If you want to add a few last minute details that really make an impact, you can add both horizontal and vertical lines across and up and down the face. These are totally optional but they add a sort of "elephant" skin look which adds a super cool textural look that I love and encourage you to try! After that, bust out your favorite white pencil!

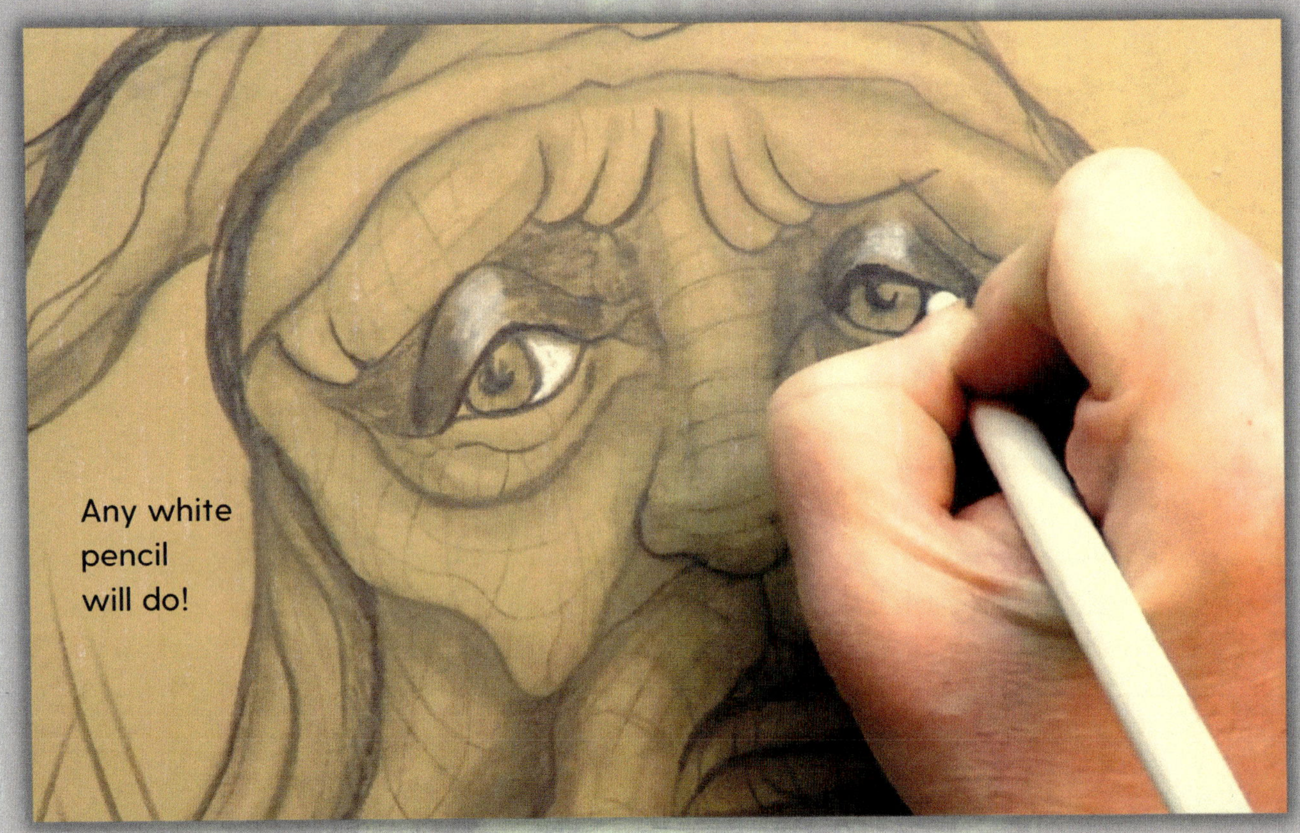

Now we are going to add pops of white highlights all over for drama and FUN! My favorite places to highlight on a face (person or otherwise!) is the whites of the eyes, the eyelids (center), top of nose, lower lip and any place that's "bumping out" on the face (so for this guy that'd be on his mustache or any bumps that would catch the light of the sun!). Then follow my highlights around the other places; they're easy to see!!

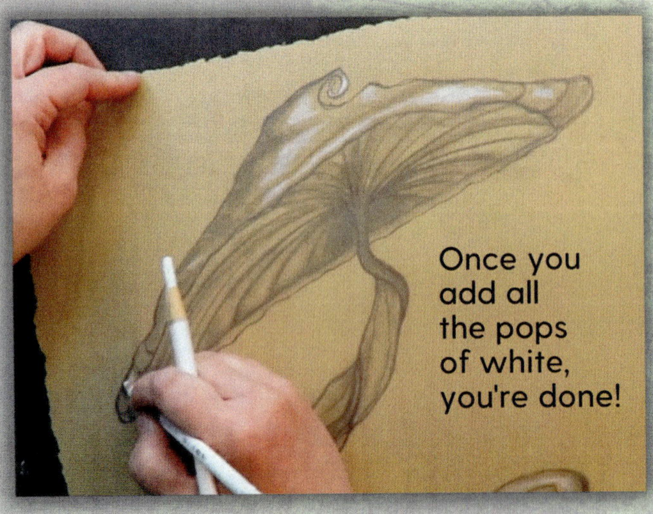

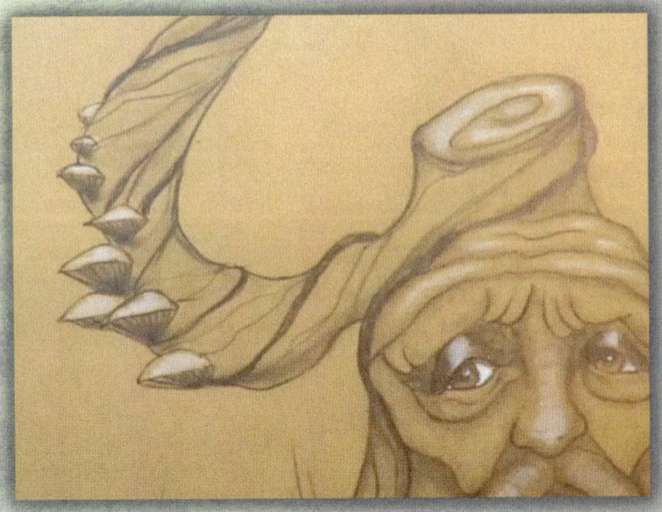

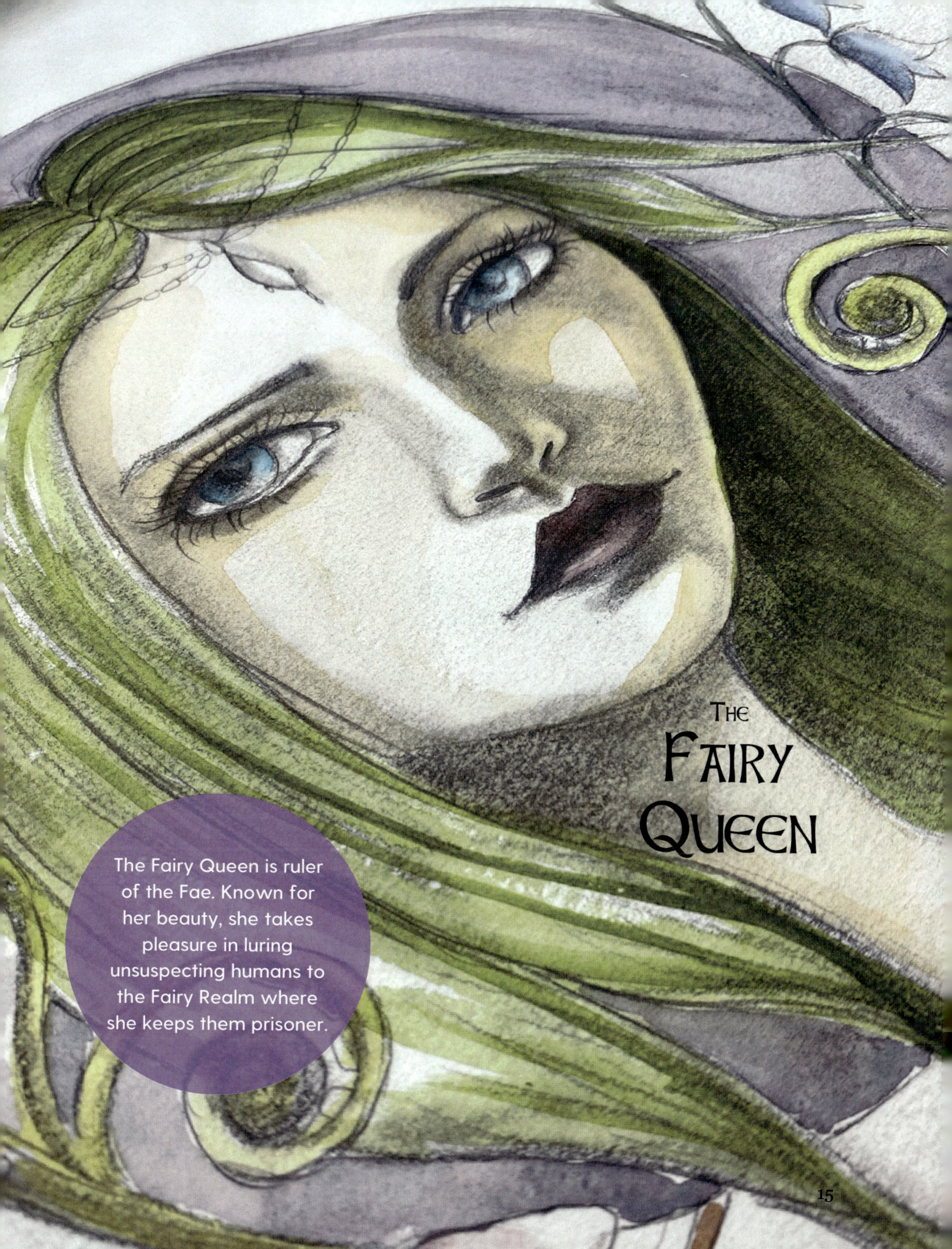

The Fairy Queen

The Fairy Queen is ruler of the Fae. Known for her beauty, she takes pleasure in luring unsuspecting humans to the Fairy Realm where she keeps them prisoner.

SUPPLIES

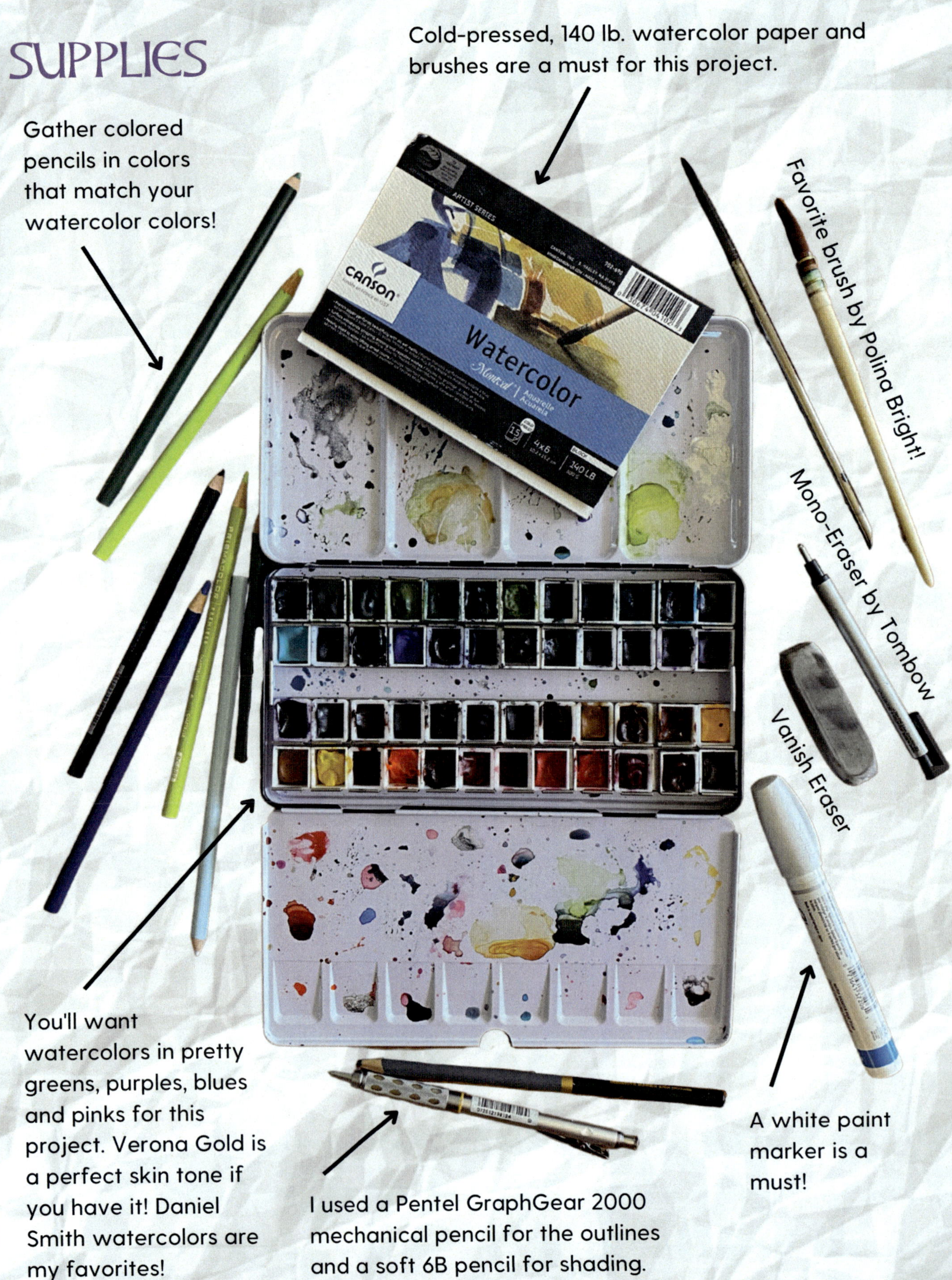

Cold-pressed, 140 lb. watercolor paper and brushes are a must for this project.

Gather colored pencils in colors that match your watercolor colors!

Favorite brush by Polina Bright!

Mono-Eraser by Tombow

Vanish Eraser

You'll want watercolors in pretty greens, purples, blues and pinks for this project. Verona Gold is a perfect skin tone if you have it! Daniel Smith watercolors are my favorites!

I used a Pentel GraphGear 2000 mechanical pencil for the outlines and a soft 6B pencil for shading.

A white paint marker is a must!

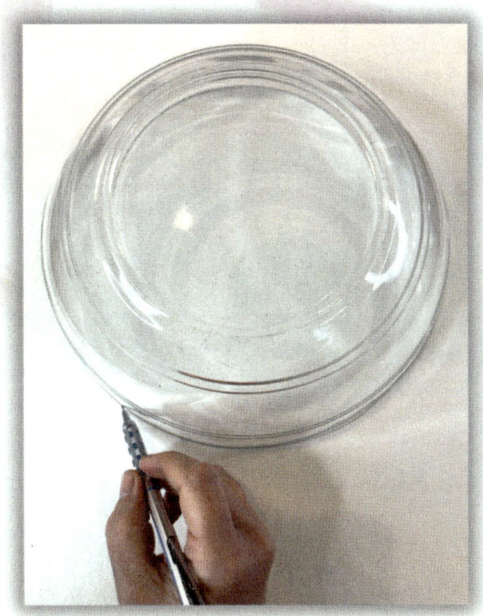

Trace a bowl to create a circle large enough to draw a face inside and flowers around it.

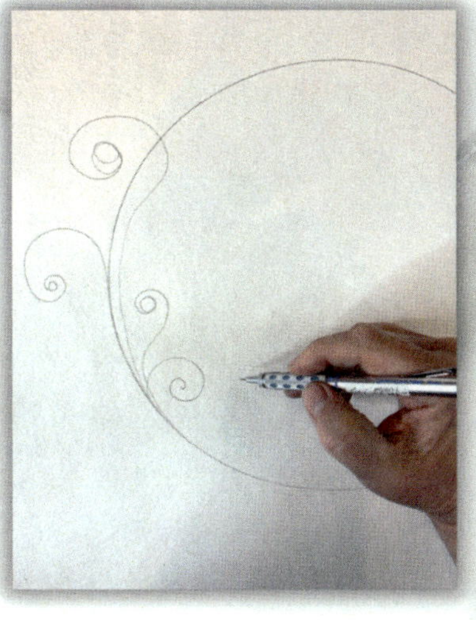

With your pencil, add swirly lines along one side of the circle, create as many or as few as you'd like.

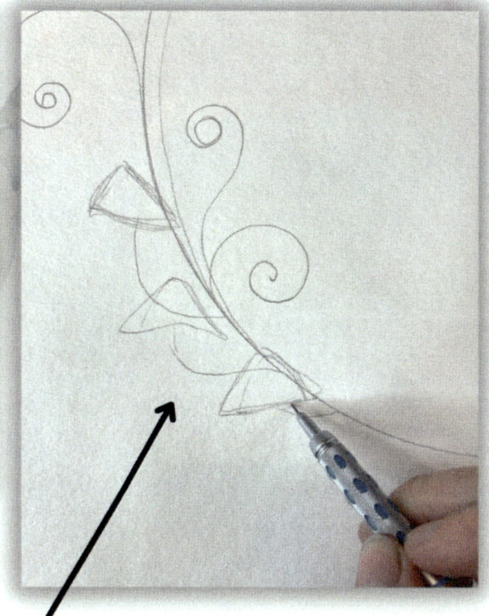

Add a trio of loose triangles with stems to create adorable little mushroom tops!

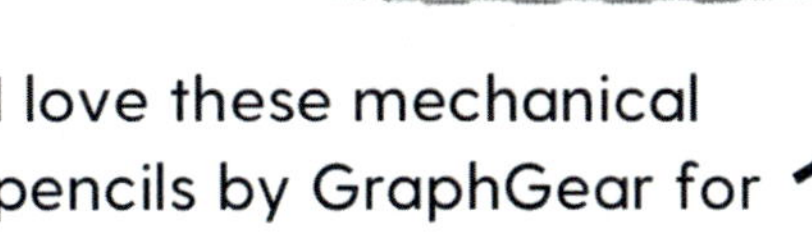

I love these mechanical pencils by GraphGear for making precise lines!

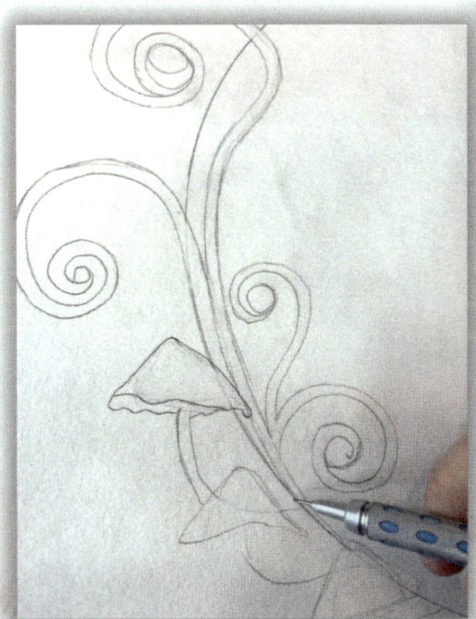

Add thickness to all your single-swirl line designs and mushroom stems. We will be adding color later.

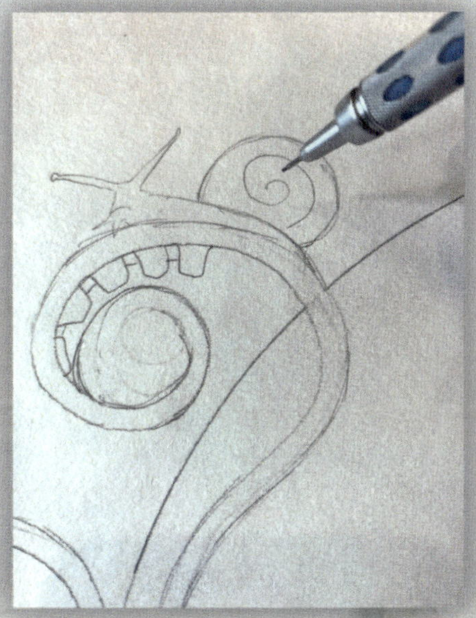

Use your imagination and have fun with the little flowers and details that decorate the sides of the circles. I added a wee snail up at the top of one of the fronds just for fun!

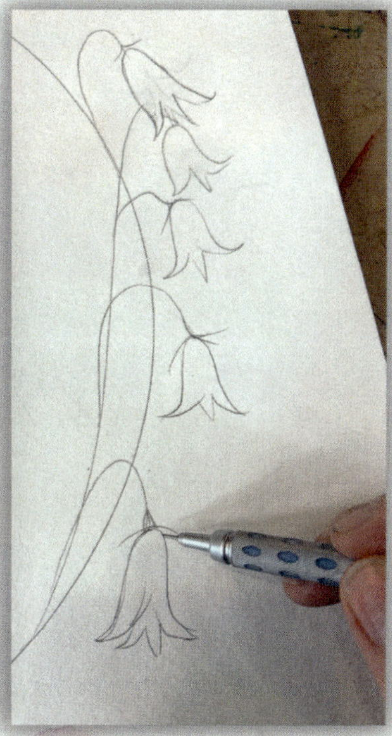

Draw a series of bell shape flowers along the right side. Add as many or as few as you like. Be creative here!

Now we will begin to draw our Fairy Queen! In the upper portion of the circle that we drew with our bowl, draw an oval for the head. The head should be "egg" shaped.

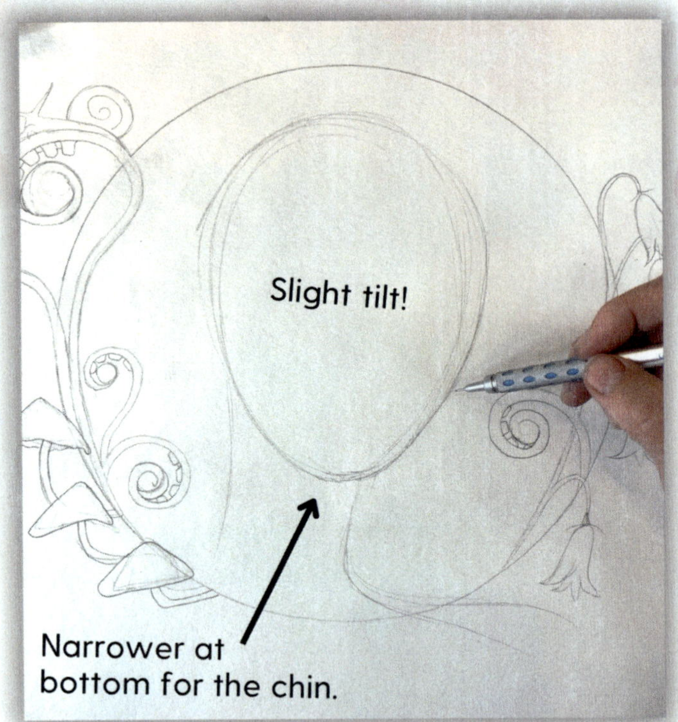

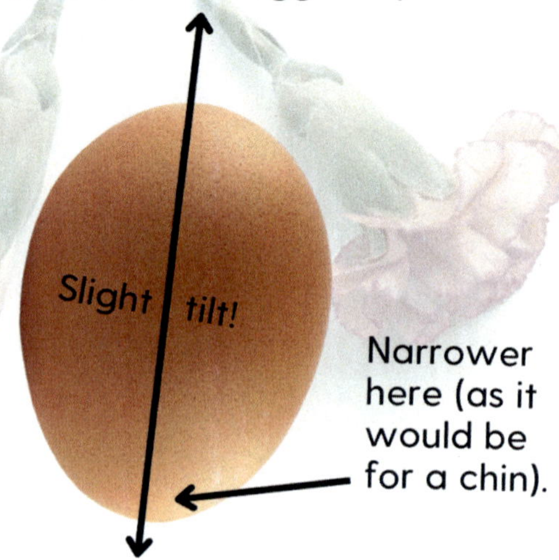

Thinking of an egg shape can help you make an oval perfect for a face! Just remember to make the chin a little narrower than the bottom. And for this project, tilt your "egg" ever so slightly!

Draw in the face guidelines as shown.

The eye line is located approximately halfway down across the oval.

The nose line is halfway between the eye-line and the chin.

The mouth line is halfway between the nose-line and chin.

Then add two lines for the neck. Note the placement of each line as it relates to the oval.

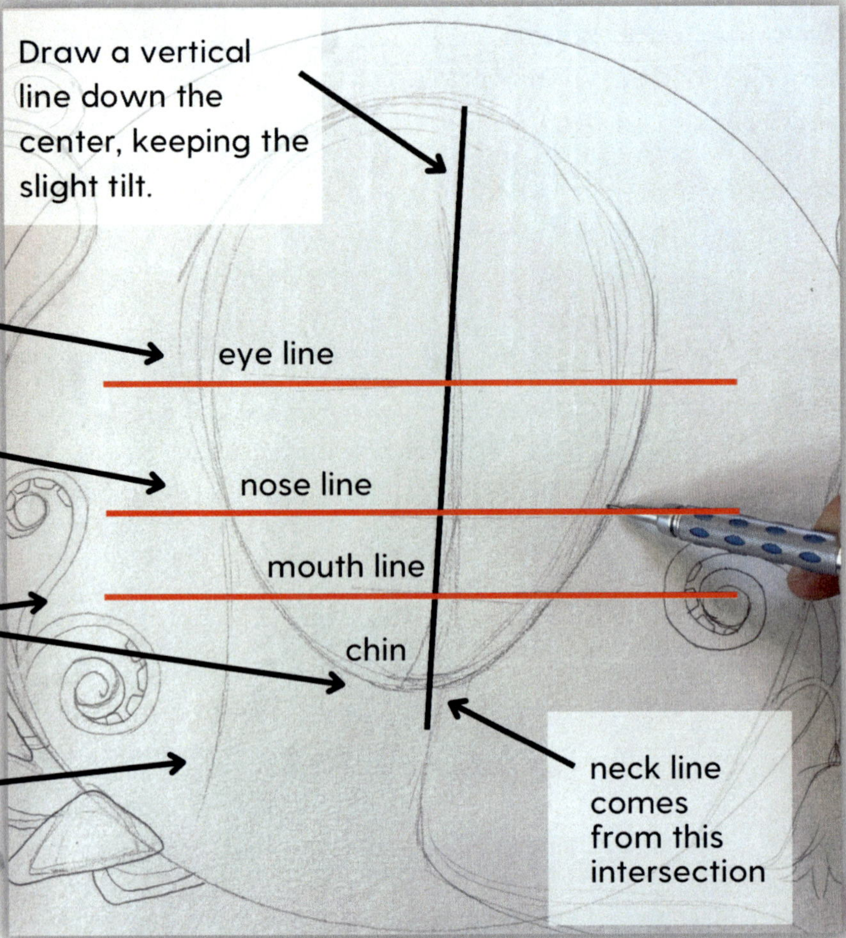

Draw a vertical line down the center, keeping the slight tilt.

eye line

nose line

mouth line

chin

neck line comes from this intersection

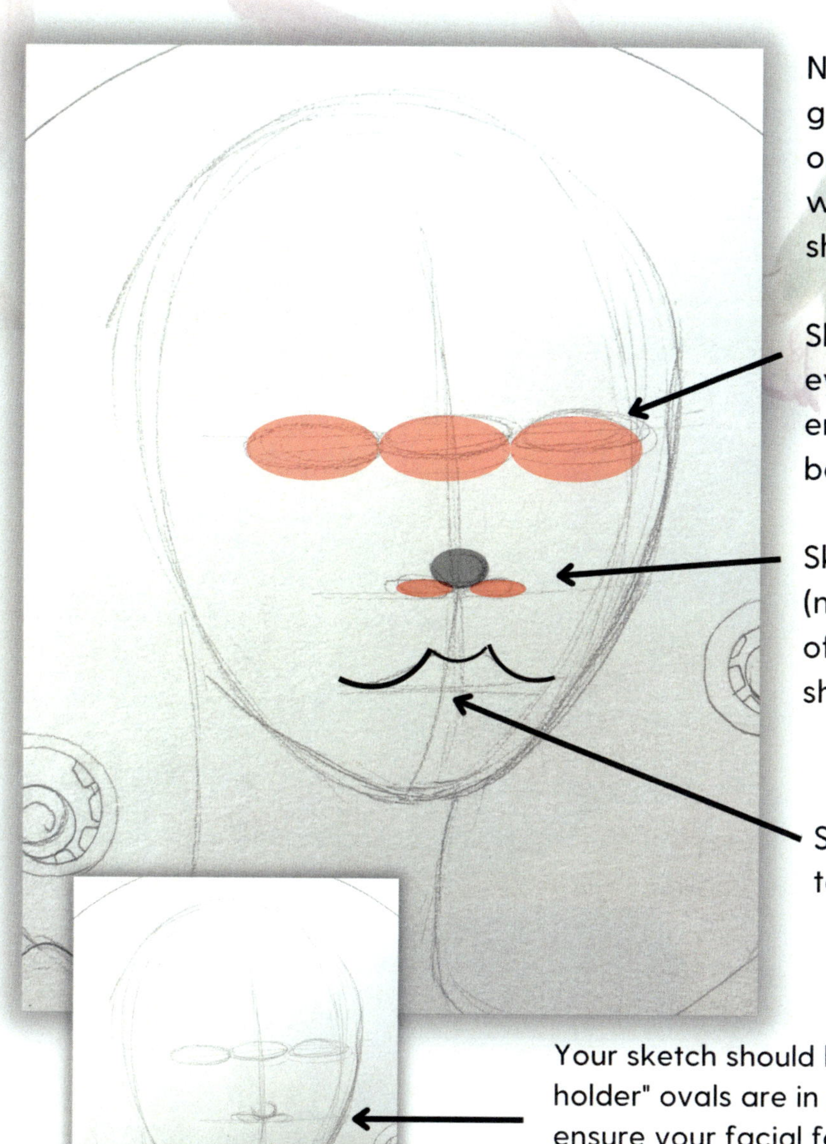

Now that the eye, nose and mouth guidelines are accurately drawn onto the oval shape for the head, we will sketch the following shapes onto the face.

Sketch three ovals across for the eyes. The third oval in the middle ensures the proper distance between them!

Sketch three ovals for the nose (note the larger oval shape on top of the other two flatter ones shown here in red).

Sketch 3 swooping lines for the top lip on the mouth line.

Your sketch should look like this when all the "place-holder" ovals are in place. Never skip this step! The ovals ensure your facial features are the correct size and shape and properly placed. Take your time making sure they are correct now. You'll thank yourself later!

When the ovals are all placed properly you can begin refining the facial features. Add a lid above each eye oval.

Then add eyebrows above them. At this stage you can also add a small tear duct coming off of each eye.

Add eyebrows and eye-lids. Add a tear duct too.

Add irises and pupils and use a circle template to help if you struggle making circles on your own!

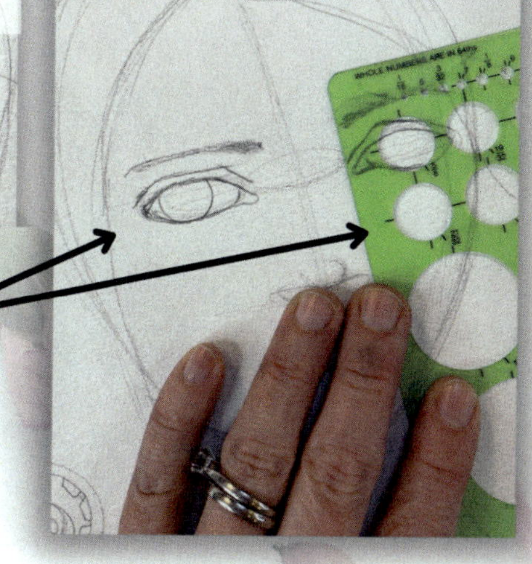

When drawing and refining all of the facial features, consider switching from a mechanical pencil to a soft pencil. This way, when you outline the eye shape, tear duct, eye-lid and eyebrows, you'll be able to see them very clearly.

Look for the letter "B" on your pencils to choose a soft one. The higher the number the softer and darker the graphite.

Cezanne® 12B

Her eyes are wonky...
Oh well!! Don't obsess over mistakes. Just keep going. It's fun!

nose bridge

nostrils

add last two lip lines

Leave an open space in the pupils to create the look of highlights.

Draw the nose bridge and outline the nostrils on either side of her nose. Then make two dark squished ovals to create the nostrils. At this point, you can add a darker line across the center of her top and now complete bottom lip.

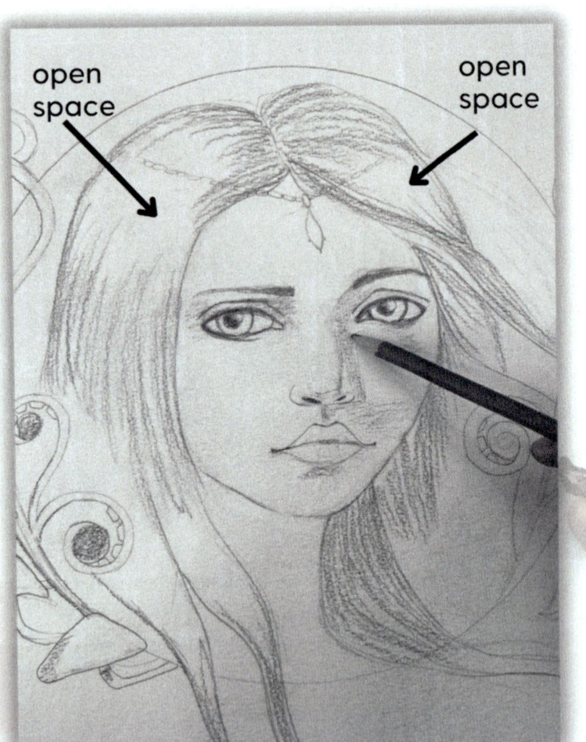

Using the side of a soft pencil, draw some lines from the part in her hair but then leave an open space before continuing with our blending stumps.

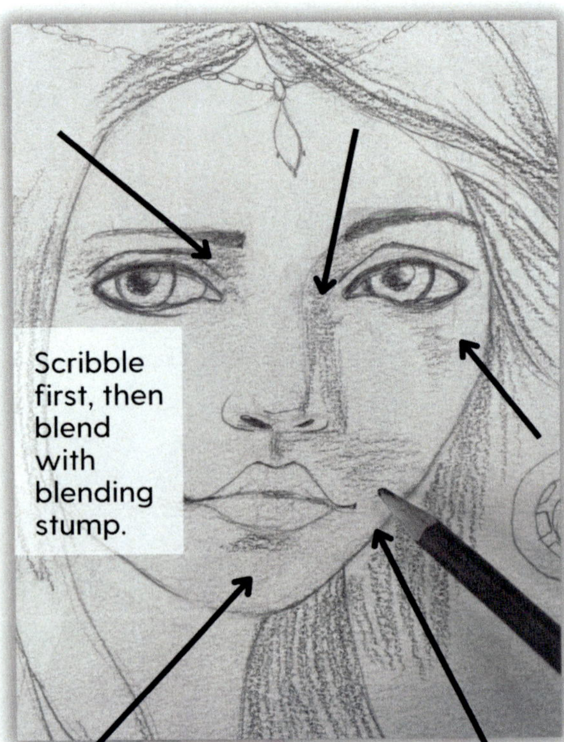

To begin shading, make gentle scribble marks down the right side of her nose bridge and face. Add more under her chin and both eyes. Blending is next!

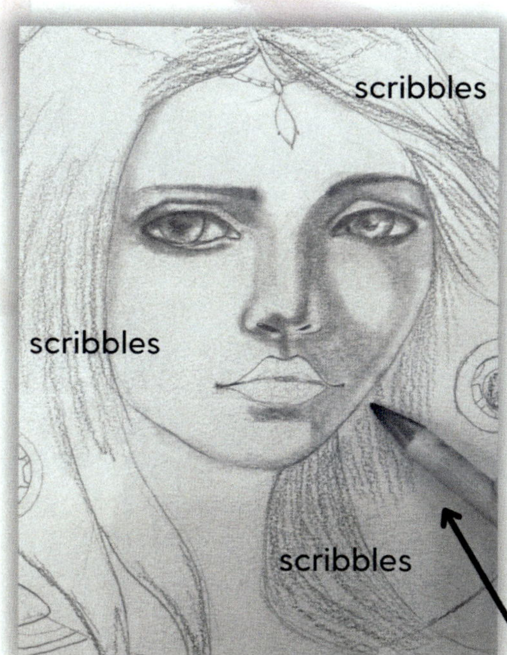

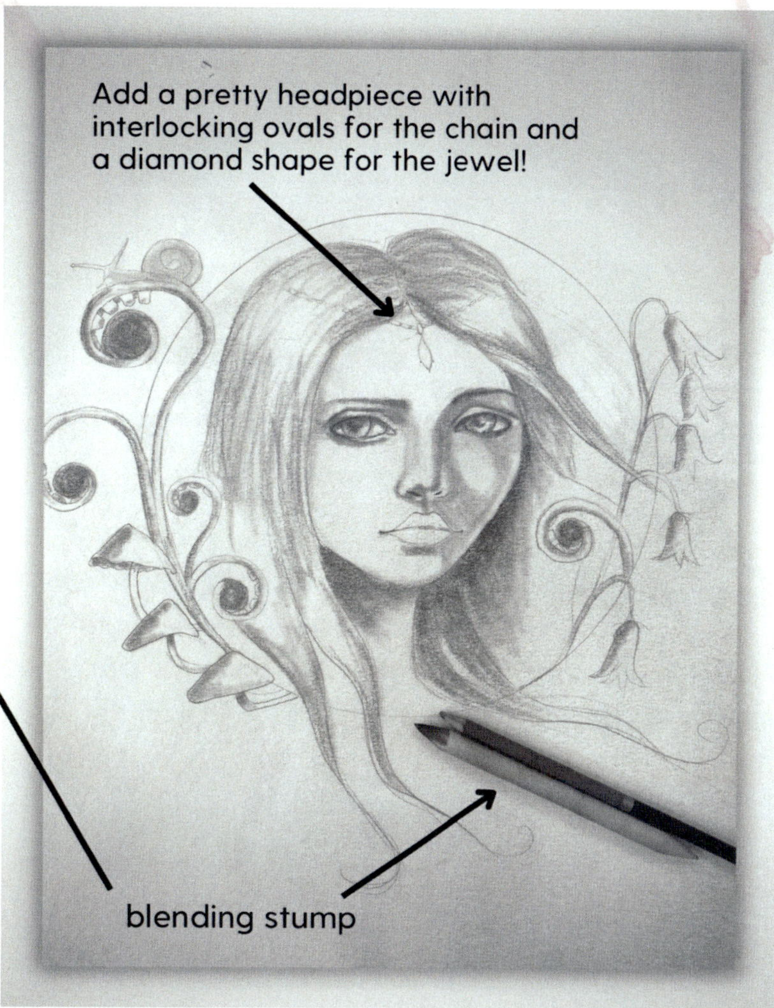

With the side of your blending stump, blend all of the soft scribbles you made until you no longer see the individual pencil lines.

Take your time adding scribbles with your soft pencil to all the areas shown. Then blend out all of the marks with your dirty blending stump. The texture of the cold-pressed paper coupled with the soft pencil lead makes blending a breeze!

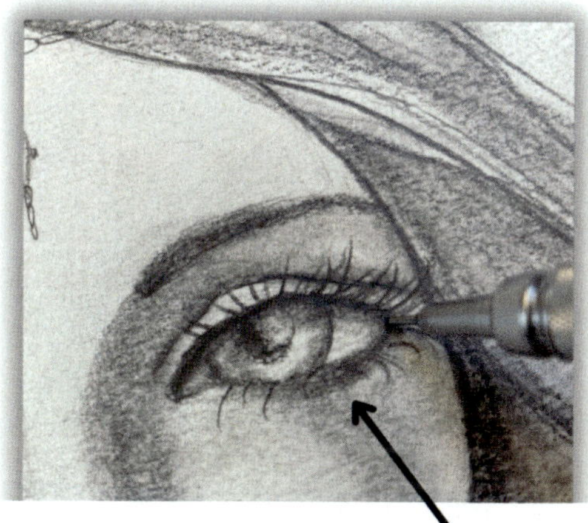

Using your mechanical pencil, draw a series of curved lines coming out from the eyelids to create stunning lashes! Then run your blending stump over the upper lid to create a shadow over the eye.

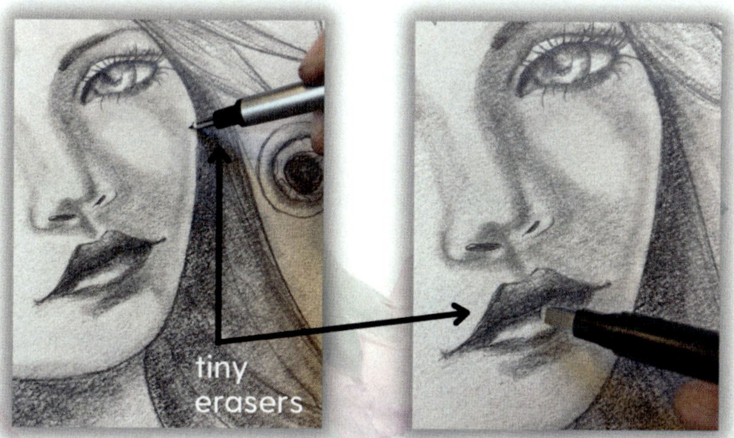

Using a super tiny eraser like the mono eraser by Tombow, carve highlights into the iris, alongside the cheek area and on the lower lip. Anywhere begging for a twinkle!

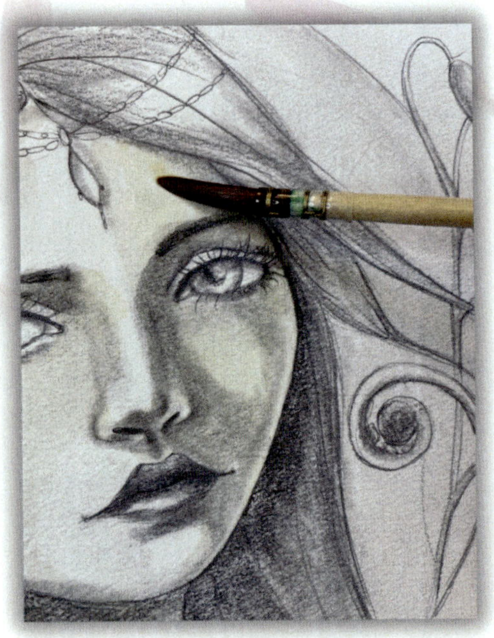

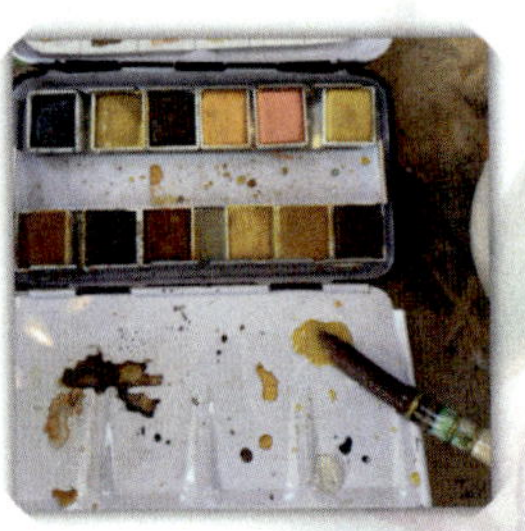

The Prima Complexion watercolor skin tone set makes choosing skin tones easy!

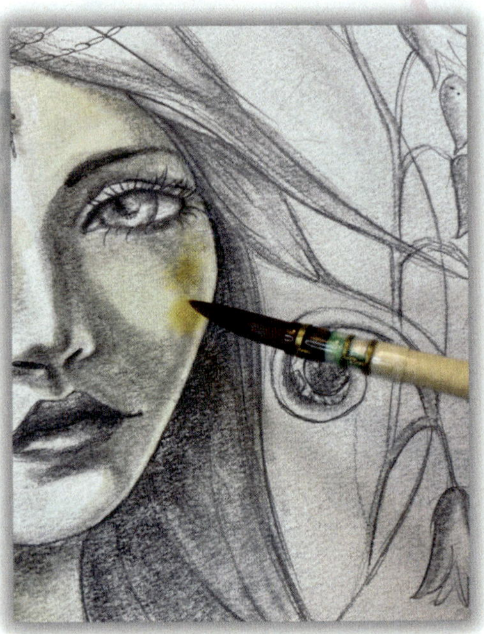

Now comes the SUPER FUN part! The best part though is that it's soooo easy. Grab a skin color that you love (in this case I'm using Chant from the Prima Complexion) and make a really watery mix of it. Then spread a super thin coat over the entire skin area. In areas you want to darken, add a second layer AFTER the first layer has dried.

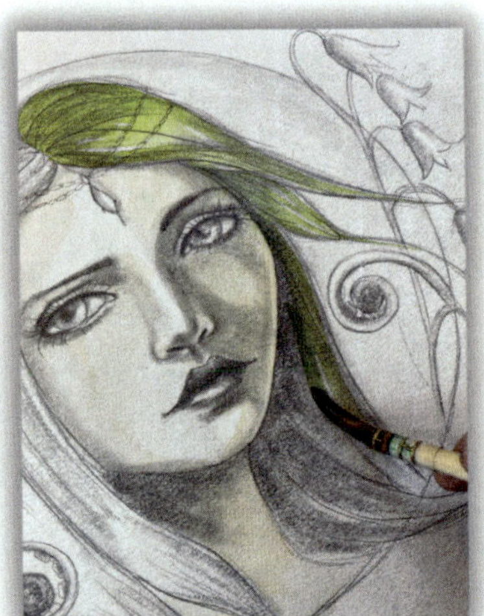

I'm using Sap Green for the hair. Choose whatever Fae color YOU love!

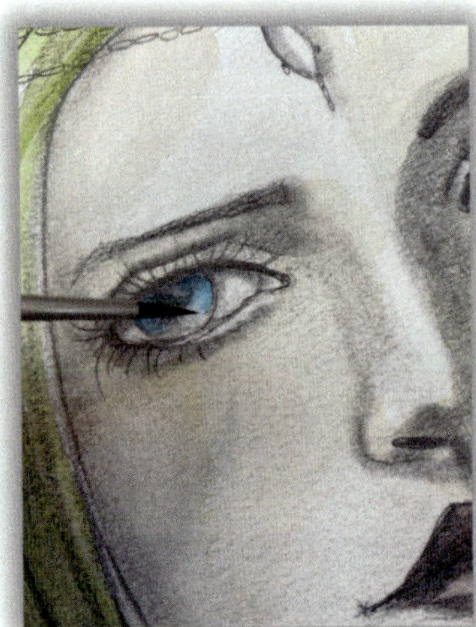

I'm using Phthalo Turquoise for the eyes because it's so striking!

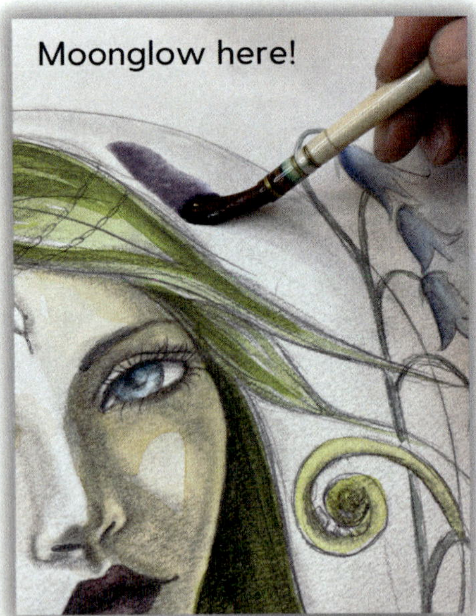

Moonglow here!

All the colors shown here are by Daniel Smith.

Now you can systematically cover each area with a delicate wash of your favorite watercolors. Wait for the first layer to dry and then add a second or third layer (when dry) anywhere you want to pump up the color. I LOVE to teach this method of watercolor to our beginner Celtic Collective students. Because all the "heavy lifting" and shading is done beforehand with graphite, this method of a simple streak of color requires very little skill. Truly anyone can do this (and so can YOU!)!

If watercolor is the fun part, finishing touches are the most satisfying! You'll want to gather your white paint pen, blending stump and colored pencils for these last moves.

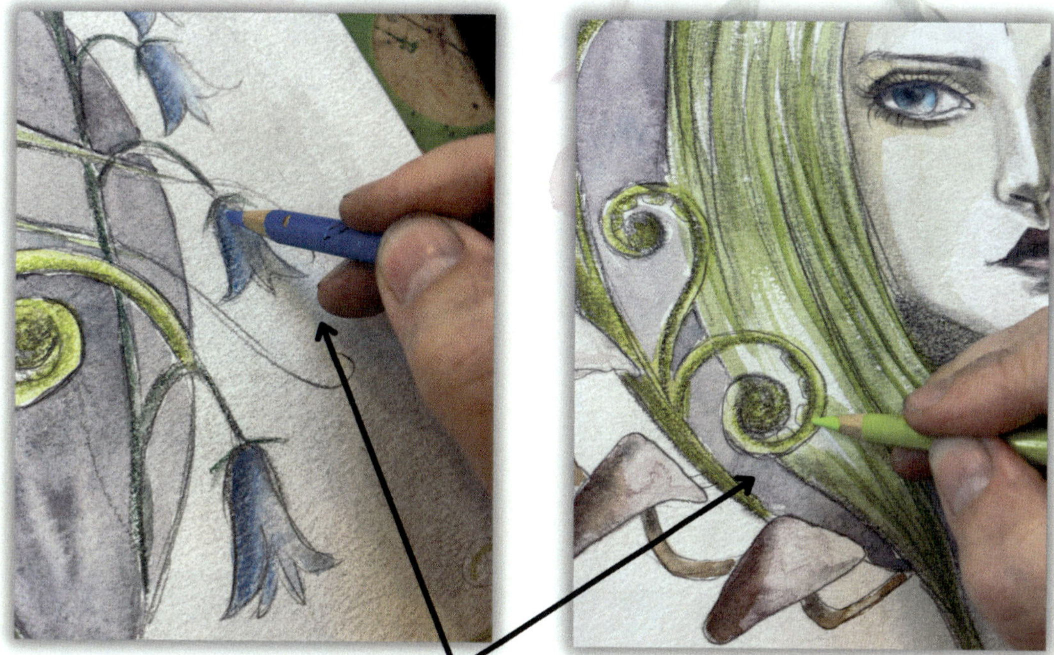

Now you can add colored pencil sketching to any areas that need a little refining. I'm terrible at painting in small spaces so I rely on my colored pencils to fill in those bitty places! You can also lighten areas by using lighter colored pencil colors, and deepen areas with darker ones!

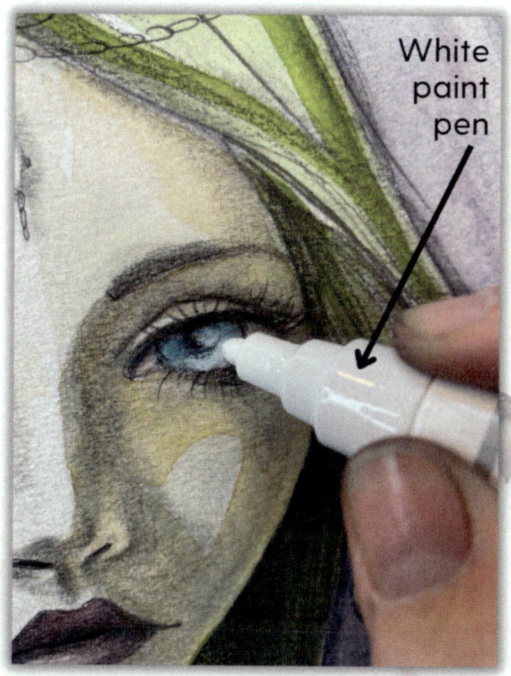

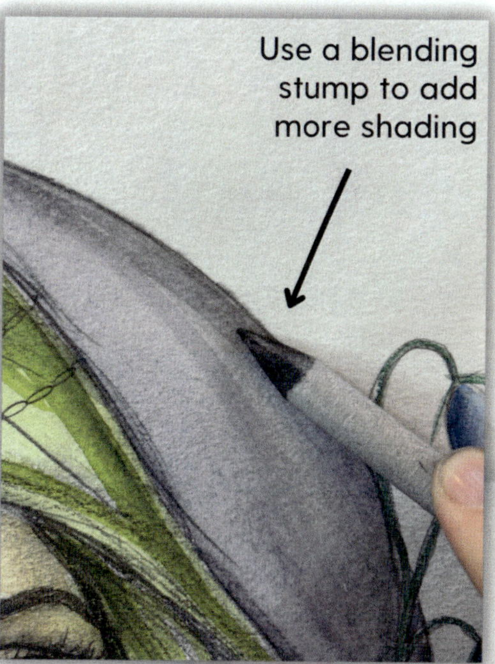

Use a white paint marker to add highlights anywhere you choose! I love to add highlights to the pupil and iris and along the lower lip! You can also add additional shading with a pencil and a blending stump. Watercolor over graphite is awesome!

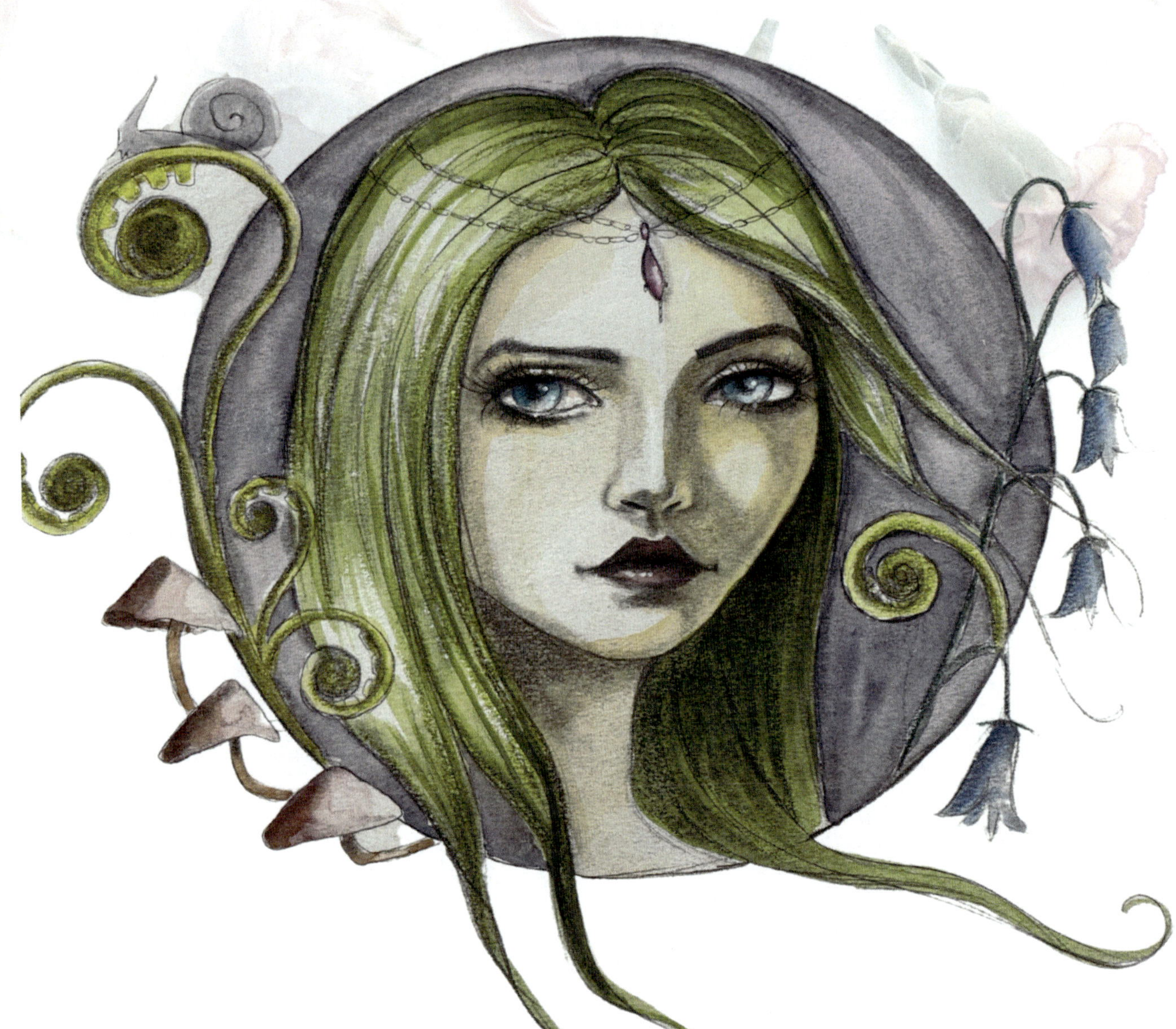

And voila! She is all done. I have to admit her eyes are a bit wonky, and that snail looks totally flat! And why did I make her hair green?

Listen. It's all WAY too easy to be hard on yourself when you're trying to make masterpieces. Please remember to be KIND to yourself! Trust me when I tell you that everyone's eyes are wonky, the snail is a DRAWING for goodness sake and her hair is green because she's FAE!! OBVIOUSLY!

I'm pointing these negatives out to show you that I am human too and YES, I see my mistakes. However, I also know that the MOST important thing is to stay positive and have FUN while you create because those attributes (even way more than your skills) will help you to keep creating and, therefore, will help you to grow your skills the fastest! Guaranteed!

Wee Hobbit Hoose

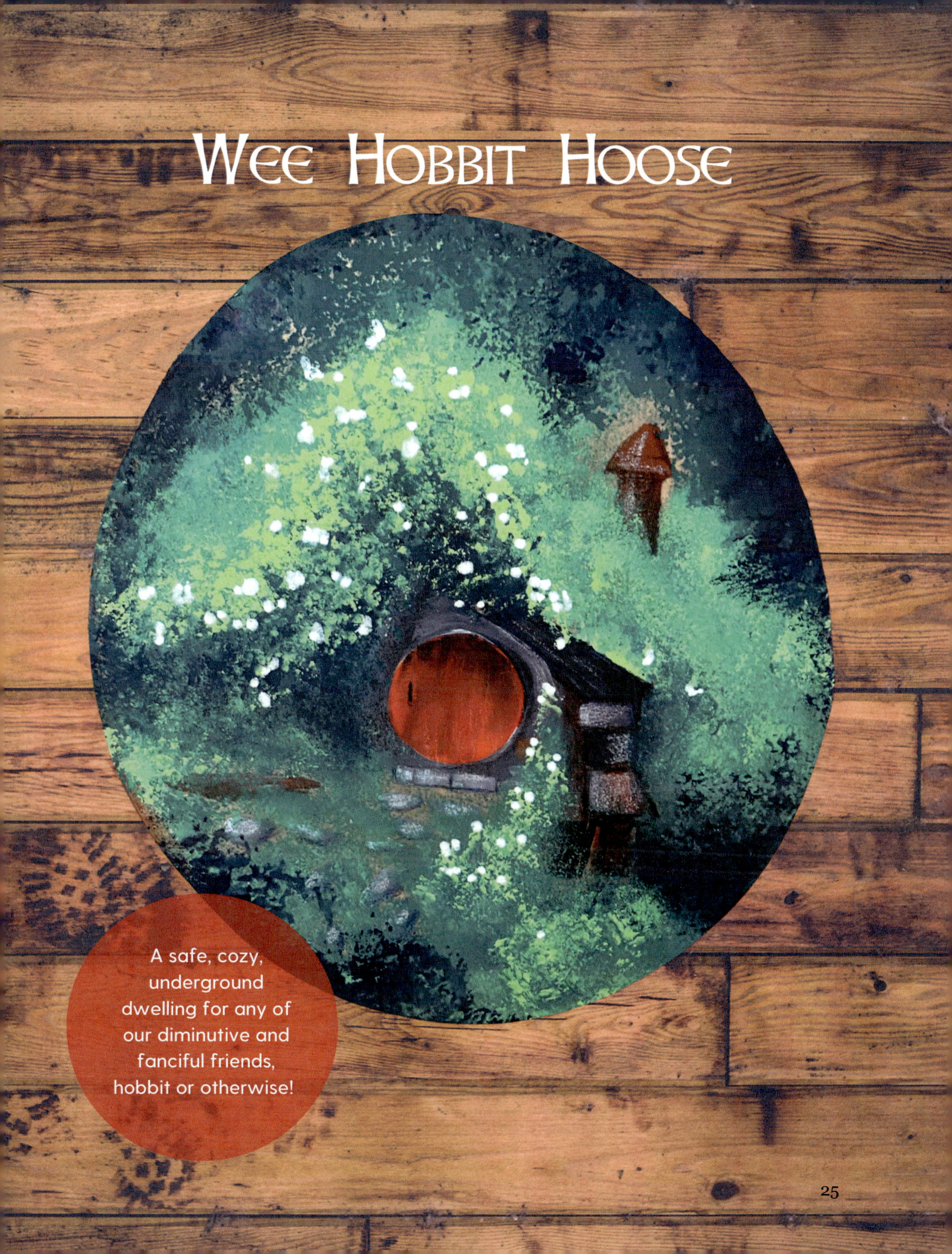

A safe, cozy, underground dwelling for any of our diminutive and fanciful friends, hobbit or otherwise!

SUPPLIES

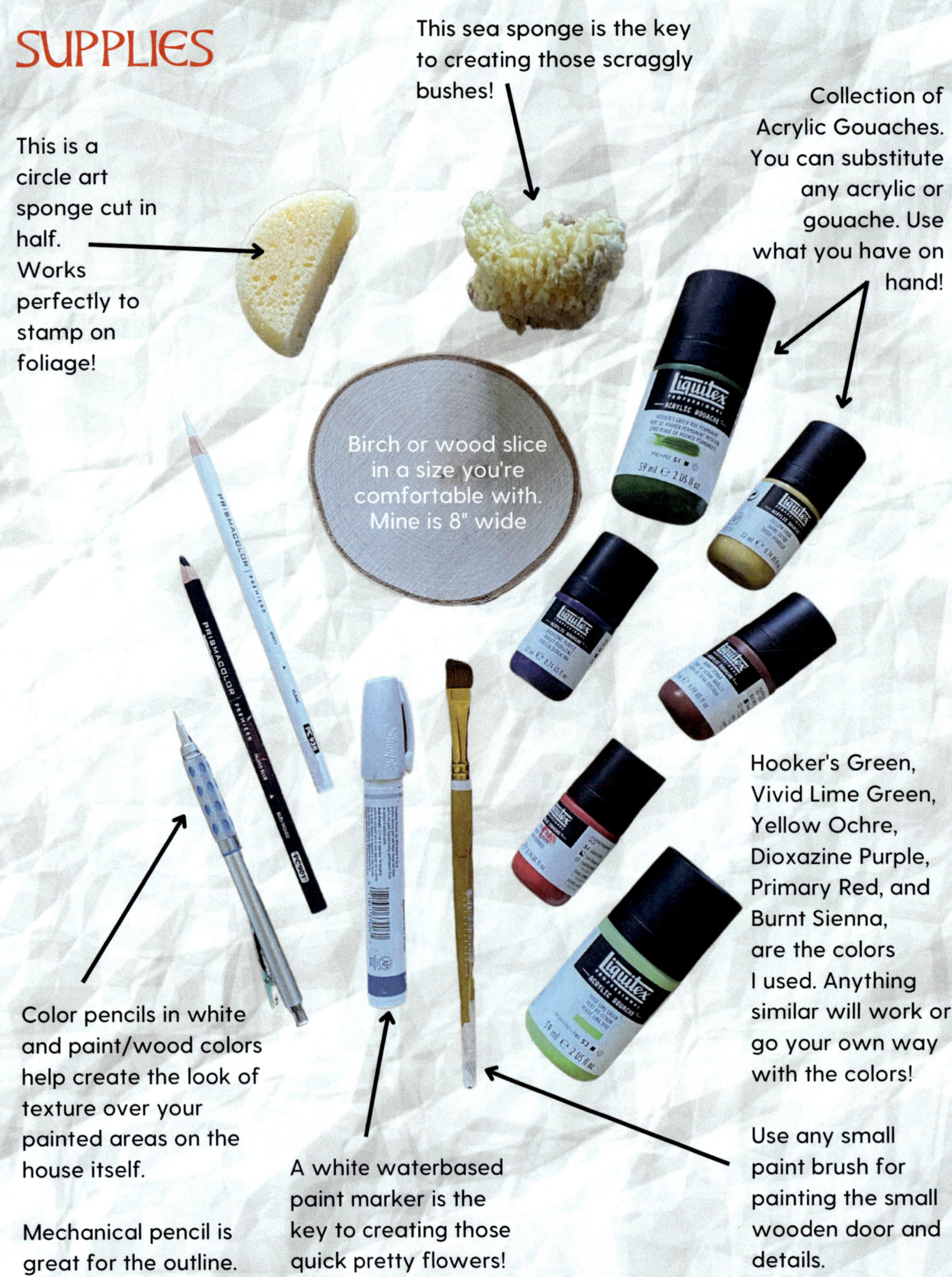
This sea sponge is the key to creating those scraggly bushes!
This is a circle art sponge cut in half. Works perfectly to stamp on foliage!
Collection of Acrylic Gouaches. You can substitute any acrylic or gouache. Use what you have on hand!
Birch or wood slice in a size you're comfortable with. Mine is 8" wide
Liquitex
ACRYLIC GOUACHE
PRISMACOLOR
Hooker's Green, Vivid Lime Green, Yellow Ochre, Dioxazine Purple, Primary Red, and Burnt Sienna, are the colors I used. Anything similar will work or go your own way with the colors!
Color pencils in white and paint/wood colors help create the look of texture over your painted areas on the house itself.
Mechanical pencil is great for the outline.
A white waterbased paint marker is the key to creating those quick pretty flowers!
Use any small paint brush for painting the small wooden door and details.

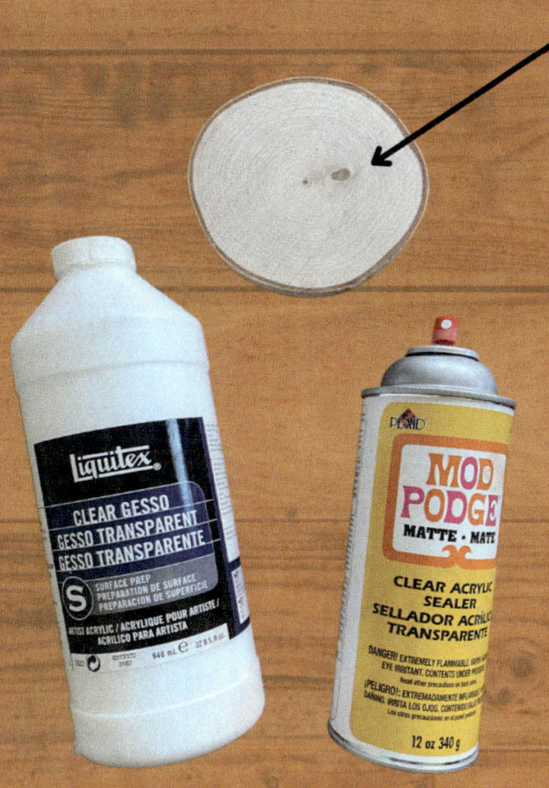

The birch (or any wood) slice needs to be treated so that paint adheres to it properly before you begin. You can either brush on a coat of clear Gesso OR you can spray it with a few coats of an acrylic spray sealer. There are many different brands to choose from; just choose whichever one fits your budget. I like Mod Podge's variety. Be sure to spray outside as fumes can be noxious!

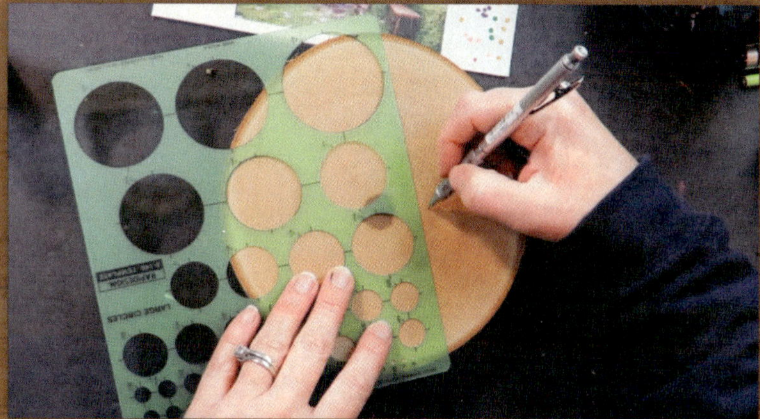

Once the wood is sealed and dry, use a regular pencil to trace a circle anywhere near the center. My wood slice is 8" tall and 7" wide and I made my circle 1.5" in diameter.

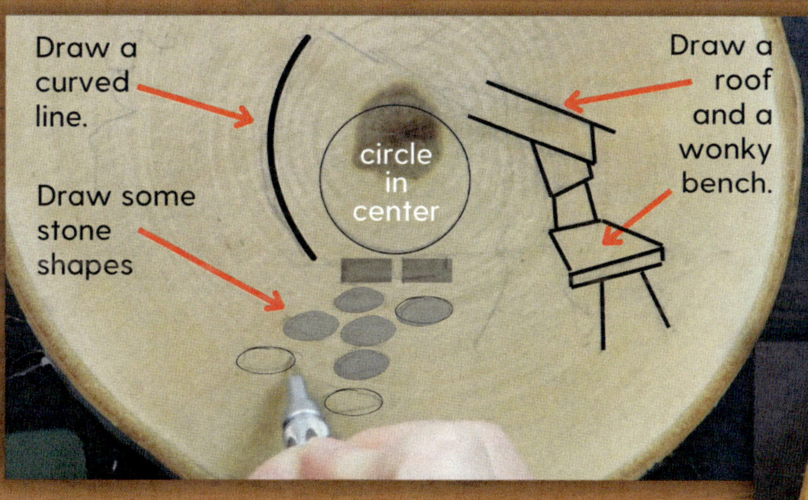

Then take your time to draw the bench, roof and messy ovals. There is very little drawing or painting in this project! Most of it is simply stamping with sponges!

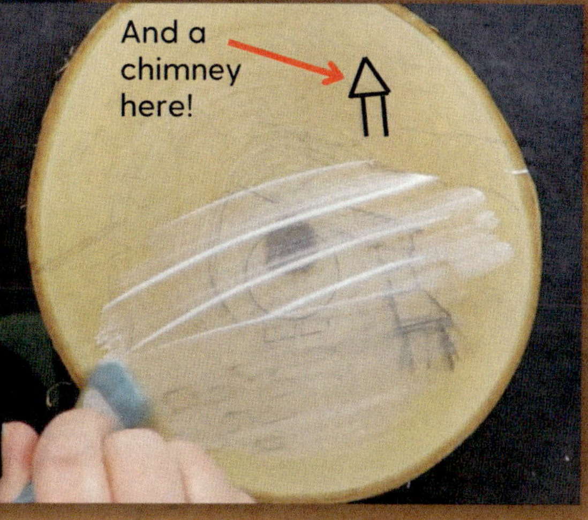

After you finish the drawing part, coat your log slice with a layer of Clear Gesso or Matte Medium to seal the wood and prepare it to be able to accept the acrylics which is our next step!

Paint the door the color of your choice (doesn't have to be red!). Then dip a paint brush in black, and then in white, and let them mix directly on the wood when you go to paint the stones, roof, house and benches! You can also try this with white and brown, or brown and black! Adding them separtely on your brush (without mixing before hand on your palette) results in this bi-colored look that is perfect for natural elements!

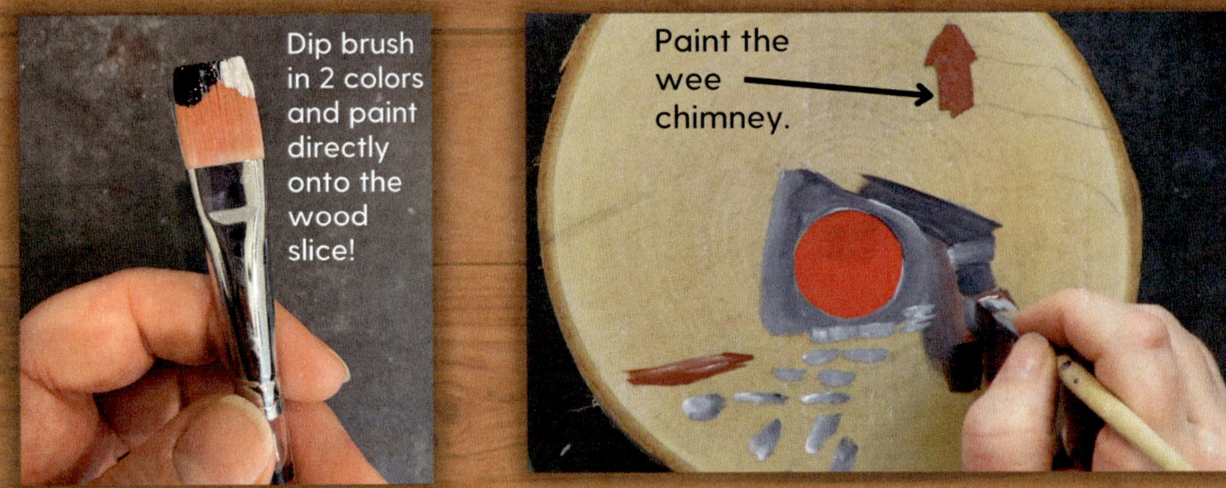

Now it's sponge-painting time! So fun and so easy! I use this EXACT (bi-colored paint) method for stamping the greenery all around the rest of the canvas.

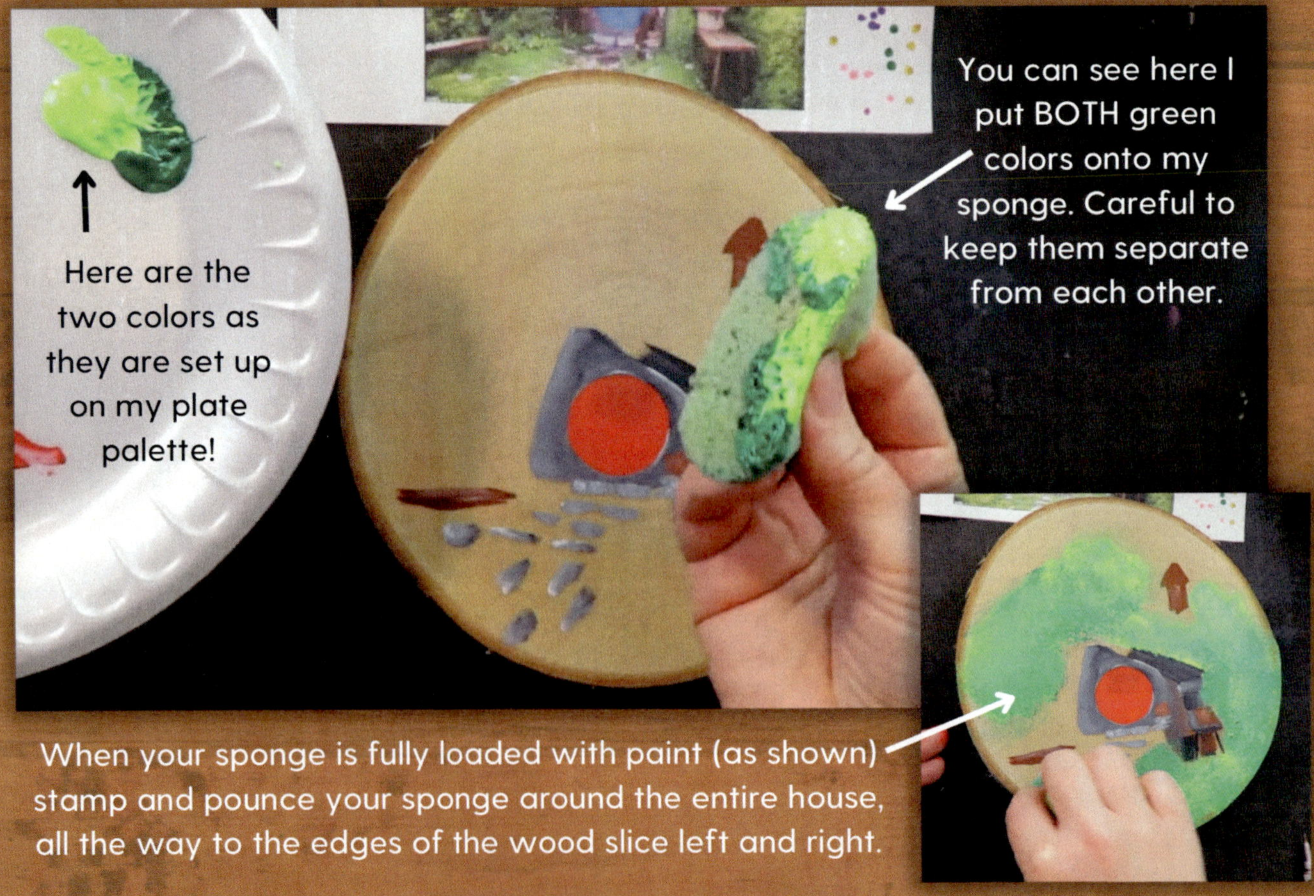

When your sponge is fully loaded with paint (as shown) stamp and pounce your sponge around the entire house, all the way to the edges of the wood slice left and right.

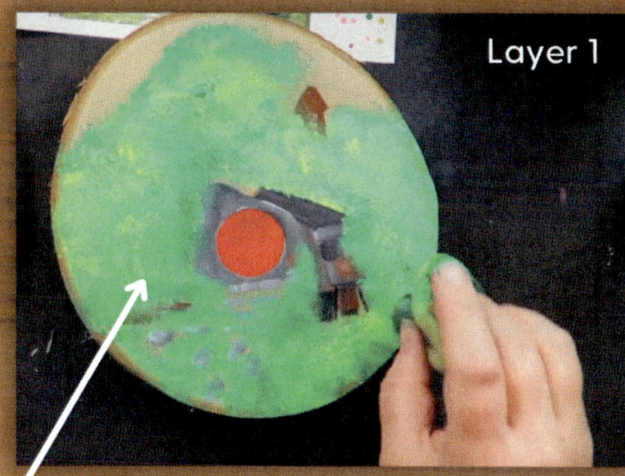

You should cover almost ALL of the wood slice with your first stamping efforts. When your slice looks like mine, let dry and wash your sponge.

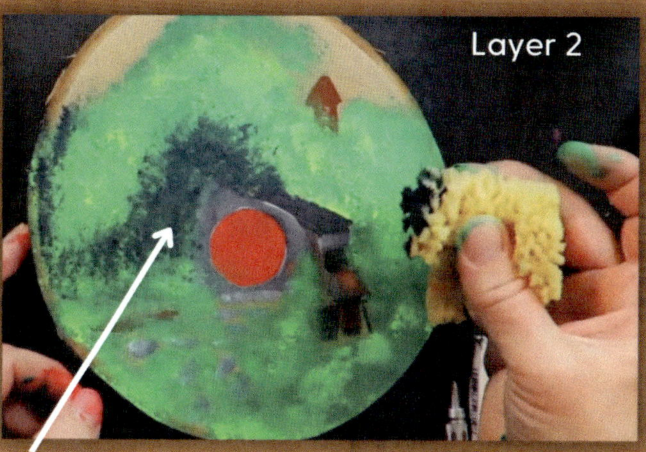

Now switch to your sea sponge and dip it into a mix of dioxazine purple and dark (hooker's) green. Stamp in area shown.

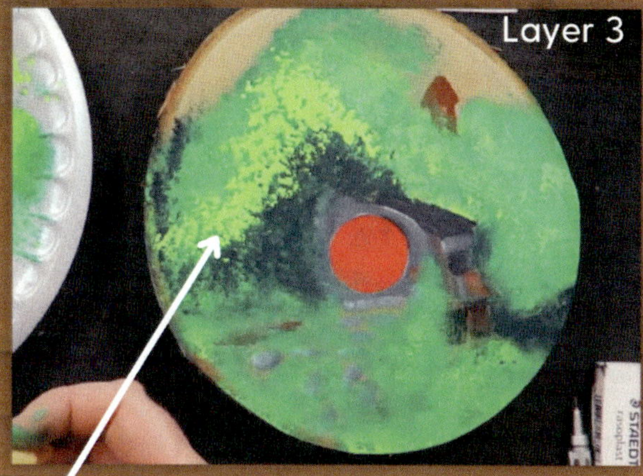

Wash your sea sponge. Make sure you dry it really well afterwards. Now load it with the light green and stamp above the dark areas we just applied.

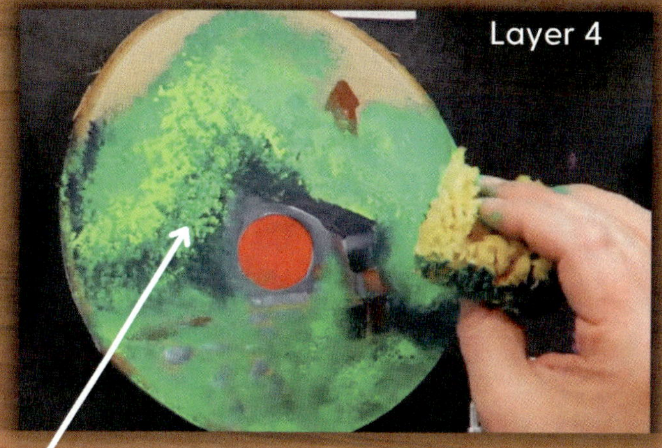

Now use a clean area on your sponge and pick up some medium green and pounce BETWEEN the light and dark areas you just added (Layer 2 and 3).

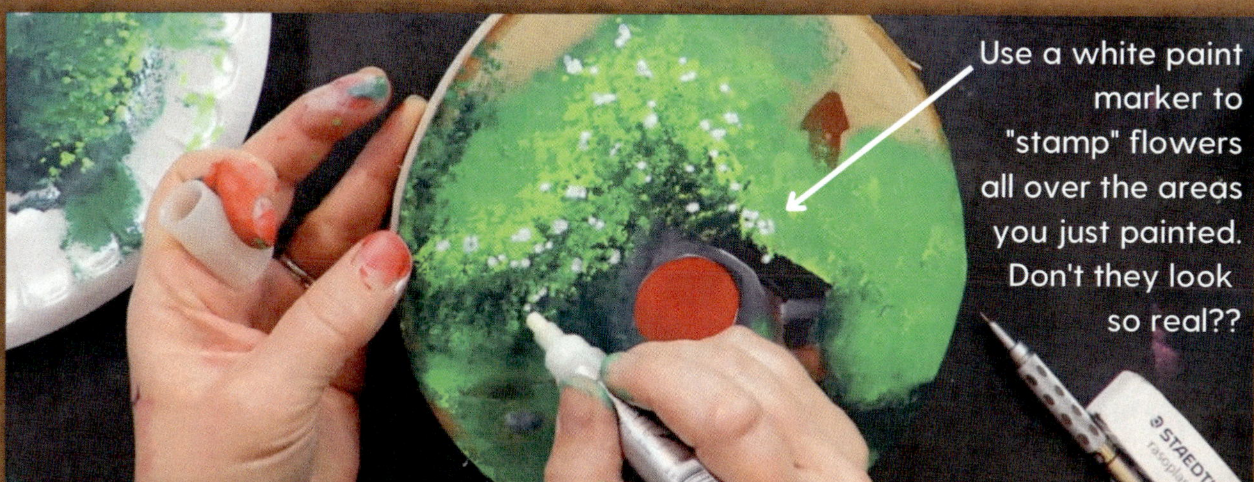

Use a white paint marker to "stamp" flowers all over the areas you just painted. Don't they look so real??

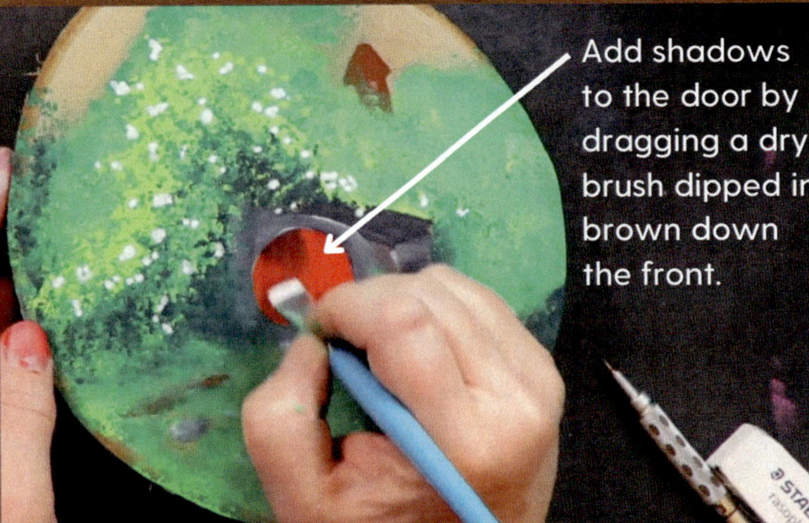

Add shadows to the door by dragging a dry brush dipped in brown down the front.

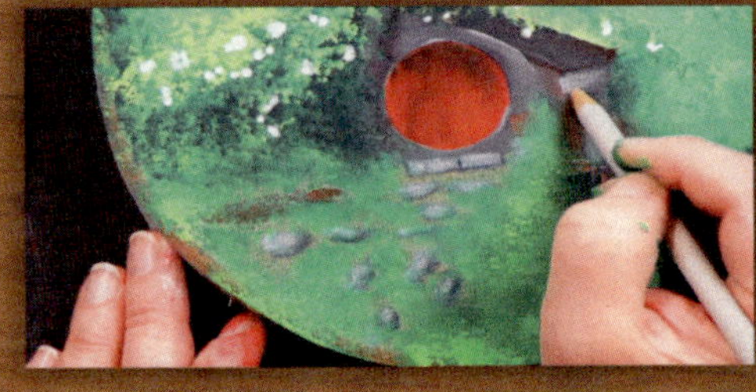

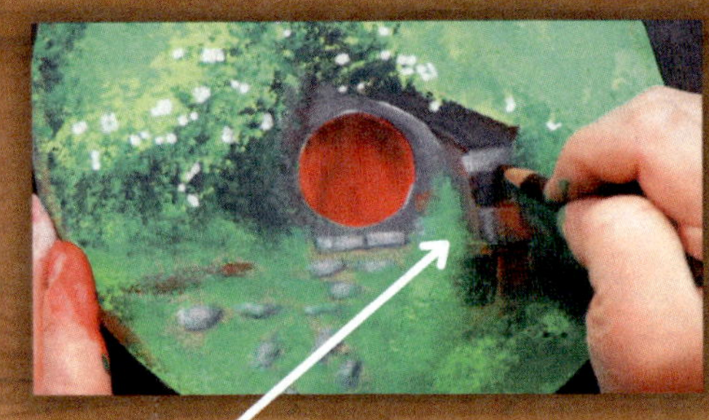

For any areas that need more definition or added texture, you can easily reach for your colored pencils to help. To create texture on the wood parts and to make it appear more weathered, add light grey color over the darker grey paint. To add definition to the stones and wood siding and roof, add navy blue pencil; it compliments the grey paint very nicely.

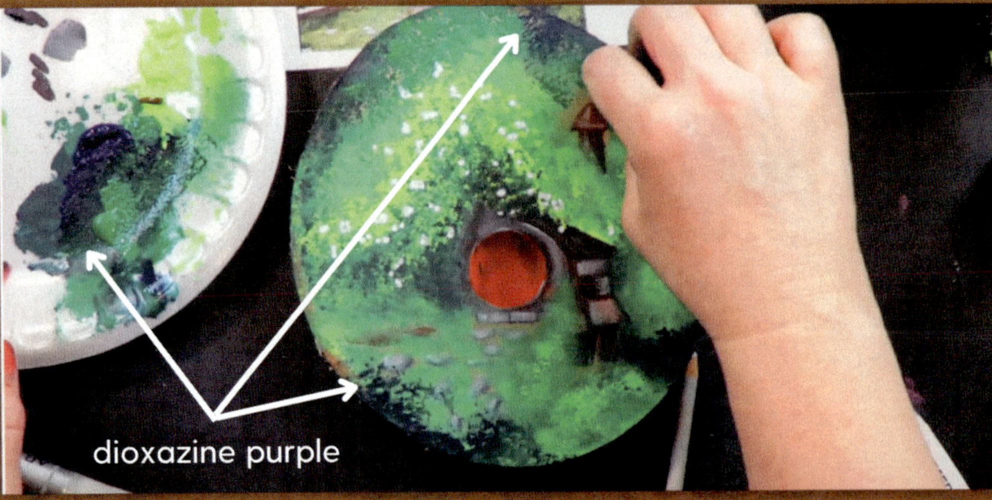

Using ONLY the dioxazine purple, stamp around the entire perimeter of the wood slice using your dry sea sponge. This really adds a lovely frame-effect that finishes off the piece.

As a final touch, add as many more "flowers" using your paint pen as you like. I added some additional blooms around the front of the house and along the right side to balance out all of those already on the upper left.

Your Wee Hobbit Hoose is now ready for its first inhabitants!

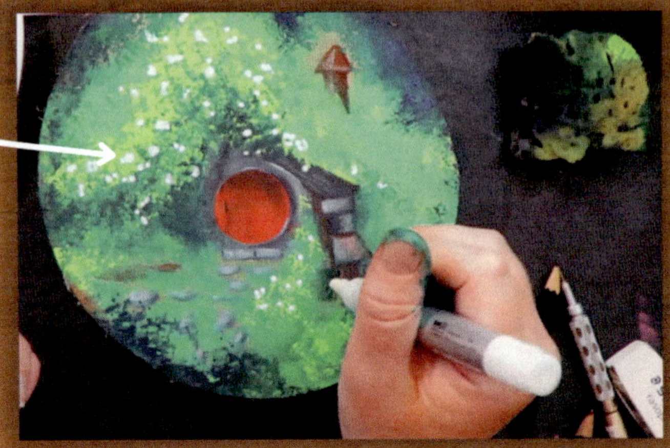

Dragon Moon

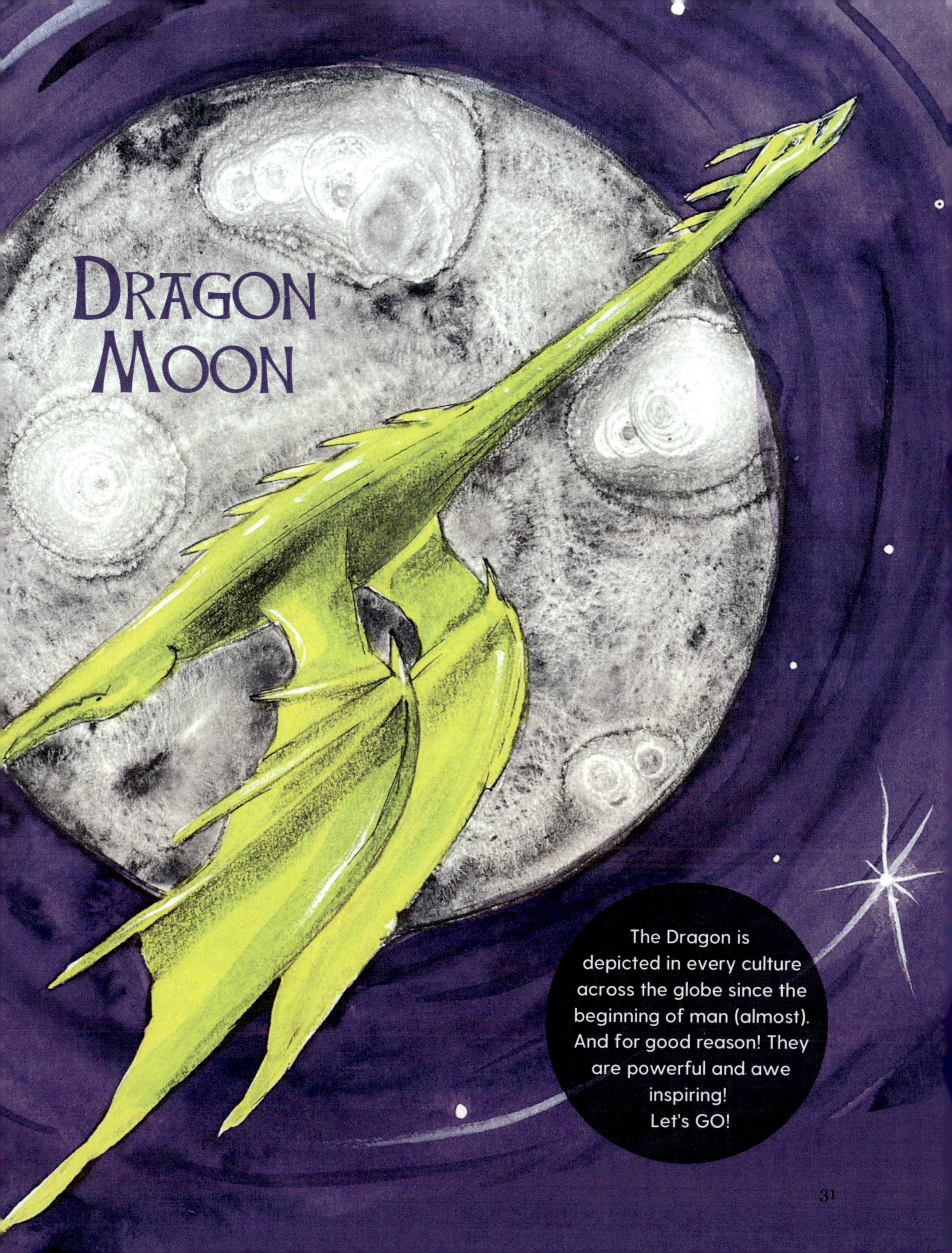

The Dragon is depicted in every culture across the globe since the beginning of man (almost). And for good reason! They are powerful and awe inspiring!
Let's GO!

Supplies

Frisket (or masking fluid)

Make sure you use a dedicated brush for it as it will destroy your water color brushes!

Your favorite white for highlights (gouache or paint pen work great too).

Regular rubbing alcohol (for moon craters!)

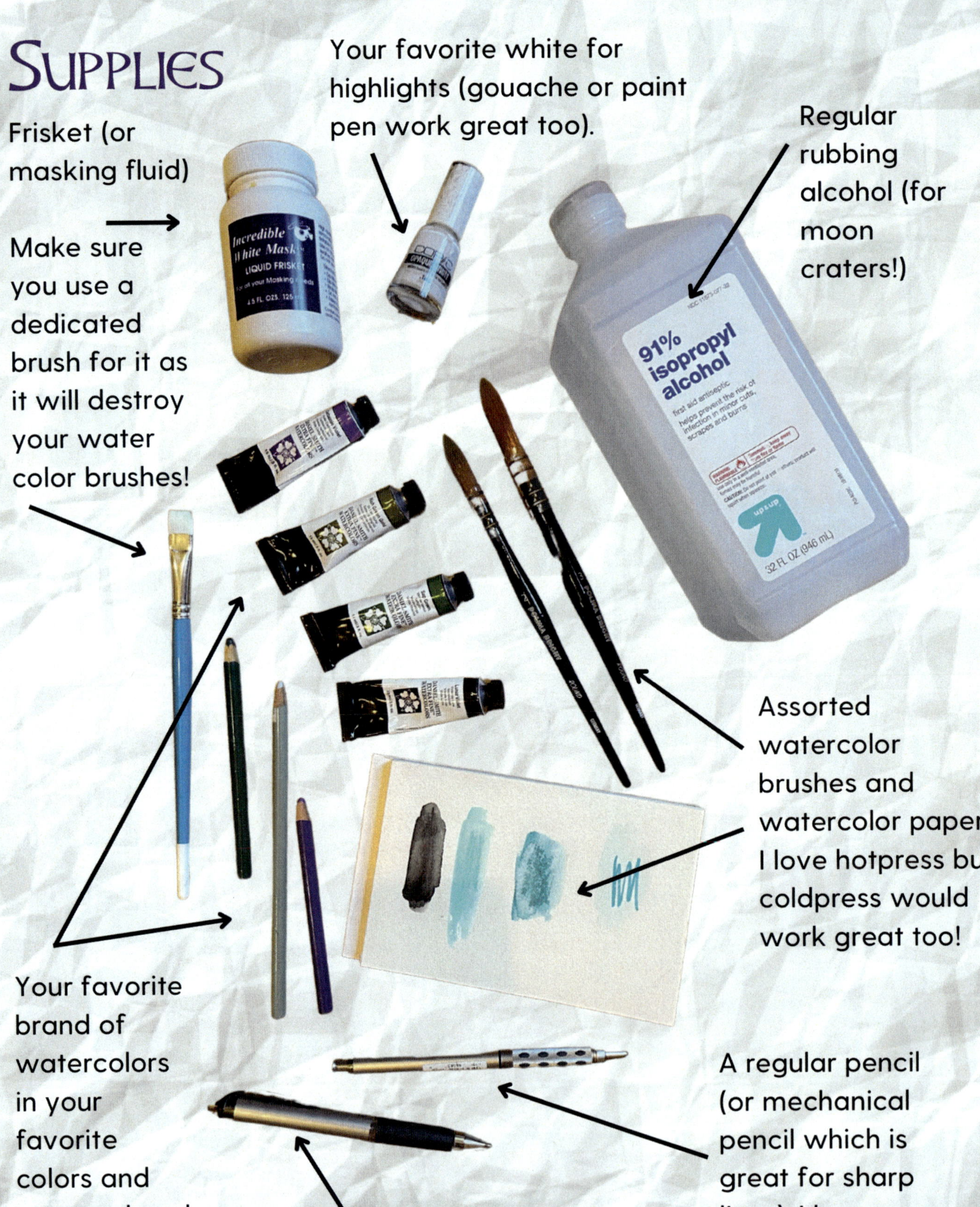

Assorted watercolor brushes and watercolor paper. I love hotpress but coldpress would work great too!

Your favorite brand of watercolors in your favorite colors and some colored pencils to match.

A regular pencil (or mechanical pencil which is great for sharp lines). I love GraphGear 2000 by Pentel.

A black gel pen is great for quick outlines or details over watercolors. A fineliner works too!

Before you even get started drawing, you'll want to size up your dragon friend. How big will the circle moon be in the middle? And how long will your dragon friend be? That's entirely up to you. But take a moment to lay out your plans on your paper before you start drawing. I only like to draw large, so of course I was going to have my dragon take up almost all of my entire 14" inch long paper! But that's just me :) Do what you're most comfortable with.

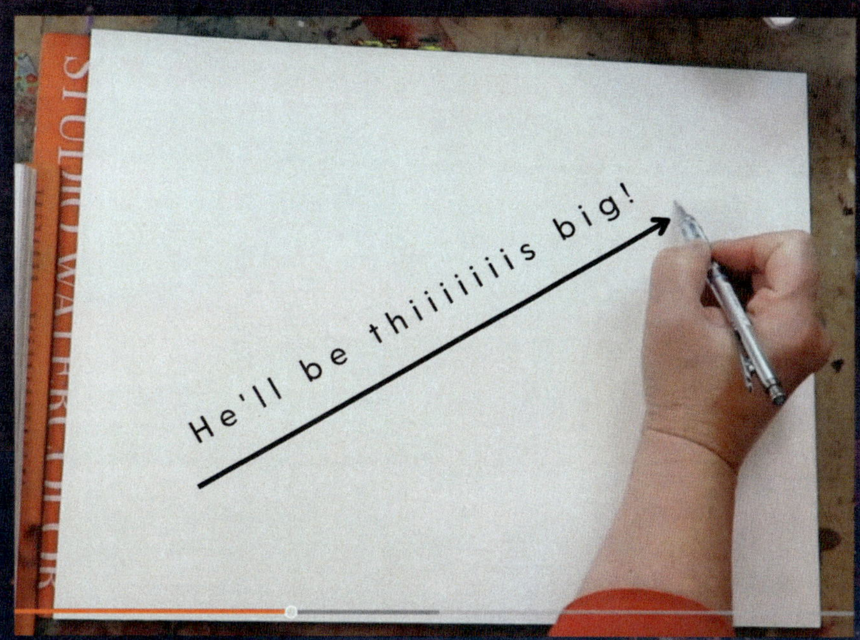

I can't overemphasize how important it is to get the scale of your subject determined correctly BEFORE you begin your art. It's soooo difficult to make changes mid-way!

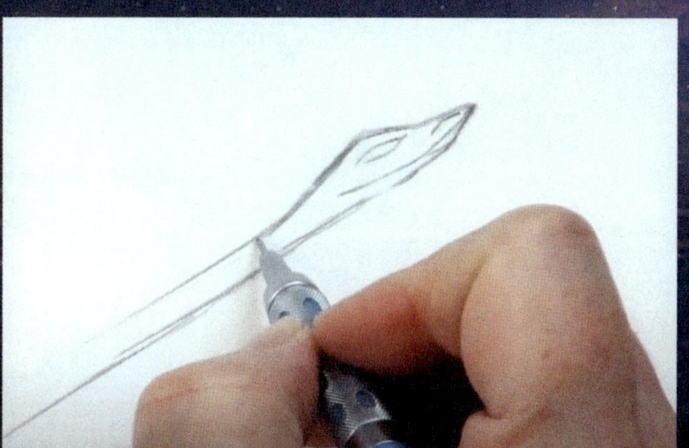

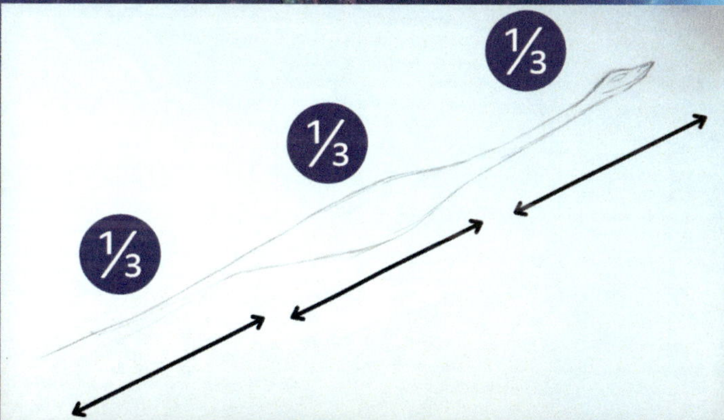

Once you know how long your dragon will be, you can start drawing. He's super duper skinny! So use a small nibbed mechanical pencil to help you make thin lines more easily. This is 0.5mm.

You can divide his body up into equal thirds if you like! The head and neck, body and tail are all about the same length. He's imaginary too, so feel free to make him all your own with any changes that you like!

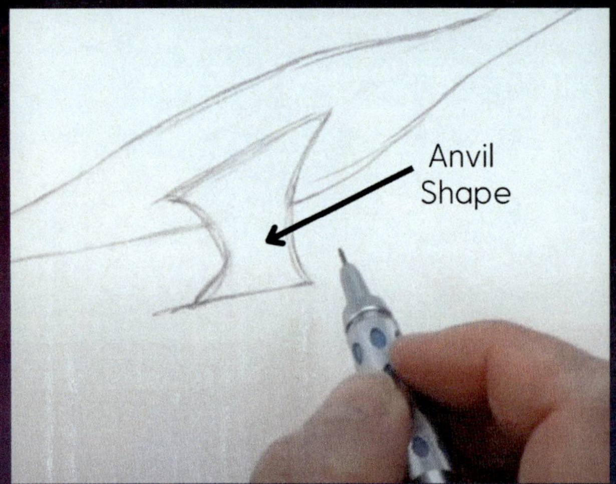

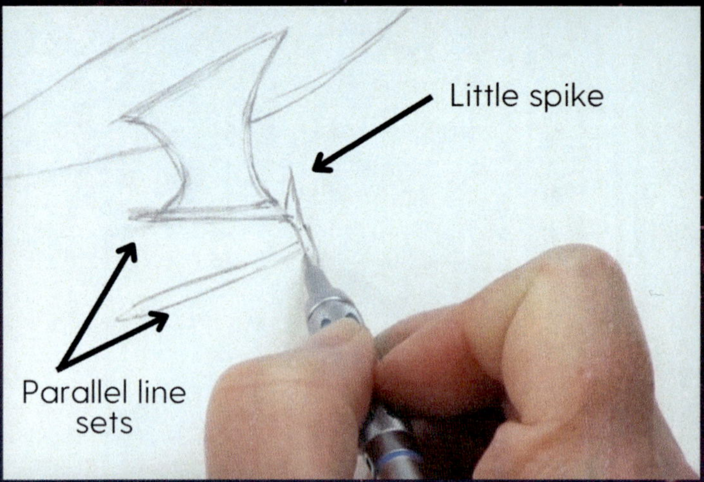

Now that we have the body sketched in, we can move onto the wings! In the meatiest part of the body, draw 2 short parallel lines. Then attach 2 curved lines on either side.

Now draw a tiny triangle for a spike, right off the end of the anvil shape we just drew. Then draw 2 new sets of parallel lines.

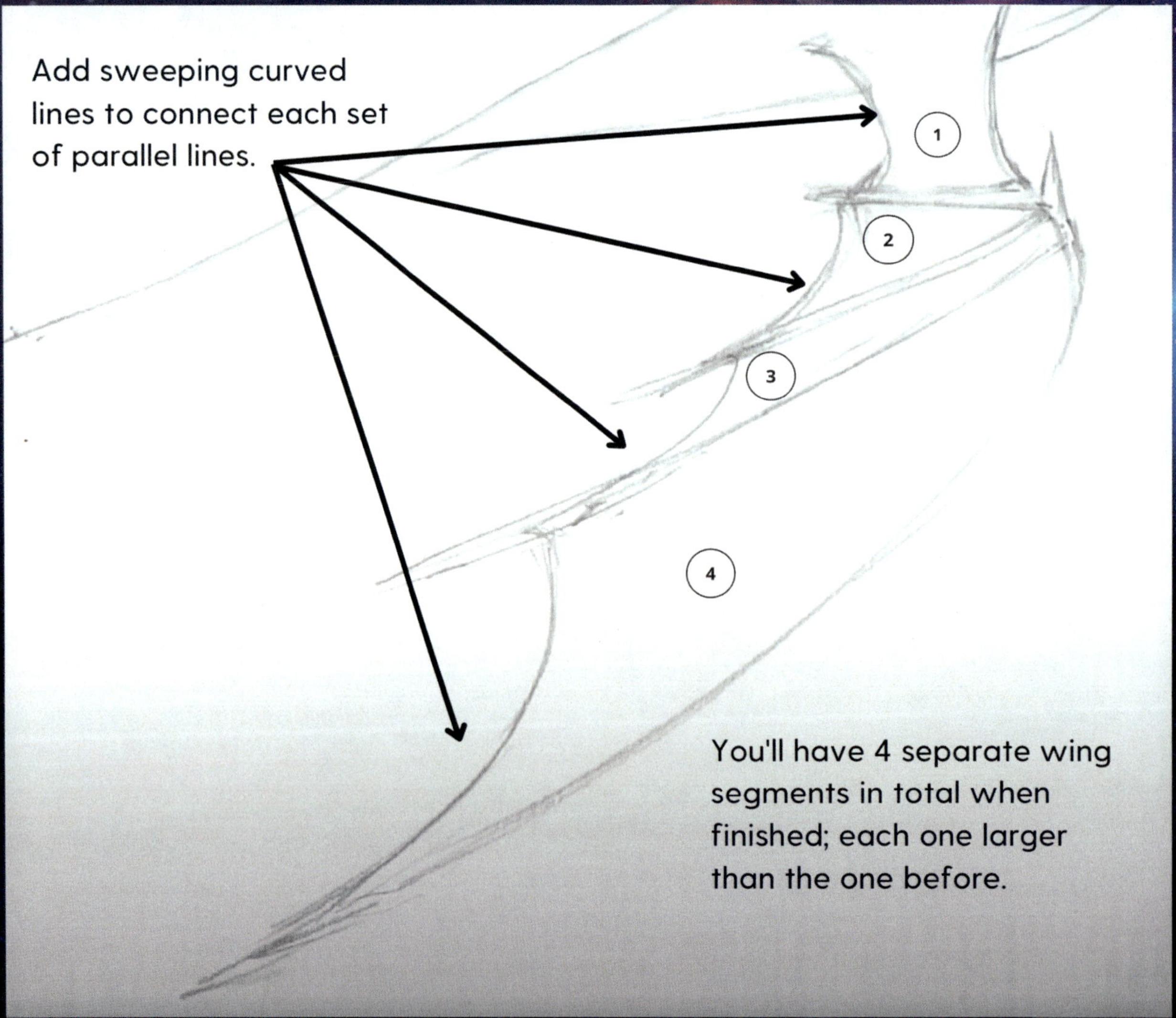

Add sweeping curved lines to connect each set of parallel lines.

1

2

3

4

You'll have 4 separate wing segments in total when finished; each one larger than the one before.

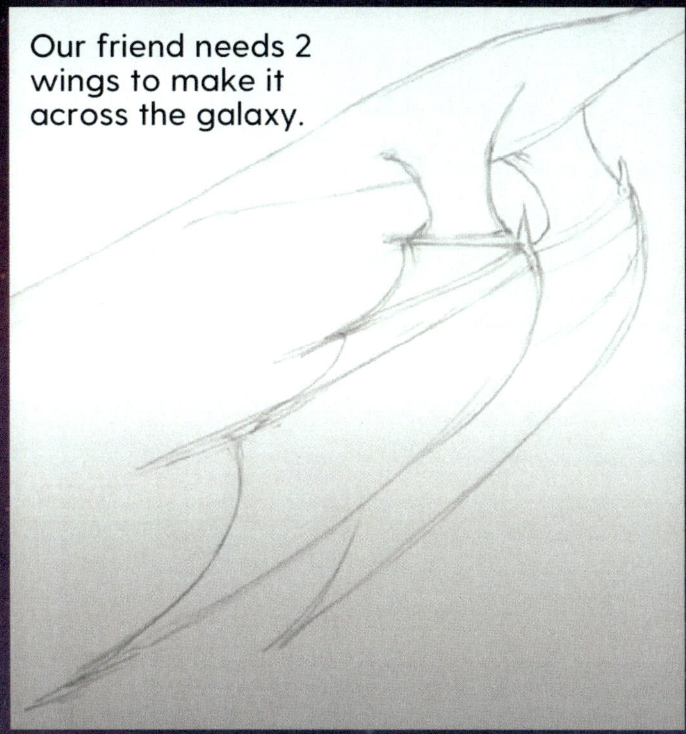

Our friend needs 2 wings to make it across the galaxy.

Draw a second wing slightly higher up but behind the first one, following the same steps we used to create the first.

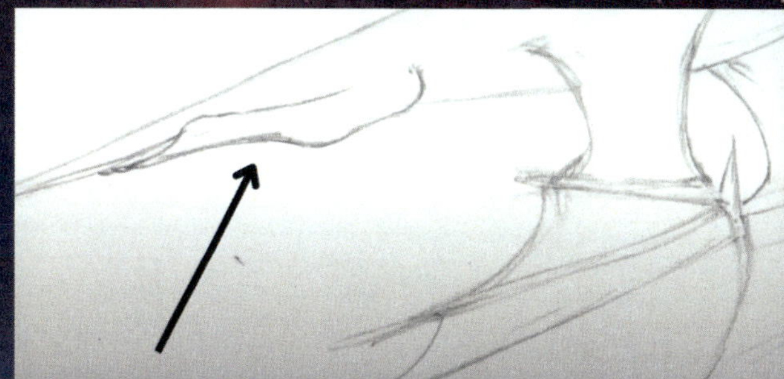

Now add a little hind leg in the space between the end of the tail and the wings previously drawn.

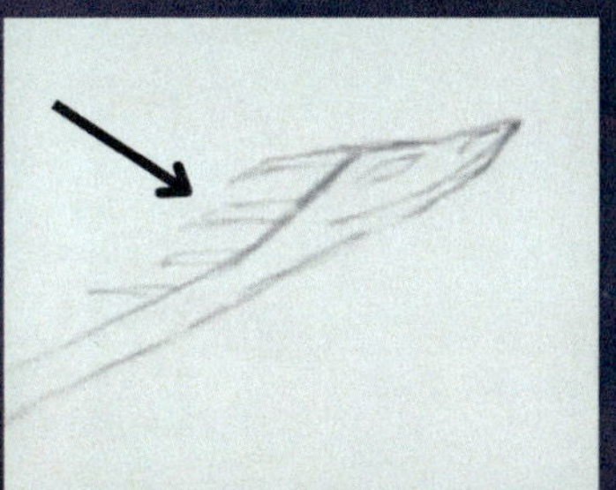

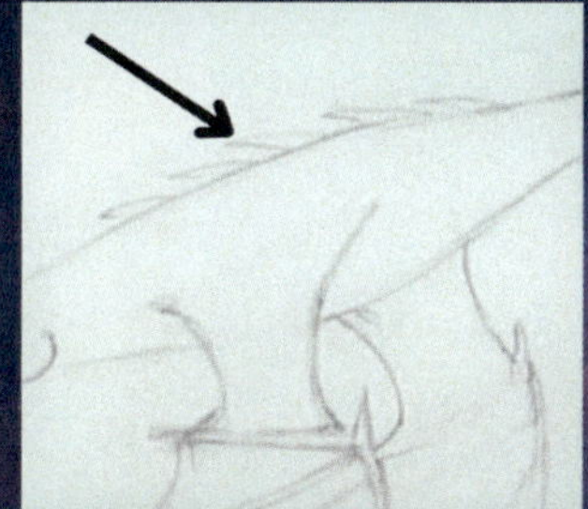

Next, sketch little spikes coming off of the back of the head and along the body. You can draw as few or as many as you like, making them as big or as small as you want!

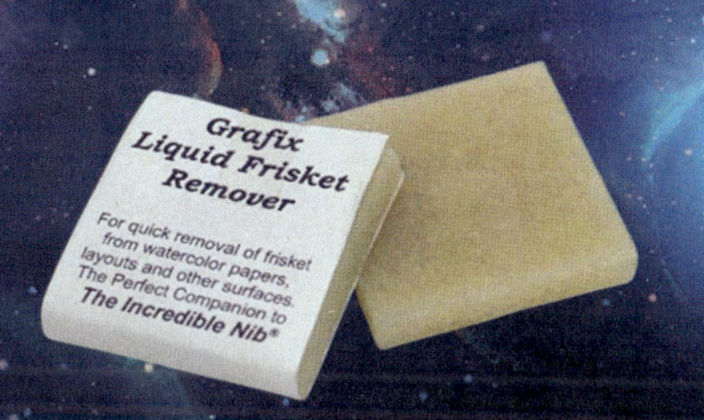

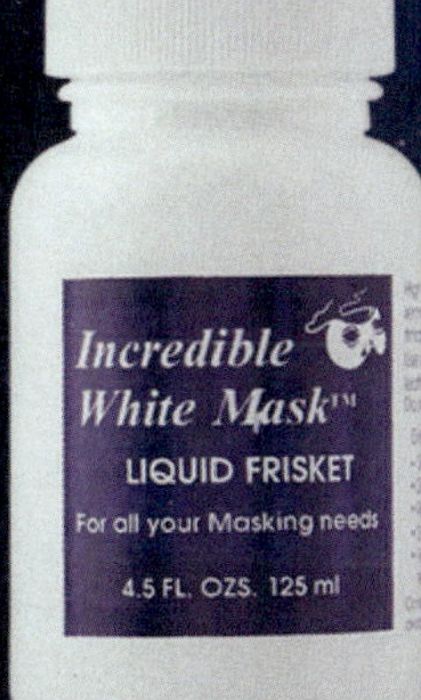

When your sketch is complete, use your dedicated paintbrush to cover the entire dragon area carefully with masking fluid. This is the brand I've come to use and love. The remover is also amazing!

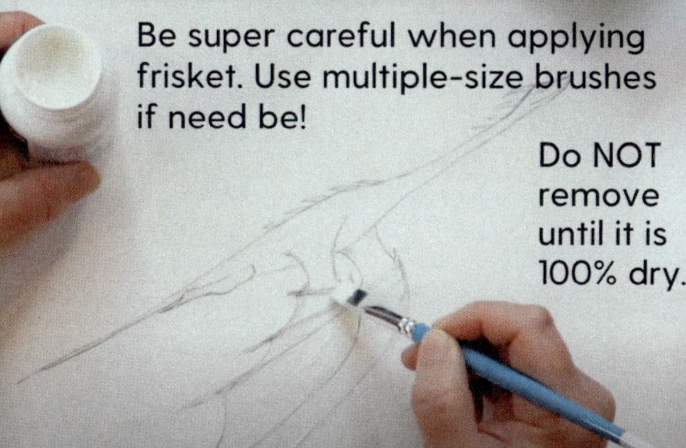

Be super careful when applying frisket. Use multiple-size brushes if need be!

Do NOT remove until it is 100% dry.

Find a bowl in your house that's about the size you envision for the moon.

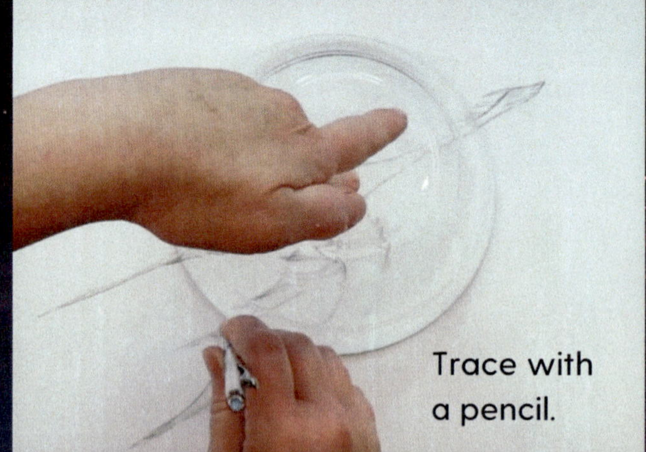

Trace with a pencil.

Now onto the fun painting part!!

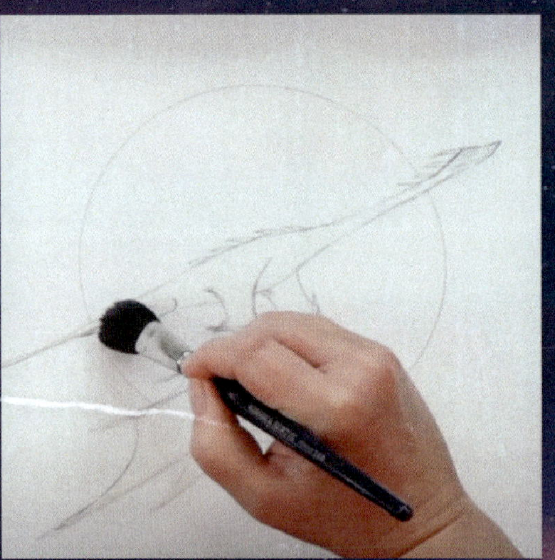

First, paint a layer of water over the entire moon circle making the paper nice and wet.

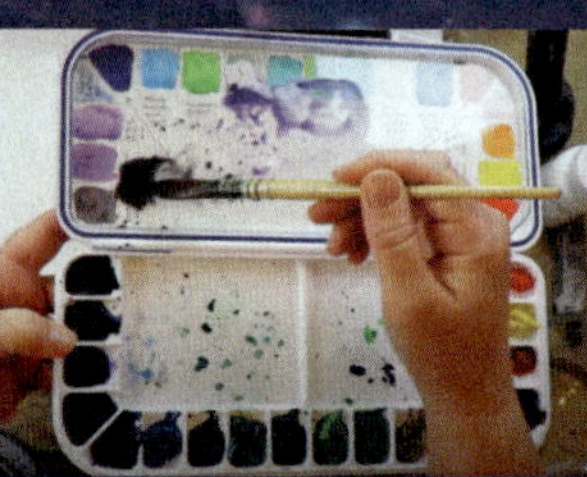

Make a water-y puddle of your moon watercolor on your palette. I'm using Daniel Smith Lunar Violet (pun intended!).

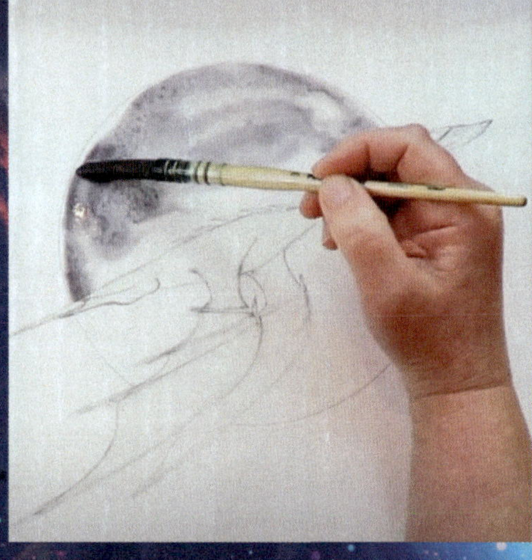

Apply your watercolor generously all around the moon region while the paper is still very wet with water.

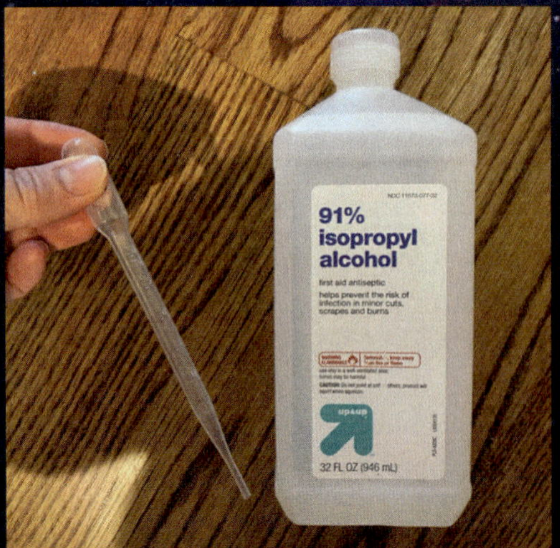

To create the craters, use a paint brush or a pipette (or eyedropper) to release droplets of rubbing alcohol over various places.

Easy and fun!

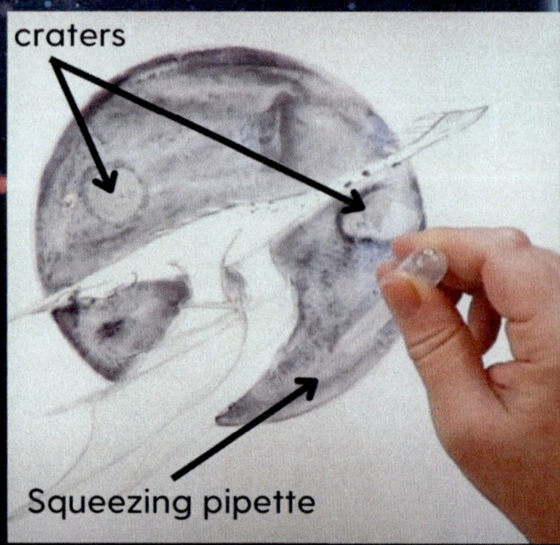

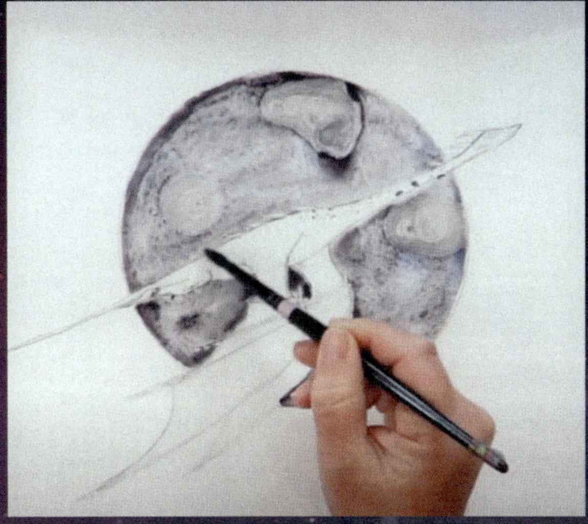

While the moon paint is still wet, feel free to add more concentrated amounts of watercolor around the dragon and craters. This will help them stand out a bit more!

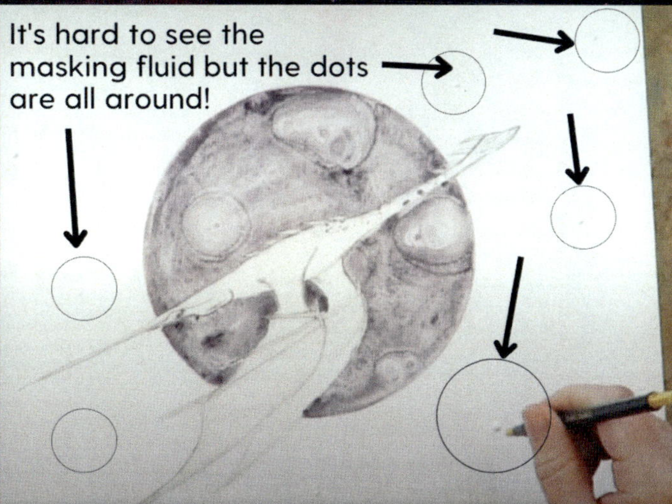

Using a paint brush or applicator, deposit single dots of masking fluid all around the moon and dragon. After we paint the background we will pull off the frisket and these will be our stars!

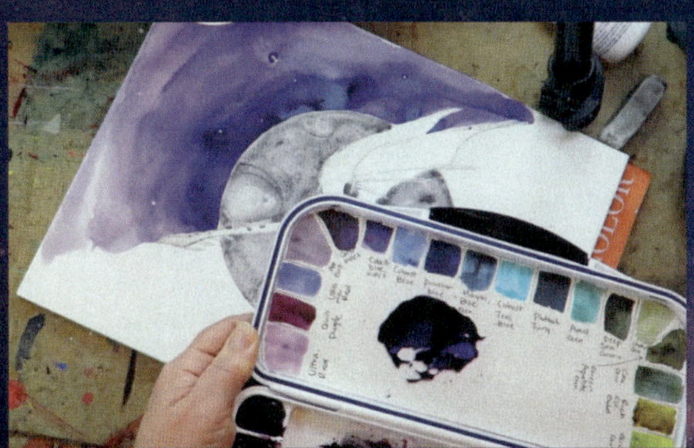

Using your favorite background sky color and some water (I'm using Daniel Smith Carbazole Violet), mix up a nice big batch for yourself so you have lots of paint and you don't run out!

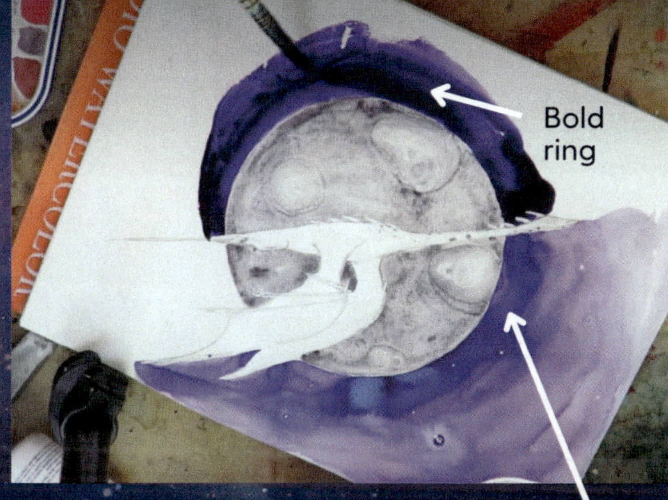

Start with a bold, concentrated ring around the moon. Add water and more watercolor (from the puddle that you made), to spread the color out to the edges of the paper.

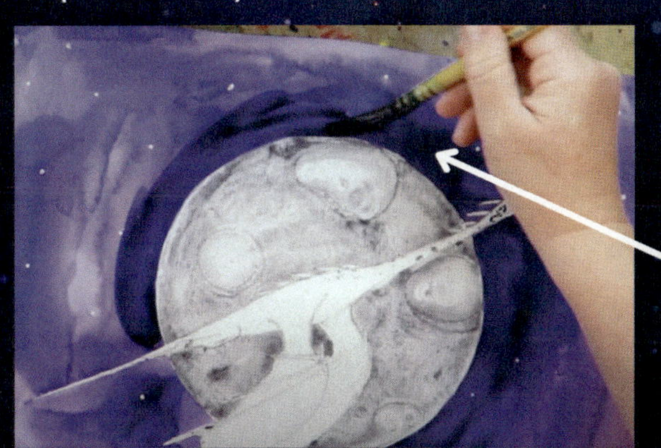

Want MORE of a concentrated look? Let your first layer dry completely and then repeat the exact same process. You'll want to move quickly and evenly. Have fun!!

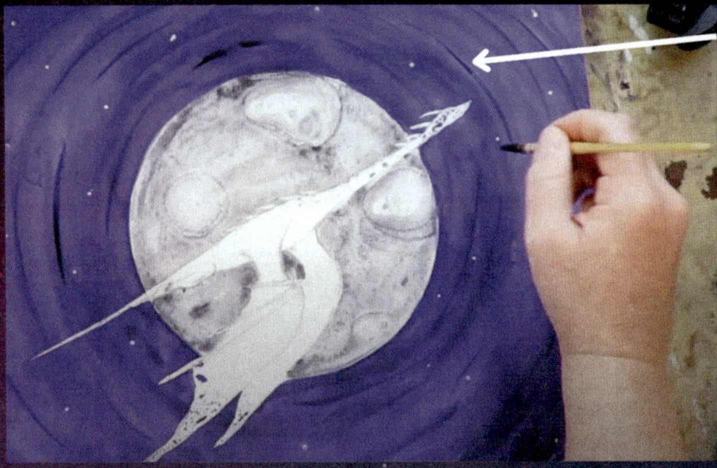

After your layers have completely dried, you can take a smaller paint brush and dip it into more concentrated watercolor paint. Moving in a circular pattern, create small curved rings around the moon.

This step is totally optional, but I really love the effect is has on the overall piece. It gives a feeling of movement.

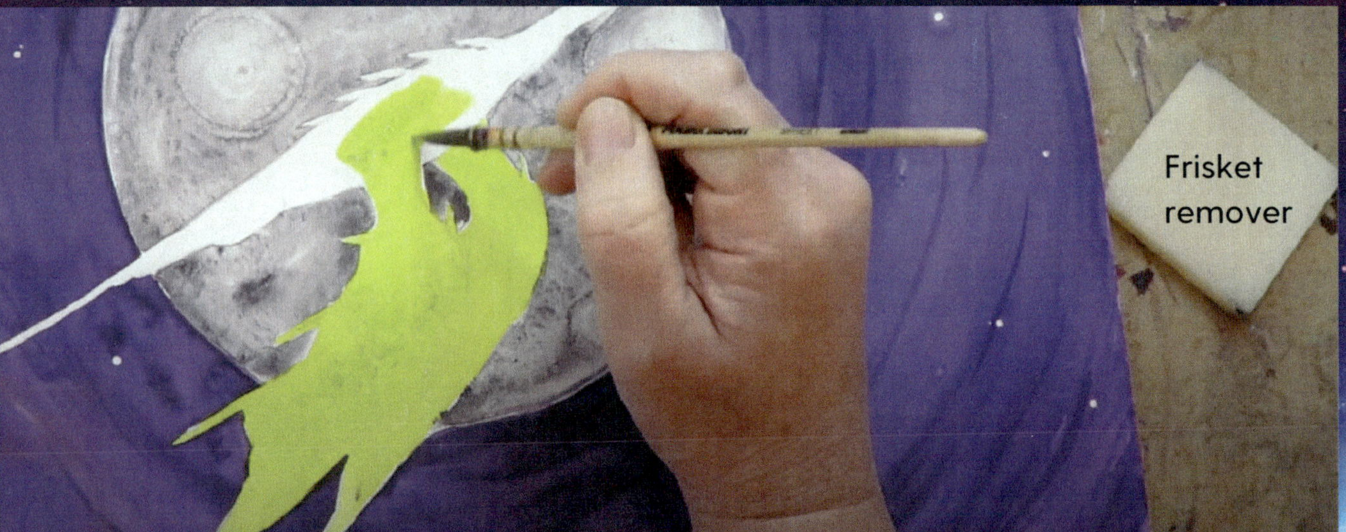

Next is the super fun part! Use your frisket remover to completely remove all the masking fluid from the sky and from the dragon's body. Then, using your favorite color, paint the entire body of the dragon. I do NOT add water to my paper before painting. Then add darker green to the BOTTOM of the dragon's body and wings. I'm using Daniel Smith's Green Gold for the first layer and Sap Green for the darker areas.

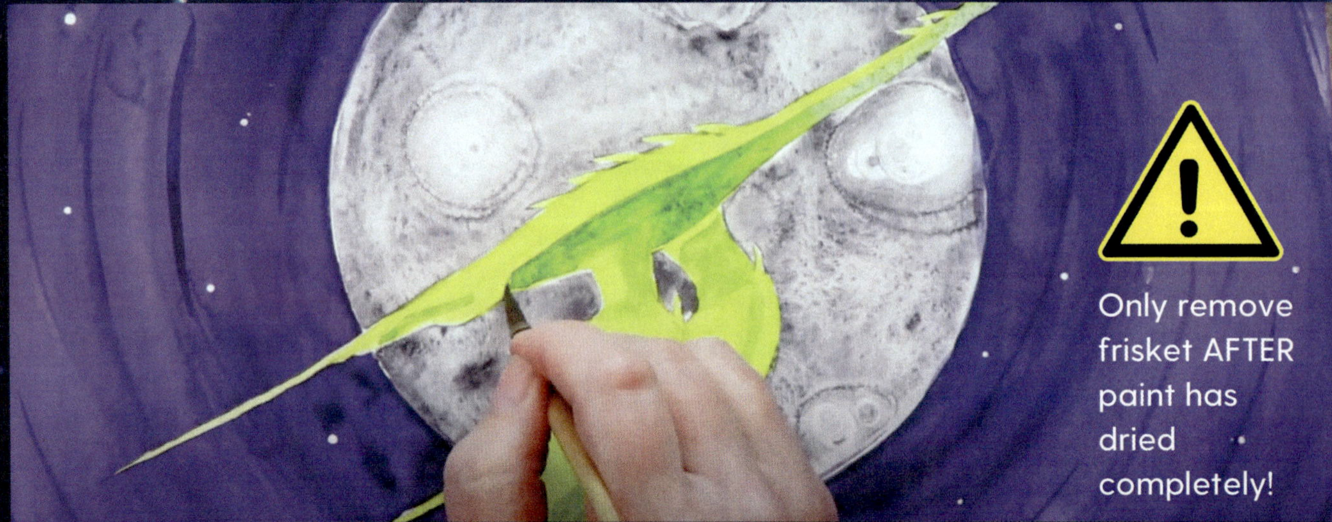

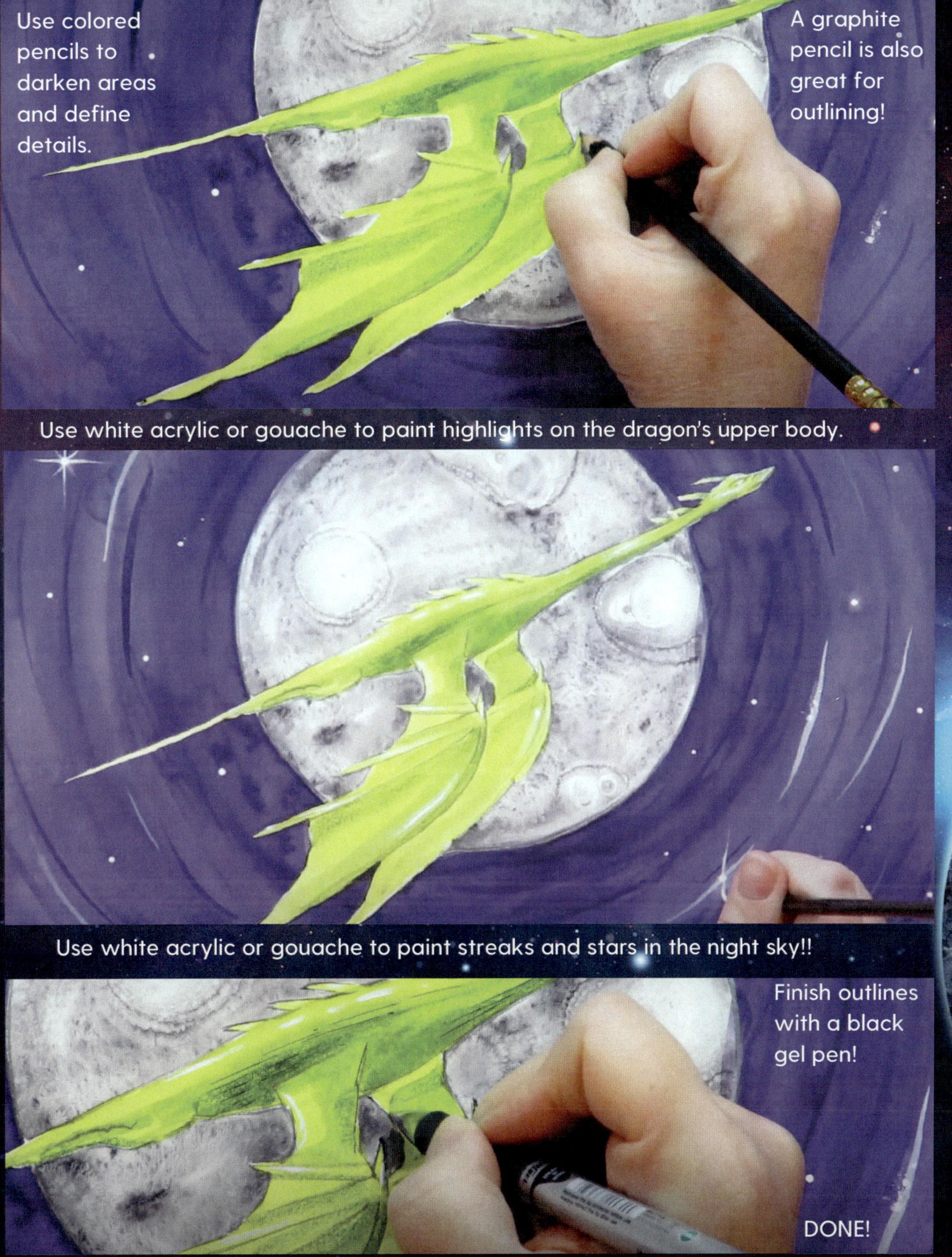
Use colored pencils to darken areas and define details.
A graphite pencil is also great for outlining!
Use white acrylic or gouache to paint highlights on the dragon's upper body.
Use white acrylic or gouache to paint streaks and stars in the night sky!!
Finish outlines with a black gel pen!
DONE!

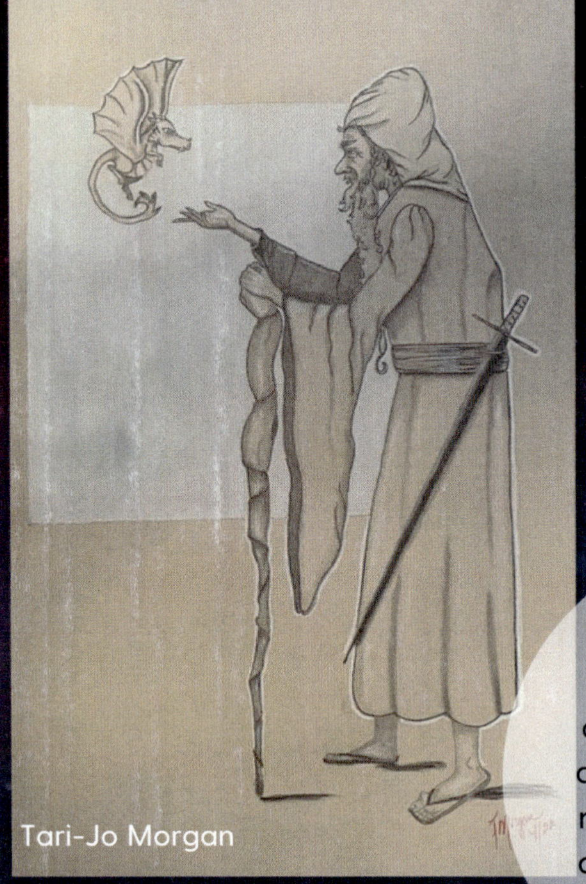

Tari-Jo Morgan

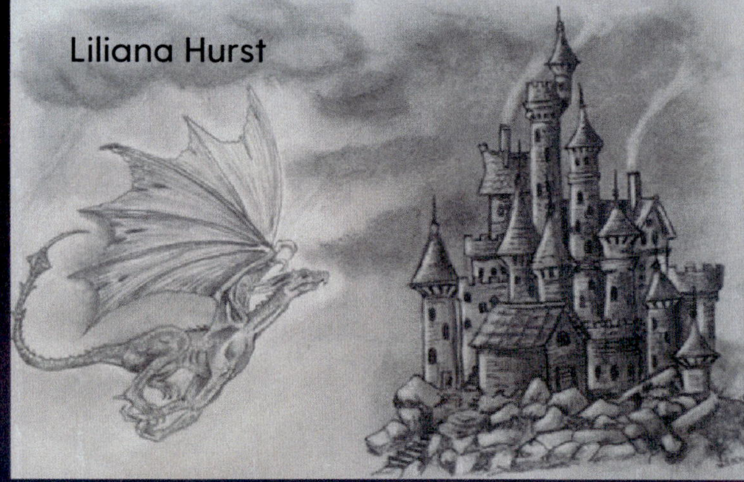

Liliana Hurst

In our art club, Celtic Collective, we LOVE drawing and painting all things mythical and magical! Here is some of our students' works from our dragon lessons!

Patricia Veneman

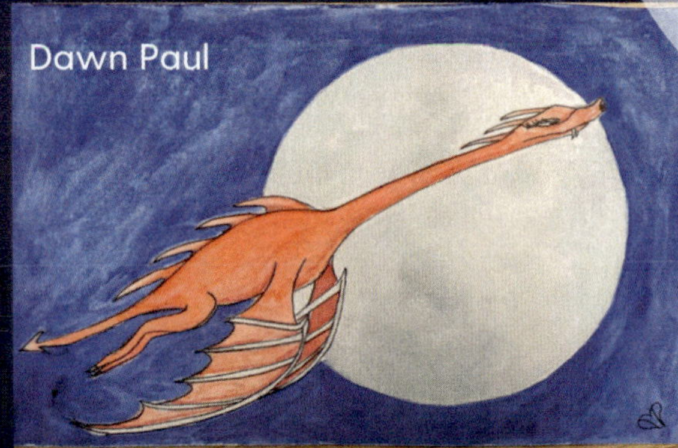

Dawn Paul

Visit 1scot1not.com/art-club.html for more info!

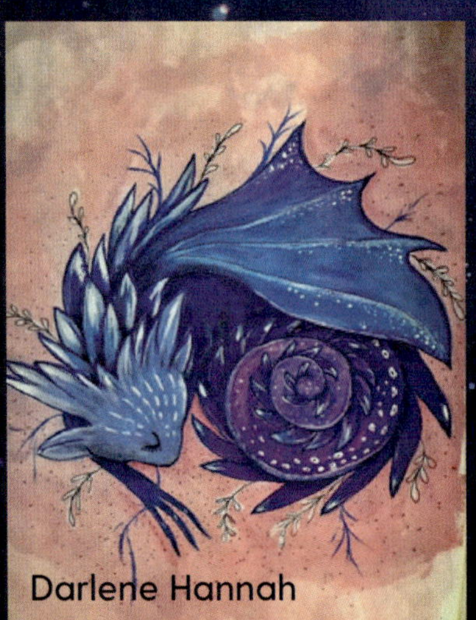

Darlene Hannah

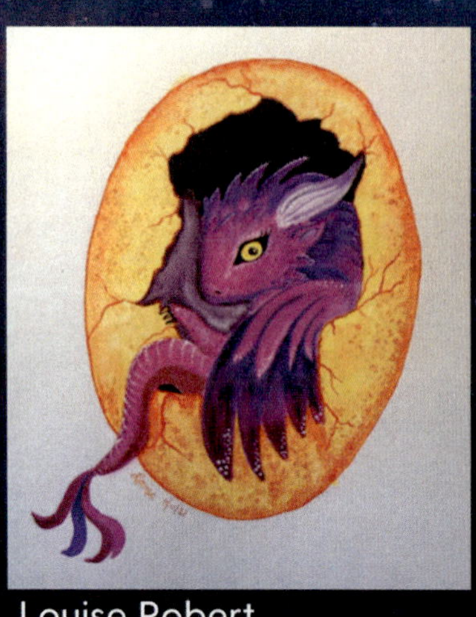

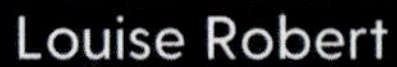

Louise Robert

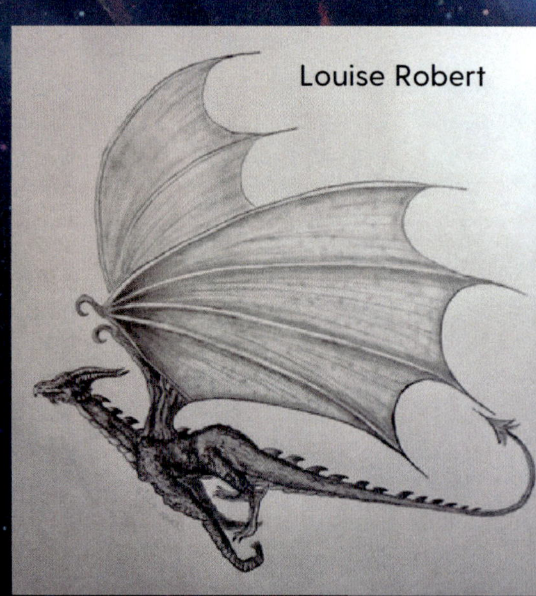

Louise Robert

Kelpie
Man Form

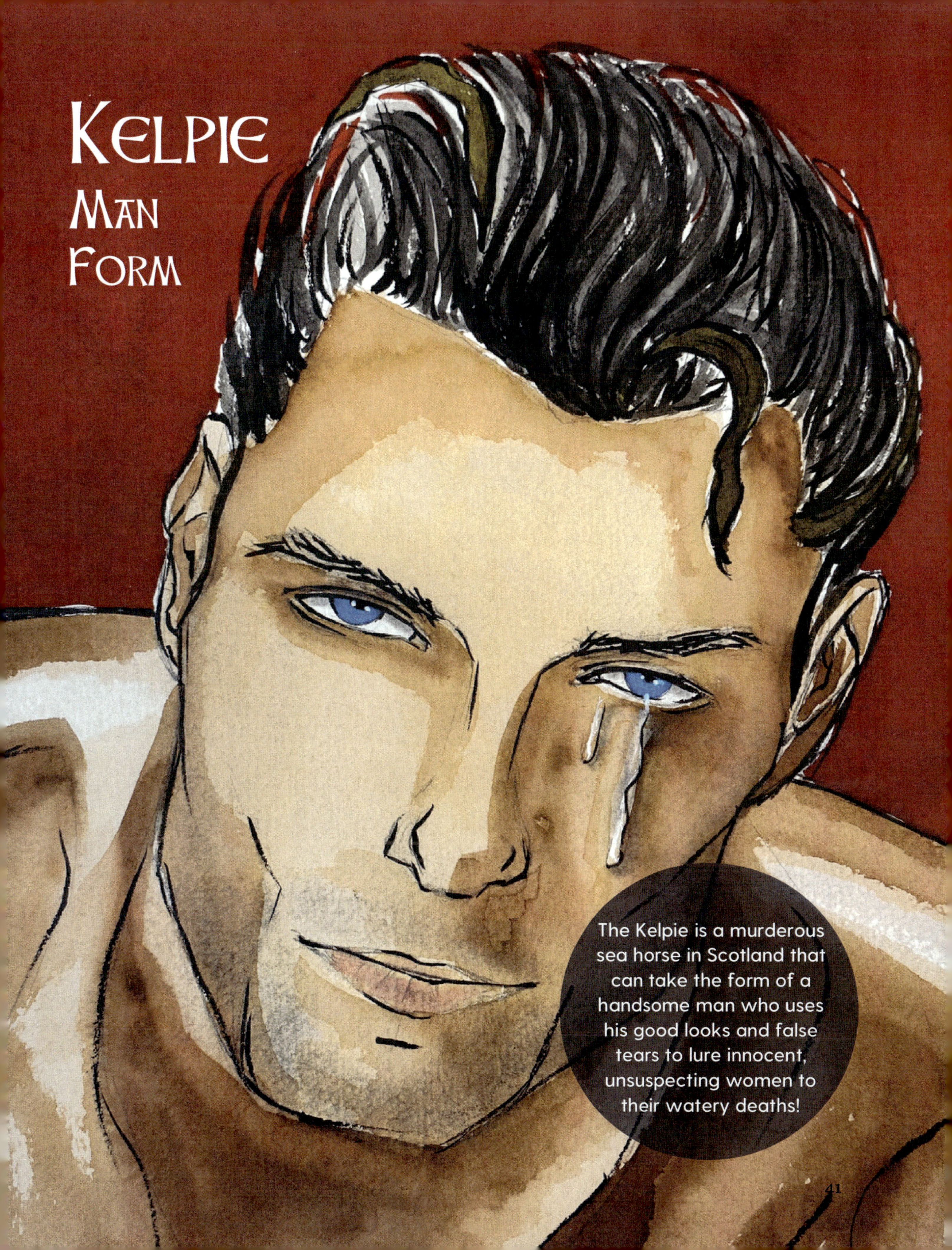

The Kelpie is a murderous sea horse in Scotland that can take the form of a handsome man who uses his good looks and false tears to lure innocent, unsuspecting women to their watery deaths!

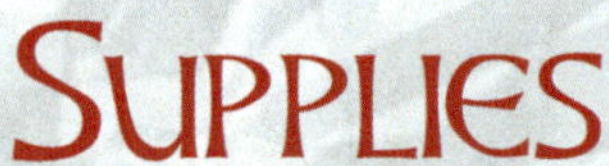

Fountain Pen Inks in red, blue, green and nude color (for skin tone).

I store my inks in wee vintage bottles!

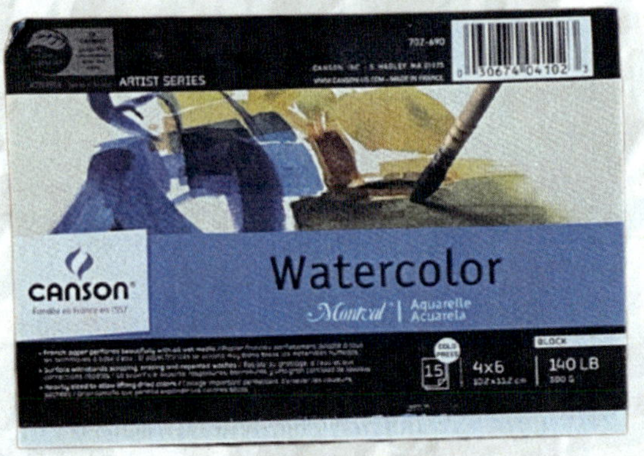

Assorted watercolor brushes.

140 lb. watercolor paper (any brand)

Mechanical pencil, brush pen, white paint pen and blending tools are great to have!

The Complexion Set of watercolors by Prima is great for skin tones! Watercolors may be substituted for any of the ink colors.

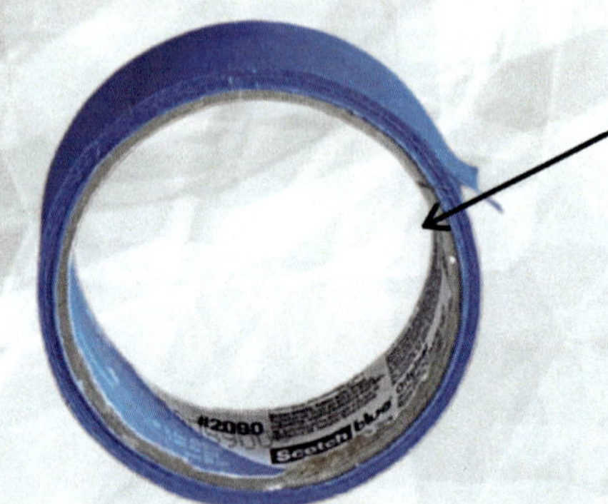

Painter's Tape creates perfect, crisp edges!

Kelpies, regardless of the horse, man or woman form they assume, always appear to be soaking wet (weird! I know!). I chose a reference for this project accordingly! This dude is handsome, naked and wet! Just like a real Kelpie!! lol!

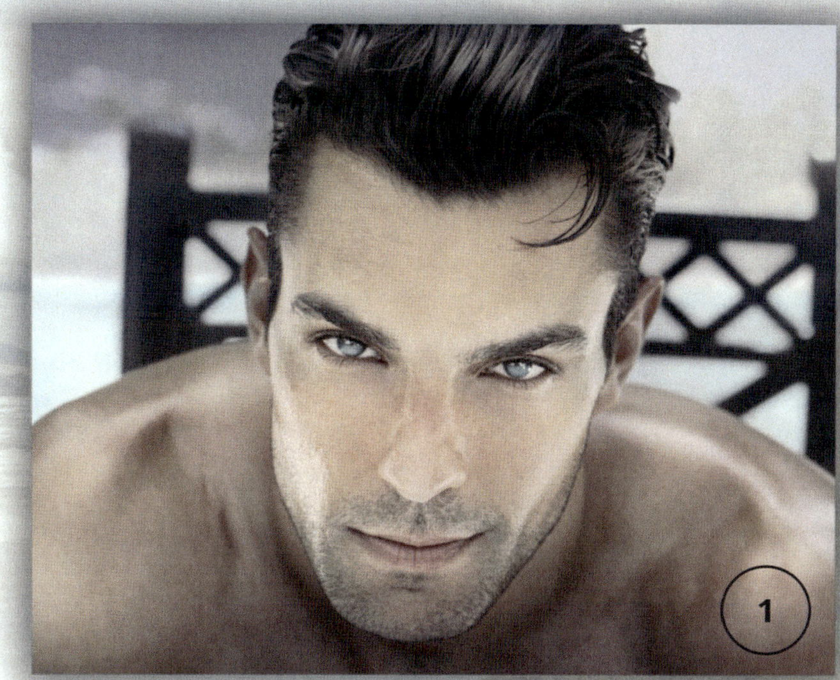

When Kelpie's take to their human, handsome man form, they often used different tricks to lure women to touch them, thereby bonding their innocent victims to them for life (so they could drown them in the depths of the deepest Scottish lochs!). One way to lure them was for the Kelpie to shed a tear in hopes that an innocent young woman would feel compelled to wipe it away. Legends confirm that this technique worked!

We will use this tear photo to help us draw one on our own Kelpie's cheek!

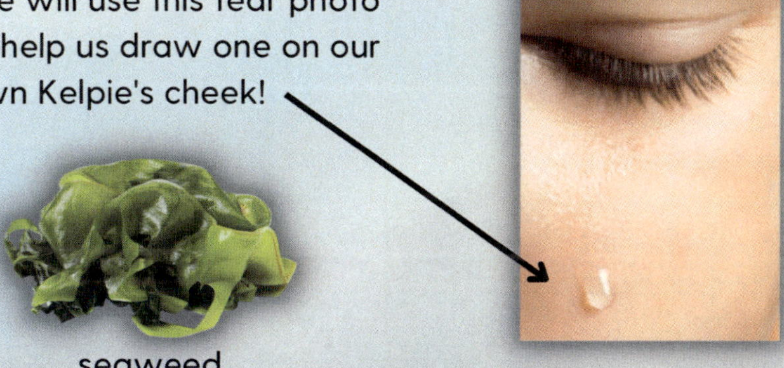

seaweed

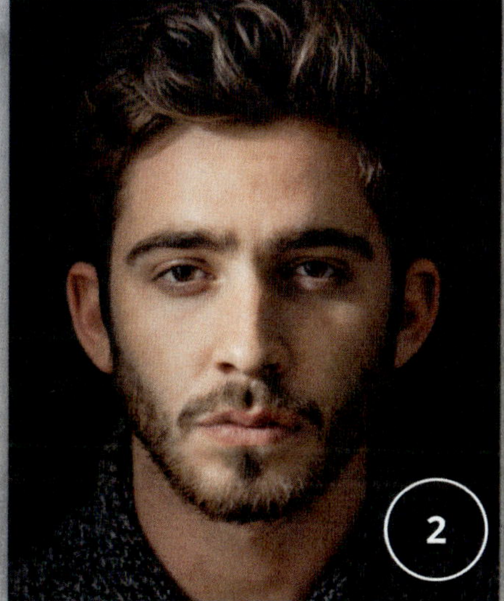

I thought the first handsome dude reference was perfect but very uninteresting in terms of shading or highlights. There was no contrast at all anywhere on his face! Choosing references that have a lot of areas of dramatic lights and darks is super fun and makes your drawings and paintings look more dimensional and dramatic too!

We will use this second reference to tell us where to make the shading on our own drawing! The last little detail here is the seaweed - which all Kelpies (in all forms) had strewn through their wet hair!

When working with wet media like inks and watercolors, it's important to use the right paper. I'm working in an art journal by Strathmore that's filled with heavy weight 140 lb. cold-pressed watercolor paper. It's perfect for super wet applications like inks! I love it!

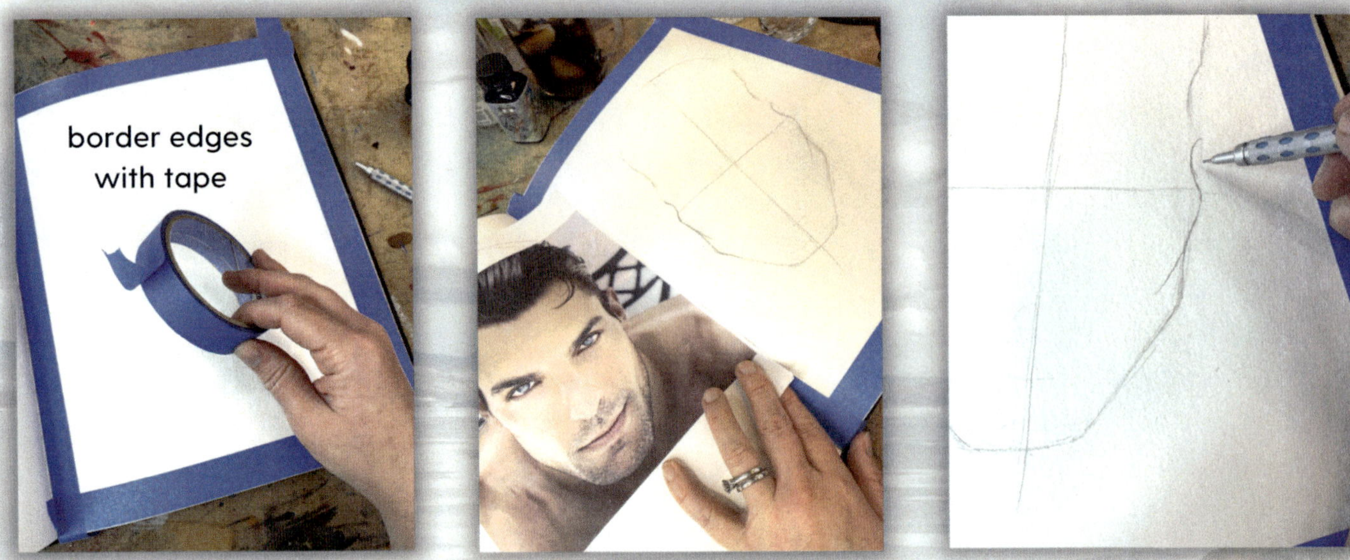

I tape the edges with painter's tape to create a crisp frame (you'll see what I mean at the end). Then I begin by drawing a large oval for the head. It takes almost the whole page and is slightly tilted (same as the model). I'm paying close attention to the curvy cheekbones! Divide the oval/head shape both vertically and horizontally with light lines.

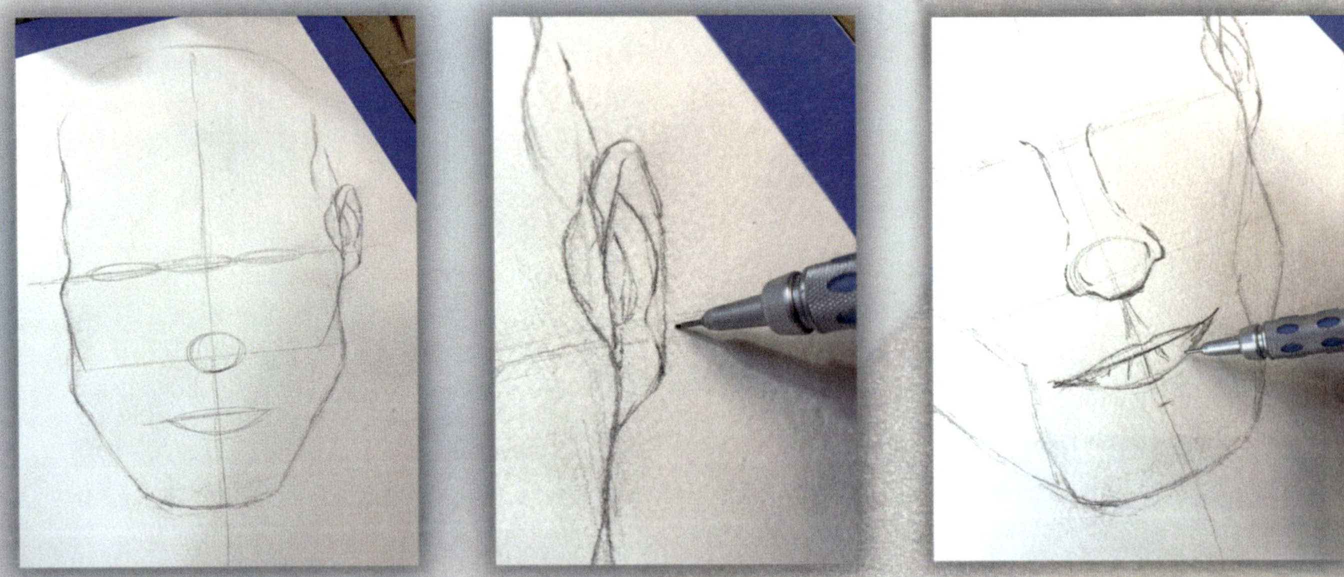

Sketch thin ovals for the eyes (draw 3 of the same size ovals across for perfect eye spacing and placement), a circle for the ball of the nose and a thin mouth. Ears line up as shown across the horizontal line. Draw the nose bridge on either side and lines on the mouth. If you need help drawing uniform circles and ovals, grab a template!

Take your time to build one facial feature at a time. The eyebrows come directly off of the nose bridge we drew in the last step. Note how they sit right on top of the eye itself.

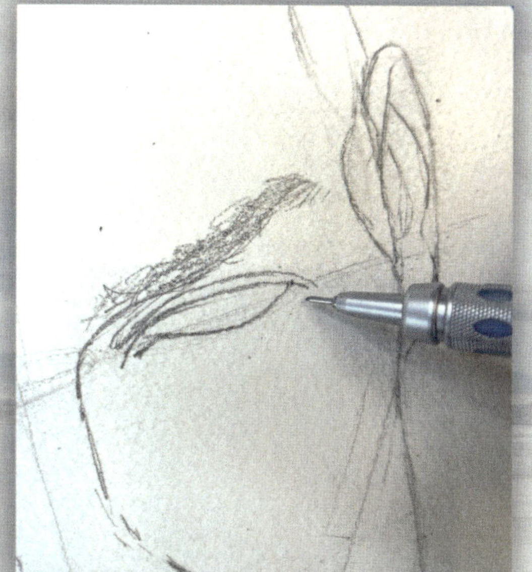

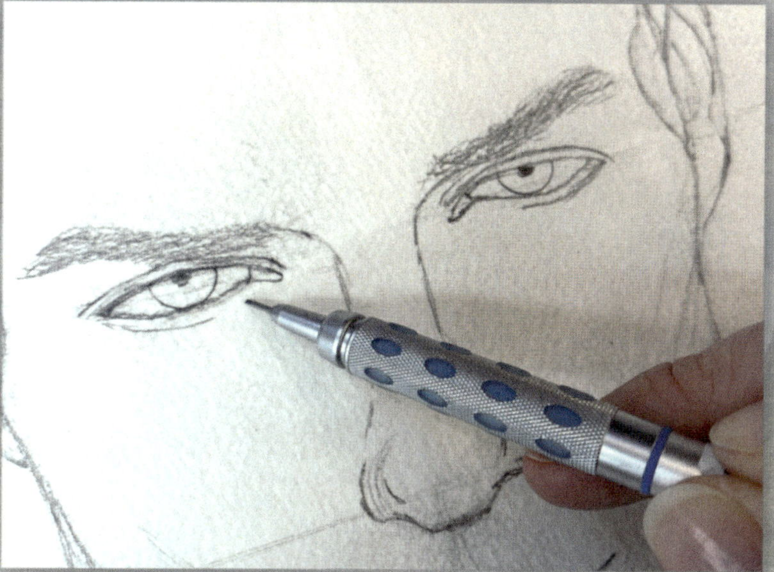

Each eye shape has a thin lid that's drawn both above and below the eye itself. When you have the two eyes drawn so they look fairly equal and even (use a ruler if you'd like, to make sure the tops and bottoms line up), add circles for the irises and pupils. Note how the irises are "cut off" by the lid so that only a half circle appears.

Draw the shape of the hair next. Notice how far it comes into the head itself.

It comes to a "V" in the center of the forehead here.

His shoulders are drawn as just a few curved lines that originate from his earlobes.

Draw in his sculpted cheekbones as well!

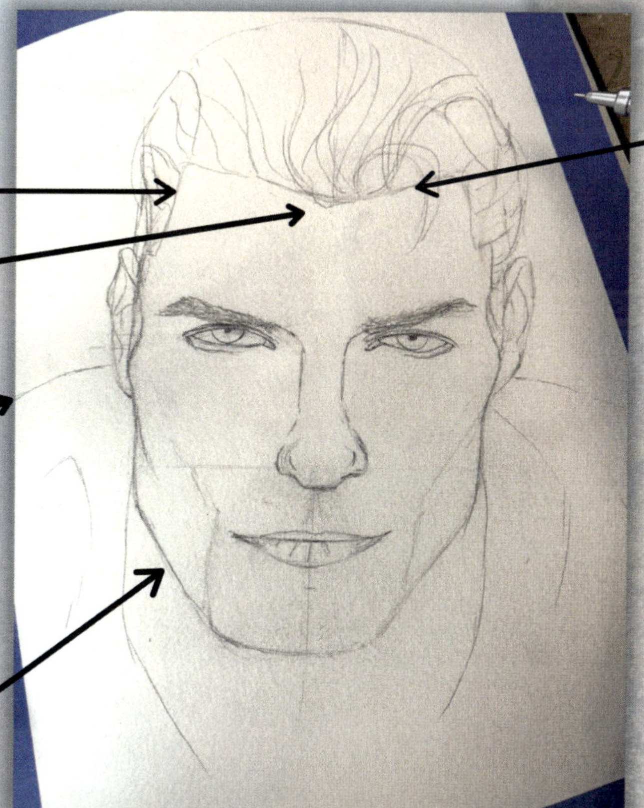

Draw hair strands that begin at the "V" in front and continue straight back towards the back of the head.

Make one piece that flops forward to the right of the "V". This will become the seaweed...the tale-tell sign that this is not a mere mortal man, but a Kelpie in disguise!!

To reemphasize what we already covered in the Fairy Queen project, it's so so crucial to draw in your facial guidelines so do not skip this step! And, as always, feel free to use a template to help you create great circles (and ovals) for all the facial features.

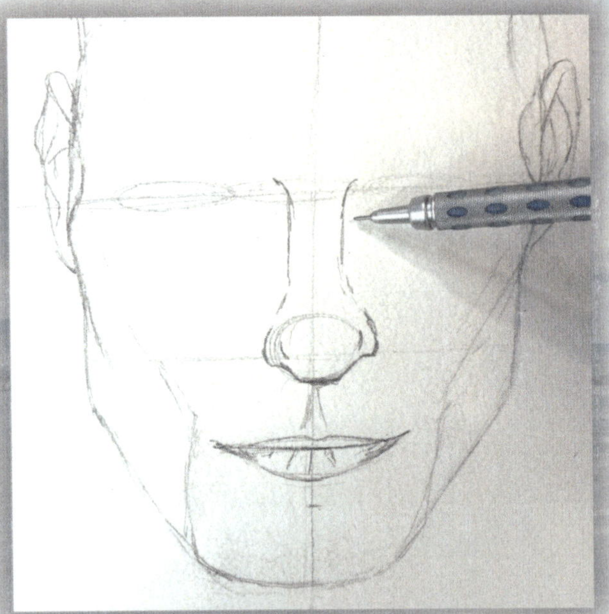

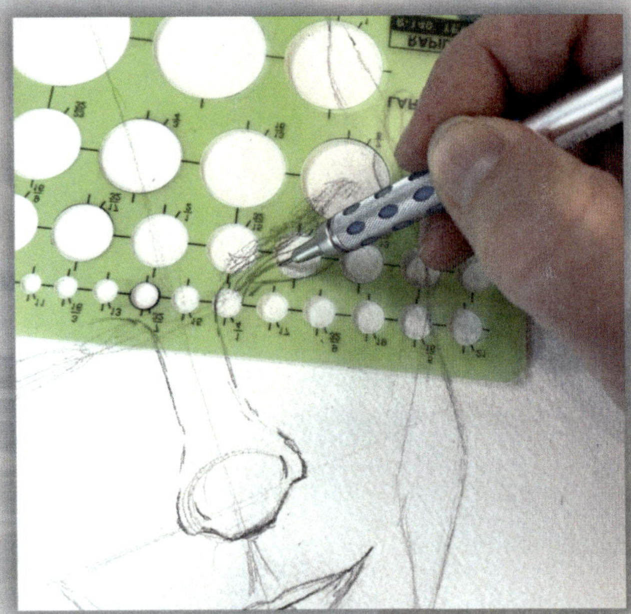

Another tip for drawing eyes that match is to draw a little at a time, developing them together rather than drawing one to completion followed by the other. This ensures even development and is much easier (I find) to make them match one another. Have trouble creating those perfect iris shapes? No problem! Use your handy-dandy circle template to help you draw them perfectly!

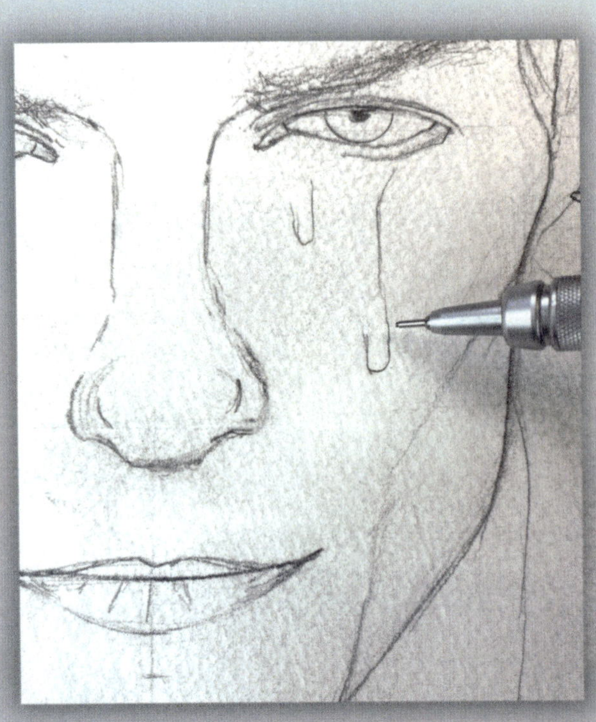

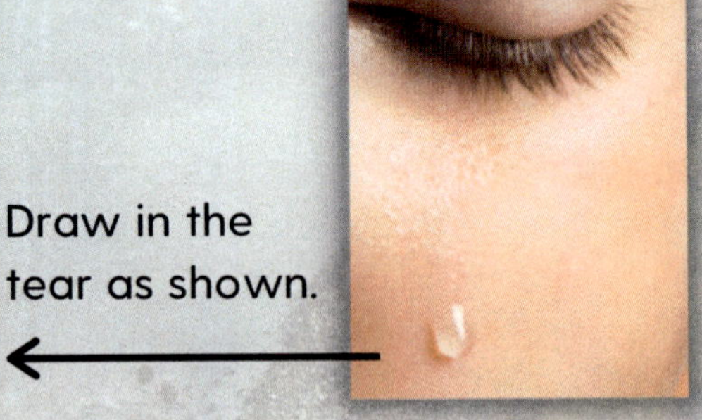

Draw in the tear as shown.

Look at a picture to help you with shapes as well as with shading and highlights, just as we are doing here!

Always feel free to lean on references to help you with your ideas or if you're not sure how to draw something. It's 100% okay to do!

Technically speaking you only use fountain pen inks to write with fountain pens but...we're artists so we're used to breaking the rules, right? Fountain pen inks come in a dizzying array of vibrant colors! Some are VERY water-soluble (will run when water is added) and some are permanent. Read the labels if you decide to purchase some so you know what to expect.

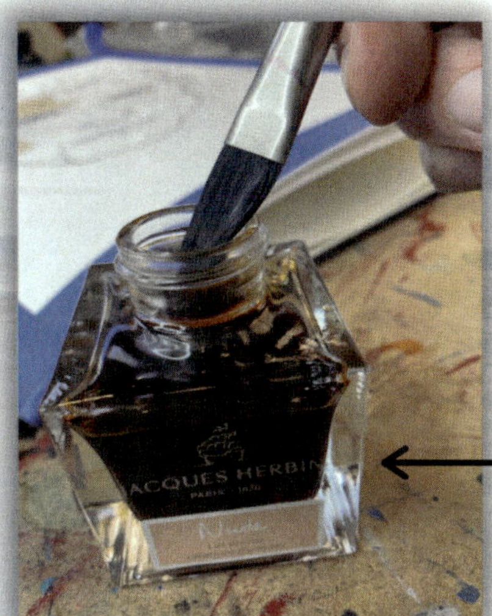

When working with inks, I dip my watercolor brush directly into the jar and then apply the ink directly onto my watercolor paper.

To feel fancy (and to be inspired), I store most of my fountain pen inks in these vintage perfume bottles! With so many wonderful colors and brands (I especially love Noodlers brand) I have amassed quite the fun collection!

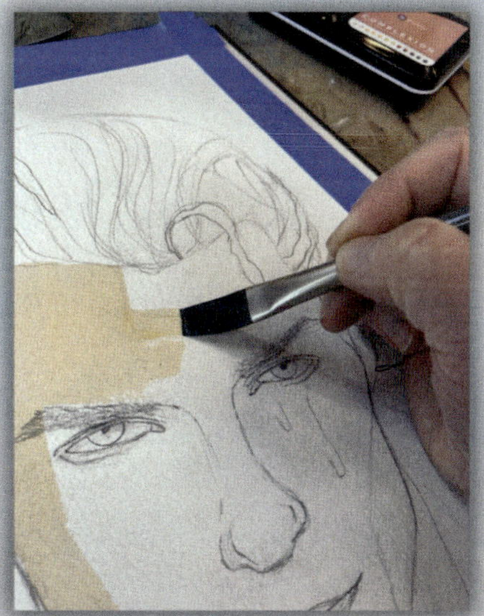

No inks? No problem, grab this wonderful set.

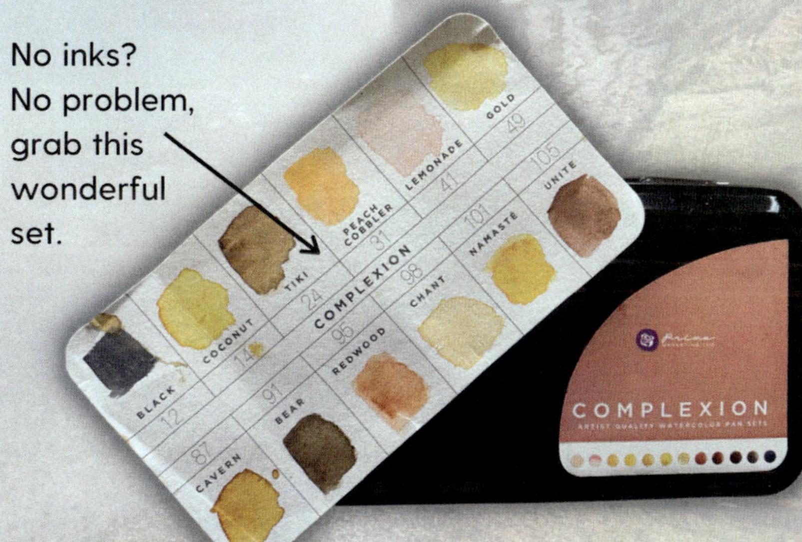

Cover the entire face and shoulder areas with a nude ink color. I love "Nude" by Jacques Herbin but it can be difficult to come by. The Complexion Set by Prima makes a perfect replacement for skin color fountain pen ink colors. Watercolors can be applied in the exact same manner (and can be used interchangeably) as inks so feel free to substitute!

Once the first layer of skin tone has been applied to the entire face, neck and shoulders, we will be adding some layers of shading with a darker color. I used Kiowa Pecan color by Noodler's Ink. If you're using the Complexion Set by Prima, Chant and Tiki would be good equivalent alternatives.

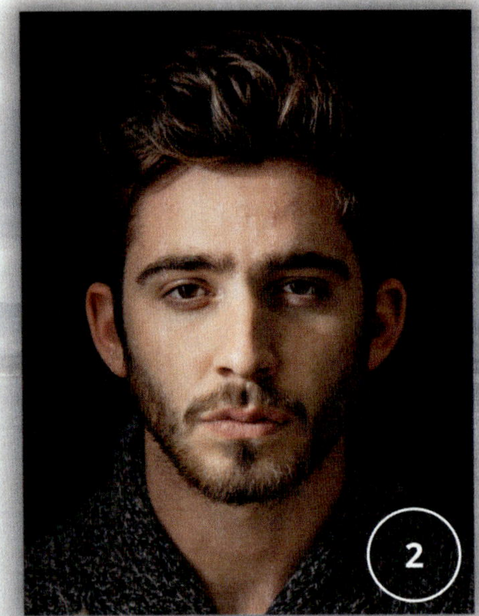

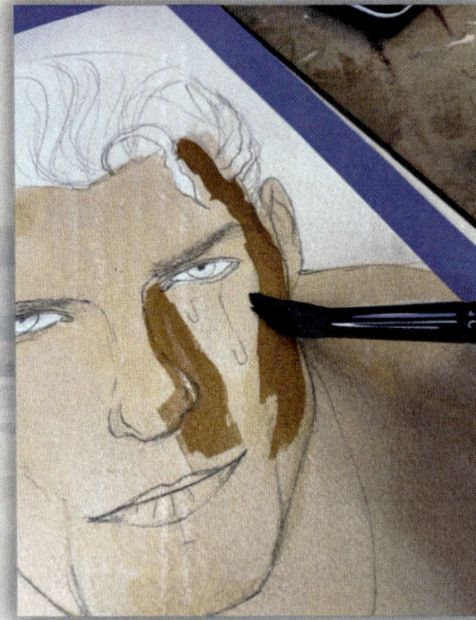

If the colors aren't blending together very well, you can add either plain water OR the first, lighter color to the areas between light and dark.

This will help both colors to blend together better.

I'm still working straight from the bottle in each case!

Remember this guy? This is the second reference. We are using THIS reference not for drawing purposes, but to help us know where to add our shading!

As you can see, the whole right side of this second reference face is nice and darkly shaded. This means that is where we'll put our darker paint!

Add the darker Pecan color (or Tiki) to all the dark areas shown. These inks (like watercolors) are watersoluble. That means the first layer will melt into the second layer and blending them together is pretty easy!

Adding areas of shading creates depth and dimension and DRAMA to our faces that you just can't achieve with only one color!

Notice the areas that DON'T get shading too. Those are just as important!

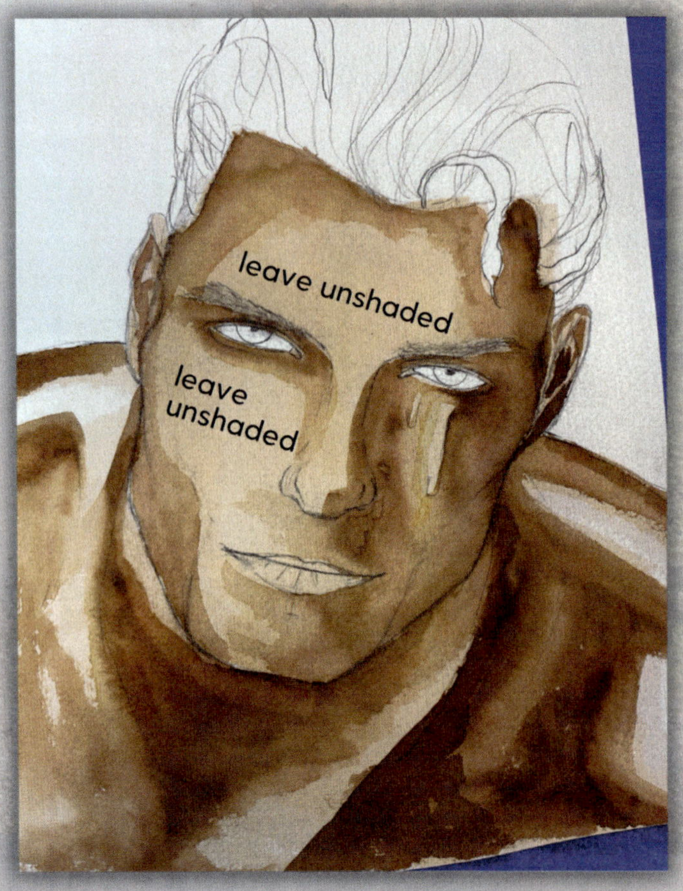

This is actually a fairly simple project when it comes to completing the colored portion! All that's next for his face is to paint his alluring blue eyes (or eyes of any color you like!), add color to his hair (and seaweed bits in green) and to fine tune the outline!

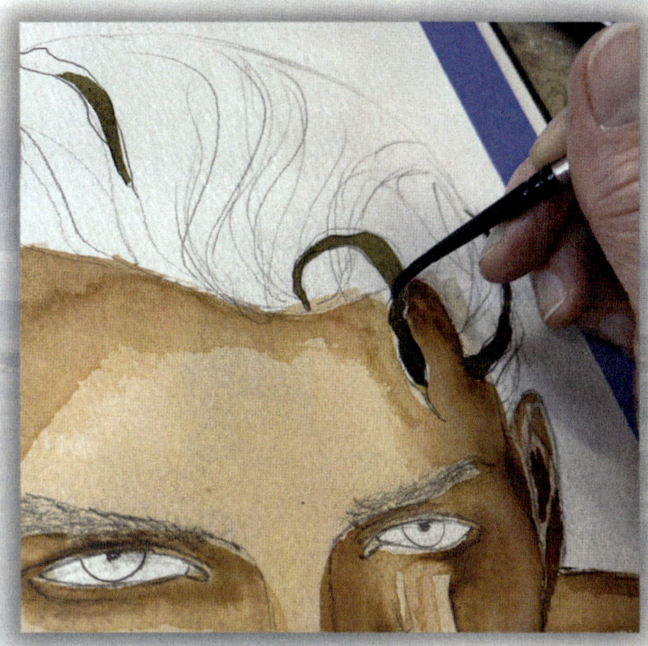

I'm using Army Green from Noodlers for a few seaweed strands!

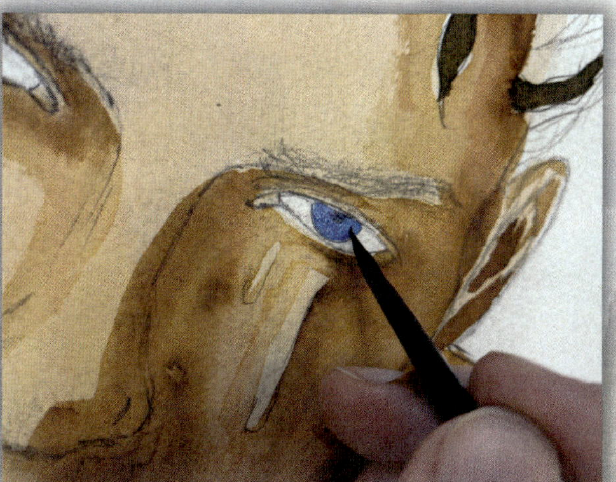

I'm using Blue from Noodlers for some brilliant eye color!!

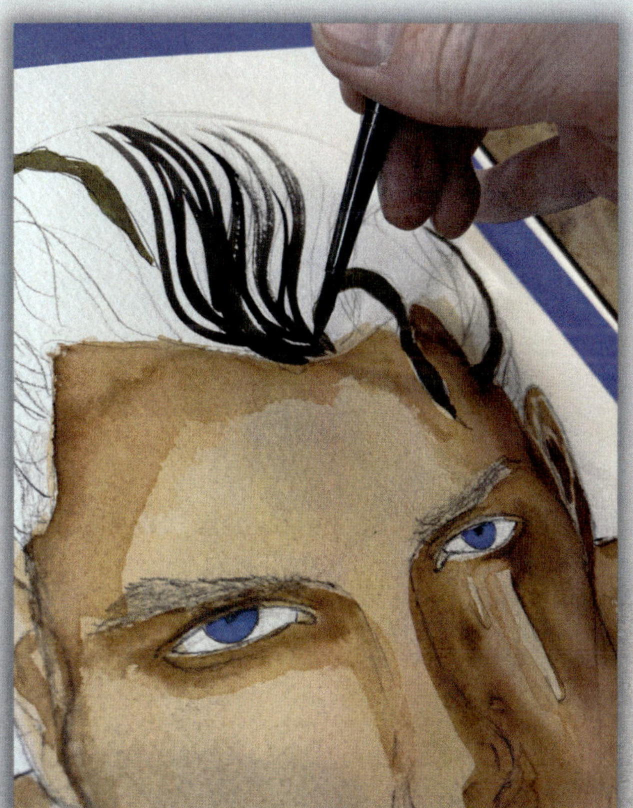

Next, using the same small watercolor paint brush, start at the "V" of the hairline and paint a series of wavy, vertical strokes to represent his thick, luscious (and wet, of course!) hair! Refer to the original reference if you need help with the directionality of his hair strands.

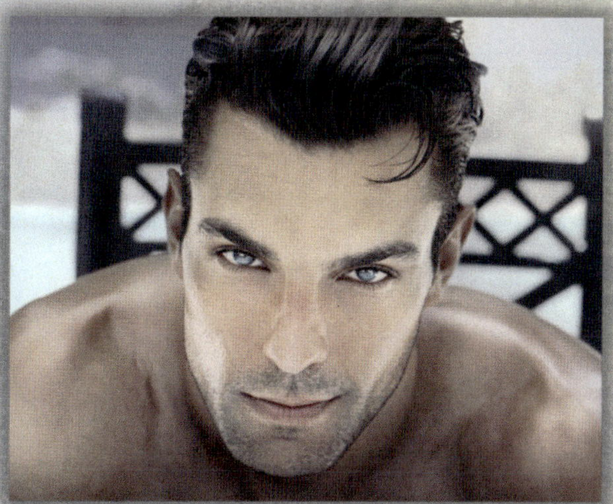

Next, I chose the appropriately named color "Widow Maker" by Noodler's to paint a blood red background! Paint right up to the tape and let dry. When you peel back the tape after your ink as dried, your lines are crisp and unbelievably clean!

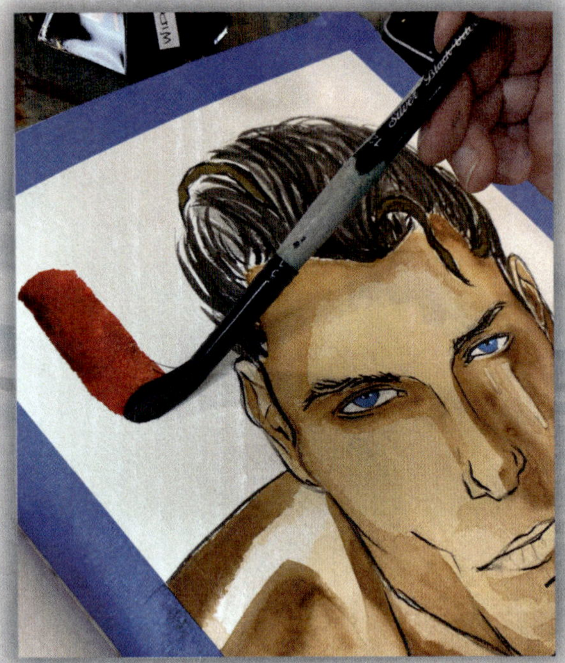

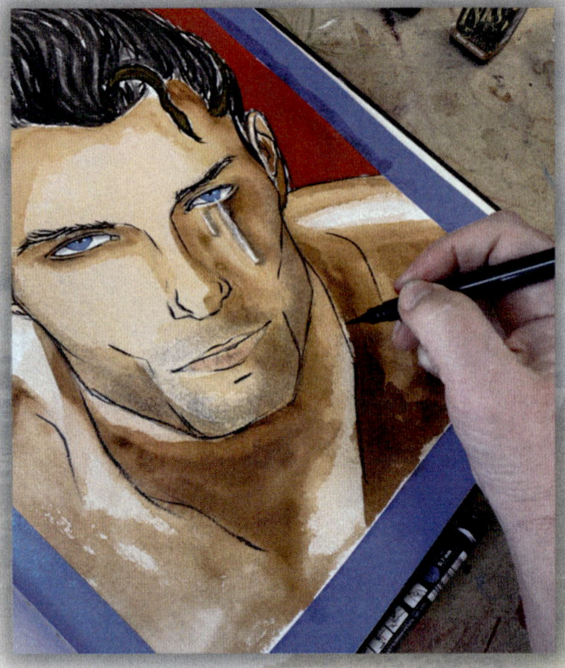

Almost finished! I LOVE to outline my faces. Outlining is easy and fun using my favorite Pentel Pocket Brush Pen which contains black permanent ink. I outline every thing from his features to the outside frame but keep pressure light so the line doesn't become too heavy or continuous. A dot of white paint pen in the eyes brings him to LIFE! Great job! Have you been lured?!?

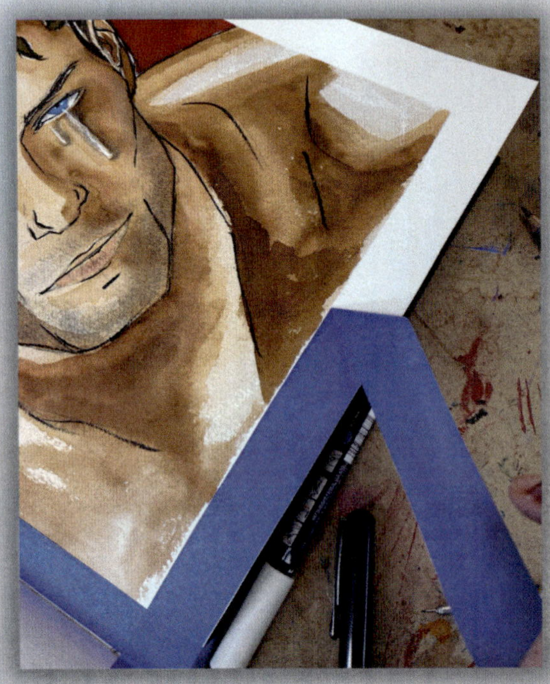

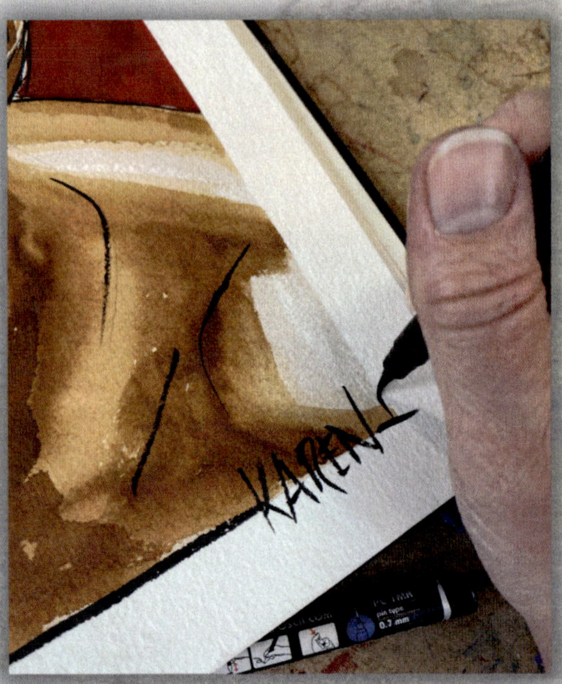

Magical Mermaid

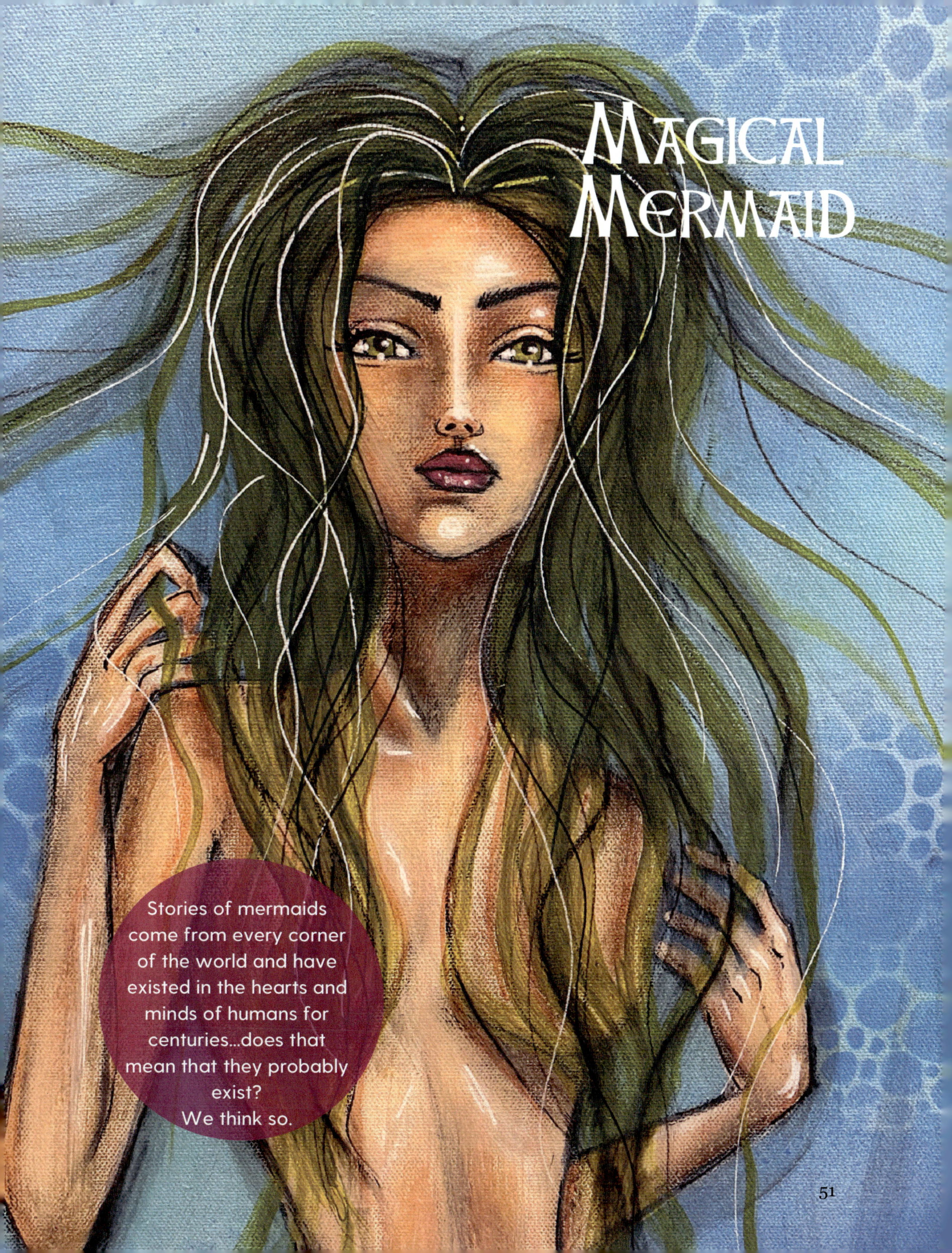

Stories of mermaids come from every corner of the world and have existed in the hearts and minds of humans for centuries...does that mean that they probably exist?
We think so.

Supplies

Mod Podge in Matte and/or in Sparkle!
White Gesso
2 - 12"x24" canvases or 1 long one
Bubble Stencil
Pitt Pens by Faber-Castell in Black, White, Cinnamon & Flesh
Large fan brush
Acrylics in flesh, magenta and green
Gelatos (gel sticks) in skin color and white
Foam brush for Mod Podge (sealer) layers
White Paint Pen
Stabilo All Pencil
Paint Brush
Colored Pencils
Magenta Glitter!
Select multiple shades of blues, teals, and greens in either spray paints or acrylics.
MOD PODGE
Liquitex
GOLDEN
LUKAS CRYL STUDIO
POSCA
BASICS ACRYLIC

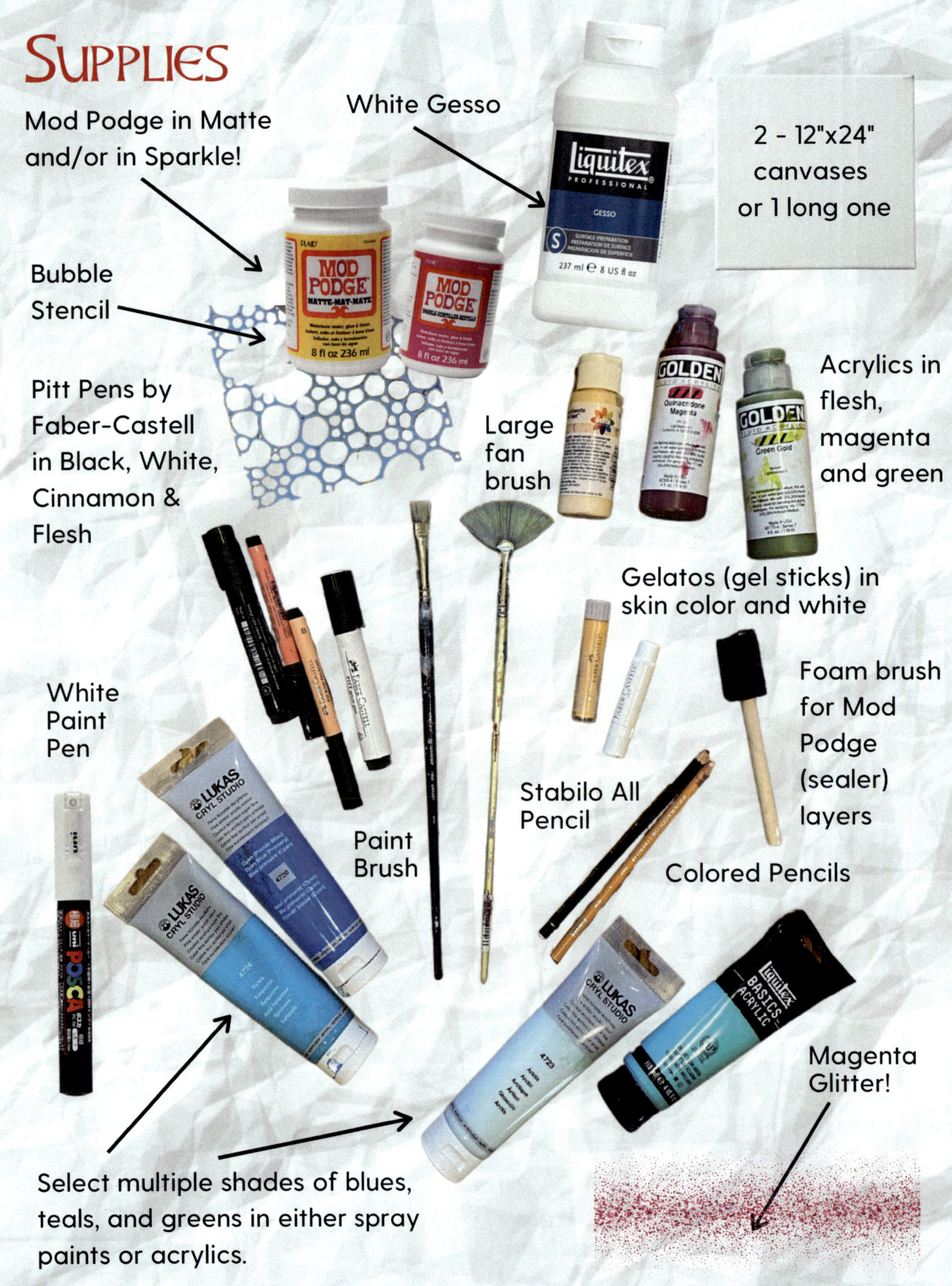

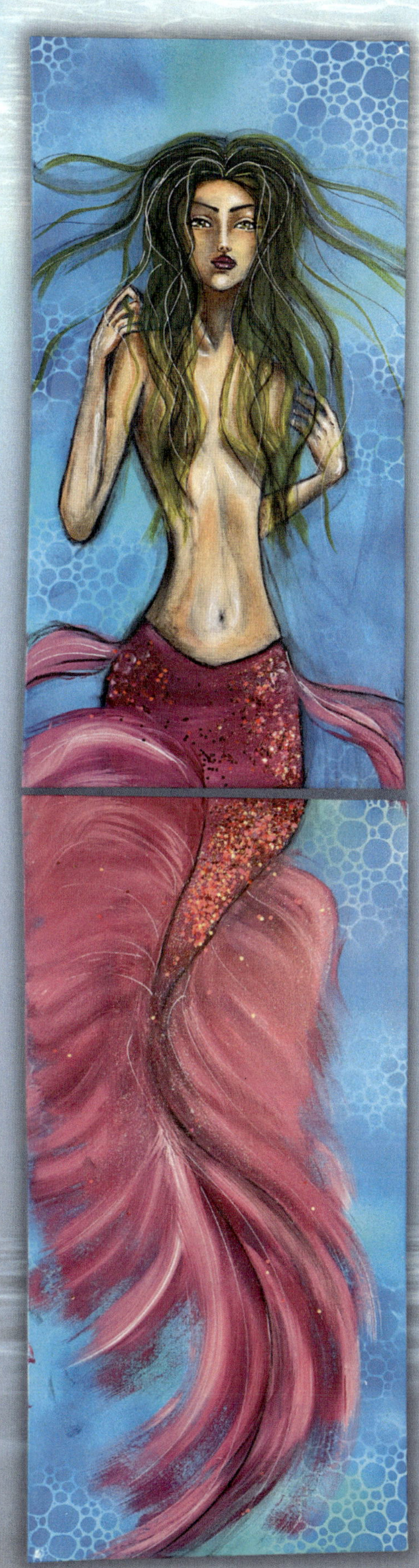

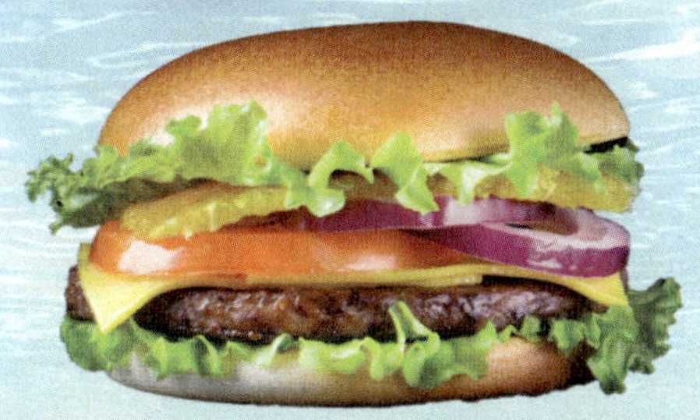

I know what you're thinking right about now...WHY is there a hamburger next to the mermaid??

Well, the answer is simple: because I'm about to teach you my FAVORITE mixed media layering system - and it works in the same way as your favorite grilled beef patty topped with all those delicious toppings!

We'll start with the plate (in this case, two long canvases) and slowly and systematically layer our art supplies in a specific order until we make this gorgeous masterpiece!

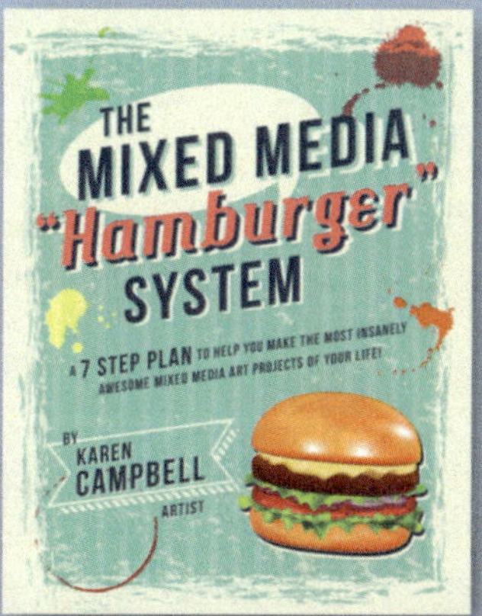

Turn the page and I'll show you each layer before delving in. If you'd like to learn more about this SUPER easy and fun way to do mixed media, you can check out my Mixed Media Hamburger System paperback book (Amazon). I also have a FREE eight-part video series that explains more about this easy-to-follow technique! Watch the free series here: bit.ly/hamburgerseries

Can't get enough of the burger? Want MORE projects and the digital book for free? Sign up for my 16-project course for beginners at mixedmediahamburger.com!

This graphic will help you see exactly what supplies we use and in which layer and in which order. This same layering technique can be (and is) used to create a HUGE range of mixed media projects!

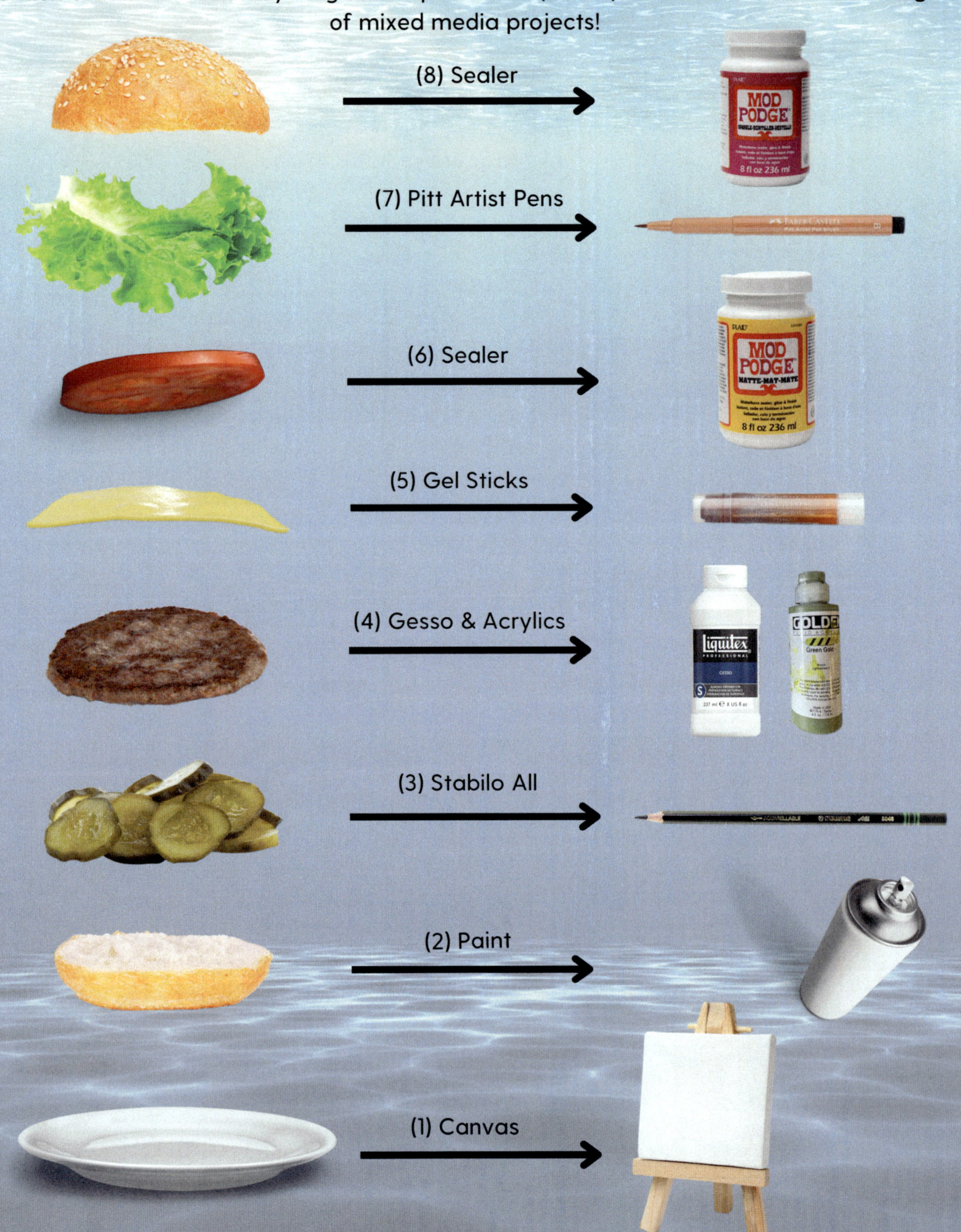

Now that you've wrapped your brain around my favorite mixed media system and the layers that are involved, let's get to work and have some fun!

First, please know you can easily do this project in an art journal or on a single canvas if the thought of working on two separate ones feels daunting. You can also easily trade regular acrylic paints for spray paints. Just coat the canvases completely with a brush, alternating your four shades of green, blue and teal.

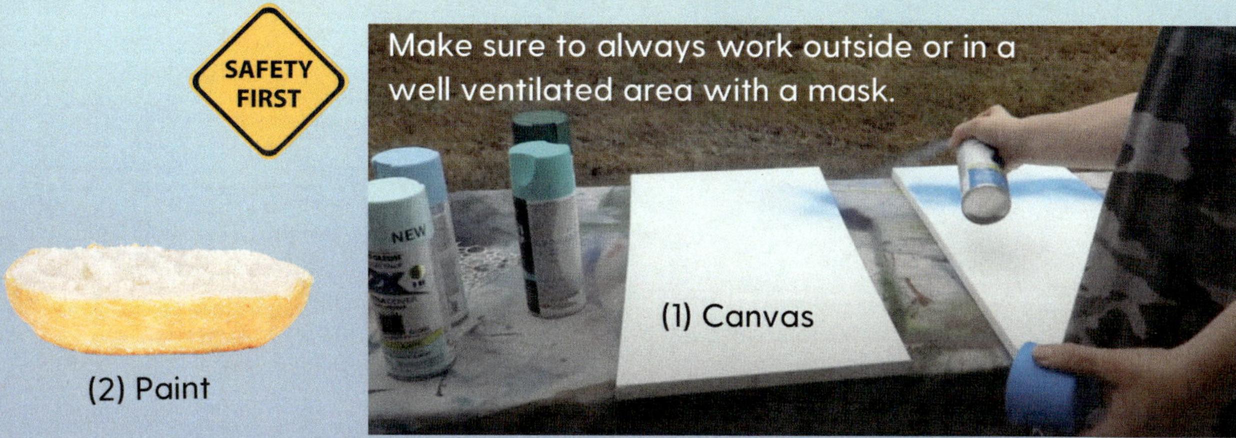

In this case, I'm using spray paints! Spray paints are super cheap, widely available and come in a TON of fun colors! Shake cans for a good two minutes before spraying. Take turns alternating as you spray each of the four colors evenly across the two canvases.

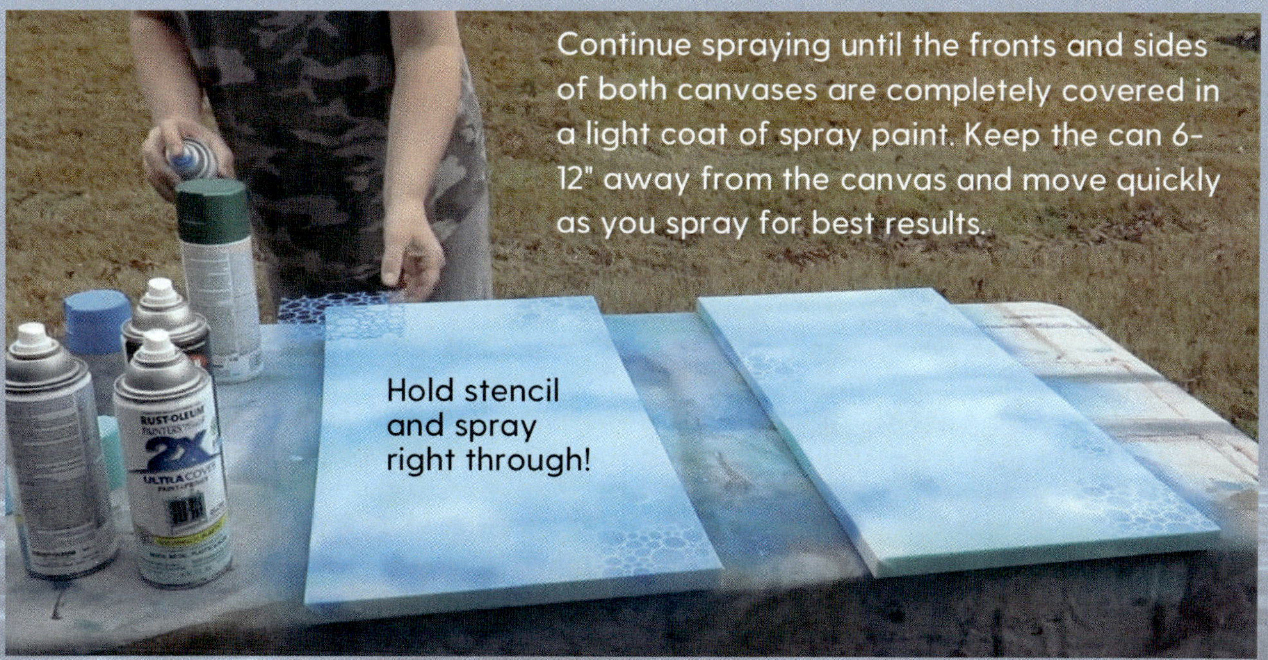

Next, grab your water or bubble stencil and place gently down on the canvas and spray paint directly through the openings of the stencil. Don't worry about cleaning your stencils, just let the paint dry there. Add bubbles to all four corners and along the sides in just one or two places. This is fast background creation and I hope you love it!

Now that the background is complete, bring your canvas inside and get ready to draw the mermaid! Use a watercolor pencil for all your drawing. I'm using a Stabilo All Pencil in black which is a SUPER fun drawing tool that is reactive when you add water or any liquid. The reason drawing with a watercolor pencil is so important (and AMAZING) is that if you make a mistake you can simply "erase" by running a wet paper towel over your lines and they will simply wipe away!

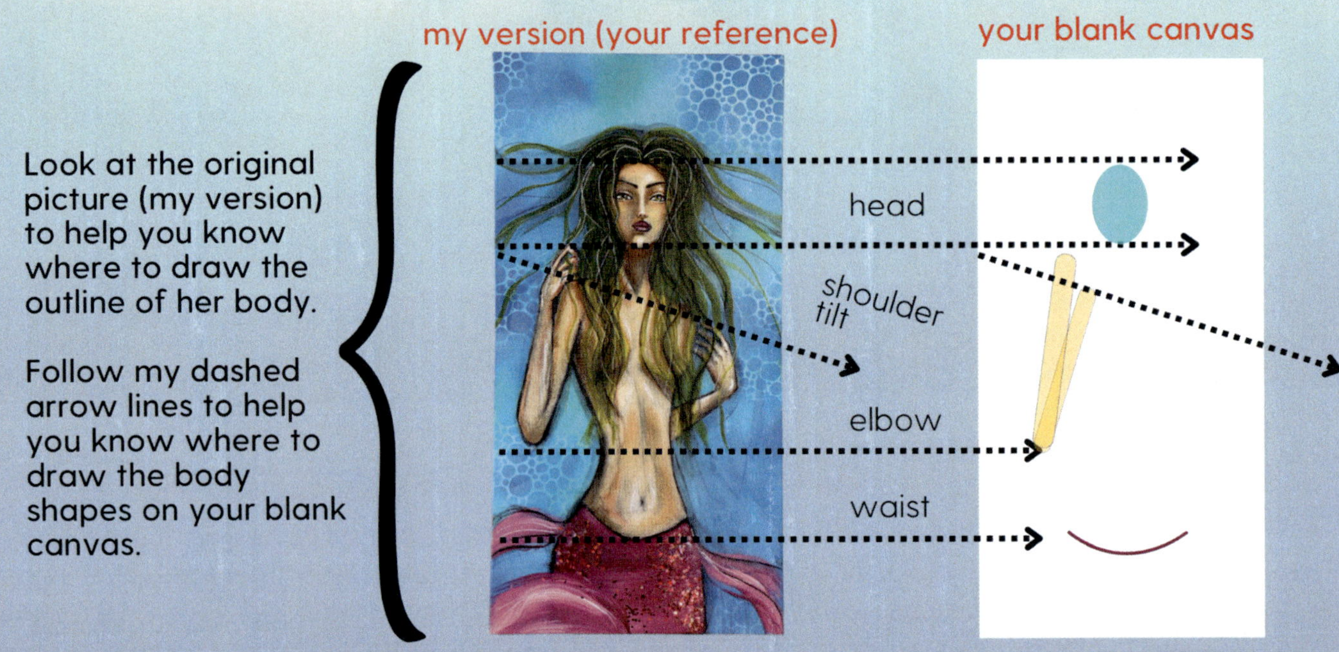

Before putting pencil to canvas, take this opportunity to plan out the scale of your mermaid. Once you start painting you can't easily make corrections so taking the time to plan out your drawing first (especially in terms of size and scale since we're working so large) goes a long way to prevent issues later on. Note the approximate location and size of her head, elbows, and waist. Now is also the time to plan out your tail swish!

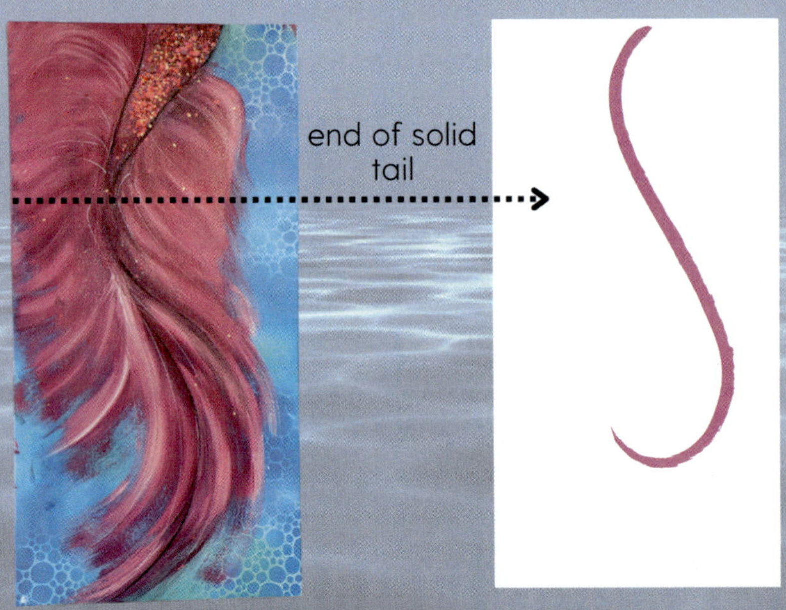

Now that the scale of your mermaid has been planned out on your canvas, you can start drawing. You can see where there are dark smudged lines in my drawings. Those were areas that I "erased" with my wet paper towel and re-drew while the area was still damp. You don't need to be too careful at this stage because all of these lines will be painted over shortly so feel free to draw and "erase" as much as you need to!

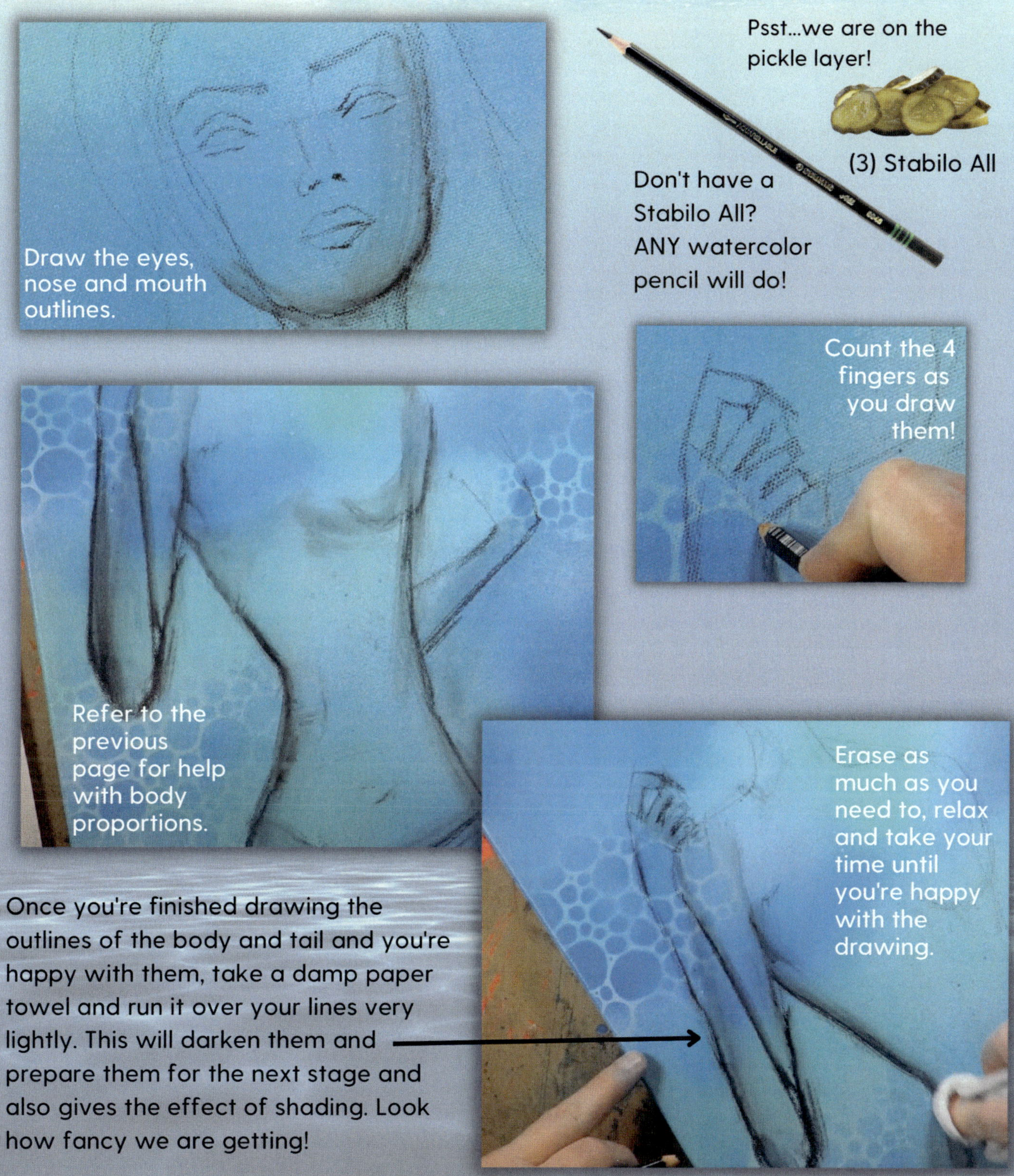

Once you're finished drawing the outlines of the body and tail and you're happy with them, take a damp paper towel and run it over your lines very lightly. This will darken them and prepare them for the next stage and also gives the effect of shading. Look how fancy we are getting!

Moving up the hamburger layers, it's now time for the burger patty layer! This means that it's time to add gesso and then to paint our mermaid with acrylics on top!

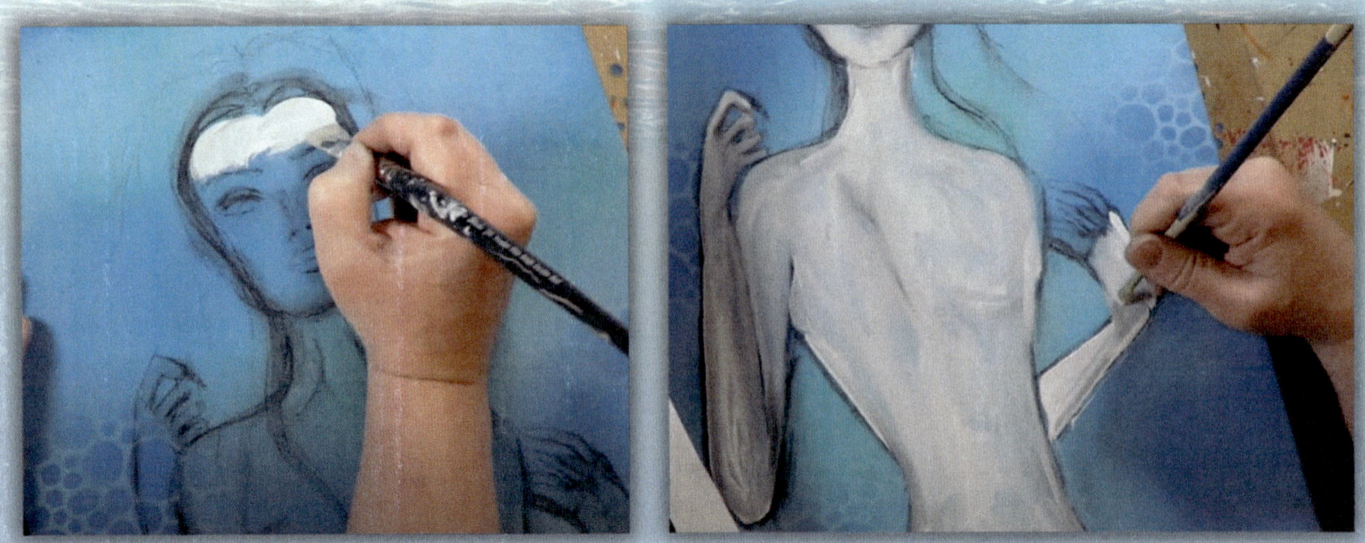

Gesso is a surface preparation product (like paint primer) that serves two purposes. First, it prepares our canvas for painting the skin color coat we will be adding in a moment. Secondly, it helps cover up the blue background so that we won't need as many layers of the skin tone that we're about to paint on top.

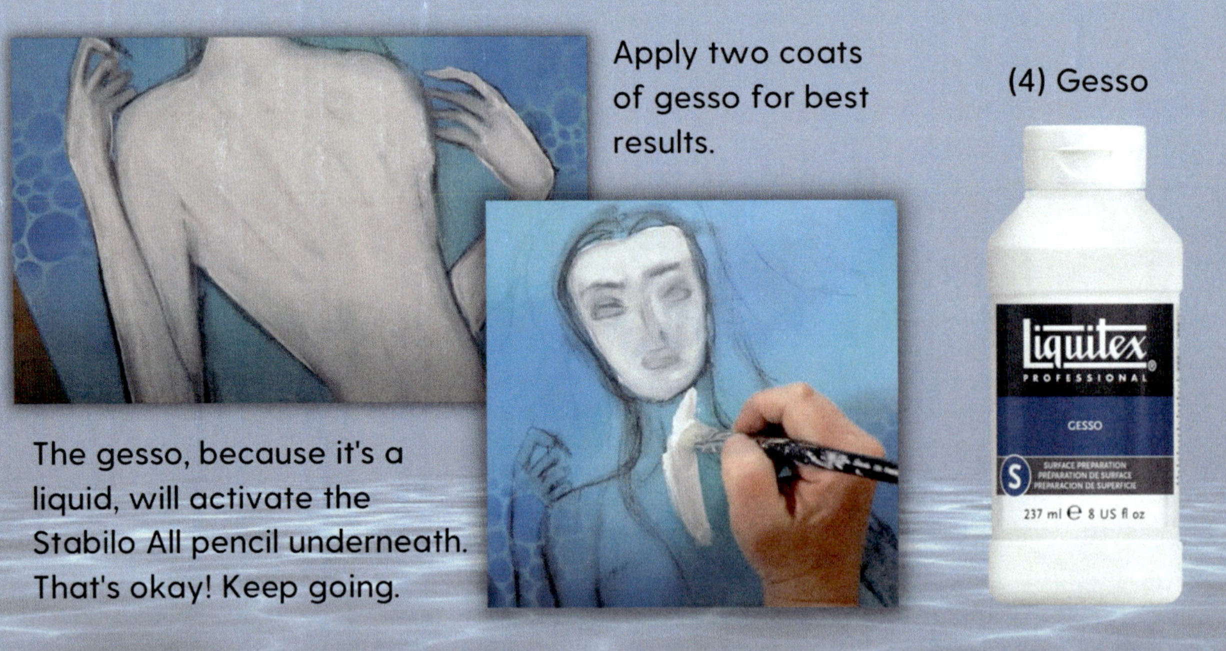

Apply two coats of gesso for best results.

(4) Gesso

The gesso, because it's a liquid, will activate the Stabilo All pencil underneath. That's okay! Keep going.

Gesso is a very common mixed media product that is used extensively. You can literally turn almost ANY surface into a paintable one by applying gesso first! Here's an important tip when working with gesso: always use a DEDICATED stiff bristled brush to apply it. Gesso is very hard on brushes and will quickly destroy your good acrylic painting brushes!

As a reminder, we are still working in the "hamburger" layer (4)!! I know this seems to silly, but I promise it's so helpful for remembering to trust the process and just keep layering!

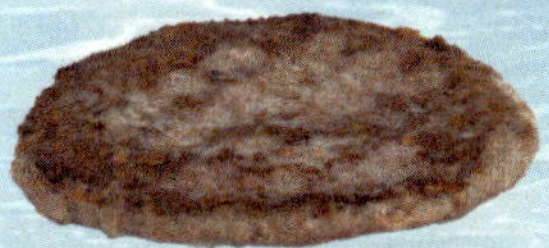

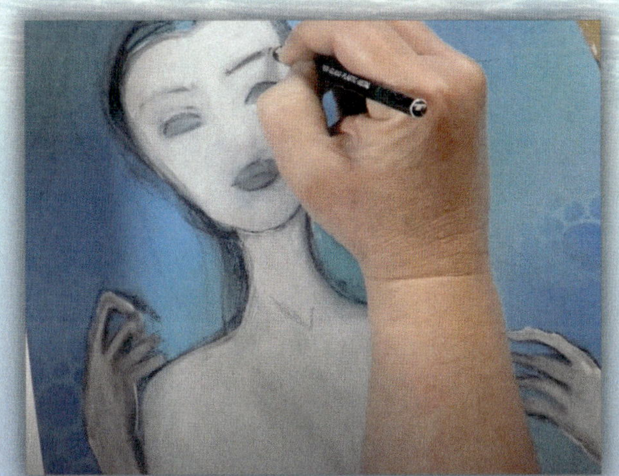

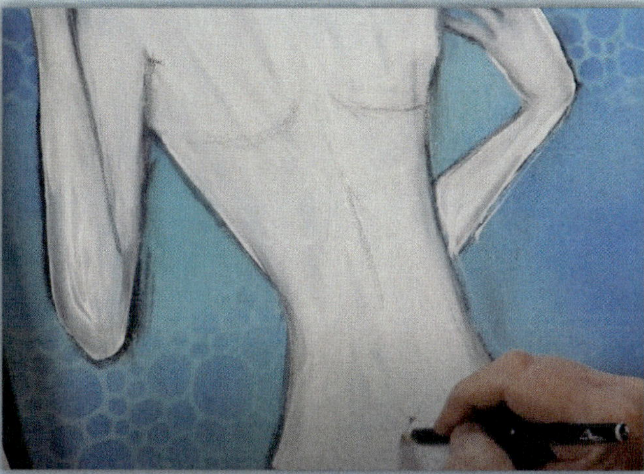

After the second coat of gesso has completely dried, redraw any parts of the body that were lost when you added the gesso. You may need to redefine the facial features, breasts, and stomach details and belly button! You can leave the tail alone as just an outline because the magenta color is opaque enough to cover the background blue completely.

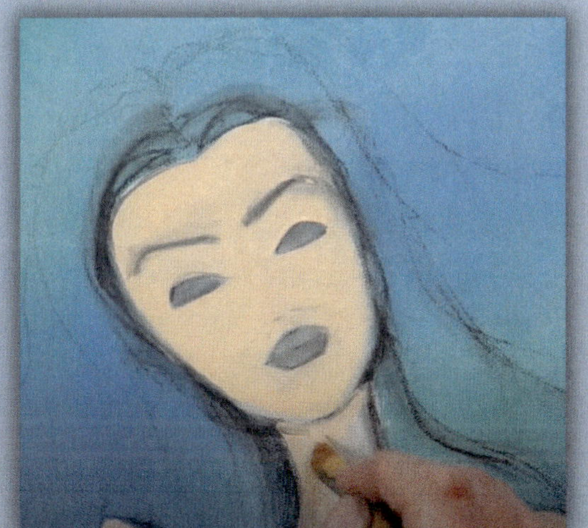

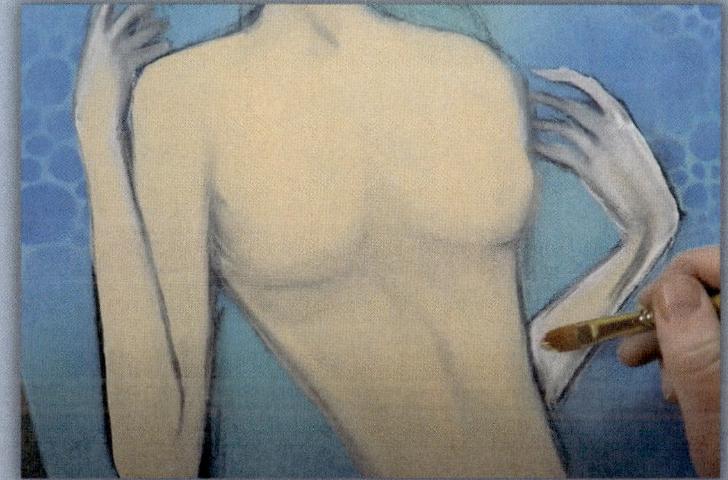

Once you've completed any re-drawing, paint the entire face and body with your skin color acrylics. Any brand or shade will work!

This is where your mermaid will assume her "ugly phase". DO NOT get discouraged when you reach this point! ALL paintings and drawings go through an ugly phase! If you stop here, that phase will win and we don't want that. We want to make a beautiful masterpiece! The only way to "WIN" is to KEEP GOING! So turn the page and let's make something beautiful today! You're halfway there!

When painting with the skin color acrylics, sometimes those Stabilo All lines can get smeared away, again! That's okay. Simply go back in and add any definition to the same areas that may have been lost: the stomach details, breasts and facial features.

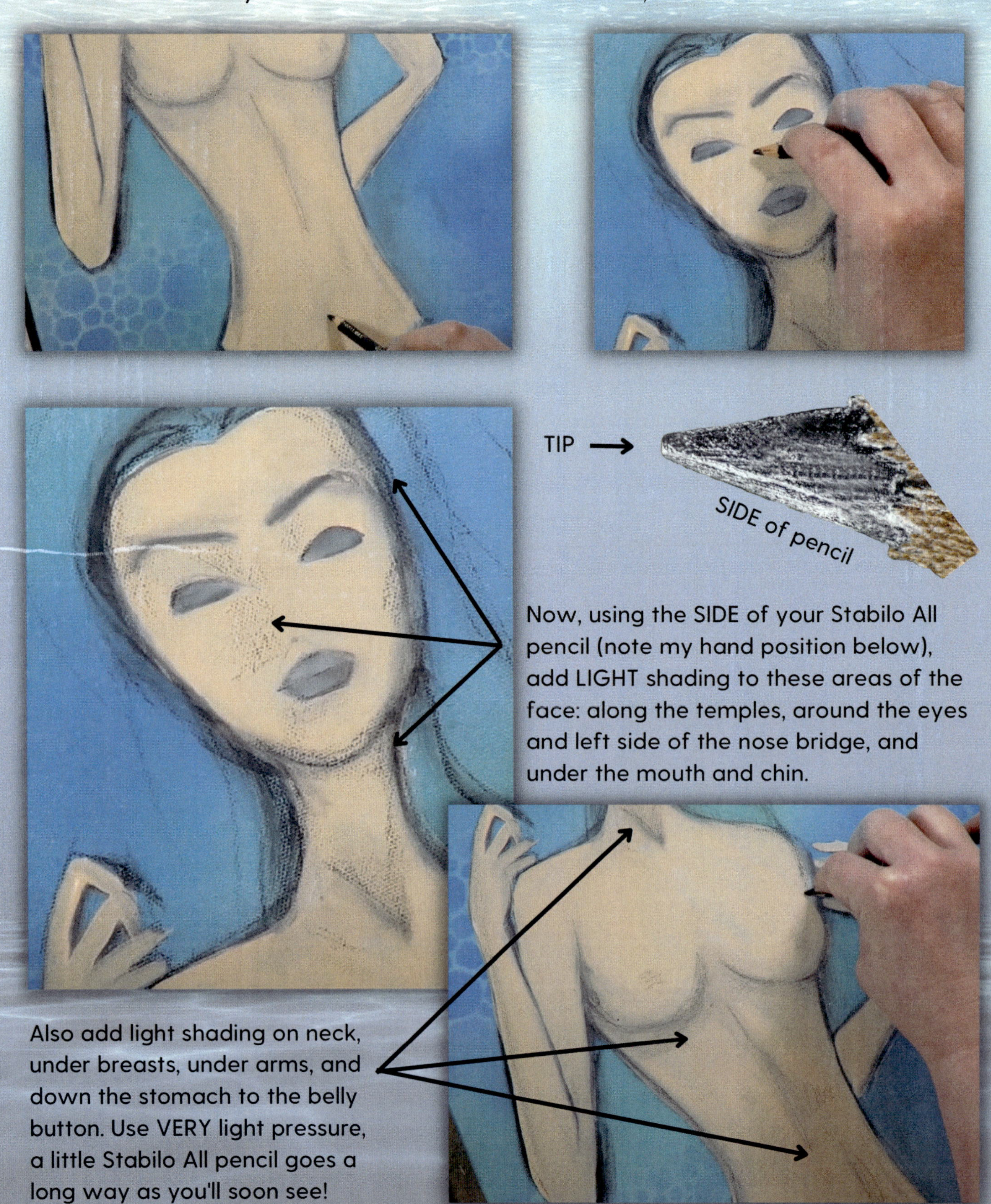

Now, using the SIDE of your Stabilo All pencil (note my hand position below), add LIGHT shading to these areas of the face: along the temples, around the eyes and left side of the nose bridge, and under the mouth and chin.

Also add light shading on neck, under breasts, under arms, and down the stomach to the belly button. Use VERY light pressure, a little Stabilo All pencil goes a long way as you'll soon see!

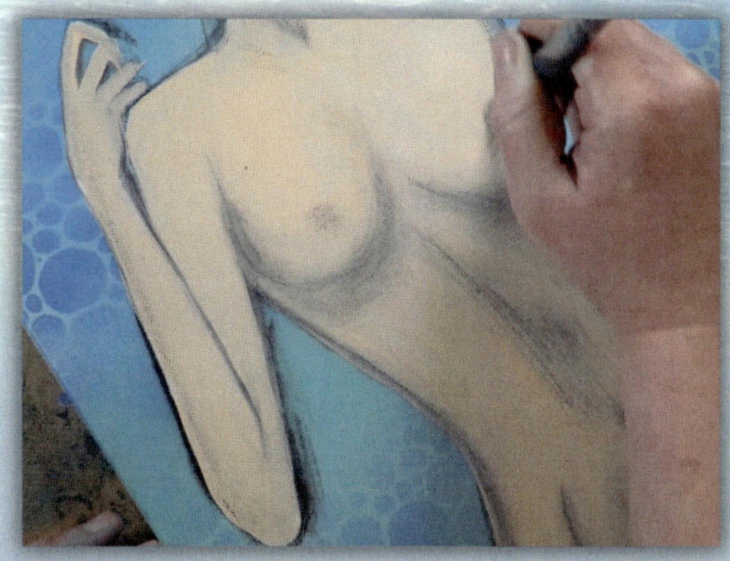

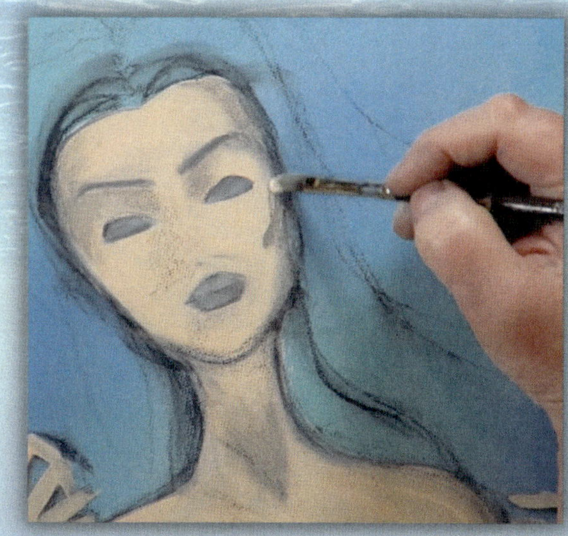

Now dip your paintbrush into the skin tone that you used to paint her body and face and gently run your brush over the shaded areas you just created with your Stabilo All or watercolor pencil. This will smear the lines and make them look like shaded areas! I know the effect looks pretty "dirty", but it's okay. Everything will come together in the end.

Now repeat this process in the shaded regions on her face. Your brush only needs to be SLIGHTLY DAMP. If it's too wet you'll wind up painting the entire region over again. We just want enough liquid to SMEAR the pencil NOT enough to have to paint it all over again.

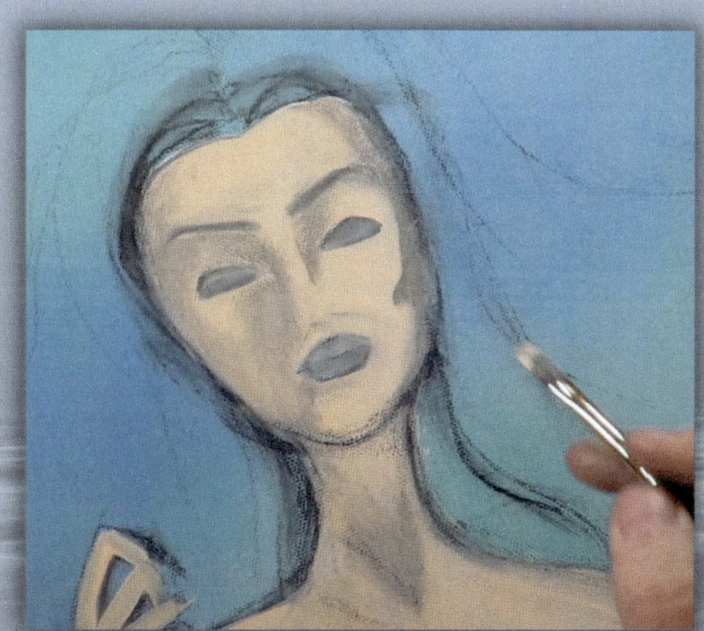

Keep blending the Stabilo All black portions with a slightly damp brush until it's smoothed over. Now your mermaid is shaded!

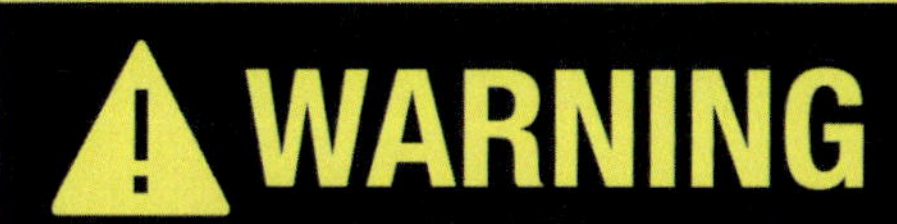

This is the UGLY STAGE
and is COMPLETELY NORMAL.
DO NOT STOP
now or you'll let it win!

The only way to get past this stage is to keeping going. Turn the page and don't give up!

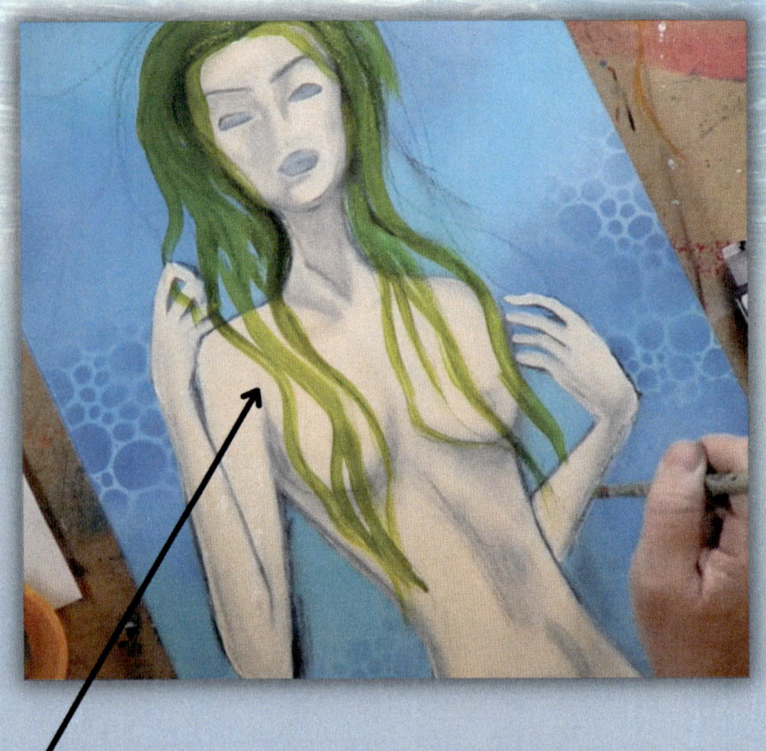

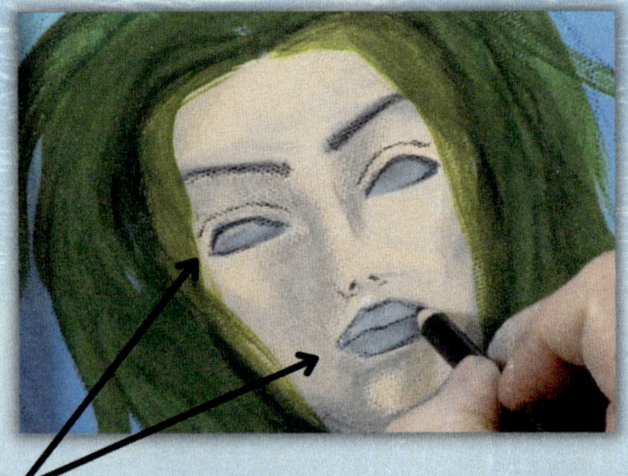

We are now switching gears and moving towards more permanent materials. This time, define the facial features with a black colored pencil that is NOT water reactive.

Using transparent green paint (I love Golden Fluid Acrylics in green gold) start at the crown of her head and paint hair strands from root to tip in a series of long, wavy strokes. You can paint green like me or use another fun color!

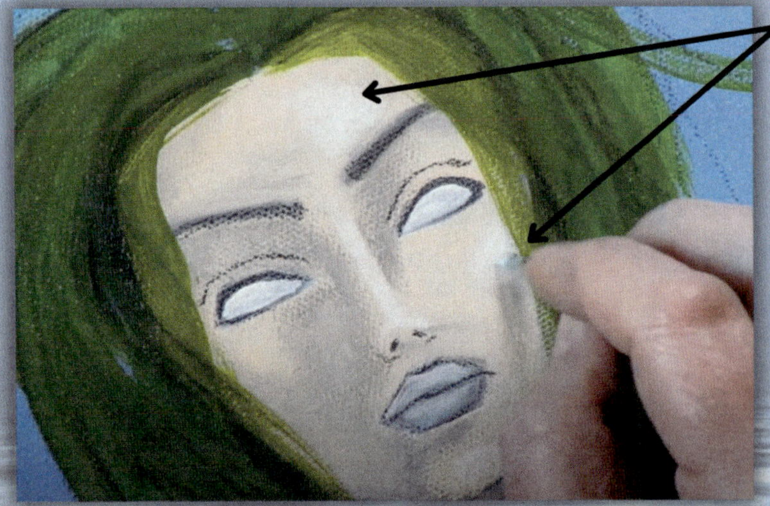

Now that the features have a bit of definition, add gesso to the eyes, on the forehead, along the top of the nose bridge, lips, cheeks, and chin! This serves as both a highlight AND prepares those areas for more layers of paint.

We are still working on the gesso and paint layer of the mixed media "hamburger" method!

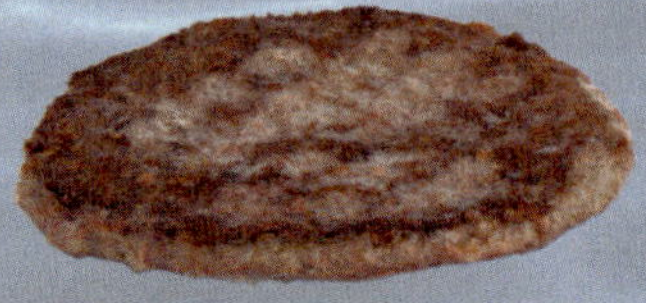

(4) Gesso & Acrylics

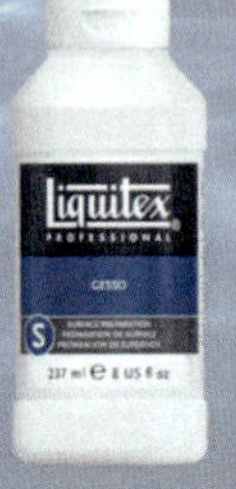

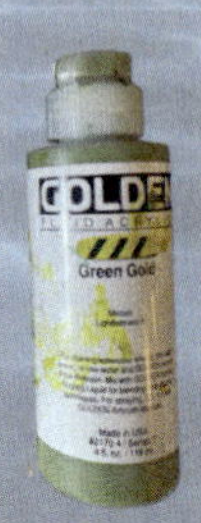

Gesso is also great for adding highlights to areas OVER your painted acrylics. It's great because it is semi-opaque so when you use just a little to blend over your dried paints it results in a lovely glow (versus the effect you'd get if you were to use white arylic paints which look solid and heavy handed).

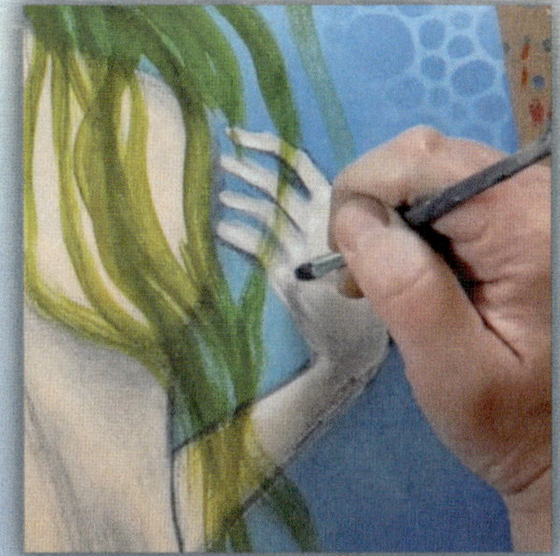

Feel free to add highlights to the back of the hand and fingers.

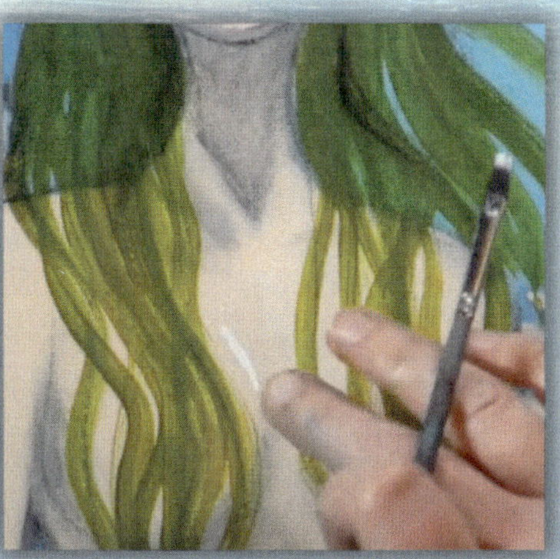

Along the exposed areas between her hair strands. You can use your finger to blend too!

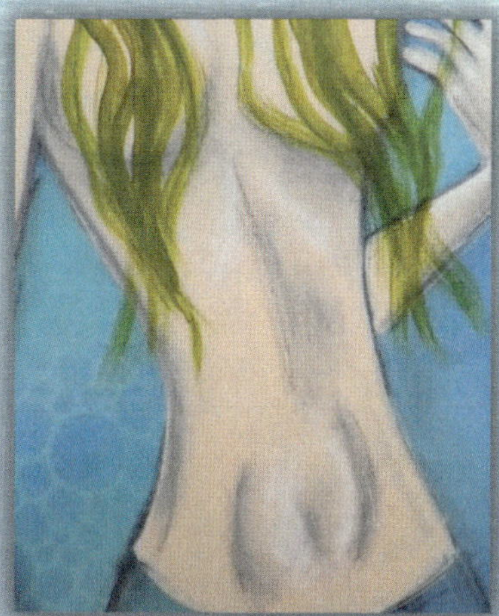

Adding some white to the belly and rib areas can add dimension too.

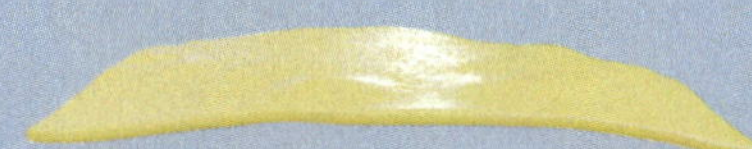

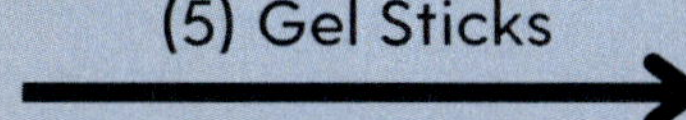

(5) Gel Sticks

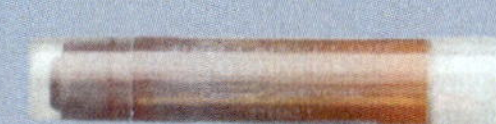

Now that the painted portion is finished, we can move onto the next layer (the cheese!!). This is a SUPER fast and fun way to add additional shading OR highlights and requires ZERO painting experience to master! I love to use Gelatos by Faber-Castell but there are MANY awesome varieties of gel sticks that will work in their place if you can't find them. Using them is SO EASY. Just scribble and then blend with your finger!

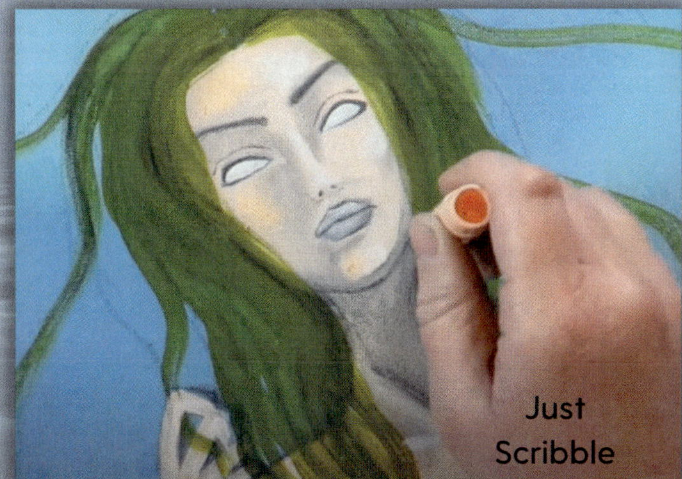

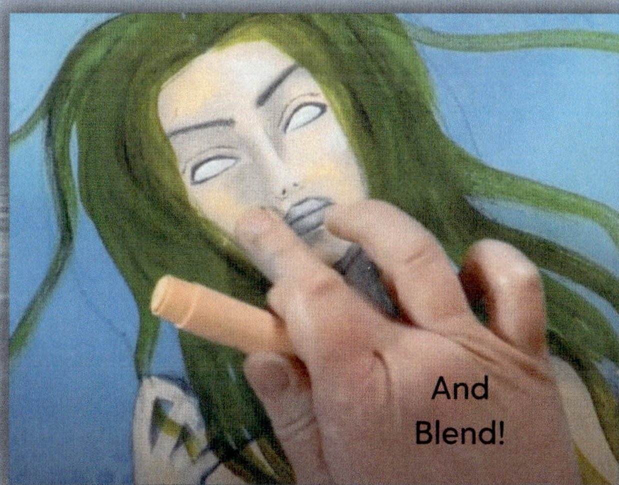

You can learn more about alternatives at this link (leads to a FREE video on YouTube)
https://bit.ly/gelsticks

Gather your Gelatos (or gel sticks in comparable shades) and work from light to dark. In any areas that need to be lighter, just go over scribble and blend with the lightest shade. In any areas that need to be a bit pinker or darker, you can use the subsequent darker shades. Again, simply scribble and then blend with your finger. It's truly that easy!

Use the image on the right to guide you on where to put the darker shades of gel sticks. I used Guava, Melon, and Chocolate in this project.

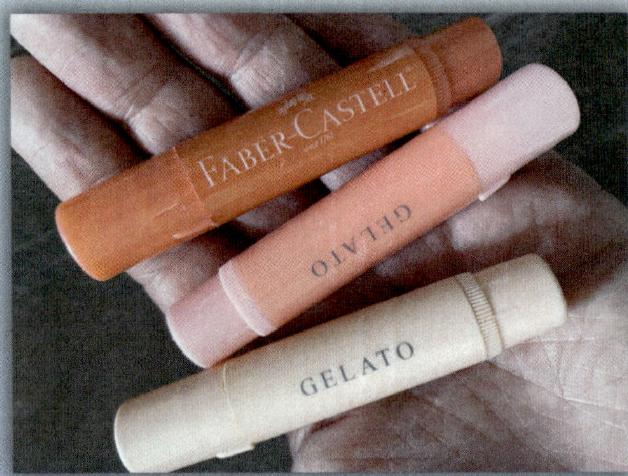

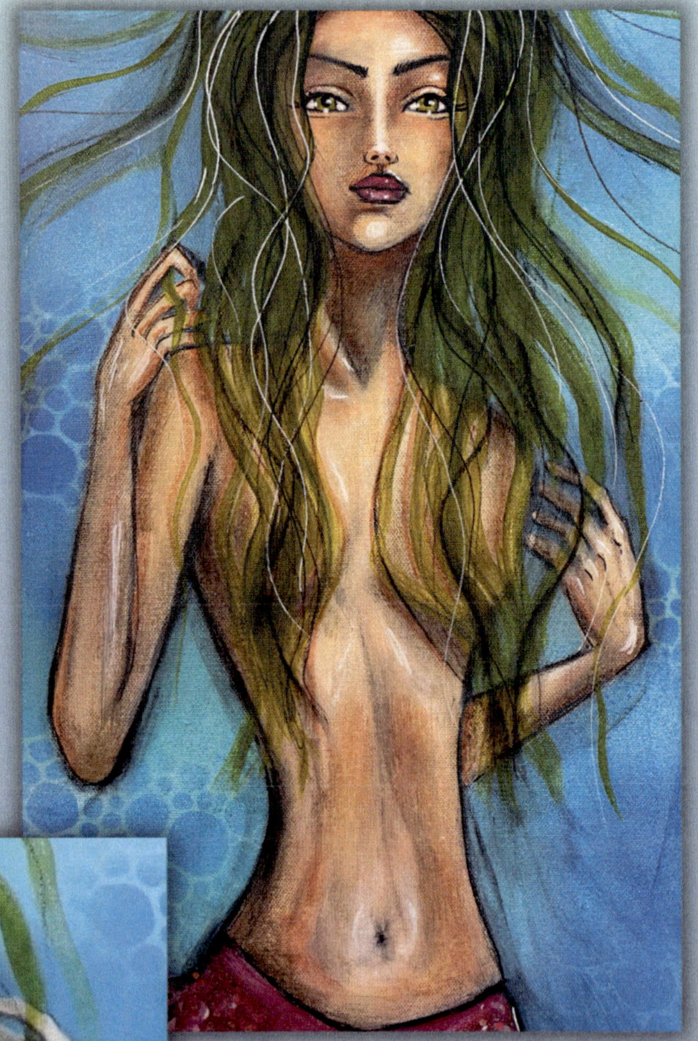

There are many shades of these fun gel sticks so feel free to get as dramatic as you'd like with the skin shading! You can also use these same sticks to add hair strands and more dimension in the tail - when we get there! But let's finish the top of the body first.

Gelatos are great because like the Stabilo All pencil, they are water-soluble. And like the Stabilo, if you want to "erase" you can! All you need is a wet paper towel!

Magic!

This is the point in the project where you need to do any last-minute painting or drawing because we are about to seal!! Once you seal, we will be changing our art supplies yet again! This is the last opportunity to add details and more easy shading with paint, pencil or Gelatos! Let's paint the lips in pink and eyes in green before we move on. You can also add more hair strands if you'd like!

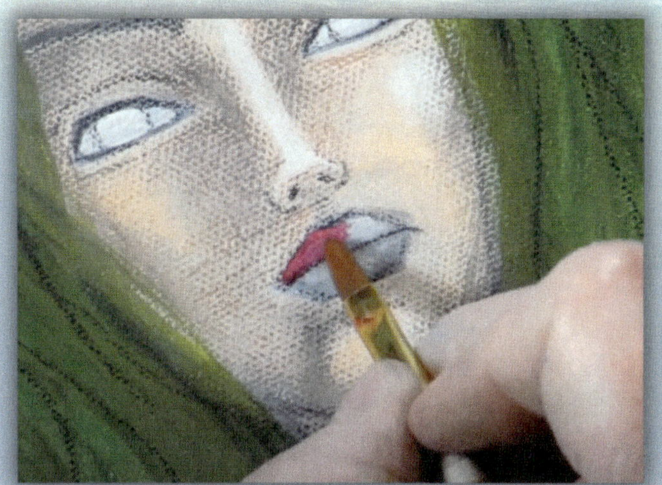

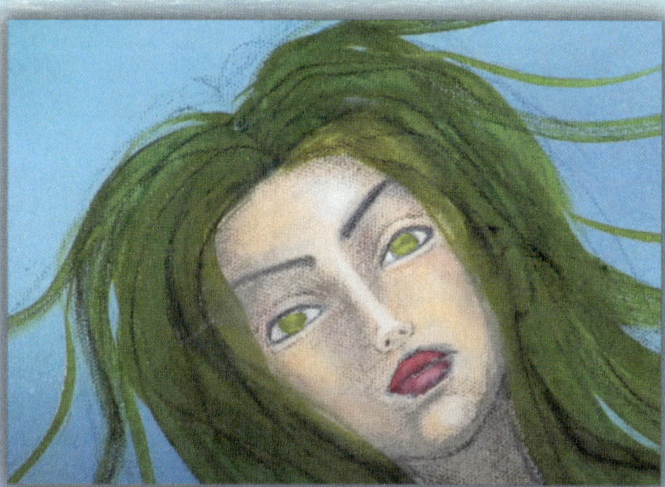

Now it's time for our sealant layer! So exciting!

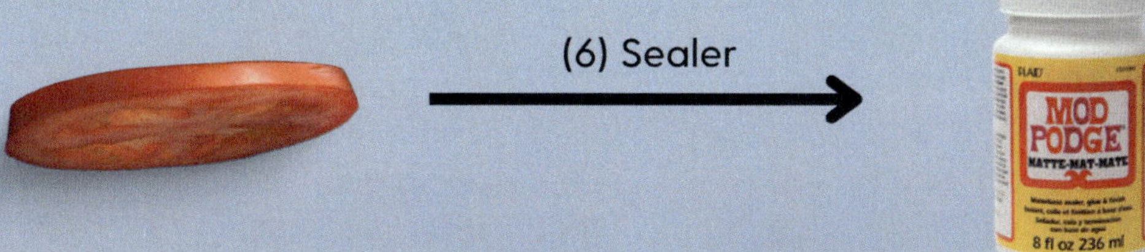

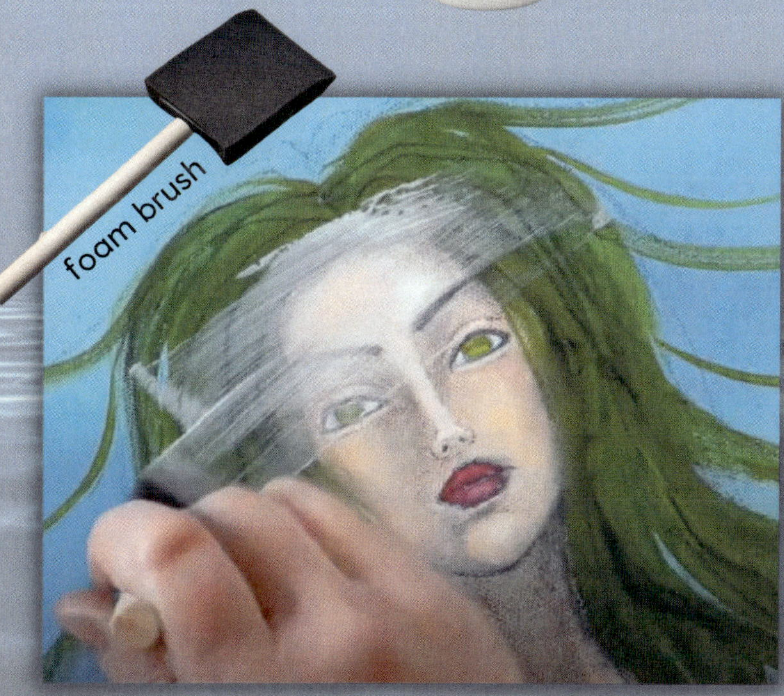

Once you're happy with all of your previous layers, spread a thin layer of Mod Podge over the ENTIRE canvas, starting with the face and moving outwards. Use a clean foam brush and change to a new clean brush frequently if yours gets too dirty as you proceed. Let dry.

If you can't get a hold of Mod Podge, there are plenty of other options. Visit to learn more: http://bit.ly/skinnyonsealers

You can wait for the Mod Podge to dry naturally or use a hair dryer to speed the drying process. With a hair dryers help, it should only take about five minutes to be able to move onto the next layer!

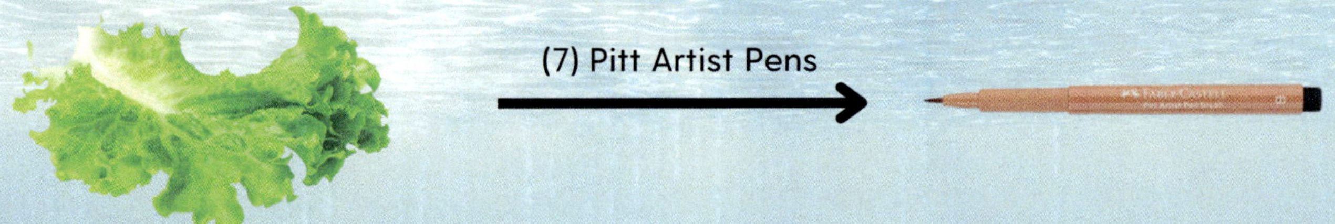

The next layer consists of adding shading in almost the exact same way we did with the Gelatos only this time we're using Pitt artist pens, also by Faber-Castell.

Pitt Pens contain a lovely permanent India ink pigment that works like paint over our sealer layer!!

Just as we did with the Gelatos, you simply apply and then use your finger to blend!

Pitt pens come in both a skinny barrel and "Big Brush" variety but they both work the same way.

I love this skin tone pack for creating all my mixed media "Hamburger" girls!

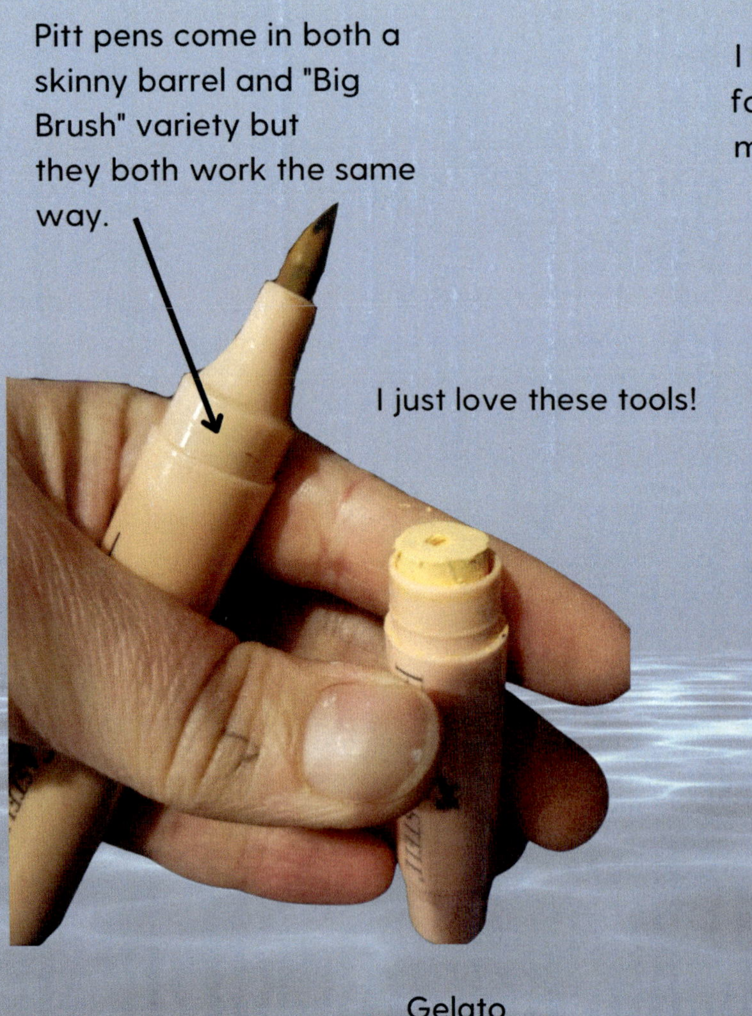

I just love these tools!

Gelato

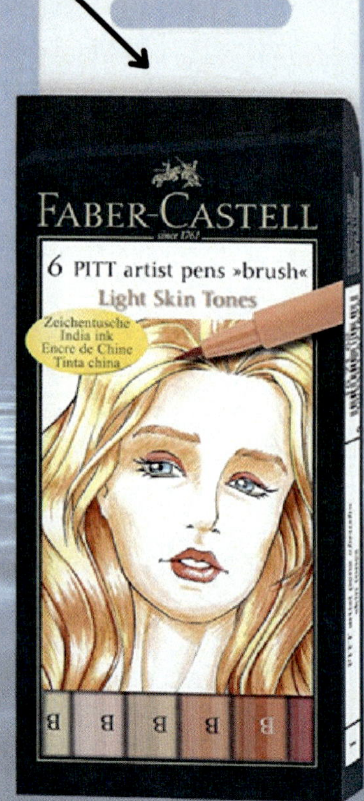

I love adding dramatic shading so I'm using Cinnamon. First I apply a strip of color. Then I blend it out with my fingers. I keep adding more bits of shading all around the edges of the face, around the eyes, and under the nose, mouth and chin.

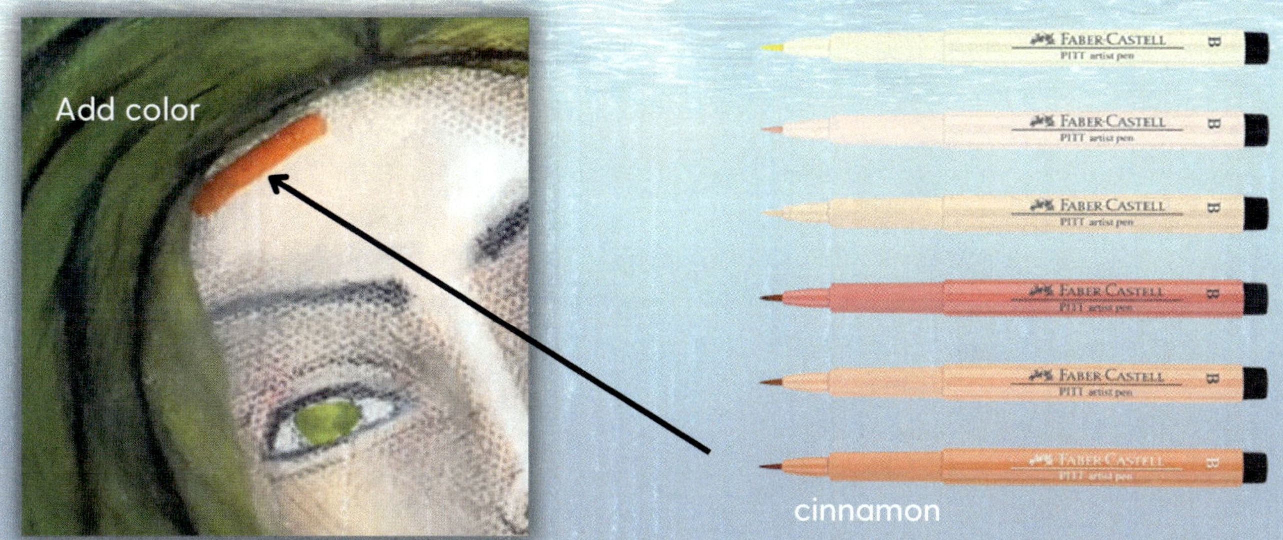

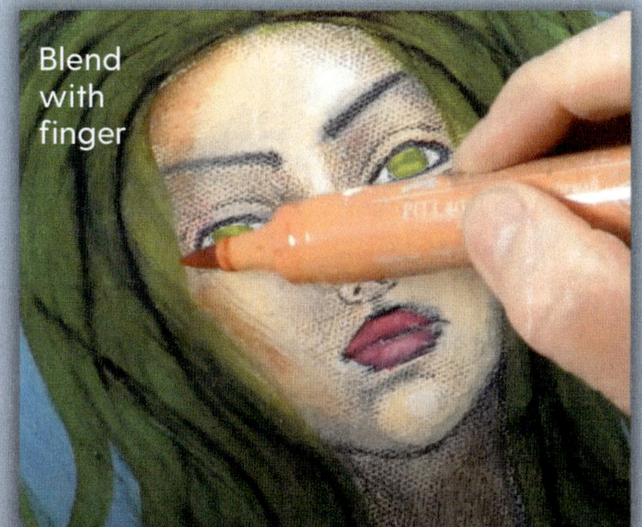

If adding dramatic shading scares you, simply add a lighter, less scary color :) There's plenty in the skin tone pack to give you lots of options!

You can also add HIGHLIGHTS by using the lightest colors or the Pitt Artist pen in white.

And you can use BLACK to add more outlines!!

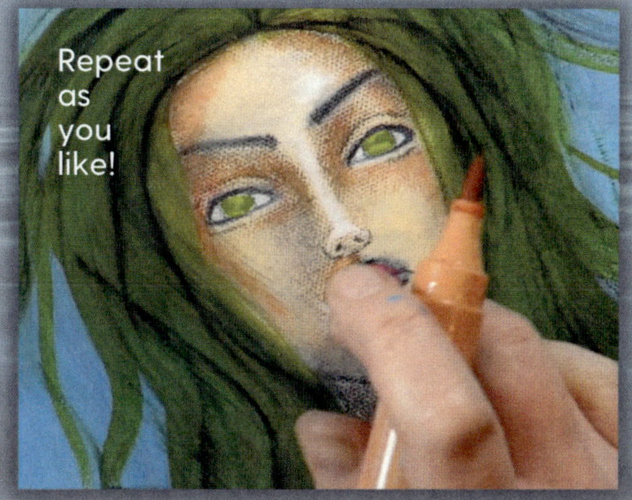

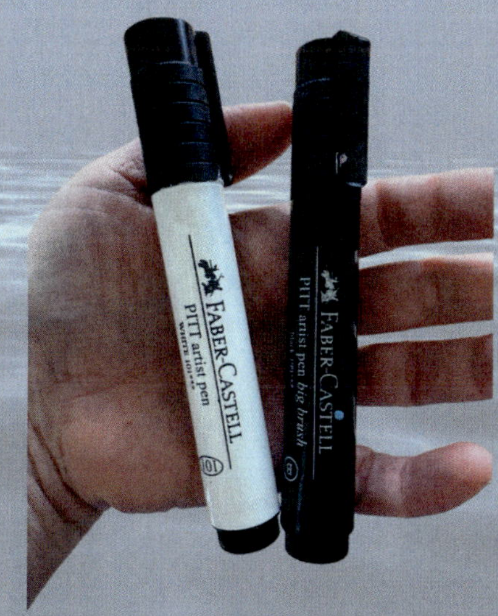

When all of the major shading has been completed, you can start in on the details. Using the Pitt artist pens in black, you can outline and fill in the facial details as you like.

Use a small nib fine liner (labeled "S") to outline and define all of the facial features.

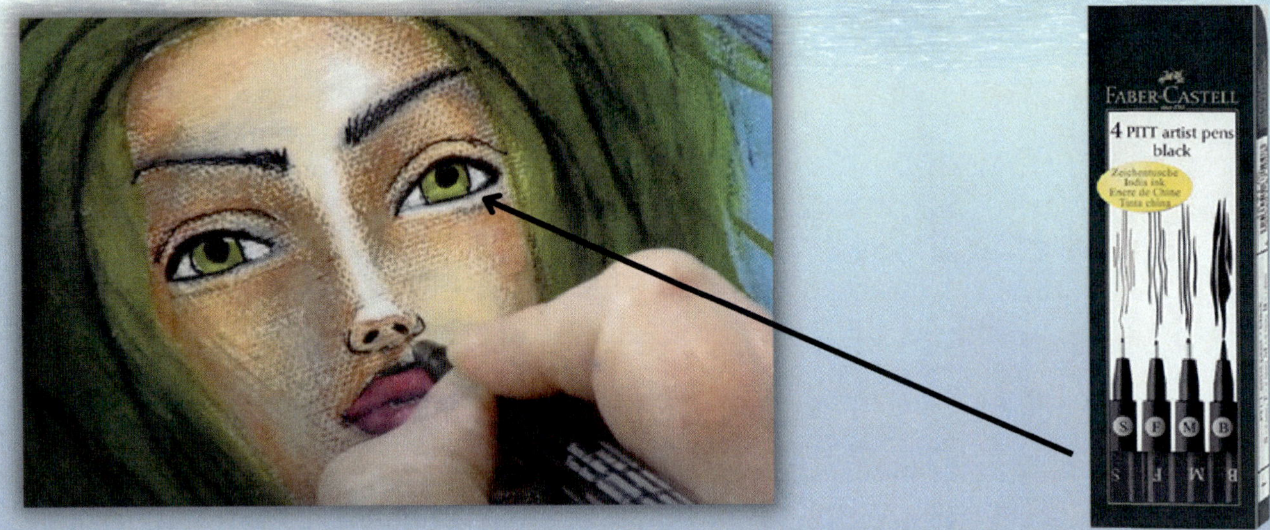

Good news! Faber-Castell also sells their Pitt artist pens in a few different fine-liner packs like this 4 pack one shown.

Having access to a broad range of nib sizes means you can apply that wonderful ink to both your large and small-scale "Hamburger" mixed media projects. These are also great to use with any mixed media and drawing projects (they do not pay me to say this! lol!).

And STILL, the good news continues!! Because of the Mod Podge sealant layer which produces a plastic layer underneath these magical markers, they remain "erasable" for a short time after application. So if you make a mistake or decide you hate the darker shading, you can use a baby wipe or wet paper towel to remove it completely!

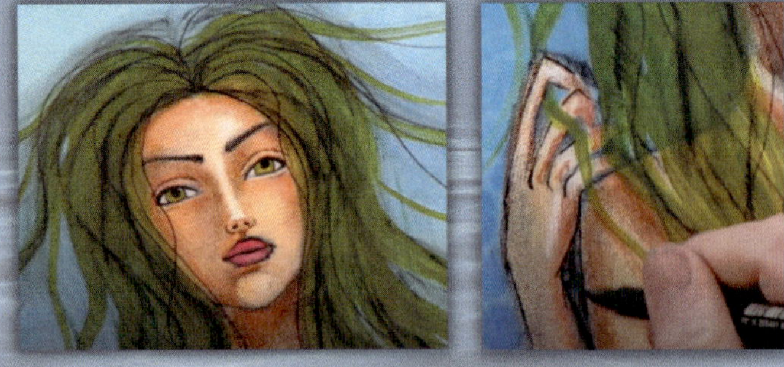

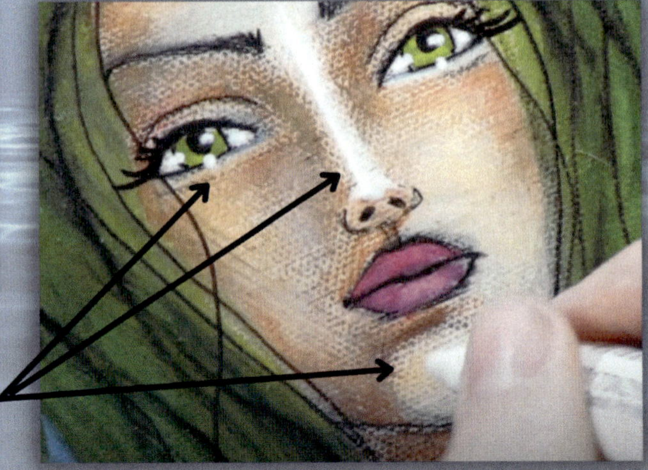

Use the black Pitt pens to create more hair strands and to outline the hands and fingers in addition to the face and facial features. Use white for dramatic face highlights!

Now we can finally turn our attention to the mermaid's tail! Phew! If you're working with two canvases like me, put them together and finish drawing the shape of the tail with your Stabilo All or watercolor pencil. Then drag a wet paper towel along each side to "activate" it so it's nice and dark and smeary as shown (left).

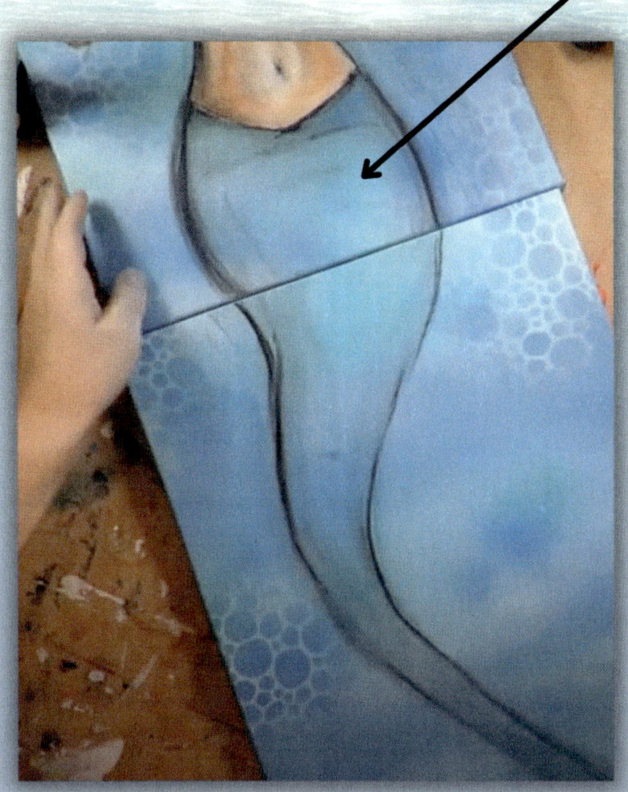

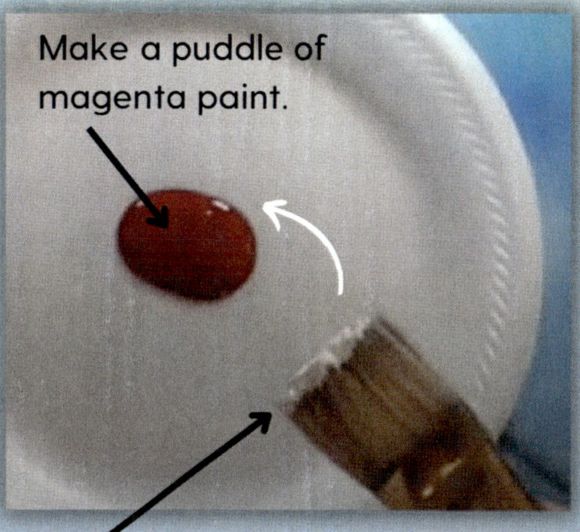

Make a puddle of magenta paint.

Using a large paintbrush loaded up with white gesso, dip your brush into the magenta paint and paint in the tail with even left to right brush strokes.

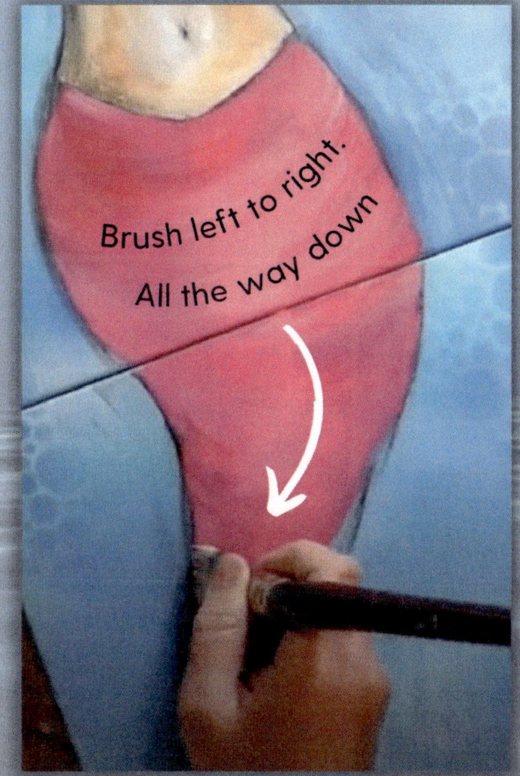

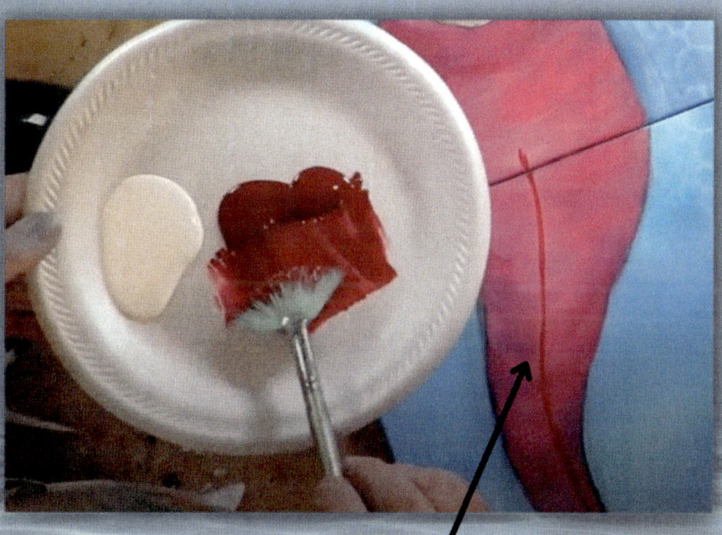

Next, paint a solid line down the center of the tail. Then dip a large fan brush into both magenta and white gesso before starting to paint the tail.

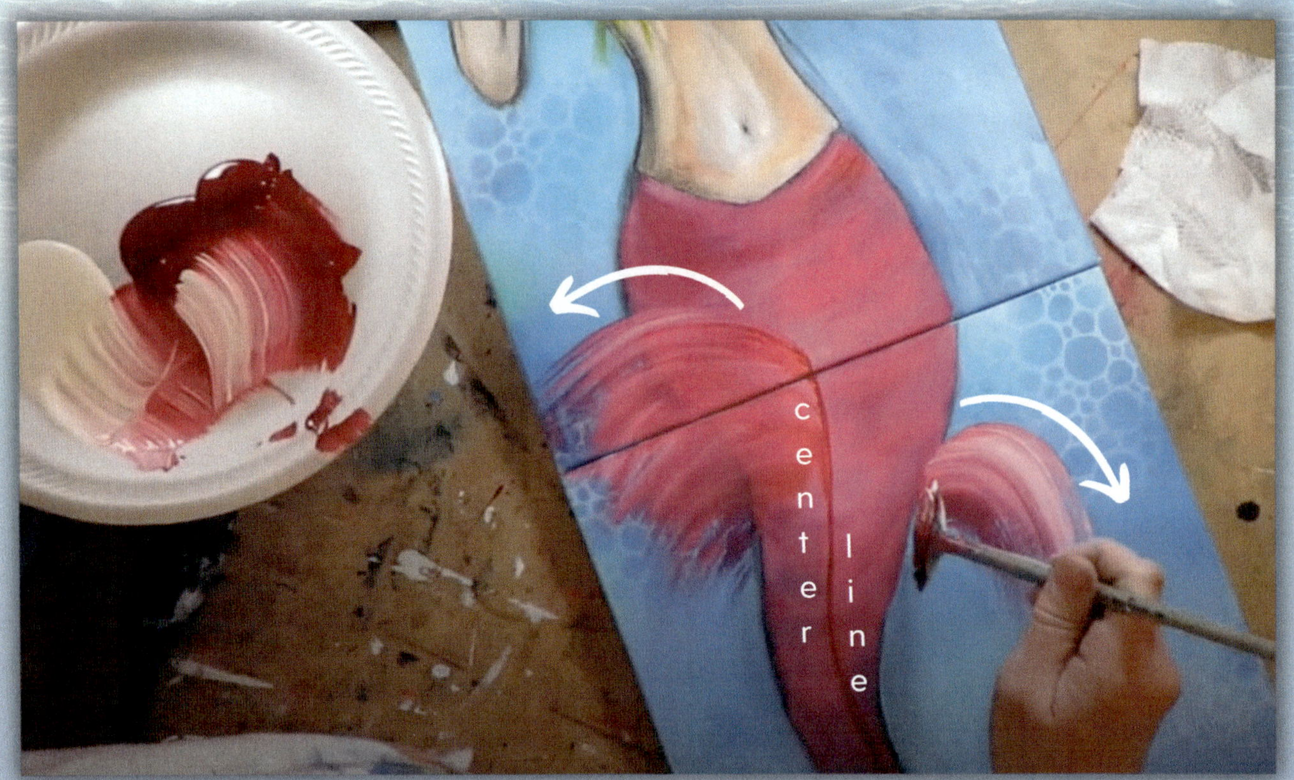

From the solid center line working LEFT first, paint curved strokes with your fan brush. Then repeat this on the RIGHT side, this time starting from BEHIND the tail (NOT from the center line).

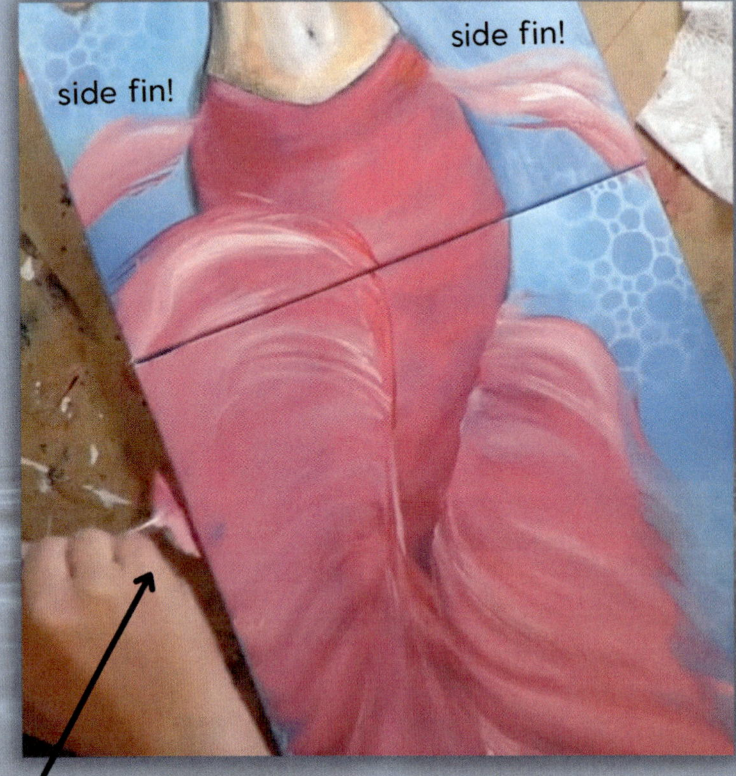

Be careful to paint around all the sides of your canvas. Add the little side fins!

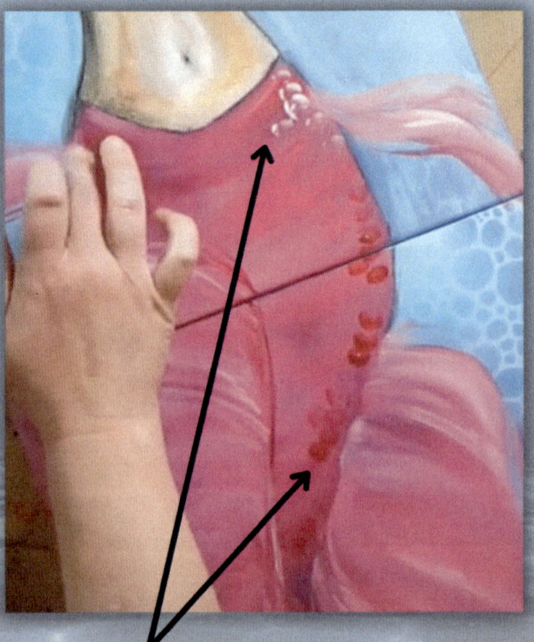

Using your fingers, finger stamp some magenta and white marks along the sides to mimic the look of scales! Having fun yet?! I am!!

In most "Hamburger" mixed media projects, I use matte Mod Podge to seal the ENTIRE canvas as the FINAL layer. In this case, we will be using Sparkle Mod Podge!! She is a MAGICAL mermaid after all! You can choose to coat the entire canvas with Sparkle or just the section of the tail. I'm choosing the Sparkle variety to seal JUST the tail (although it would look STUNNING on all of her!!).

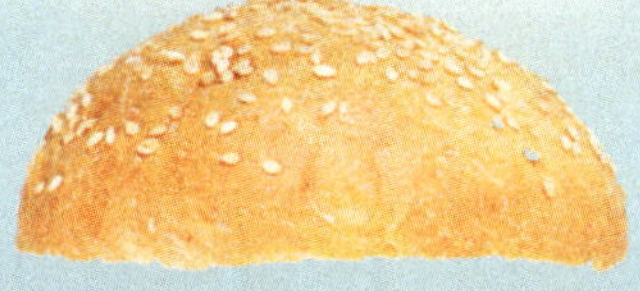

(8) Final Sealer Layer!

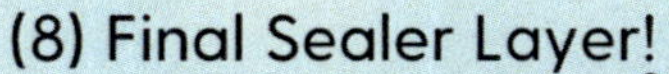

We made it to the end!

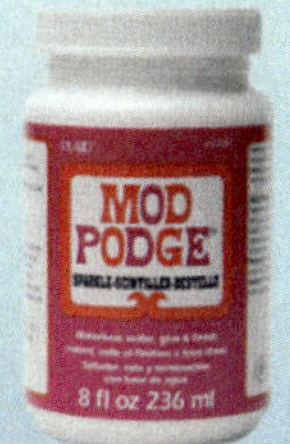

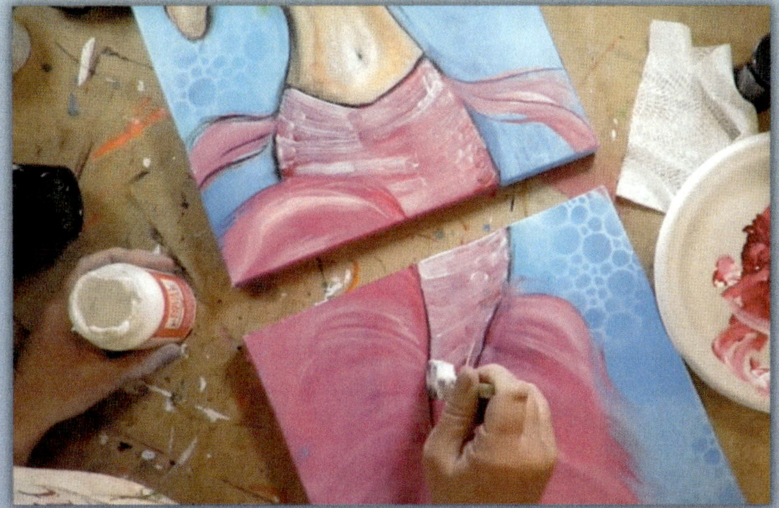

Using your handy-dandy foam brush from earlier (you can wash those out and re-use them dozens of times), coat the entire tail with Sparkle Mod Podge.

While it's still very wet, sprinkle large magenta glitter as desired! I limited myself to the sides but you can absolutely go crazy with it everywhere if you want to!

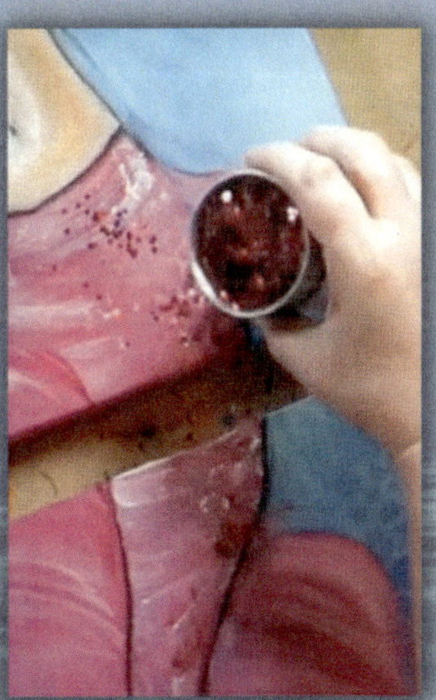

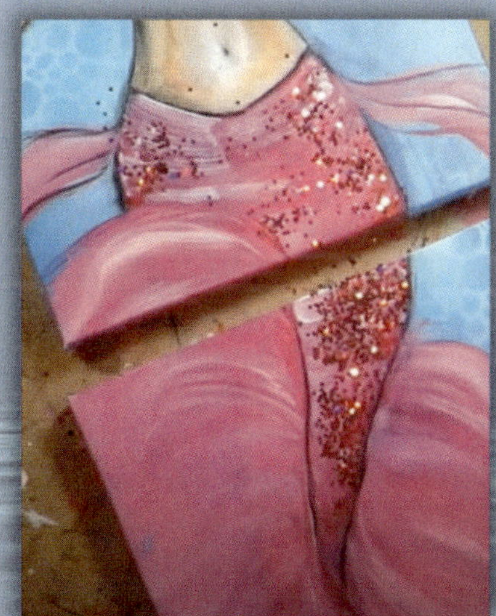

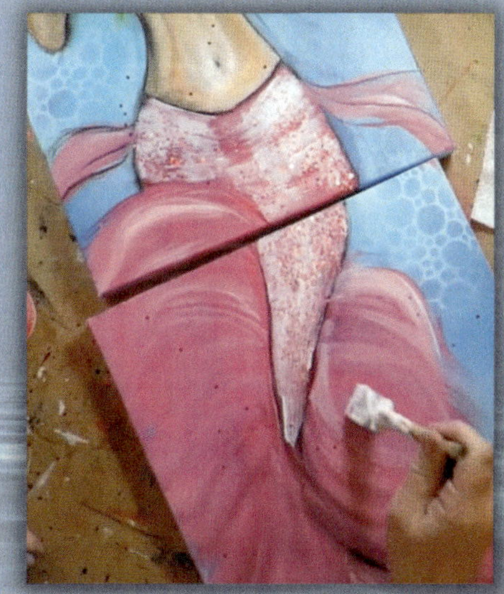

Shake any excess glitter into a trash can. Then, for extra drama (and security), add another generous helping of Sparkle Mod Podge over the whole tail. Coat the entire mermaid from top to bottom with either Matte or Sparkle Mod Podge to seal and to freeze all layers underneath.

Technically, you can absolutely consider your project complete at this point. However, because your last layer is the Mod Podge, you can still go in and add more details, shading OR pops of highlights because Pitt Pens (as we know) work great over the sealant. You can also use paint pens if you prefer.

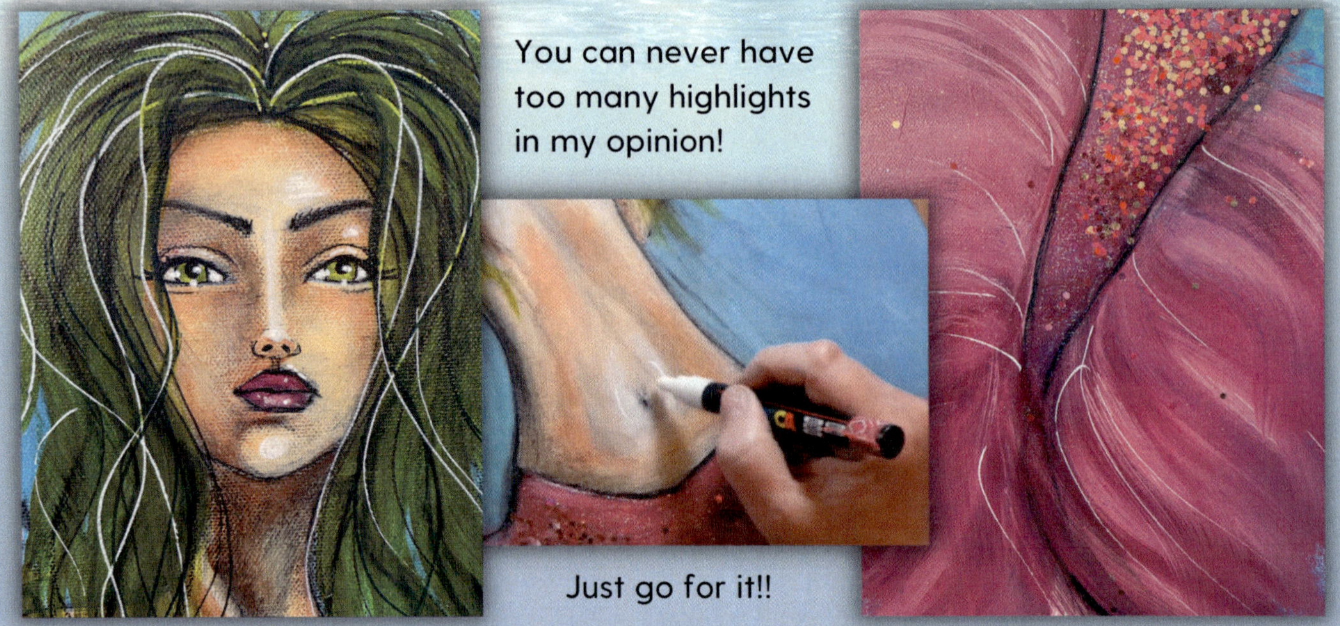

You can never have too many highlights in my opinion!

Just go for it!!

Hair strands, eye sparkles, lip shine, glowing chin, and eyelids, reflected tummies, and accentuated tail swipes are ALL great spots to add highlights!

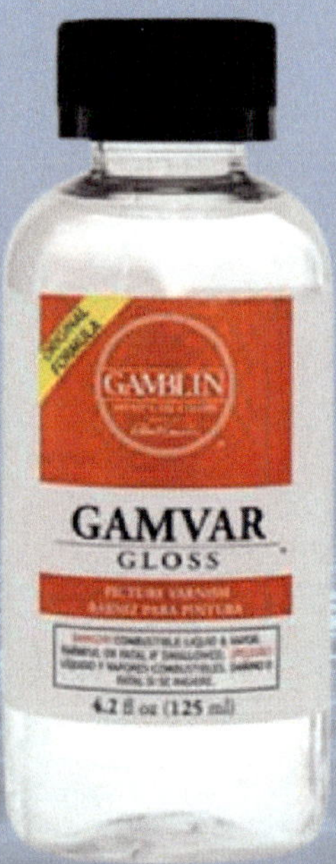

Just be sure to add a final layer of sealer when you're all done! As a super extra bonus step, you're welcome to apply a spray or brush-on varnish on top of your final Mod Podge (or whatever sealer you're using) layer.

There are amazing top-coat/varnish products that will add a brilliant shine OR a lovely diffused matte look, depending on the finish option.

If you're sensitive to aerosol sprays, look for a brush-on variety like this awesome product from Gamblin.

To learn more about some fun finish options I've tried and tested, visit: https://bit.ly/bestvarnishes

When all that is complete, stand back and be AMAZED at the magical mermaid masterpiece you just created!!!

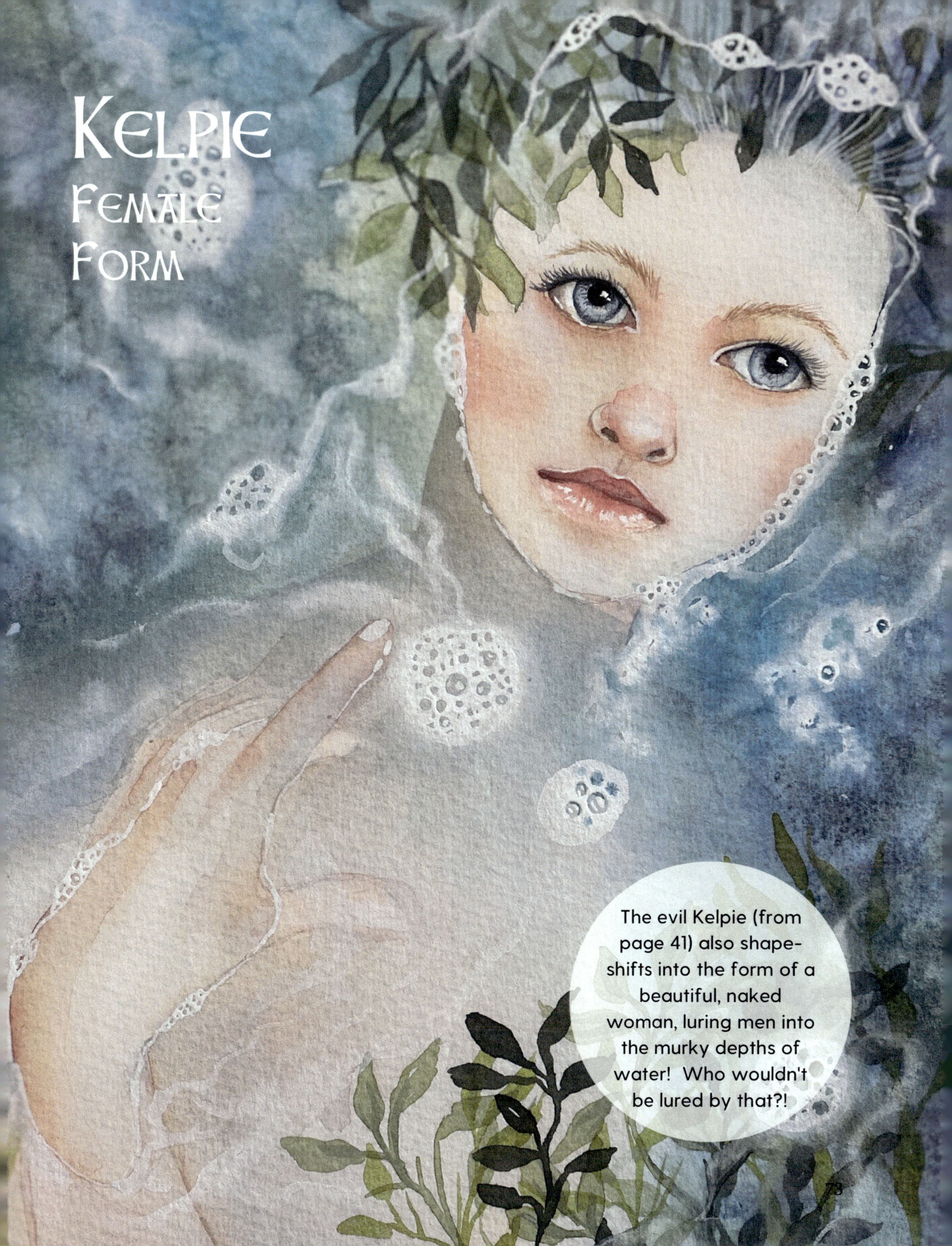
Kelpie
Female
Form
The evil Kelpie (from page 41) also shape-shifts into the form of a beautiful, naked woman, luring men into the murky depths of water! Who wouldn't be lured by that?!

Supplies

Selection of watercolors - any brand will do. I am using mostly Daniel Smith, Schmincke and Winsor & Newton.
Opaque white paint like Dr. Ph Martins Bleed Proof.
Table Salt
Selection of paintbrushes
Watercolor pencils
Graphite pencil to transfer your drawing.
140lb. watercolor paper
Painters tape to make a nice clean border.
Water to clean brushes!
MILLFORD

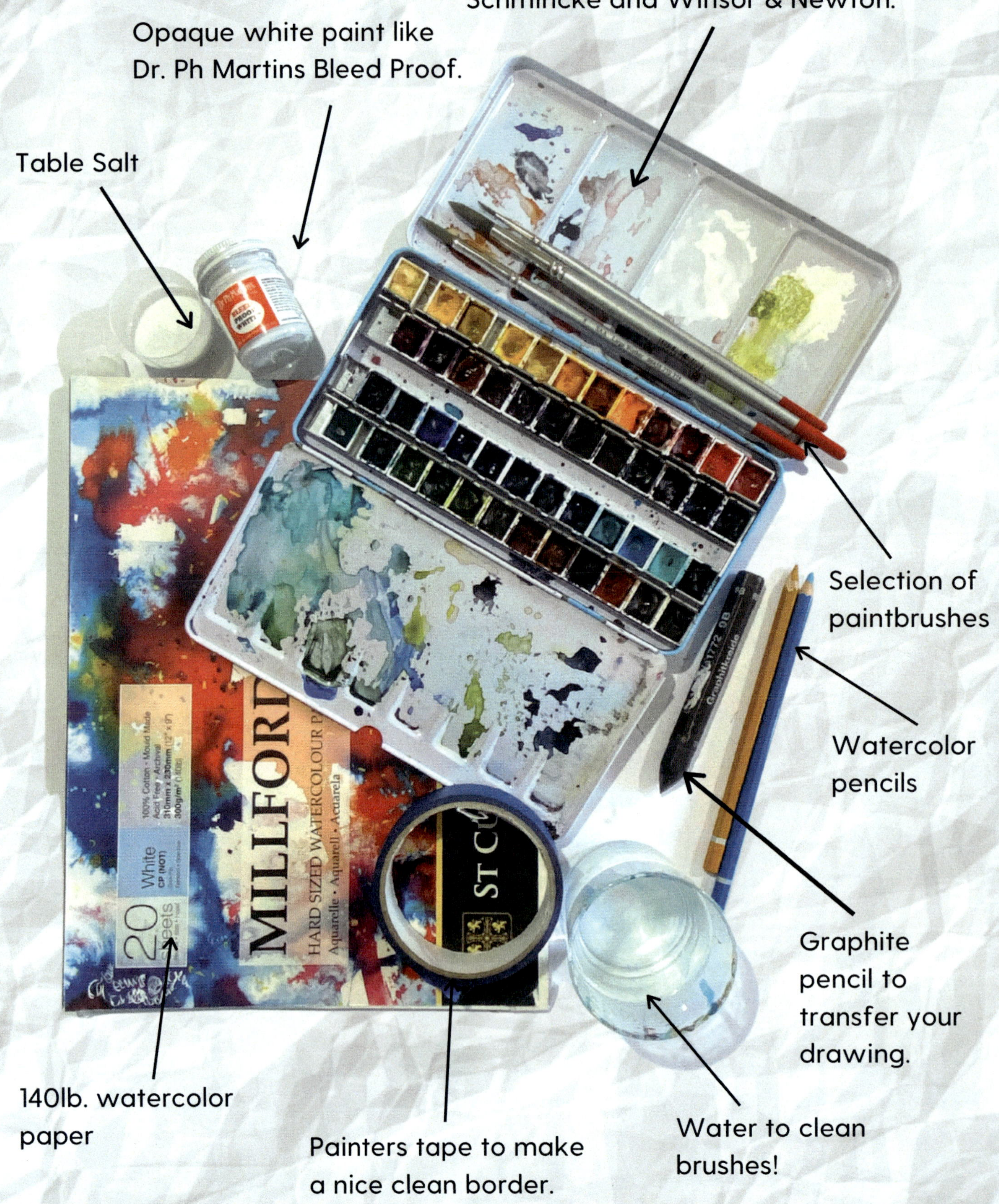

First, let's find an awesome photograph of a woman emerging from water.

There are lots of great images on Unsplash or Pixabay which are copyright free (or you can use this one!).

I liked this one because you can see how she is under the water, and the bubbles are a cool effect that I wanted to paint.

Kelpie women are very alluring and I felt that this photo showed that slightly sexy side but is also appropriate for this book!

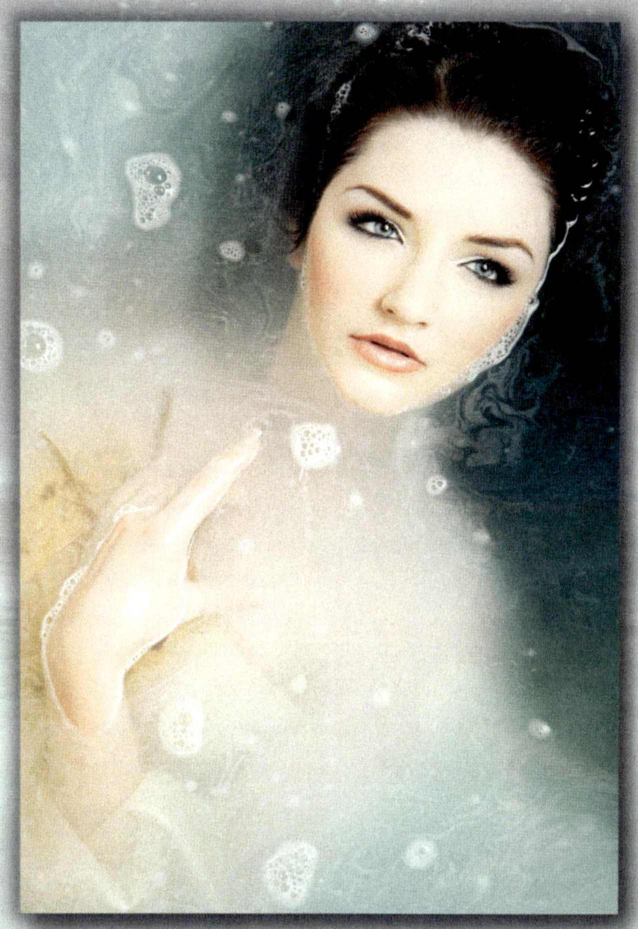

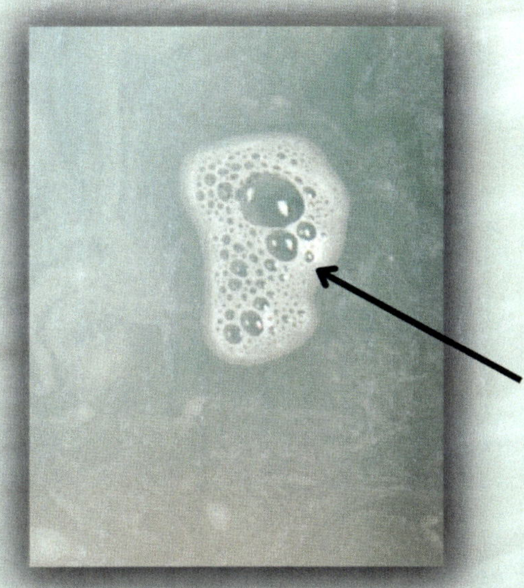

I love these bubbles! We will be using these as a reference to paint them in later. Blowing up the images to a larger scale helps you to see the details really clearly so you can paint them more easily.

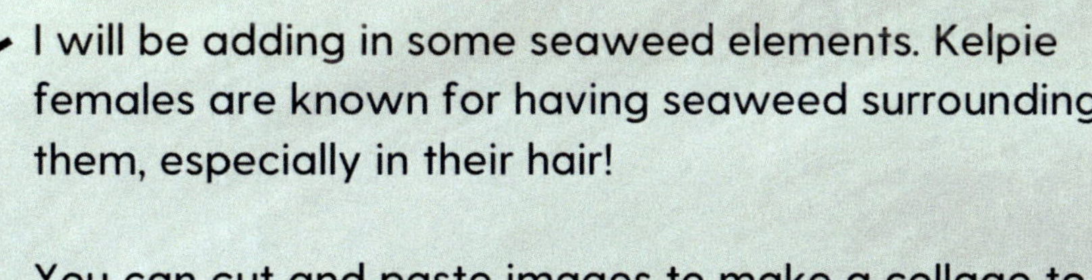

I will be adding in some seaweed elements. Kelpie females are known for having seaweed surrounding them, especially in their hair!

You can cut and paste images to make a collage to transfer, or, if you have a computer or iPad, you can collage these elements together digitally to make up your composition.

Once you have your composition laid out (either in your head, on paper, or on your computer), you're ready to sketch them down on paper.

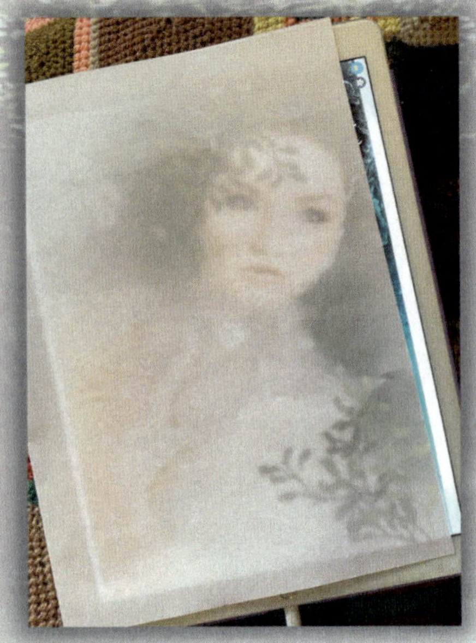

First you need to trace your image. You can use a sheet of tracing paper OVER your iPad image OR use a light box if you have one. Both are handy for transferring an image onto a new sheet of paper.

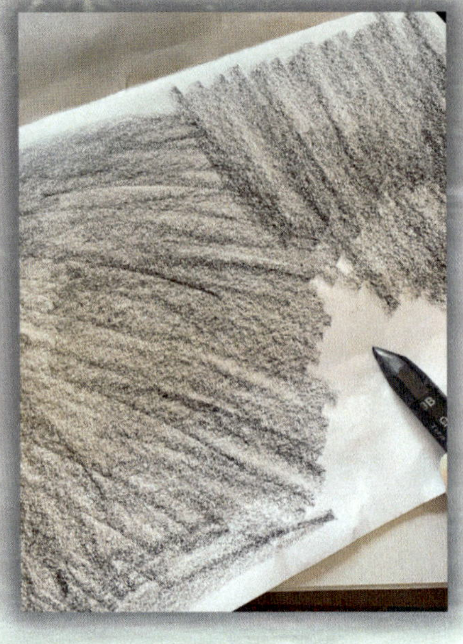

Then, turn it over and scrub some dark graphite pencil all over the back.

Next, turn this back over and lay it gently on top of your watercolor paper.

Hot tip from Karen: this method creates very light lines. For DARK transfer lines, use carbon transfer paper.

Now, trace the image with a sharp pen. The image will now be transferred onto your watercolor paper. The line may be faint but that's okay. You can also use transfer paper to complete these same steps.

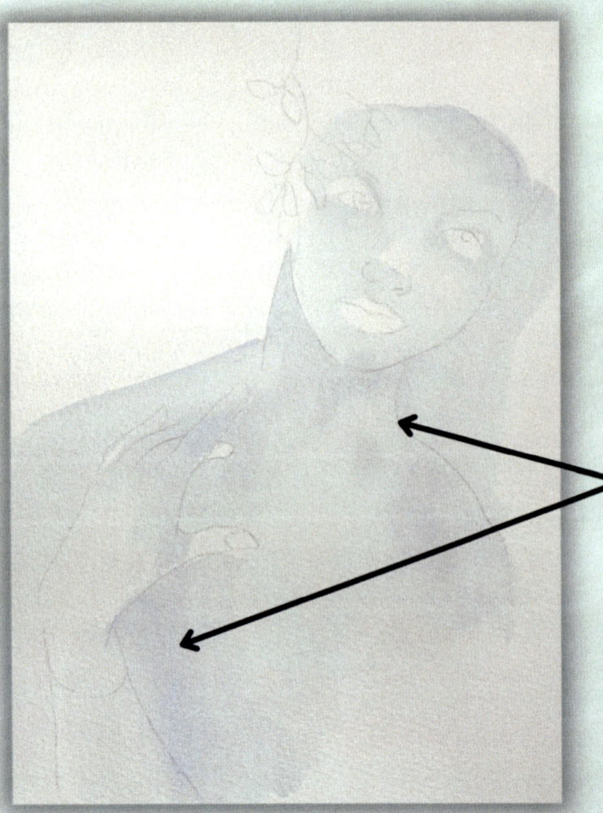

I like to tape the edges of my paper with painter's tape. That will create a nice white border at the end of the project.

I start off by mixing up a nice, pale watery mix of blue. I am using cobalt blue for this, but any blue will do so just use what you have!

Cover most of the girl's form with a watery mix of this paint. Add darker areas where the shadows are in the photograph or just follow me!

Use a fairly large brush and let this layer dry completely before continuing. You can use a heat gun or hair dryer to speed drying time.

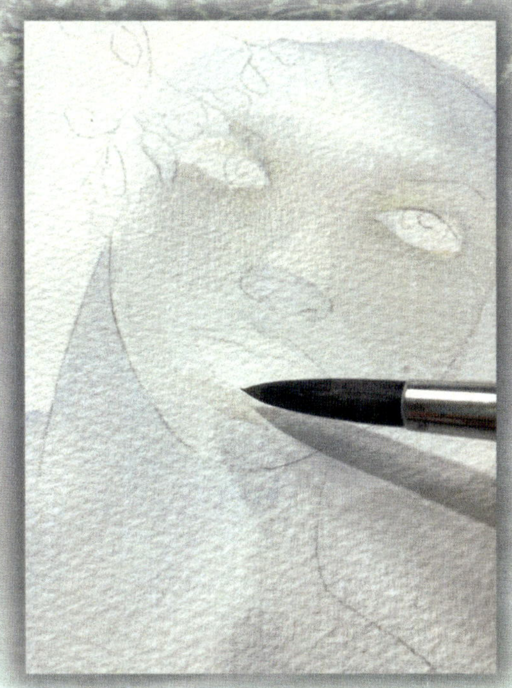

Once your blue paint is dry, you can start to lay in the first layers of watercolor on her face and body. First, mix up a pale skin tone with Naples Yellow with a small amount of Alizarin Crimson. (Refer to my watercolor skin tones cheat sheet on how to mix up a skin tone - see page 127).

With watercolor, the more water you add to your pigment, the paler the color becomes. Apply the paint to the main areas that are in shadow, and then wash out your brush and blend it out so that it is paler in the lighter areas.

Let each layer dry before adding the next so that you get beautiful glazes and depth of color.

Next, we will paint the background using a wet-on-wet application. Before we dive in, let's quickly go over exactly what that is! It's simple, really.

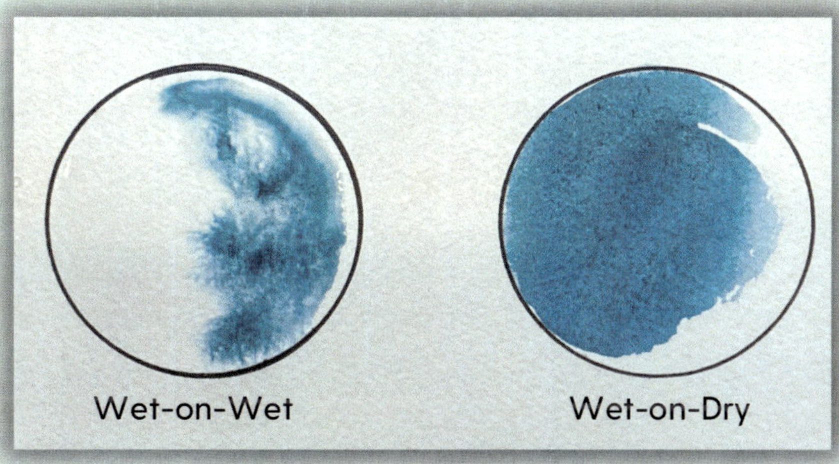

In watercolors, wet-on-wet describes the process of wetting the paper with clean water first and then dropping in the paint to let it move around the paper as it pleases.

Wet-on-dry is where you apply paint directly onto a DRY piece of watercolor paper.

Both are correct ways to paint with watercolor! Both are commonly used within the same watercolor projects but have very different results, as you can see!

Now let's continue with the background. You can use a selection of your favorite blues and greens using the wet-on-wet application I just described. The main colors I'm using are Cobalt Blue and Sap Green.

While the paint is still wet you can sprinkle some salt on it and let it dry. This is one of my favorite ways to add subtle texture into the backgrounds and large, wet areas.

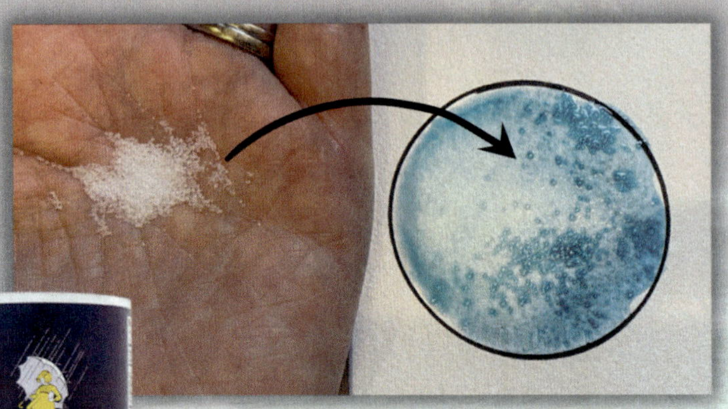

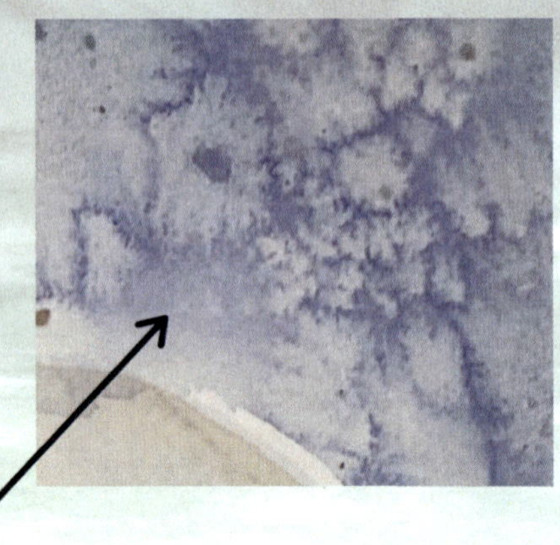

Once the paint and paper are both dry, brush the salt away to reveal lovely, sparkly textures! For this project, I sprinkled salt lightly and randomly around the background areas. It's a gorgeous effect!

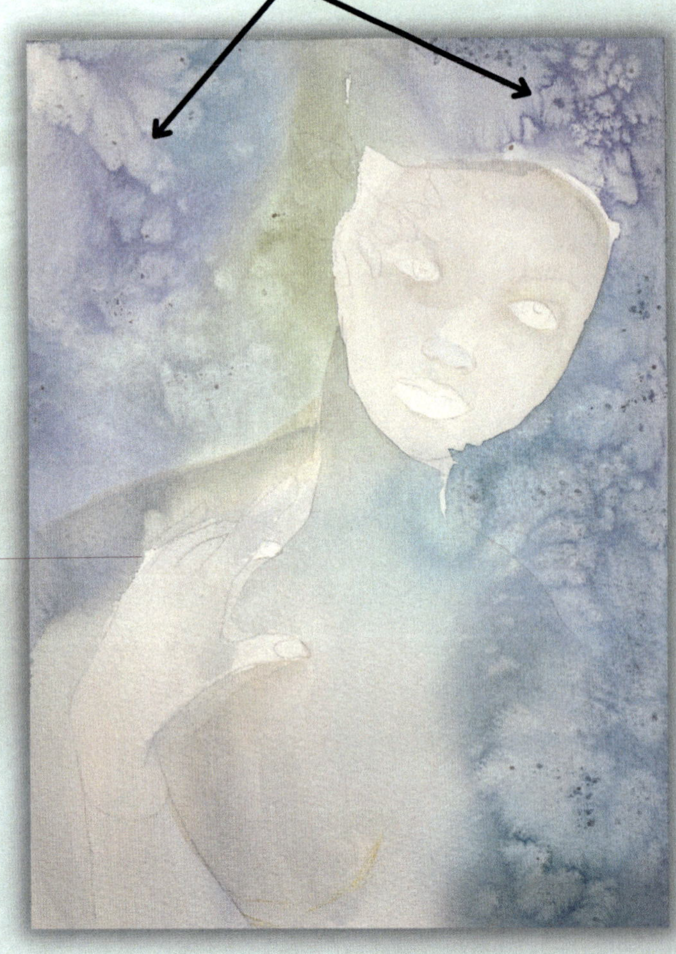

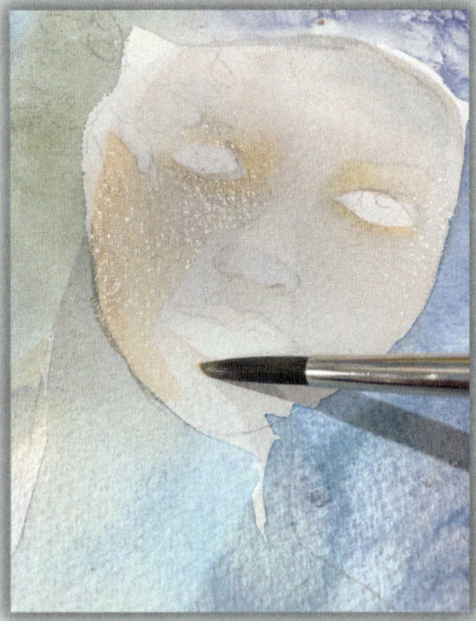

Next, keep adding layers to the face with your skin tone mixture. For this project, it's the area around the eye, under the mouth, under the chin, and in the dip under the nose.

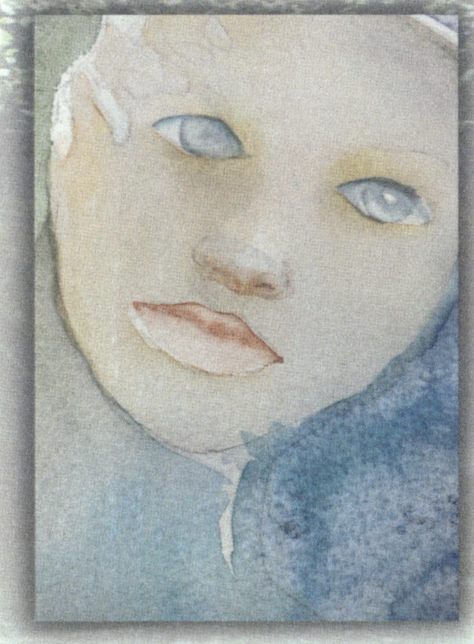

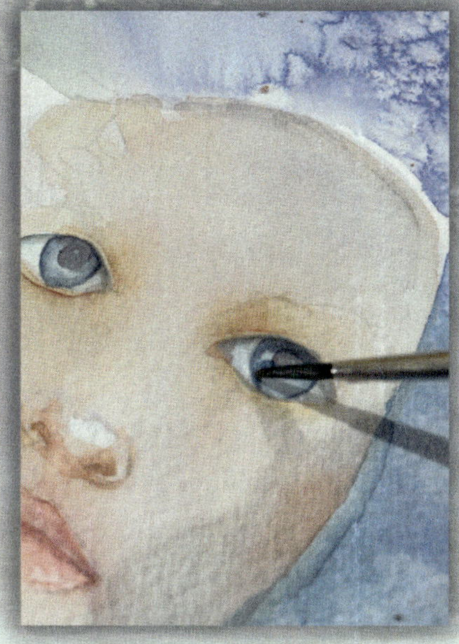

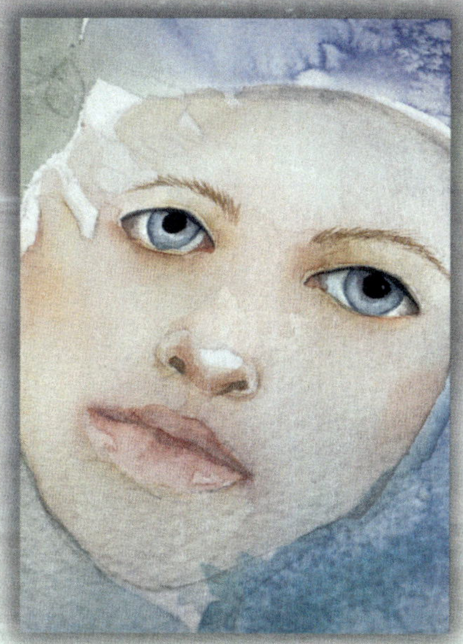

Begin by building up the blues for the eyes and some pink or peach for the lips. Paint these lightly to begin with. Make sure the skin around the eyes is dry before you begin!

You can then add more layers to make some parts darker. You can let the eyes dry slightly while you move to the lips, and vice versa.

Do not paint the pupils black until the blue of the iris is dry. Watercolors dry lighter than when applied, so you may need to add more layers to darken them.

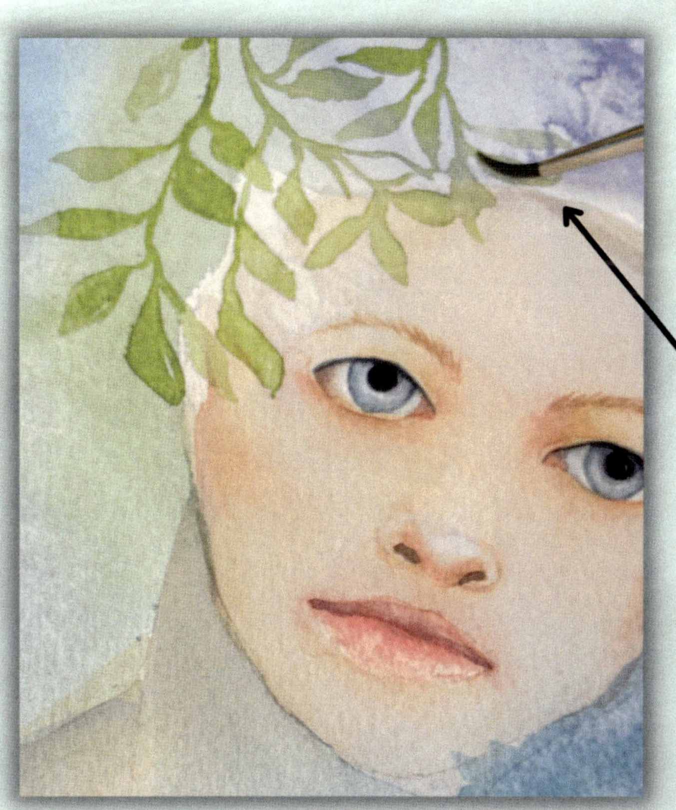

Now that the background is dry, it's the perfect time to paint in some seaweed shapes on top.

Use a medium-sized round brush and your favorite greens.

Press down with a round brush (as shown) to make the perfect leaf shape!

Then lift up and use the tip of the same brush to paint the thinner stalks.

If you have some overlapping leaves, paint them once the previous layers have dried so they don't go muddy or lose definition.

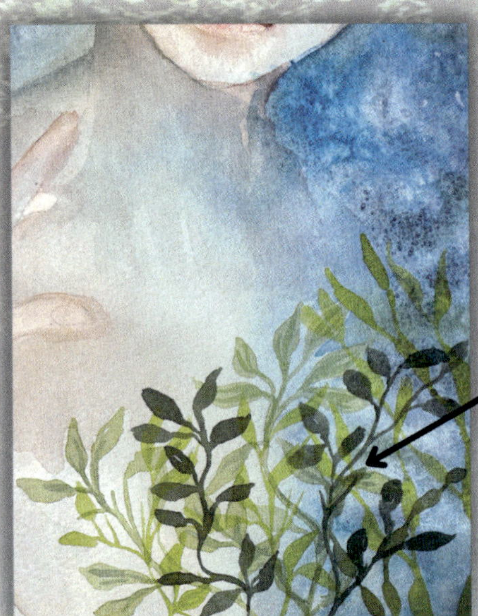

You can help create depth by adding a second layer of seaweed in darker green. As you can see, I added 2 layers of seaweed (a light layer and then a darker layer on top) to both the areas over her head, as well as in the lower right corner.

Add more blue and green into the background, to darken it up and add depth and dimension, as well as color!

Feel free to paint some more pink onto her cheeks and nose at this stage.

More seaweed can be added along the left-hand side, near her hand to balance out the composition as a whole.

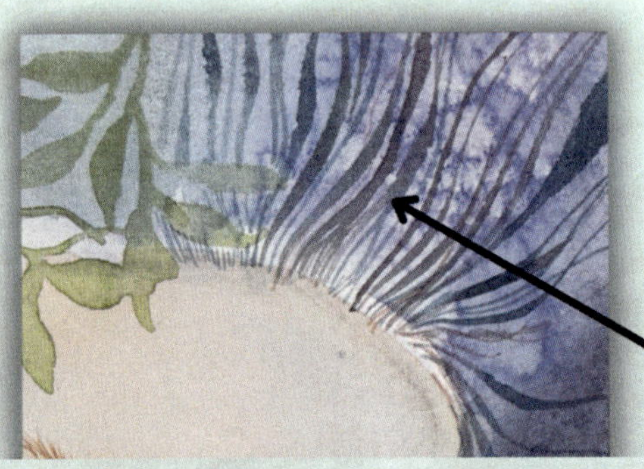

Add in some fine lines using a small liner brush for her hair. You can vary the thickness of the line by how hard you press down with your brush.

We both love watercolor brushes by Polina Bright: www.polinabright.com/karencampbell and use coupon code KARENCAMPBELL to get 10% off your whole order!

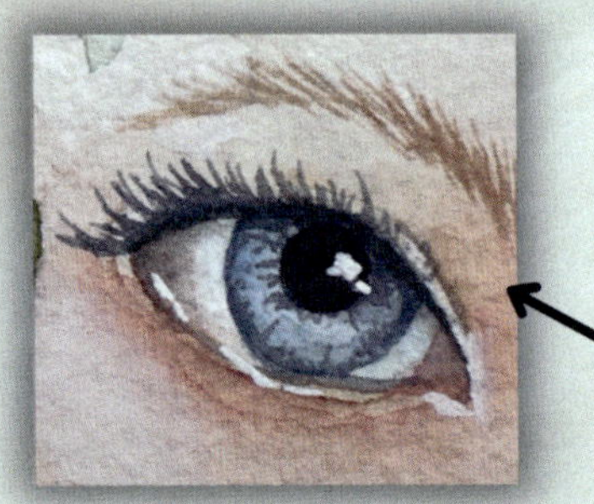

Don't forget to also use a fine brush to paint on her eyebrows and eyelashes!

Painting these bubbles is super fun! Make sure your background layers are completely dry before you begin.

Then grab your white! Ph Martin Bleed proof white is the best one for this but you can also use white gouache or Copic opaque white.

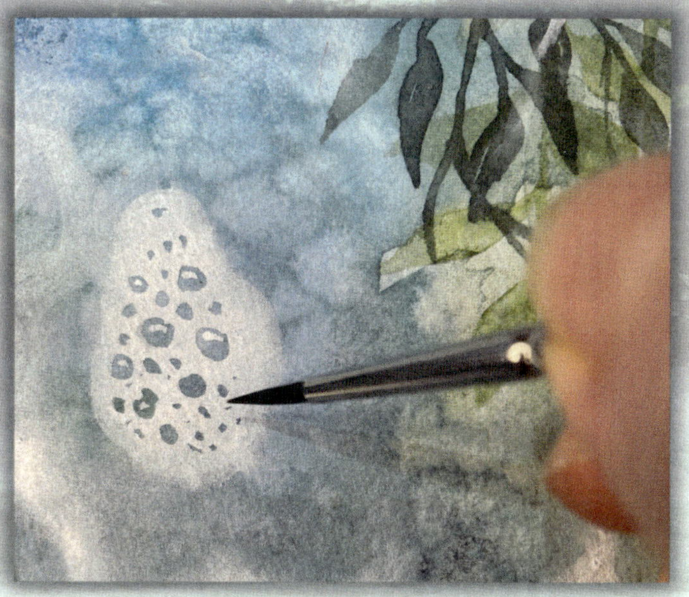

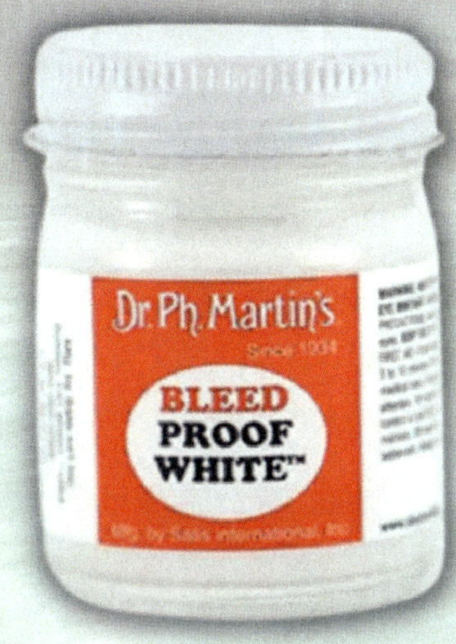

Begin by painting lots of circle shapes of various sizes, leaving the inside of the circle empty (so you can see the background showing through). Once you have done that, fill in the space around them with more white.

Finally, you can paint tiny highlights in some of the circle shapes. Use a small brush for this to get more precision.

If the paint is too thick feel free to add a little water.

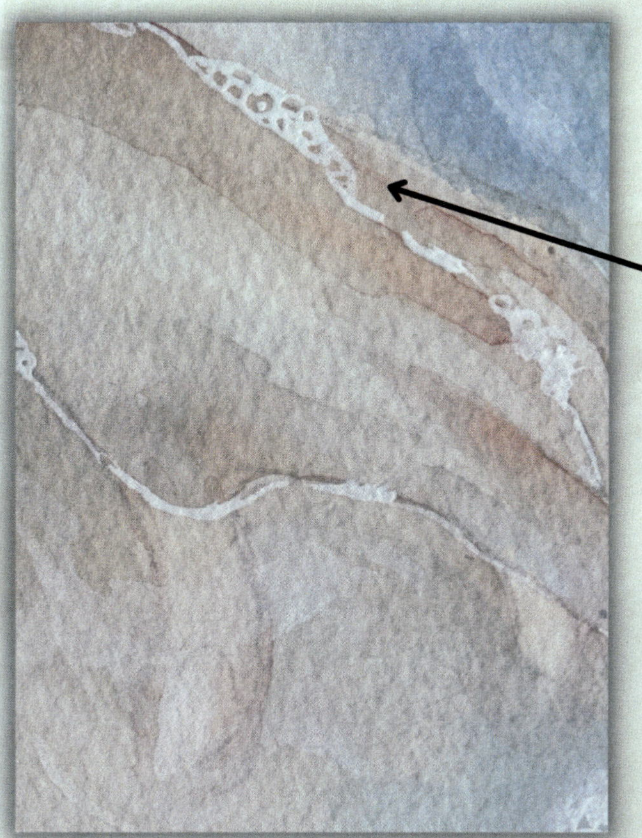

Continue to paint bubbles around your picture in various places. You can see here I painted some around the hand which gives the illusion of the hand coming out of the water somewhat.

It's a super effective technique!

Turn the page to see where you can also paint these bubbles around her face too. The effect is that it looks like her face is rising out of the water!

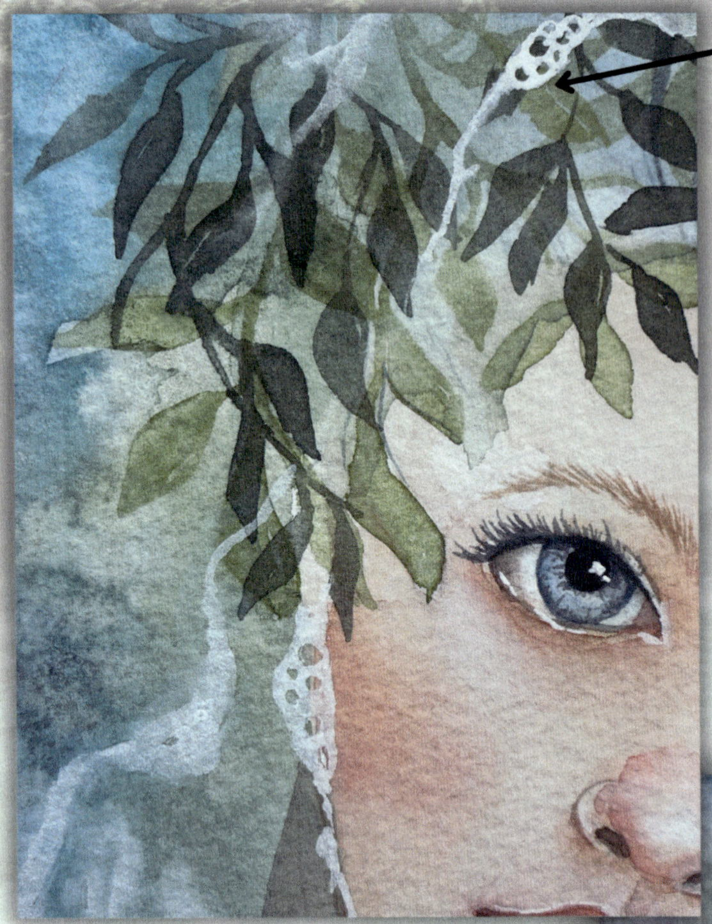

I continue using the opaque white to create highlights in the painting and more bubbles.

This is the part where everything "comes together" and she starts to come alive!

Even though this is a super fun part and you might be itching to get to it, try to leave it till the end!

Feel free to add watery patches around her. Just water down the opaque white slightly and apply it loosely with your paintbrush.

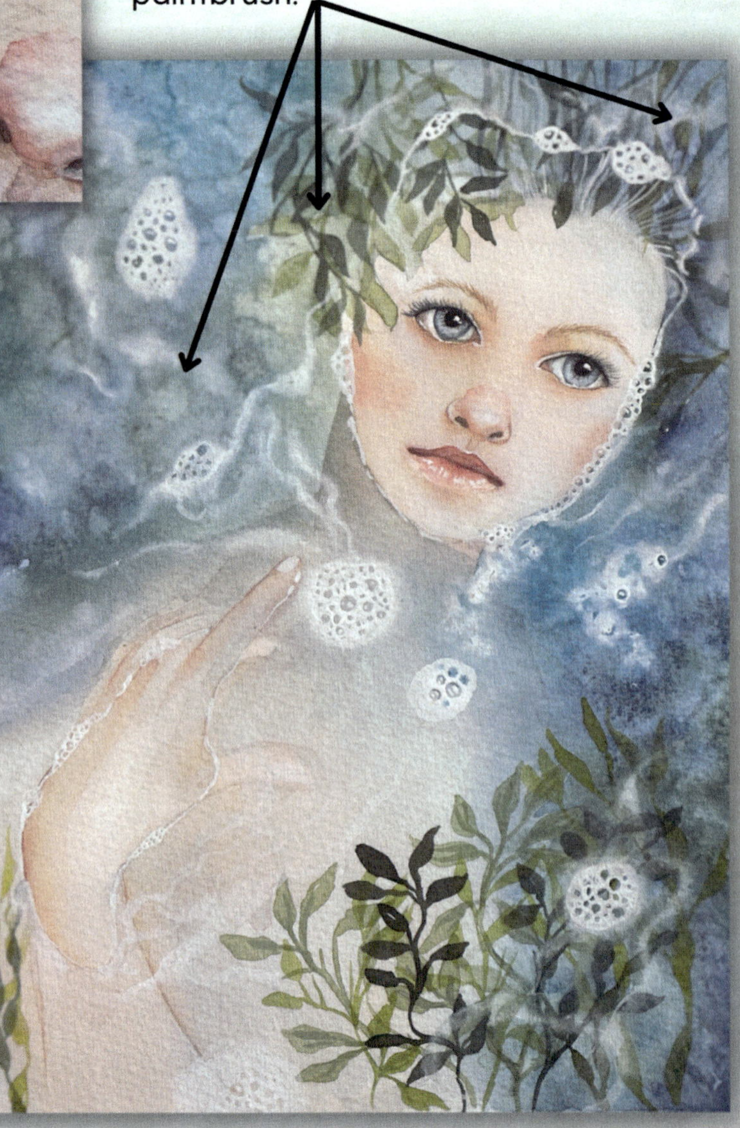

You can also add white highlights to the following places on her face to make a big impact: in her pupils, on the tip of her nose, and on her bottom lip.

You can also apply white highlights to her cheekbones and in the corners of her eye nearest the nose.

Do this sparingly and blend it out with a damp brush to make it look more natural.

She is done! I hope she doesn't lure you into the water with her!

You did a great job!!

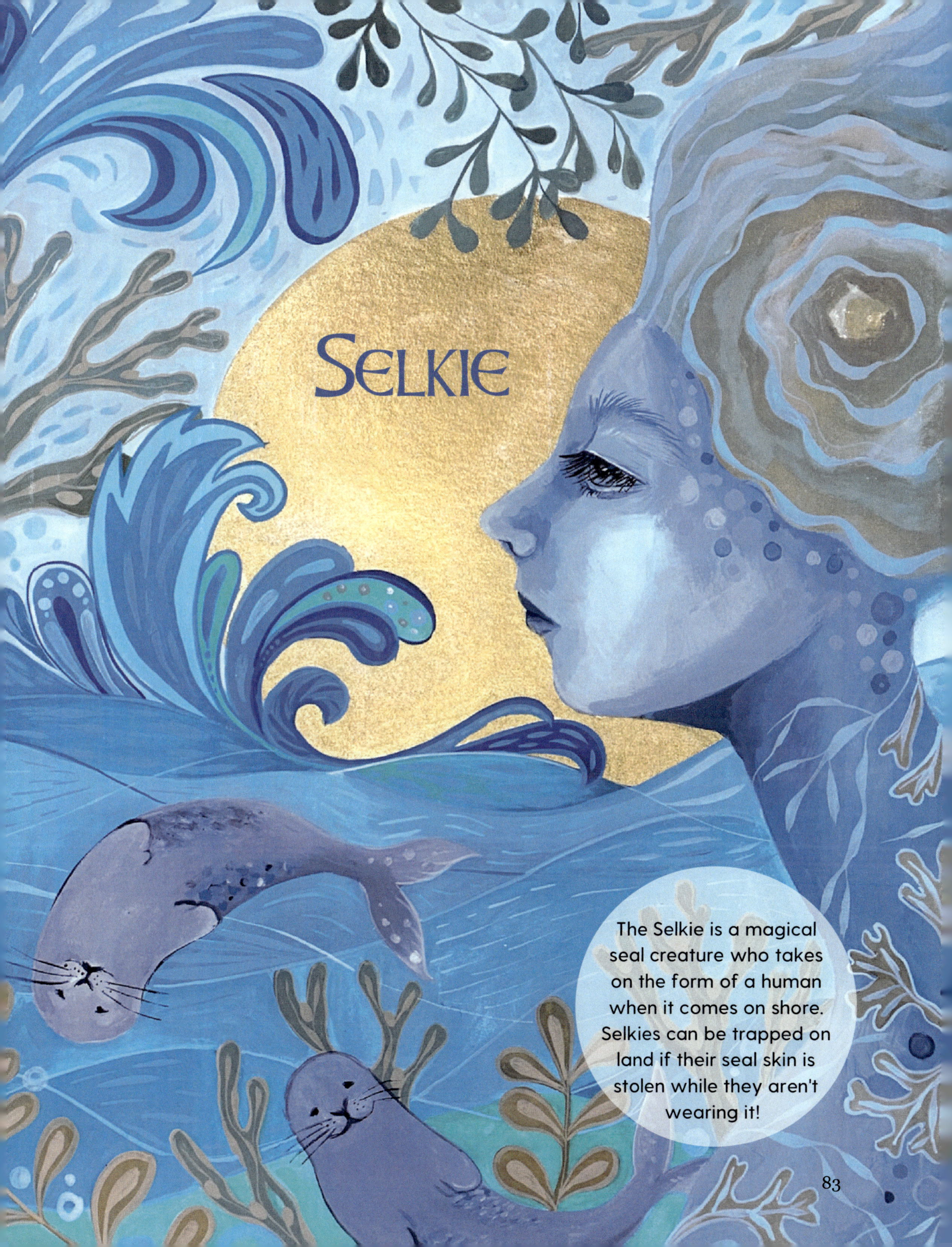

Selkie

The Selkie is a magical seal creature who takes on the form of a human when it comes on shore. Selkies can be trapped on land if their seal skin is stolen while they aren't wearing it!

SUPPLIES

Watercolor paper 140 lbs.
A stay-wet palette is not compulsory but is a very handy tool for painting with acrylic gouache!
CANSON
Metallic watercolors
Water for brushes
Colored pencils
Selection of paint brushes
Acrylic or traditional gouache

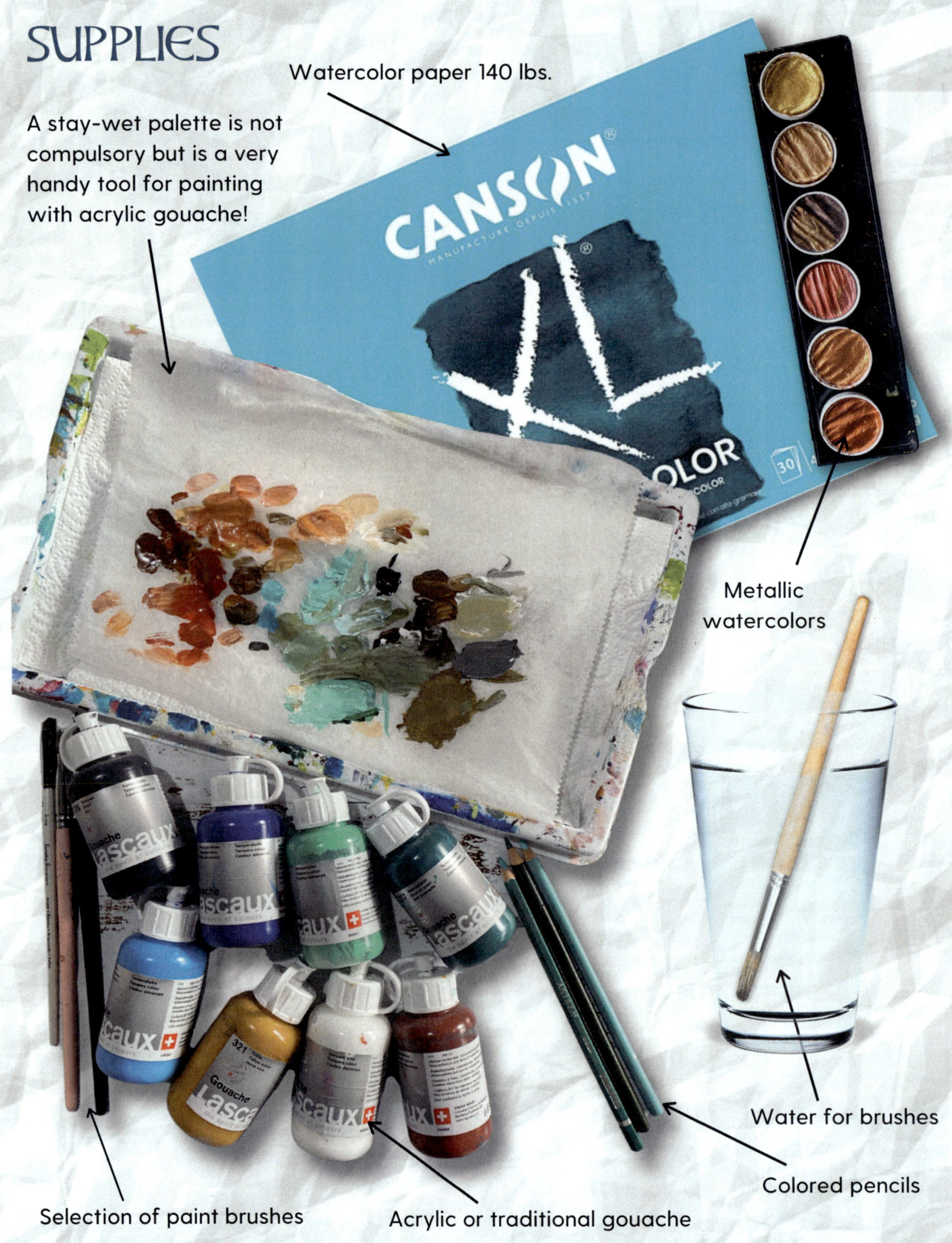

Gouache & Awesome Alternatives

Gouache has been around for centuries but it may be new to you! So what is it? Well, it's watercolors with a twist! So like watercolor, it remains water-soluble (even after dried) and never becomes permanent. But UNLIKE watercolor, it is extremely matte (or flat, with absolutely no sheen or granulation to it) and it's also totally opaque - so you can't see through it.

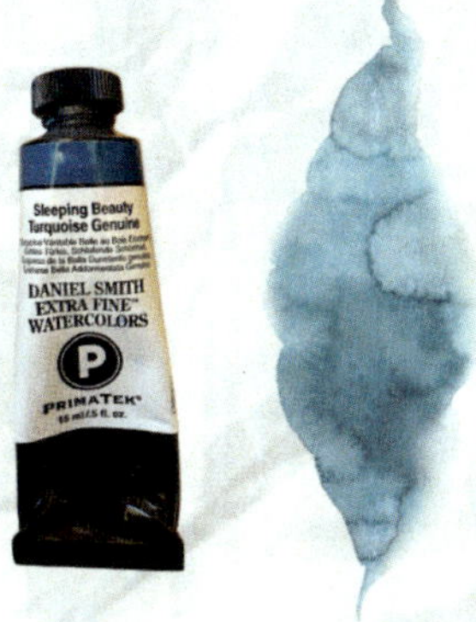

Watercolors are transparent and remain water-reactive.

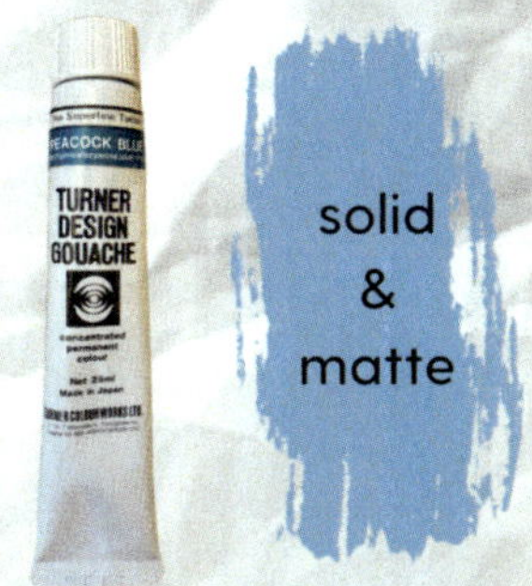

"Traditional" gouache is opaque and stays water-reactive. Fine art brands can be very pricey.

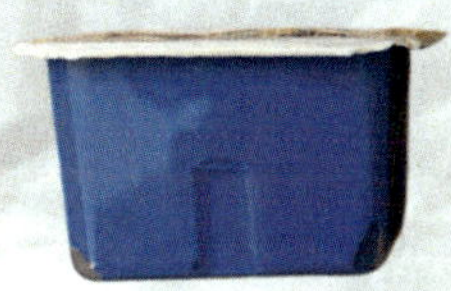

"Traditional" gouache is also available in these very cheap gel cups, perfect for those on a budget. You need to add water to these however, in order to achieve the desired consistency.

What's known as "traditional" gouache is available at a few very different price points. Due to its ability to remain water-reactive, it can be a bit tricky to work with, since adding any new layers has the power (and tendency) to re-activate all the layers underneath. Unwanted blending in a paint project can be frustrating! So, in response to this, manufacturers have invented different products that mimic that lovely opaque and matte effect but that are PERMANENT, so they are a little easier to paint with.
Here are some excellent alternatives to traditional gouache that you may be interested to learn about!

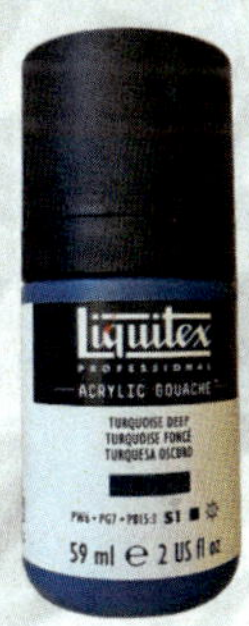

Acrylic Gouache has the flat, matte and opaque qualities of traditional gouache but is permanent when dry, making it easier to layer and work with.

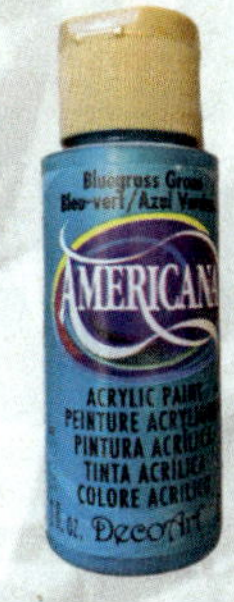

Interestingly, a lot of inexpensive craft acrylic paints mimic the look of gouache due to their matte appearance!

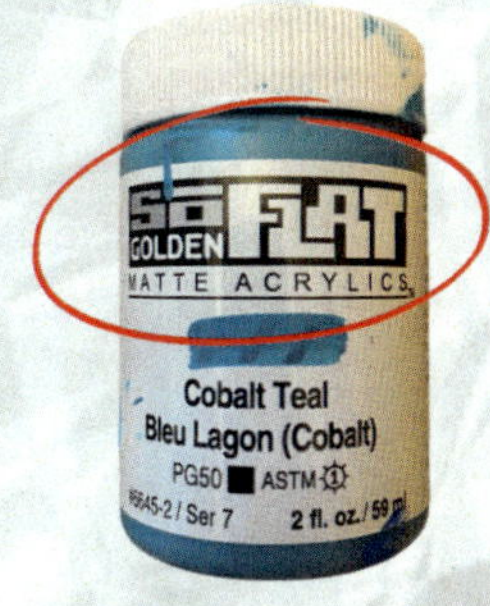

Look for the word "matte" when shopping for acrylics. These will all be great substitutes for gouache!

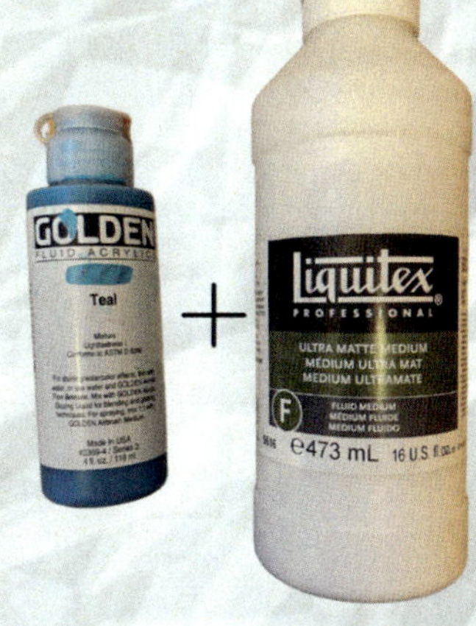

You can make your own matte paint by stirring in some Ultra Matte Medium into your regular acrylics!

Selkies are shape-shifting creatures that change from their seal form into human form when they come ashore. In Scottish folk tales, it is common for selkie women to be kidnapped by human men. Hiding the Selkie's skin forces the now landbound woman to stay ashore. Then, the man convinces (or forces) the Selkie to marry him and bear his children. In some stories, the skin is later found and the Selkie is then finally able to reunite with her underwater seal family.

If you want to do a painting with story-telling elements, it is often helpful to begin by gathering images that will help you tell your visual story.

So here, I wanted to have a woman who looked a bit "otherworldly," as if she came from the sea. I chose to have her in a background of sea-related imagery which includes water, seaweed, and seals.

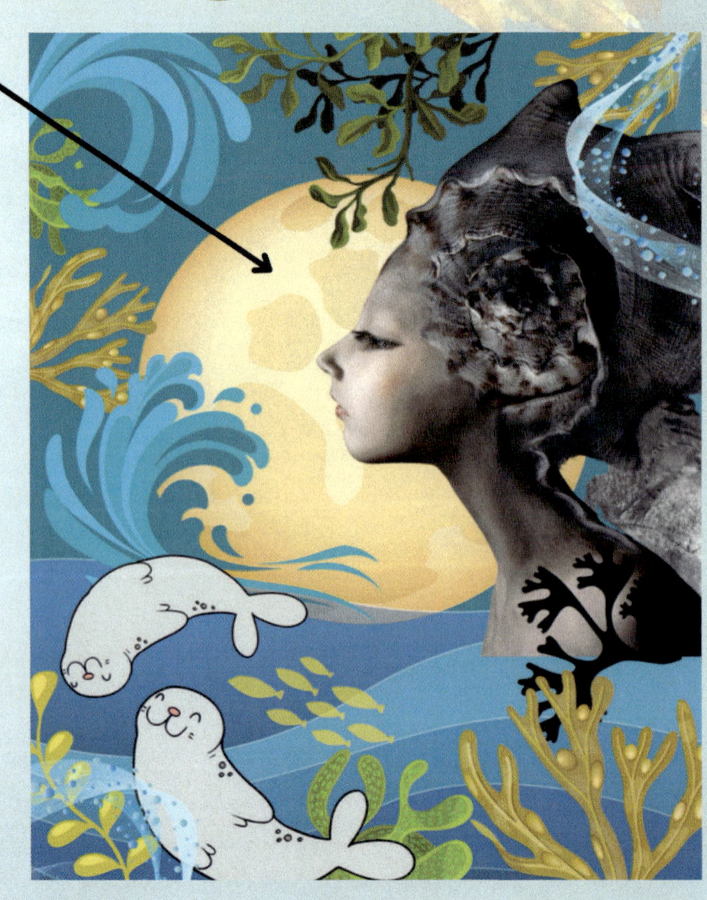

You can find royalty-free images on Pixabay, Unsplash, or similar sites and either print them off and cut them up or make a digital montage on your computer or other device.

Spend some time moving the elements around, before deciding on the final composition. When you're satisfied, sketch out your final design onto watercolor paper.

This means that you will be happy before you begin drawing - and save you from a lot of erasing!

On heavyweight watercolor paper, begin by sketching out your composition in a gold-colored pencil following your picture collage. Start with the face, as that is the most important part of the painting. Because we are painting in gouache, you do not have to worry about erasing sketch lines as they will be covered over by the paint.

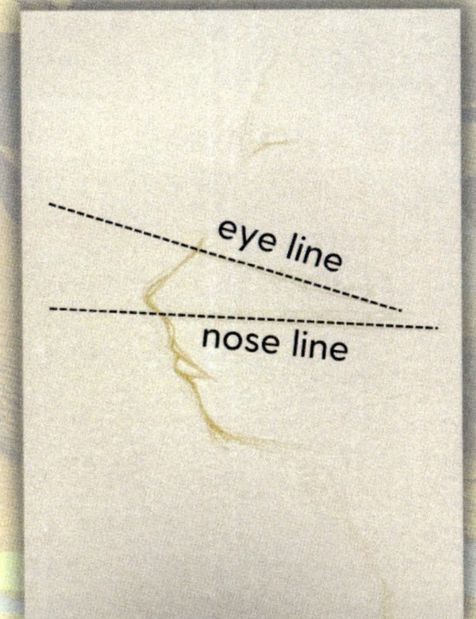

Sketch out the main shape of the profile, paying attention to the angles of the face. Follow my guidelines for proper eye and nose placement.

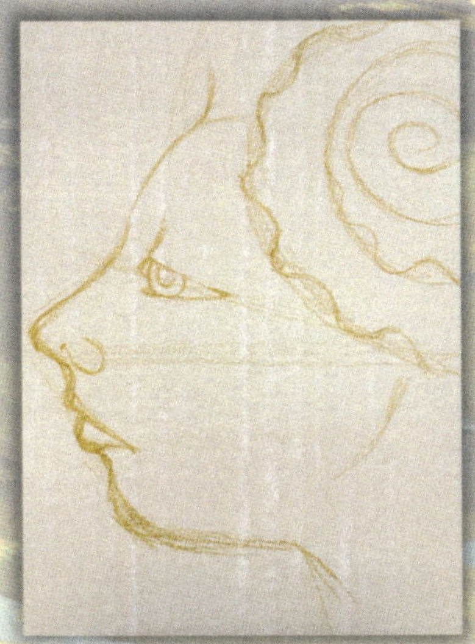

The eye at this angle looks a bit like a wedge of a pizza!

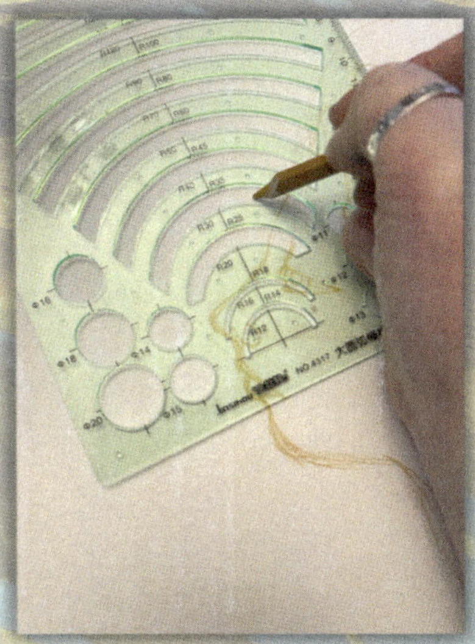

Use a template to draw the moon in the background behind the head as shown. No template? Use a bowl!

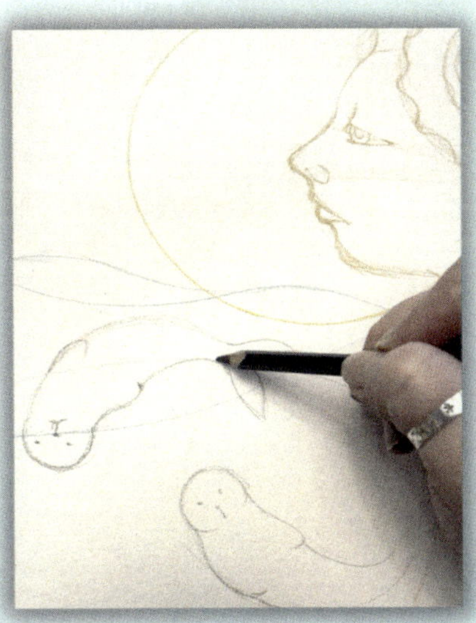

Use different pencil colors to draw in the additional sea creatures and elements.

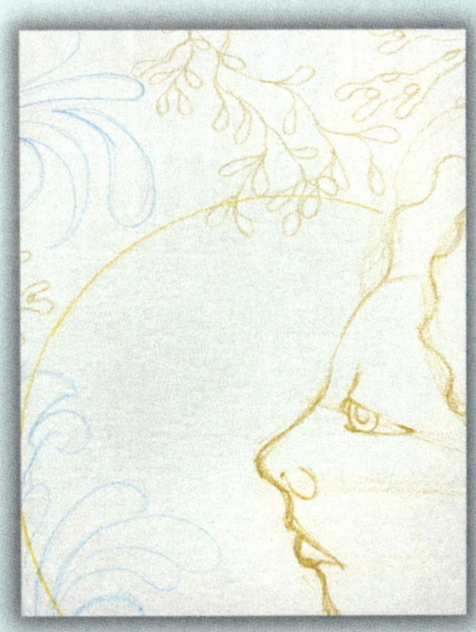

Draw in the main shapes but not the small details at this stage.

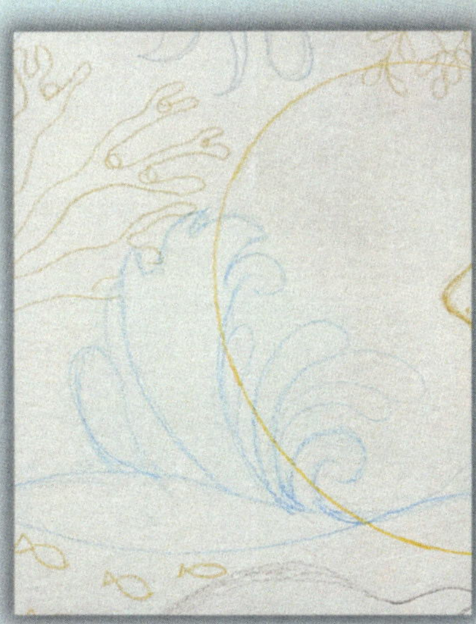

We will be painting the main areas first and address the details later.

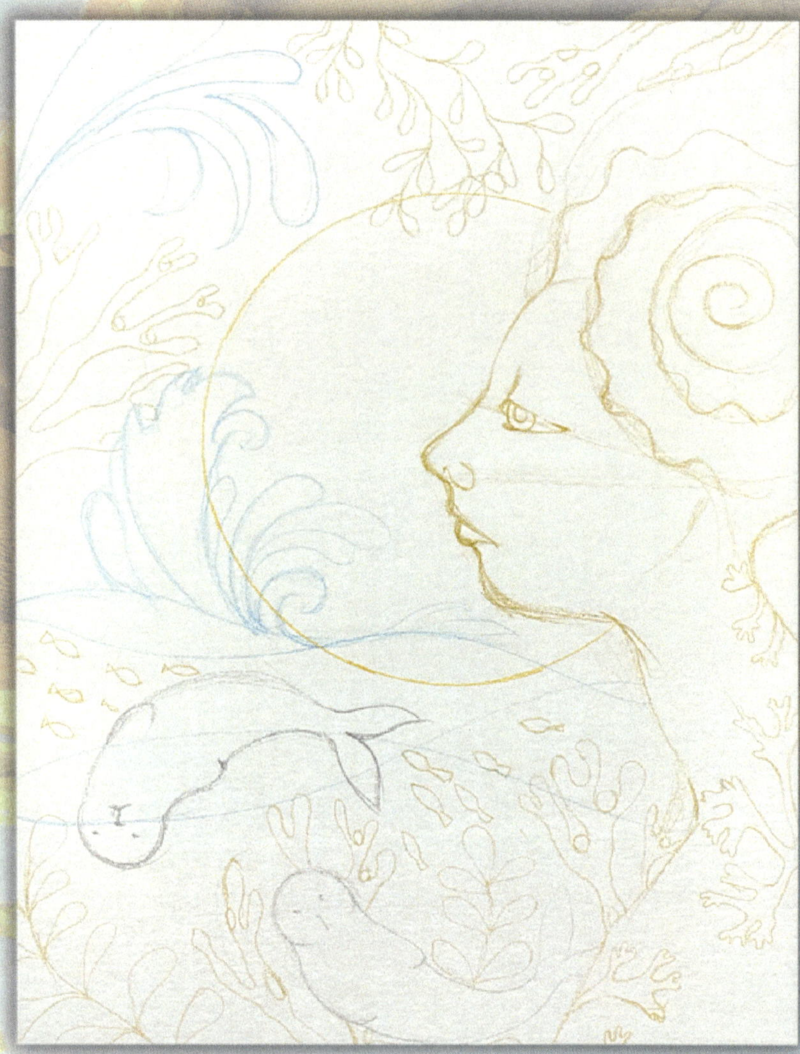

Here is what the completed composition looks like.

You can see that I have laid out the main shapes rather than smaller details.

If you feel nervous about drawing a complicated composition like this, you can also trace your composition montage using a light-box or transfer your design using carbon paper.

You are now ready to start painting!

To help keep your paints wet as you work, you can use a stay-wet palette for your gouache if you have one.

A stay-wet palette will prevent your gouache from drying out while you are working. It is especially handy if you are using acrylic gouache, as I am. You can make your own stay-wet palette easily by using a Tupperware box with a lid and lining it with wet paper towels and a piece of deli (or wax) paper.

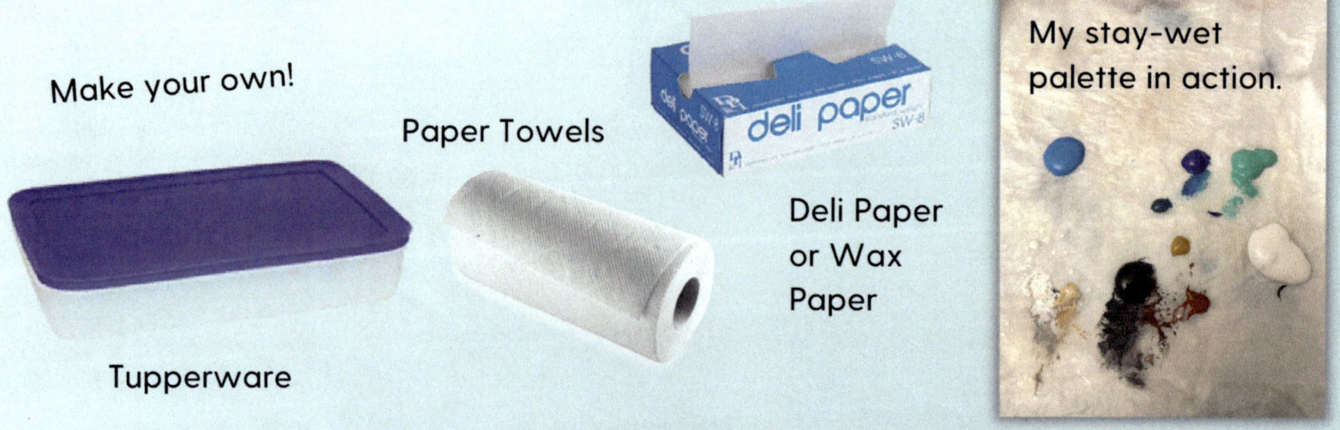

Remember that you only need to put out the colors you need for each area, rather than all of the colors for the whole painting! We will focus on one subject at a time.

We are going to start off by painting the gold moon. I used gold watercolor for this but you can also use gold gouache (or acrylics) if that's what you have. Use a fairly large brush. As previously mentioned, it doesn't matter too much if you go over some of your lines as the gouache will eventually cover over everything.

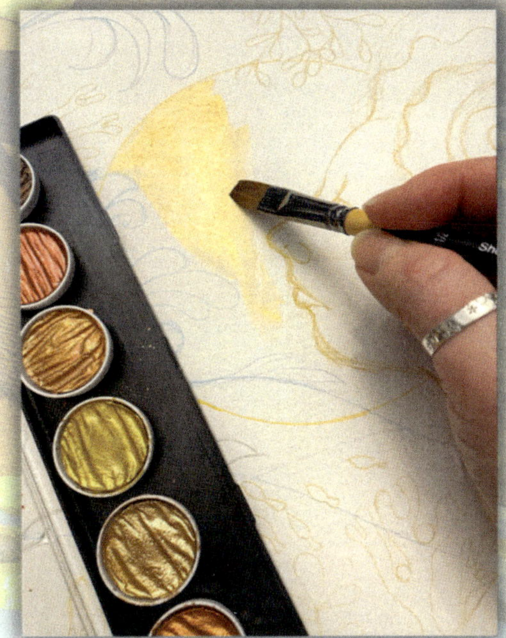

To get good coverage, paint several layers if necessary. Let each layer dry completely before painting the next.

Once you have completed painting the moon, you are ready to start painting the Selkie!

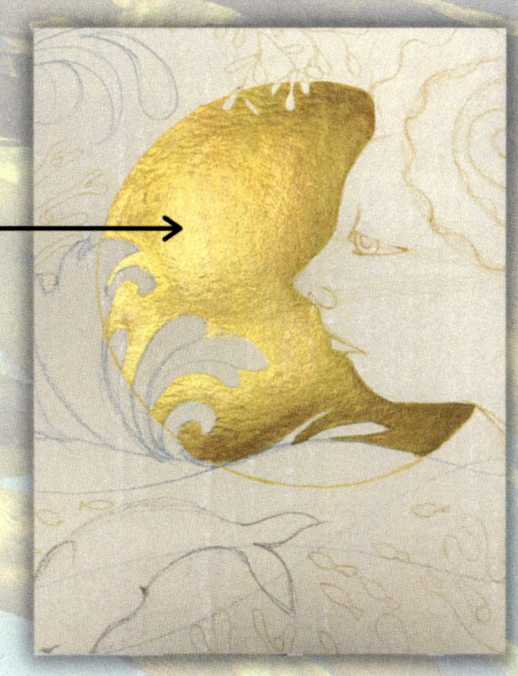

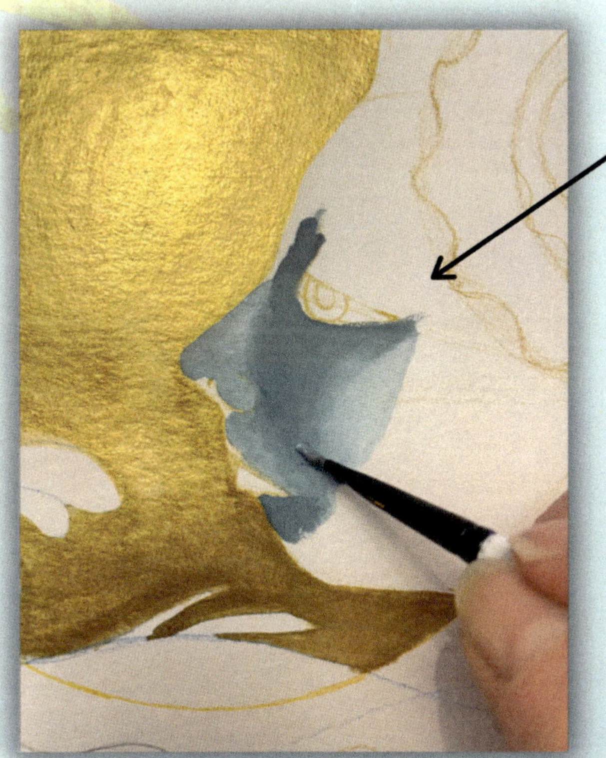

Mix up some blue-grey tones and begin by painting in the first layers of the face. With three shades ready to go, we are set to paint the face like a pro!

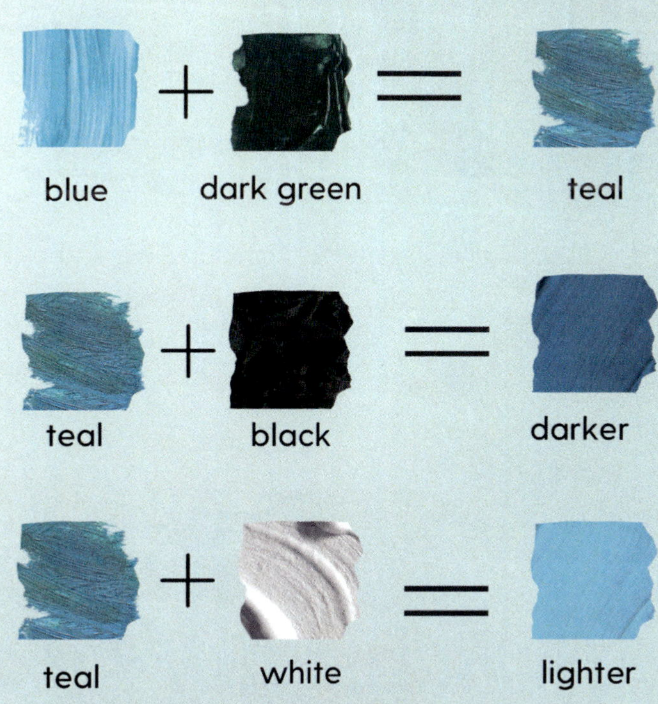

Use a larger size brush to begin so you can work quickly and blend as you go!

Paint darker tones in the shadows around the eye socket and under the chin, and lighter tones on the cheekbones and down the bridge of the nose. You don't need to worry about perfect blending! Just do the best you can and have fun!

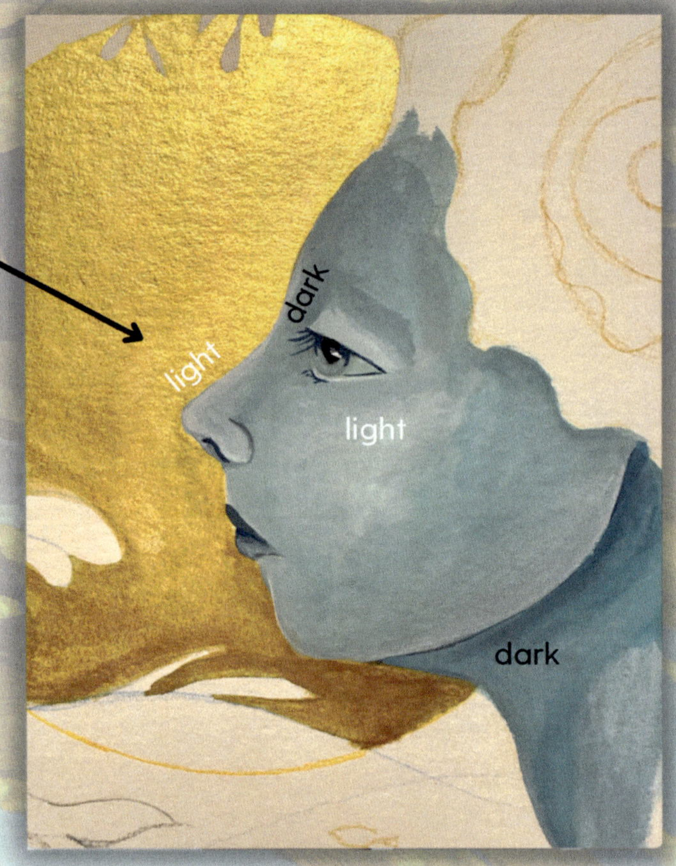

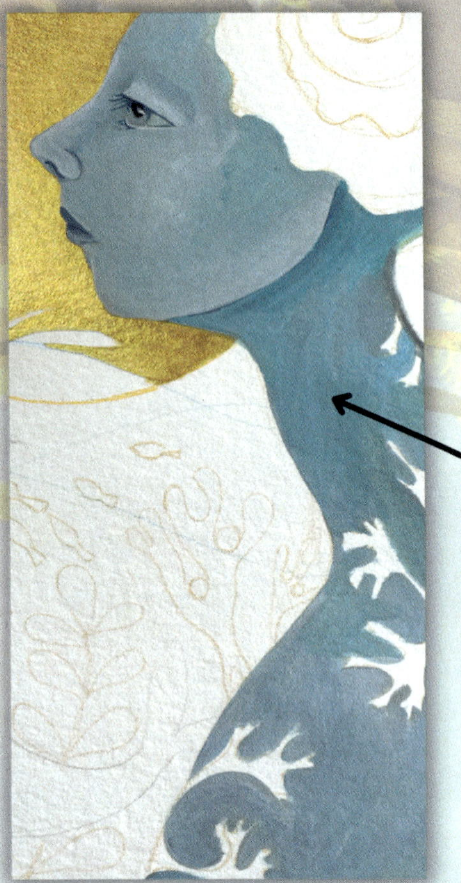

Continue to paint the first layers of blueish greys down the neck and body. Notice I left out the areas where the seaweed will be. You don't have to be too neat at this point as it's only the first layer.

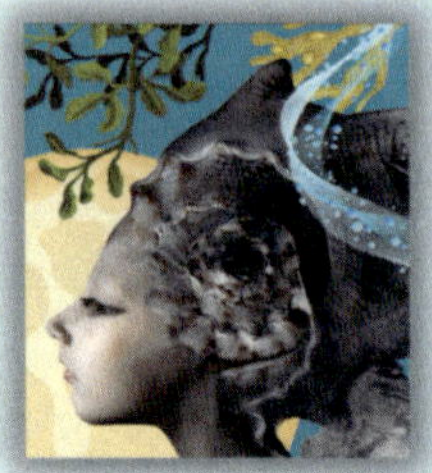

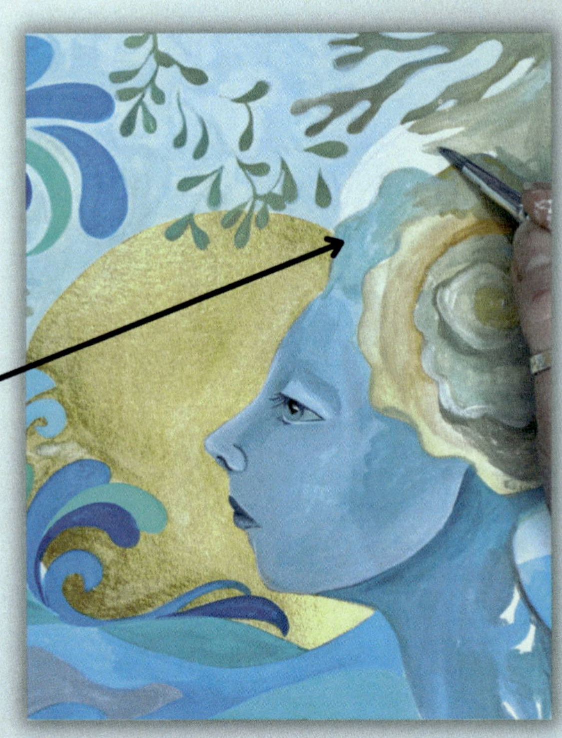

We will talk about the background later. For now, we are just sticking with painting the Selkie's face!

For the hair area, I chose to paint a shell instead of real hair. The reference image I found had the shell shape and I thought it fit the sea theme perfectly.

Paint in the colors for the shell/hair loosely, blending them while still wet on the page.

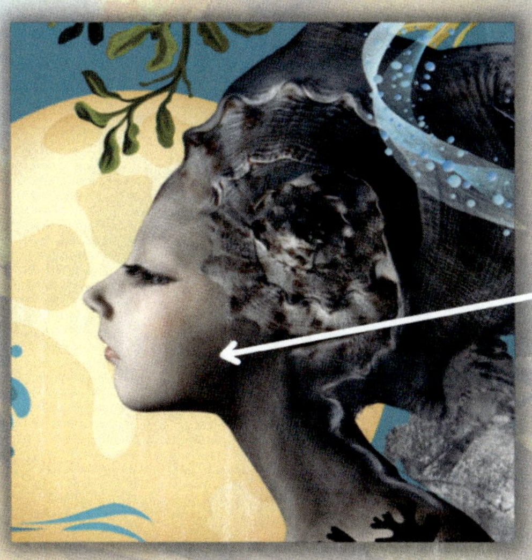

Once your first layers are down for the face and "hair" you can begin to refine them even more. Look at the original photo to see where the lights and darks really lie.

Her cheeks really seem to be glowing! Those can be kept rather light. Note how dark the areas under her chin and down her neck are. You can add additional black to your blue-grey shades to get the most dimension and drama from those regions of darkness.

Now, let's switch gears and discuss color blending for a moment! If you want some of your areas to have smooth color blends, then gather up several brushes: one for the first color, one for the second, and a third used to blend the two colors together.

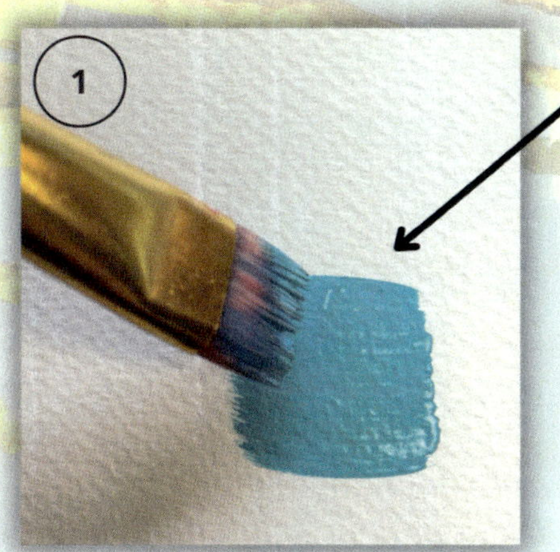

Start off with your first paint color. Apply it with the first brush.

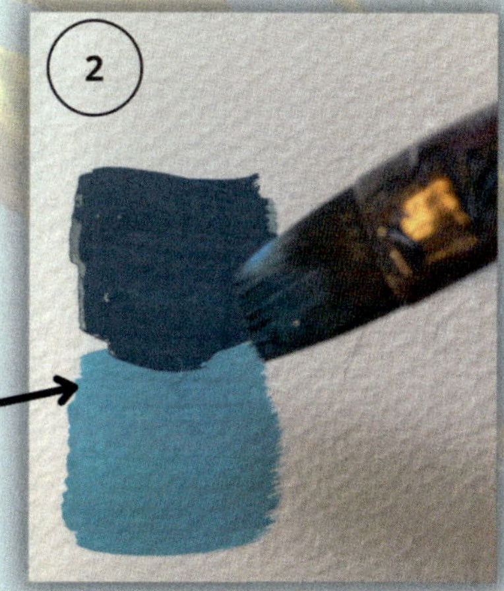

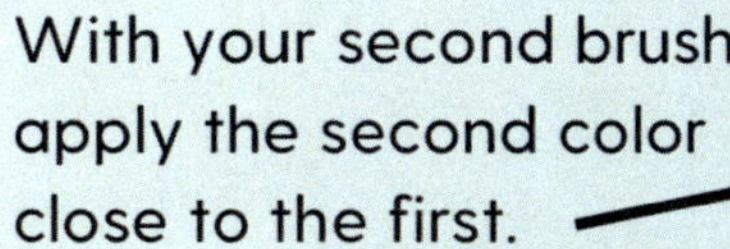

With your second brush apply the second color close to the first.

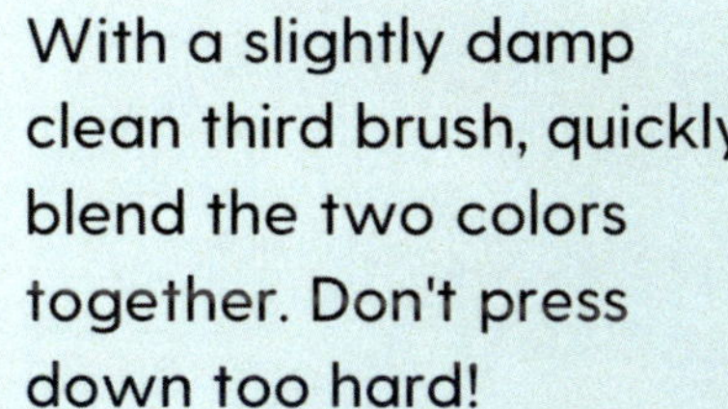

With a slightly damp clean third brush, quickly blend the two colors together. Don't press down too hard!

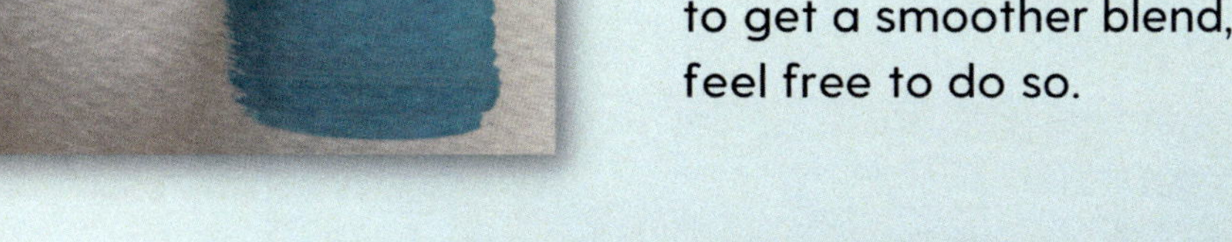

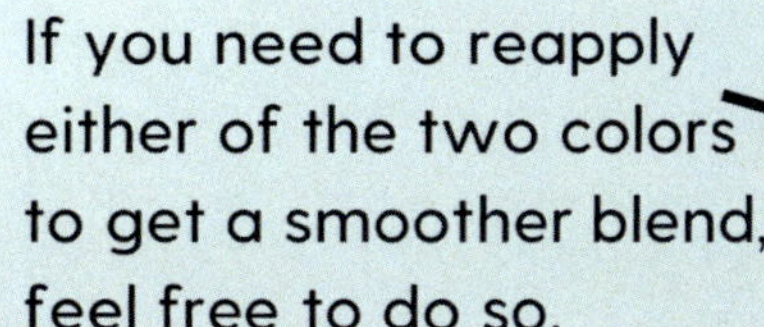

If you need to reapply either of the two colors to get a smoother blend, feel free to do so.

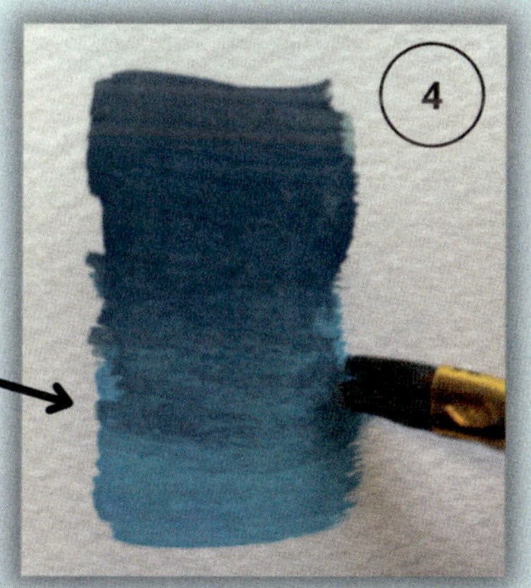

Be patient with yourself while you paint. Working with gouache (especially if you're a beginner) can be very tricky! Don't worry if your blending isn't super smooth; it's all good and, like everything, just takes practice.

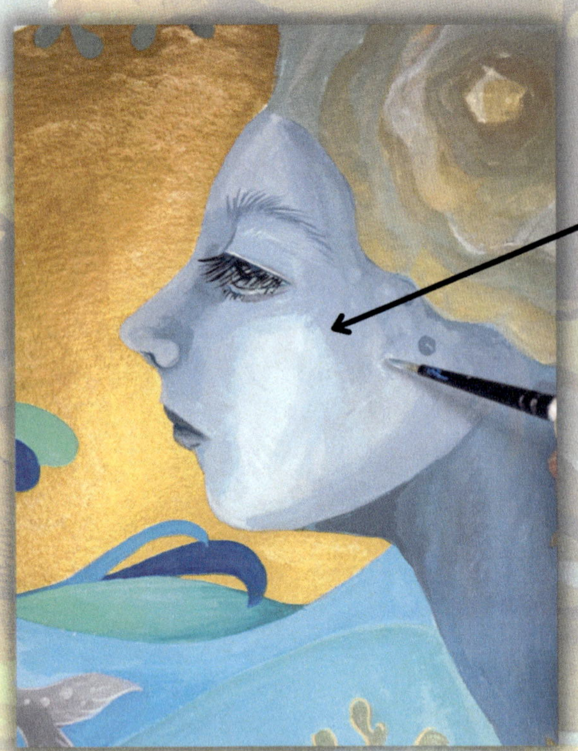

You may need to add lighter areas to her cheekbones, forehead and nose if your first layer wasn't light enough. Use the color blending tips from the previous page to help you blend the colors.

With a fine-detail brush, add in some thin lines to show the eyelashes, eyebrows and nostrils.

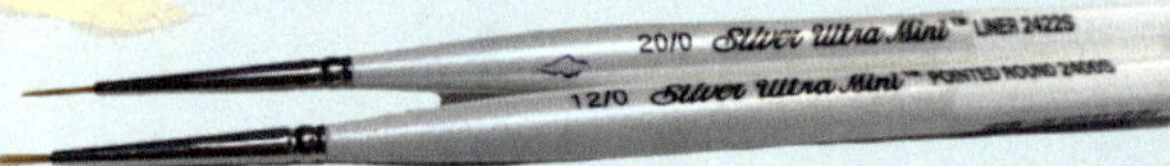

I love these detail brushes by Silver Ultra.

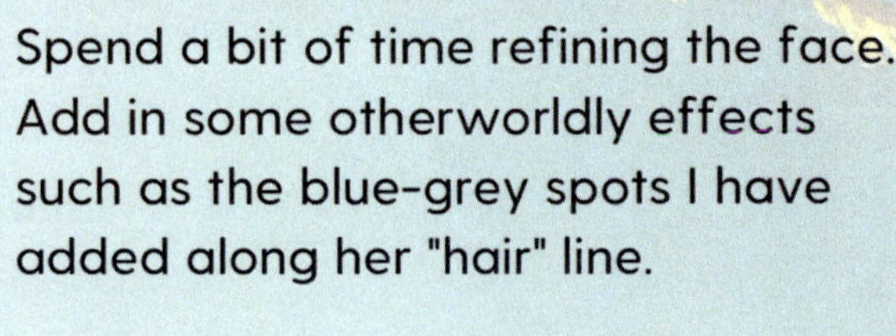

Spend a bit of time refining the face. Add in some otherworldly effects such as the blue-grey spots I have added along her "hair" line.

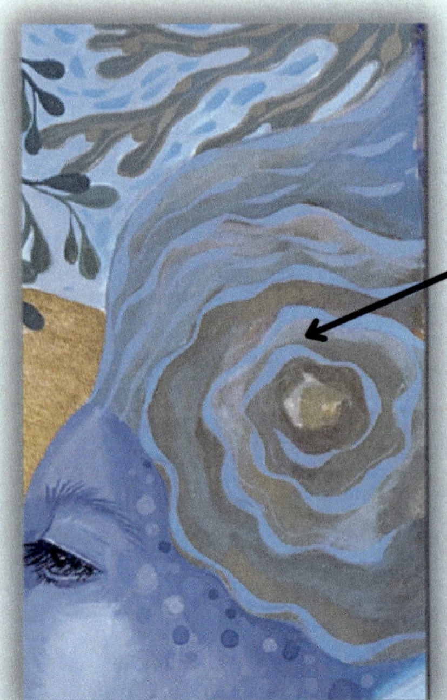

Add in more details on the second layer of the shell headpiece. I used a pale blue and painted thick and thin lines around the spiral.

The patterns on the shell do not have to be true to life or match your reference photo! I love making these soft squiggle lines!

We are now going to move on to painting the background elements! Let's look at our original sketch and the reference photo once more. We want to paint seaweed, waves, the seals and the rest of the background colors.

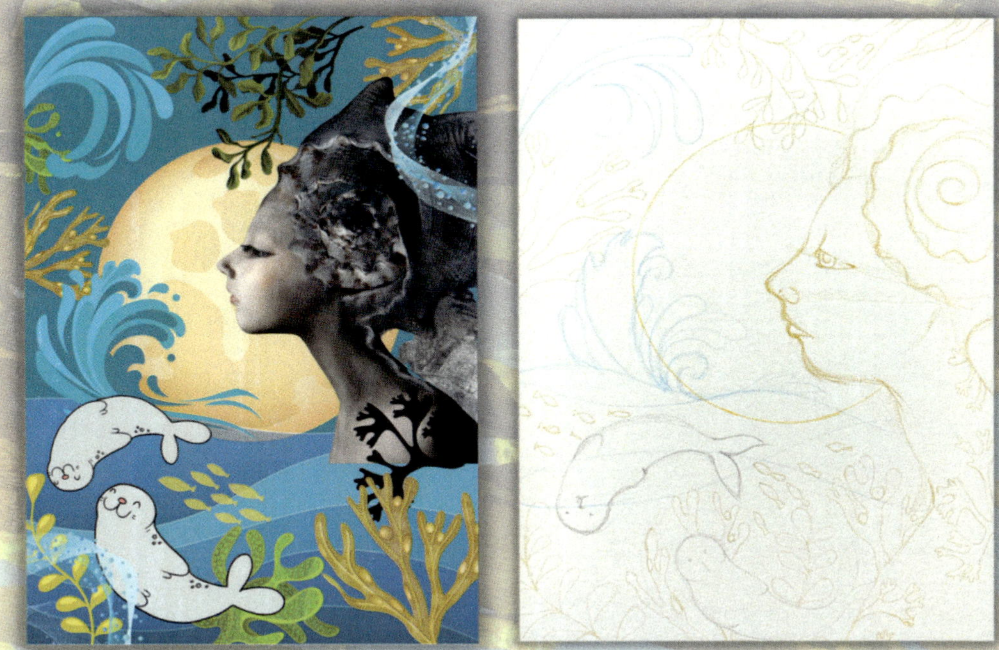

It may seem daunting, but if you have spent some time sketching out your composition properly, this next part of your painting is relatively simple!

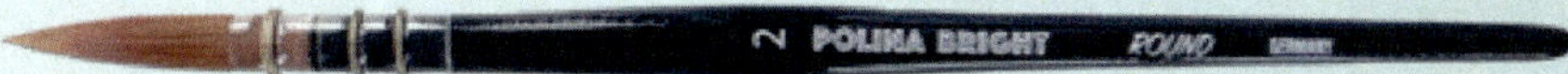

It is a bit like "paint by numbers". You can work your way around the painting adding in each color for each section.

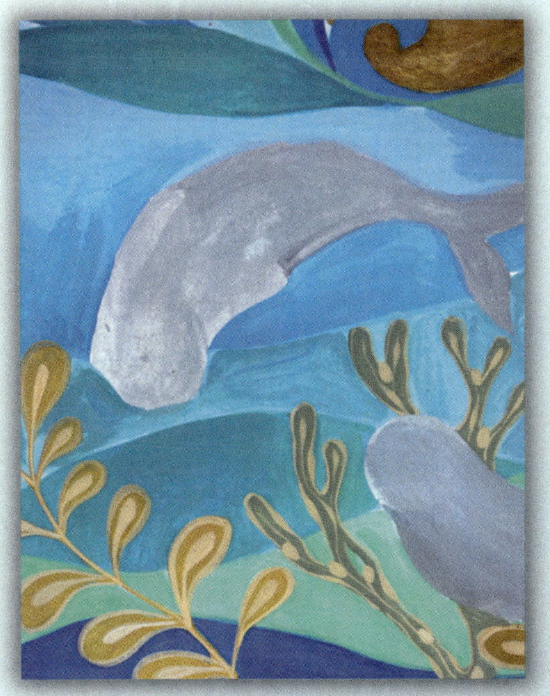

Do not worry about small details at this point, we are still just working out the larger elements.

Use a larger brush and paint each section in different shades of blues, greys and greens. It helps to move around the page so that you are only working on one dry area at a time. You can use a hair dryer to speed up the drying process if you like!

If you use a color in one area of the painting, be sure to repeat it in another area too; this helps to create cohesiveness in your composition.

Continue painting in the background colors for the sea, using different shades of blues and greens. You may need to do two coats and that's okay. It's normal for the first coat of gouache to go on unevenly. Make sure you mix up enough of the color you are going to use so you can do a second coat.

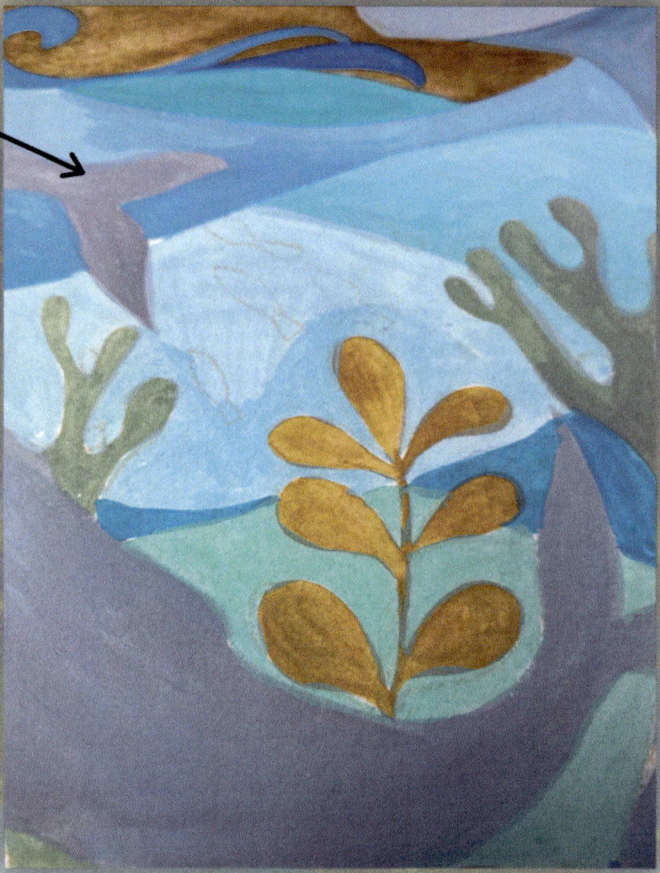

As you can see in all of these pictures, there isn't even coverage so we know that one coat is not enough.

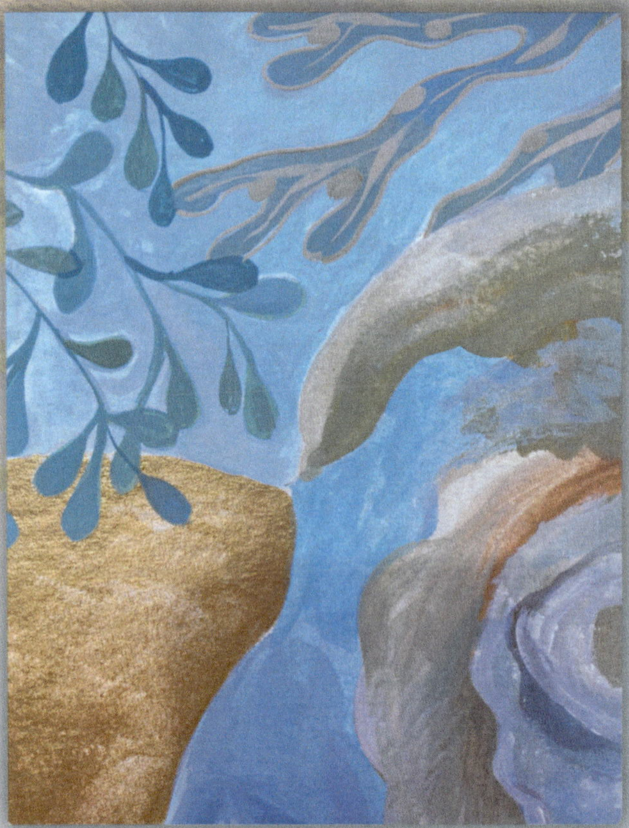

At this point, you can begin to add in some of the smaller details. Paint in lines along the seaweed, with little circle details.

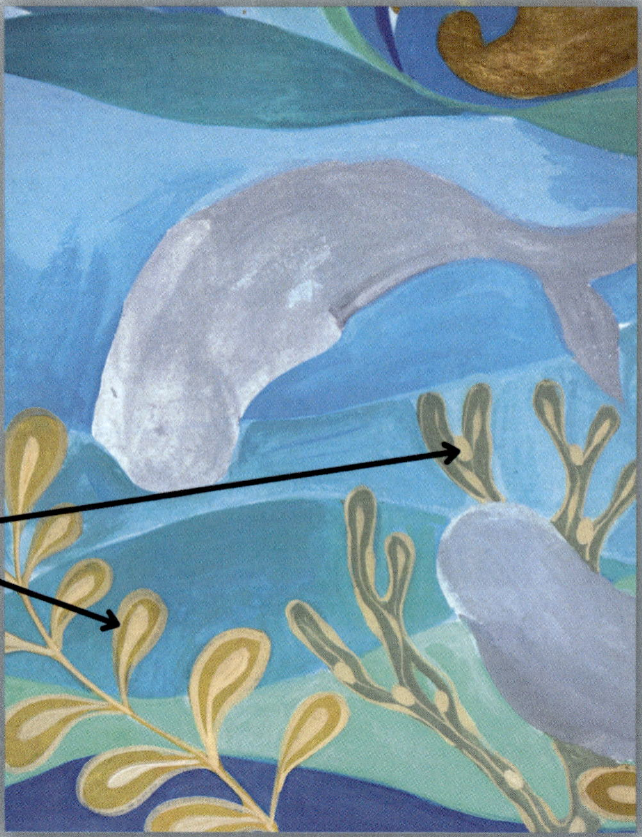

Feel free to make these as whimsical as you'd like! Remember, this is the home of magical sea creatures! So have fun filling in all the little details!

For the large background area, mix a pale greenish blue with a lot of white. It can look quite interesting if you blend in a few different variations of this so the color isn't flat. Do not worry about painting the fine stalks of the seaweed: you can paint them on top of the light green background afterwards.

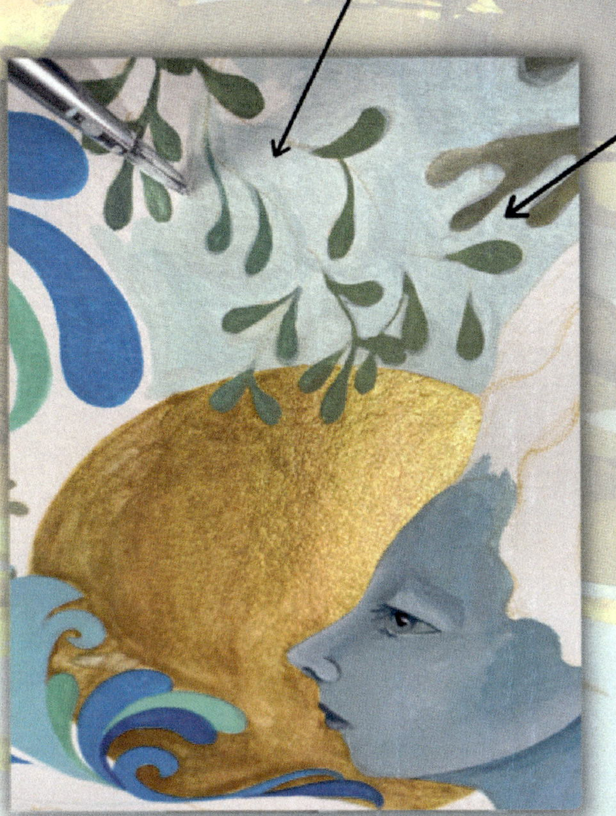

Use a small brush to get into the more awkward areas and a larger brush for the larger areas. Paint all the areas above the sea line in the same pale blue-green.

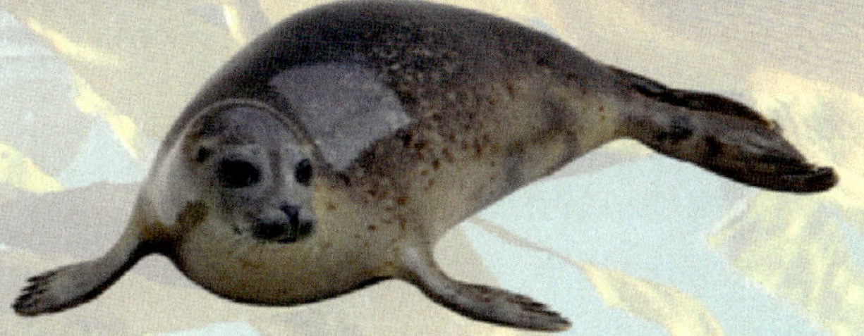

For the seals, use a similar color to your Selkie maiden. Paint similar dot markings too just under the fins. Use a small detail brush for the facial features but don't make them too complicated.
Simple is better. Aren't they so cute?!

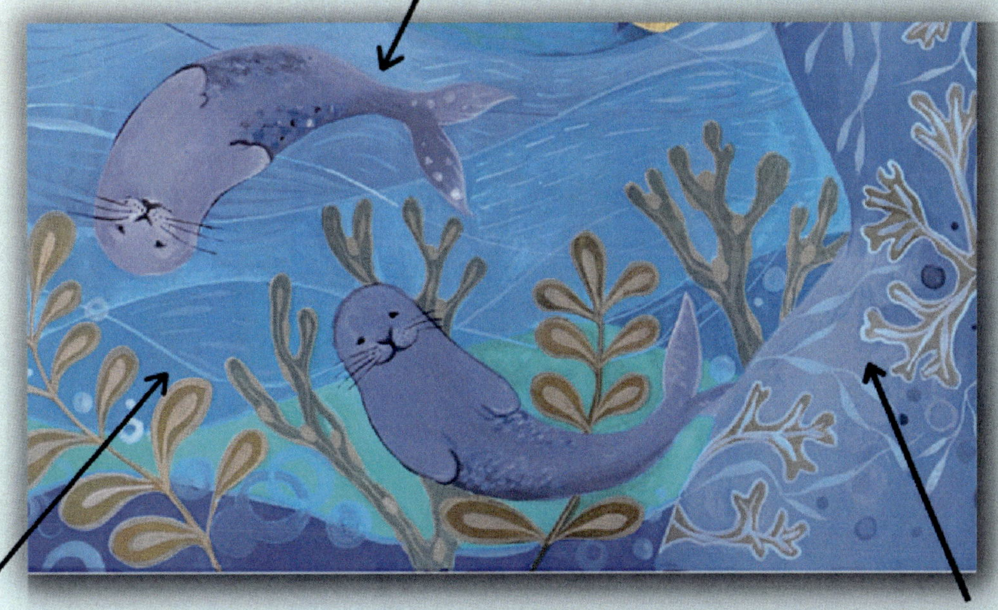

Now we can add light shades of blue to indicate the movement of the waves.

Then we can finish the details on the Selkie's shoulder and neck. Paint some pale blue markings all over these areas.

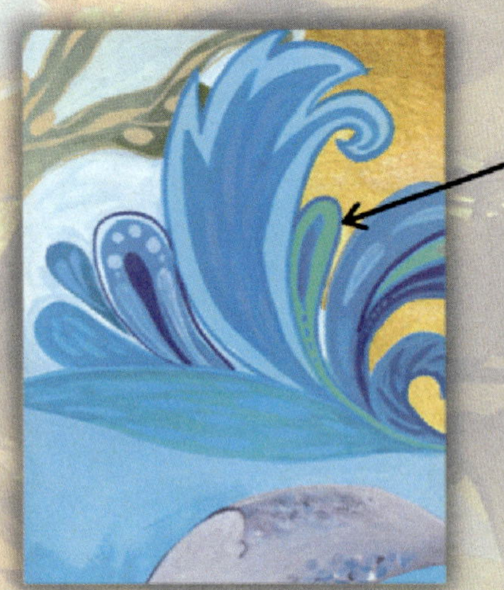

To finish off, you can really go to town with all the little details! Use a smaller brush and paint in any extra details you like to include on the waves, sea, plants, and everywhere!

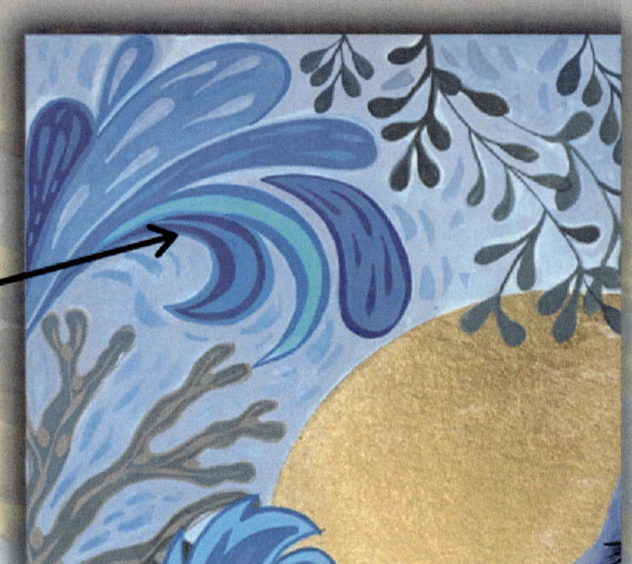

These details are not supposed to be realistic! This is a fantasy painting so feel free to use your imagination!

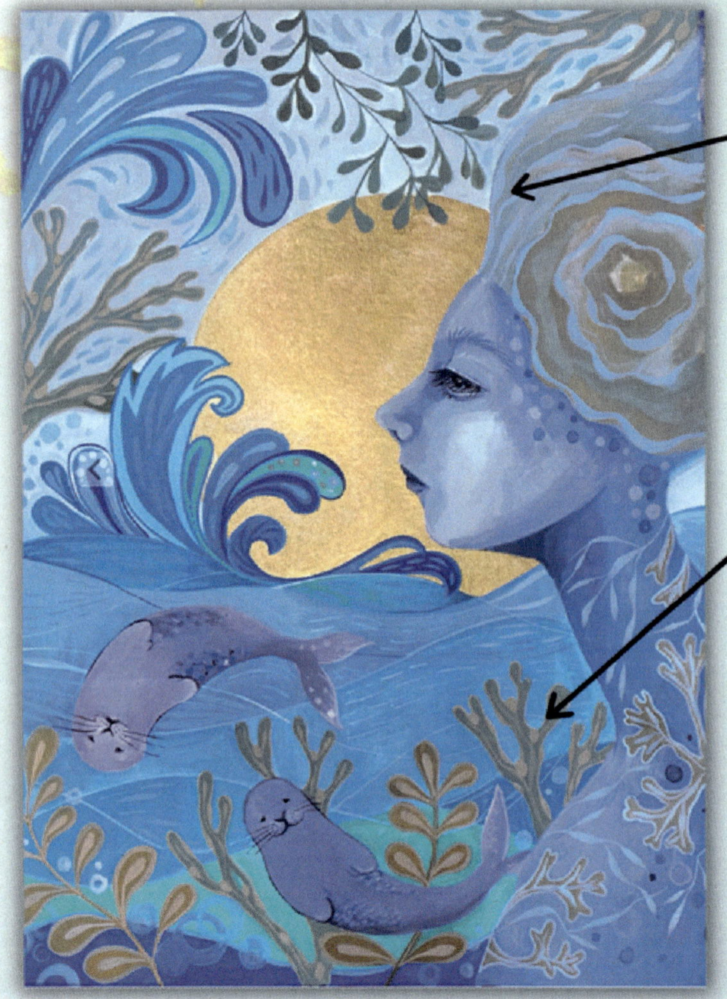

Have fun adding details and any other marks as you like into the background sky!

These wavy short lines help to give the painting a sense of movement in this area. But feel to add your own marks of movement!

Paint in a second color on the seaweed to show the wee bubbles you can see in some of them!

Most importantly, have fun painting, and remember, use your imagination! Your Selkie is waiting for youuuuuuu!

MAGICAL UNICORN

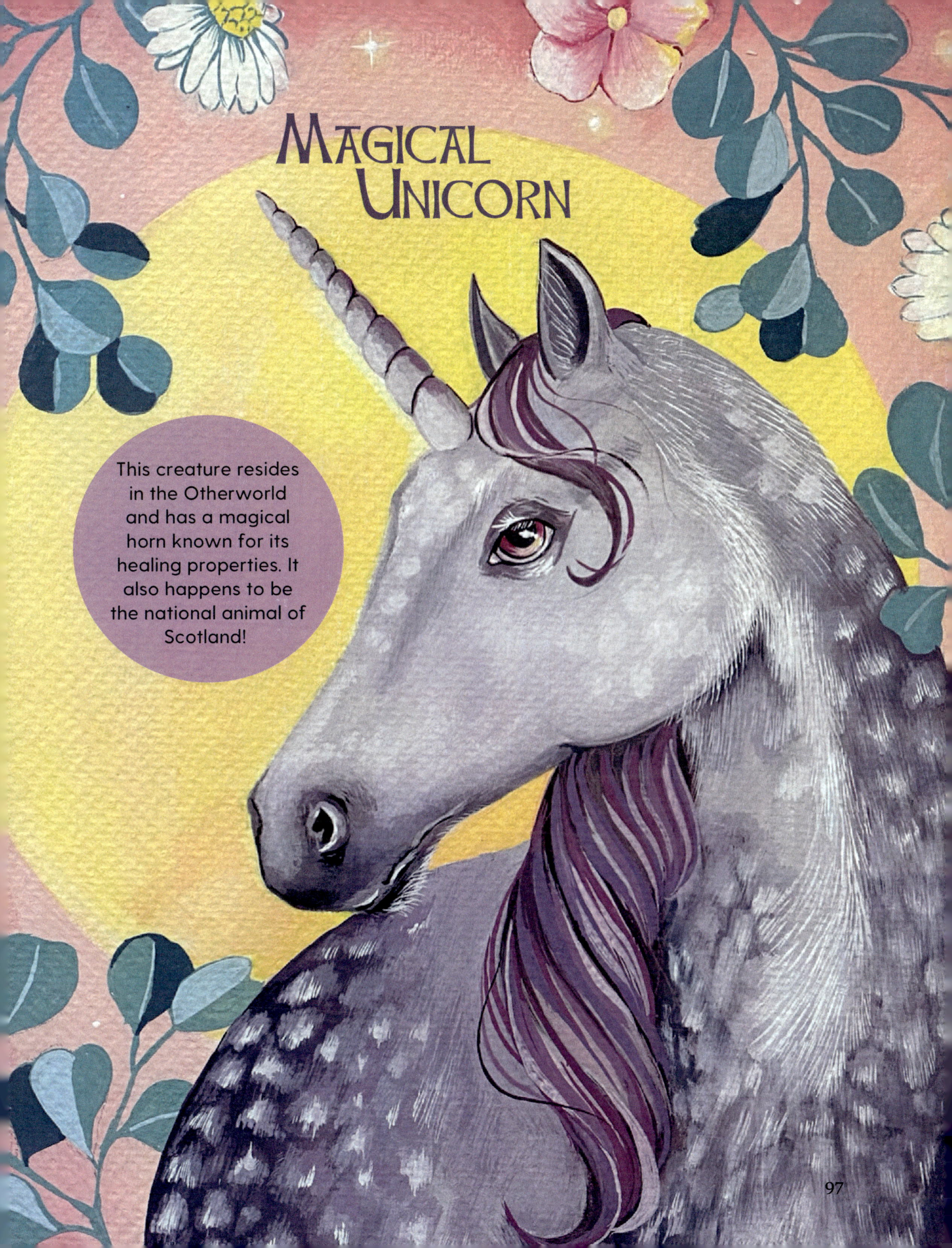

This creature resides in the Otherworld and has a magical horn known for its healing properties. It also happens to be the national animal of Scotland!

Supplies

Pencil for sketching out design
Watercolor paper 140 lbs
A stay-wet palette - great for acrylic gouache!
Jar of water
Selection of paintbrushes
Acrylic gouache (or alternatives shown in previous project)
Colored pencils for sketching out design
CANSON
MANUFACTURE DEPUIS 1557
CANSON
Gouache
Lascaux
Gouache
Lascaux

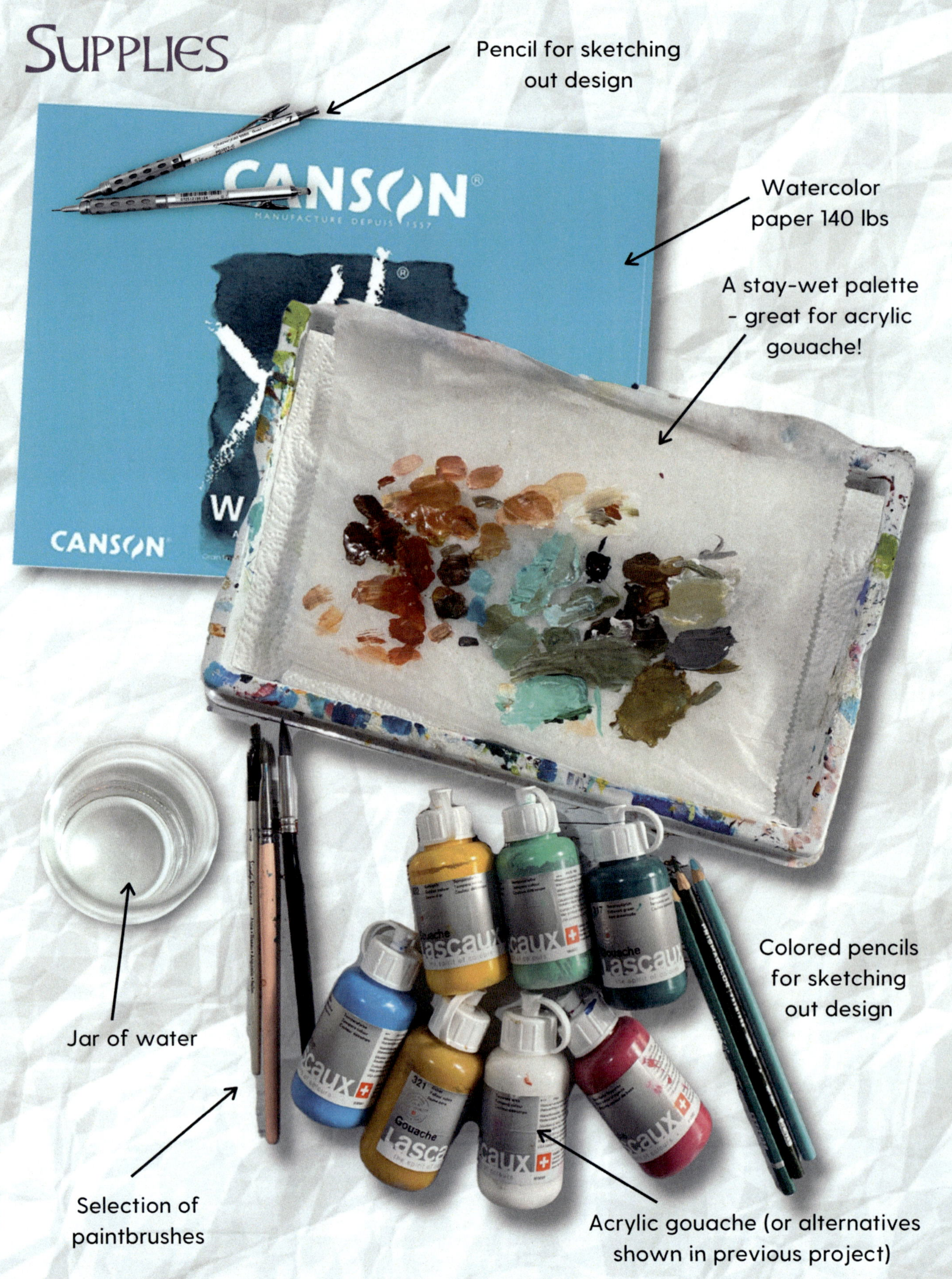

We will begin with a photo montage of royalty-free images. If you have an iPad or computer you can play around with the placement of the elements you want to include. Sites like Canva and Paint are great for this!

Just select your images and then play with varying arrangements until you've found a collection of good ones that you love.

The ones on this page are some I've collected that we'll use for our project.

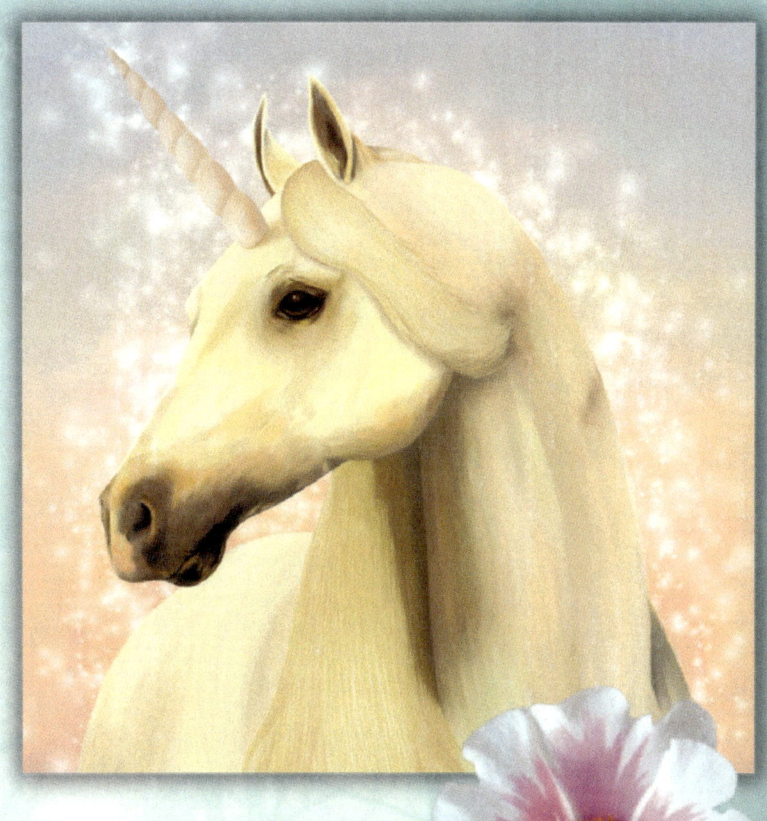

If you don't have a computer or are not comfortable with any online programs, no worries. You can still print off images and cut them out and paste them onto a larger sheet of paper OR just use magazine cutouts or objects from your environment! It helps if you make a mock-up the same size as your piece of watercolor paper. I sourced a picture of a unicorn for you here, but even a good horse picture would do for this! You can just add the horn using your imagination!

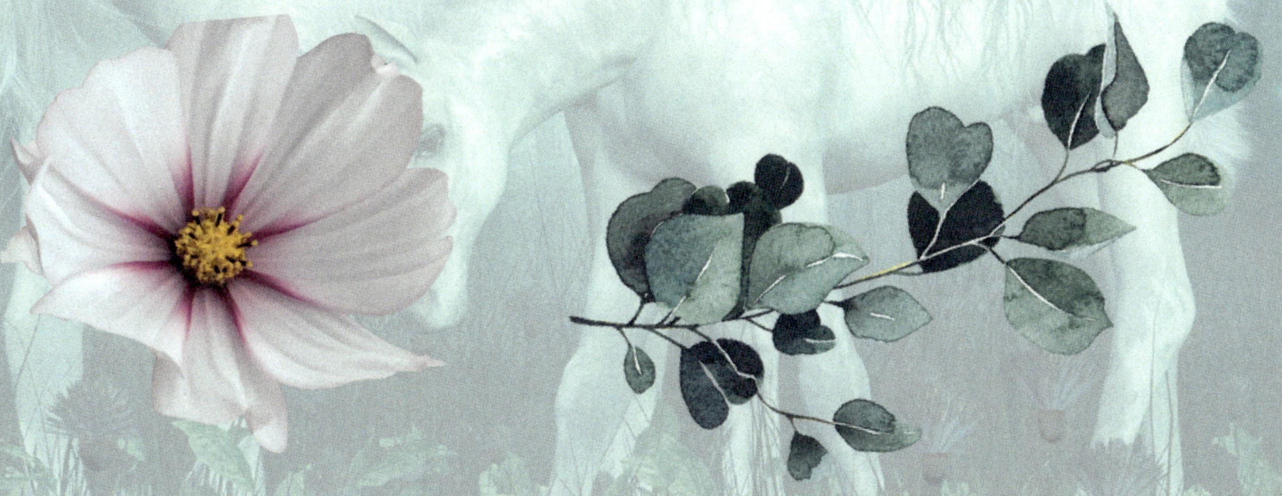

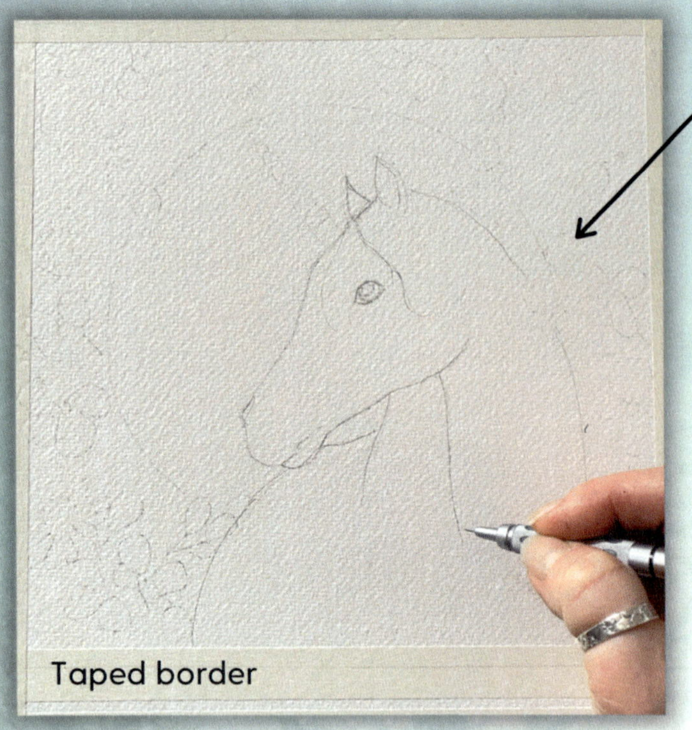

Use a lightbox or carbon transfer paper to draw out your composition from your reference image.

This is not cheating!

You are going to be putting a lot of work into the painting part so giving yourself a head start by getting the proportions right is very important!

Do not sketch in the smaller details as you will be painting the background first and painting the leaves on top. Details are always added last.

To create a lovely white border when you're finished, tape your paper onto wood or whiteboard prior to painting. Use painter's tape or masking tape to adhere your watercolor paper nicely onto the board. Applying gentle heat from a heat gun directly over any stubborn-to-lift areas will help you to remove it with ease later if it's too sticky!

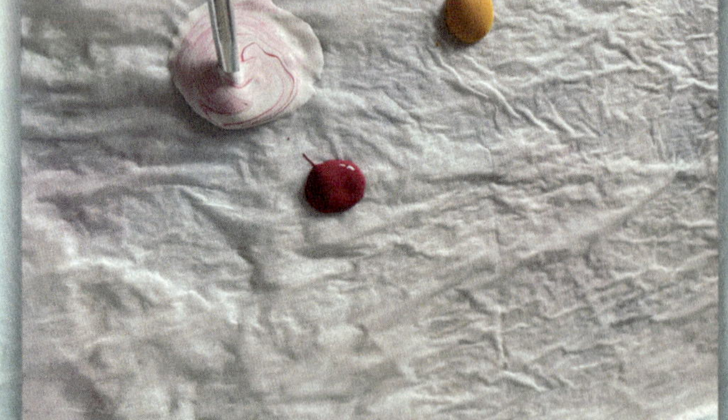

Mix up your background color in a stay-wet palette (see the Kelpie project for directions on how to create your own) by using pink, some yellow, and lots of white.

Gouache works well when a fair amount of white is added! Pink and yellow make a lovely peachy pink tone. You may also need to add some water to the mix to get it to the right consistency. This is especially true if using less expensive brands.

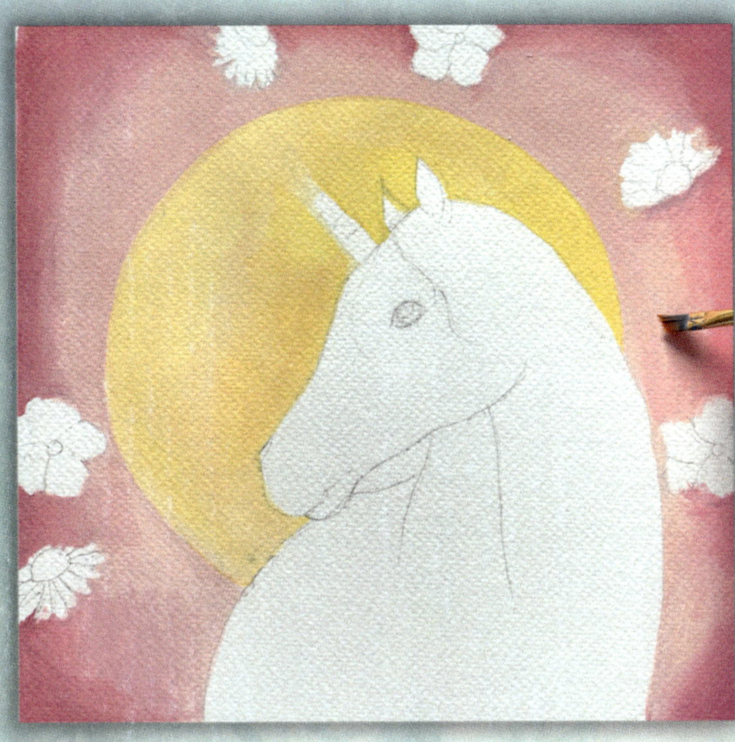

Begin by painting in the background and the moon.

You may need to do two coats to get even coverage.

Paint with a large brush and do quick strokes of darker to a lighter color to make it look like the moon is glowing.

Once you have painted the background, begin painting in the flowers using the same pink/yellow/white combination.

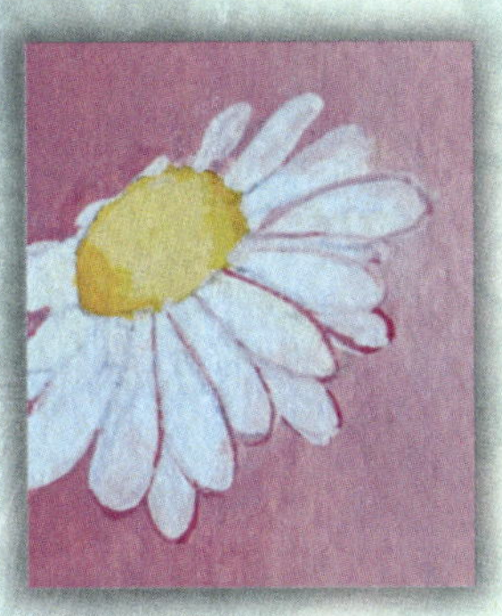

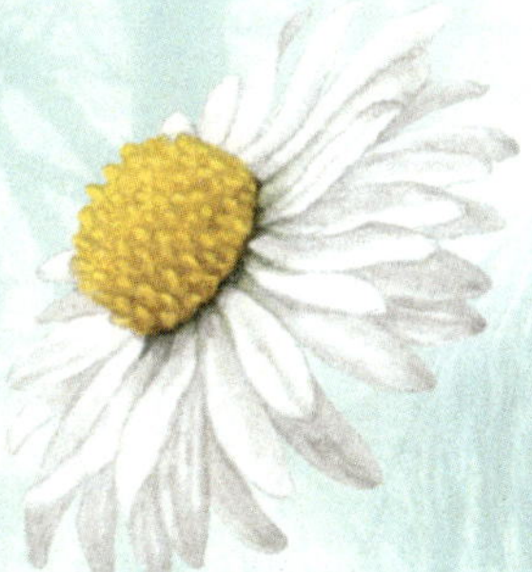

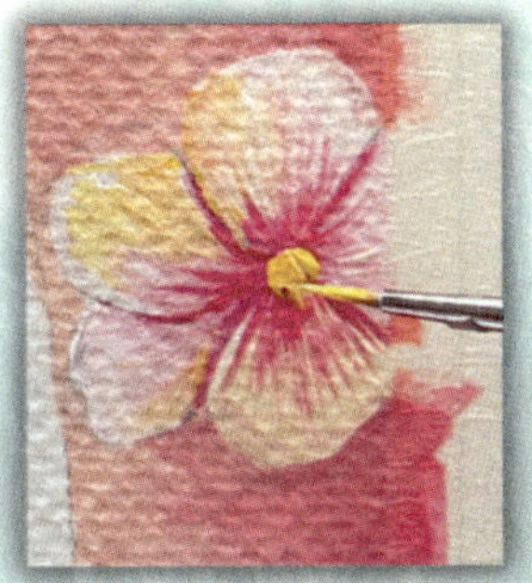

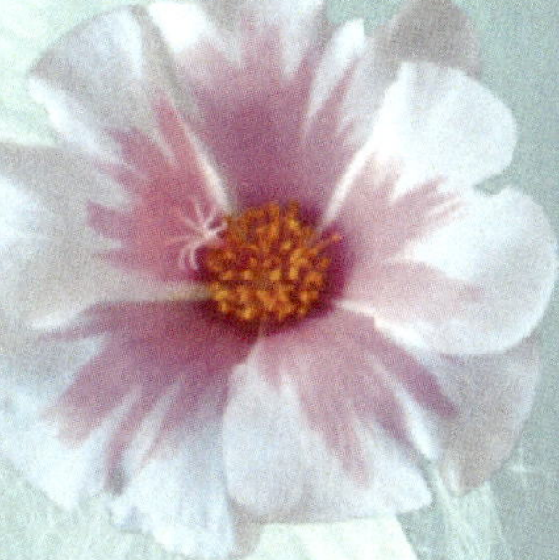

Look at your references to help guide you on how to create the overall flower shape. Start out by painting the main color first. Paint each flower type at the same time so you are mixing the same color and can be consistent. Experiment with color mixing till you get the color you want! Have fun with it!

The daisy petals shown here (right) are outlined in the same green that the leaves are painted in. Turn the page and I'll show you how to mix your own 4 shades of green that we'll use for all the leaves in the project.

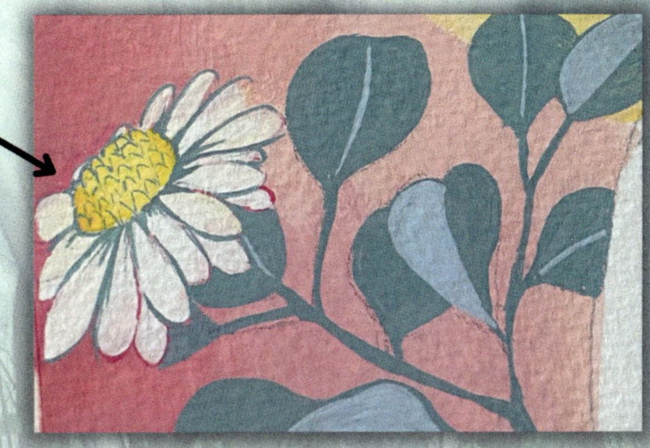

Prefer working straight from the tube? That's okay too! Just add white or black to create your shades if that's easier for you!

To create the shades of green for this project we will start with Shade 2. This green shade was made by mixing a combination of turquoise, some green, some yellow ochre, and white. Make sure if you are mixing, you make enough to paint all the leaves.

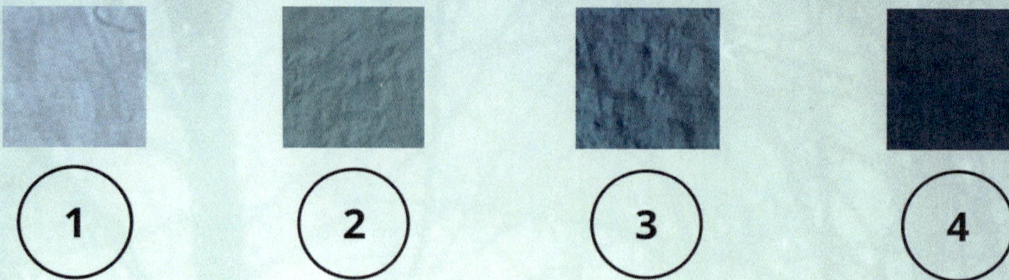

To create the 3rd Shade, simply add a bit more blue to the mix. To create Shade 1, simply add a bit of white to Shade 3! You can also make this nice darker shade of teal color (Shade 4) by mixing blue, a small amount of green, and a small amount of black! Now we have FOUR shades of green in our painting and we're ready to fill in all of our leaves step-by-step.

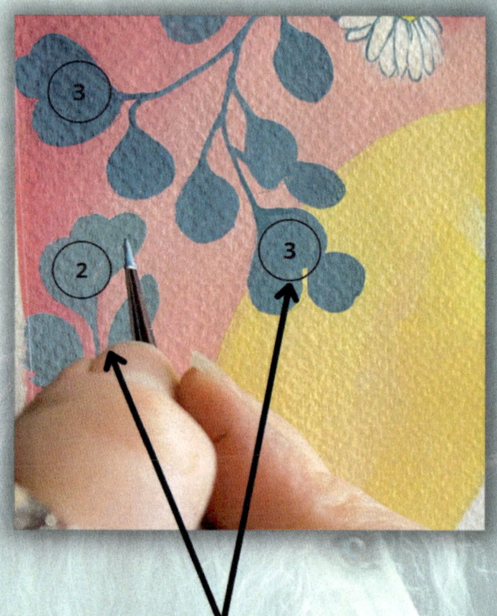

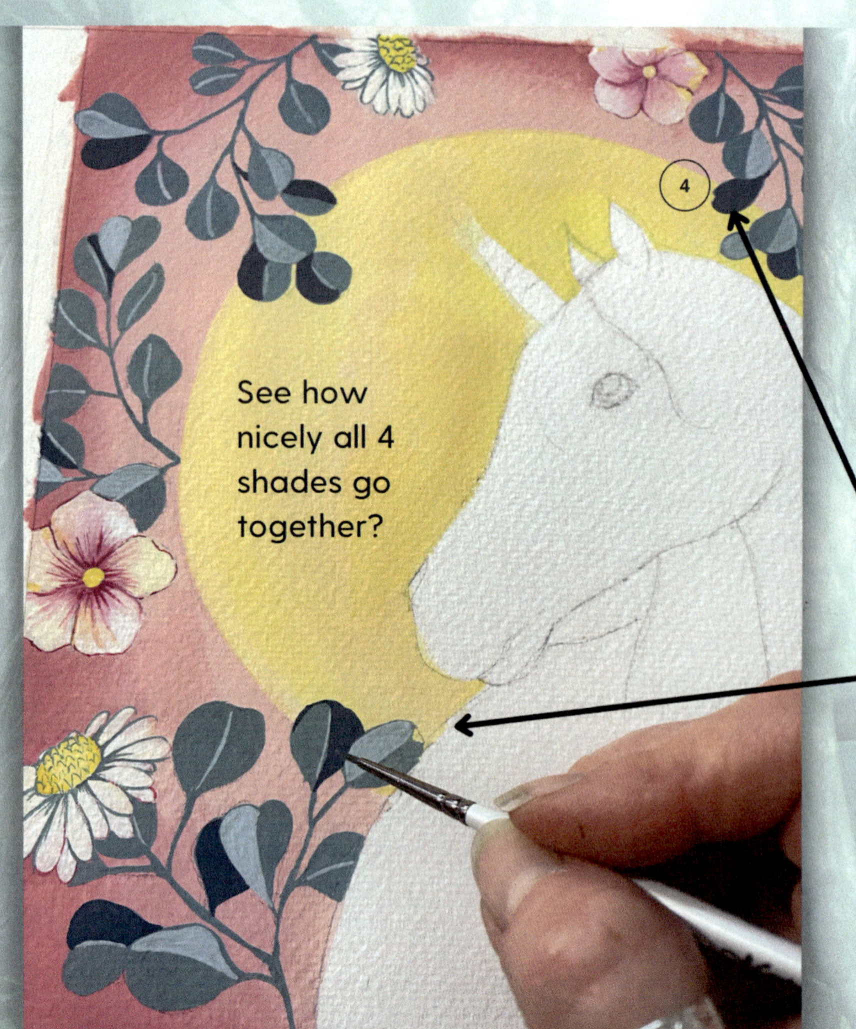

Paint half of all of the leaves and stems in Shade 2. Then the other half in Shade 3.

Go back and add a few (that are in the back) in Shade 4 and you're good to go!

Adding the lightest color (Shade 1) to the veins of the leaves and only half of SOME of the leaves will make your composition more illustrative and interesting!

Don't over think it; just do a lovely mix of all shades.

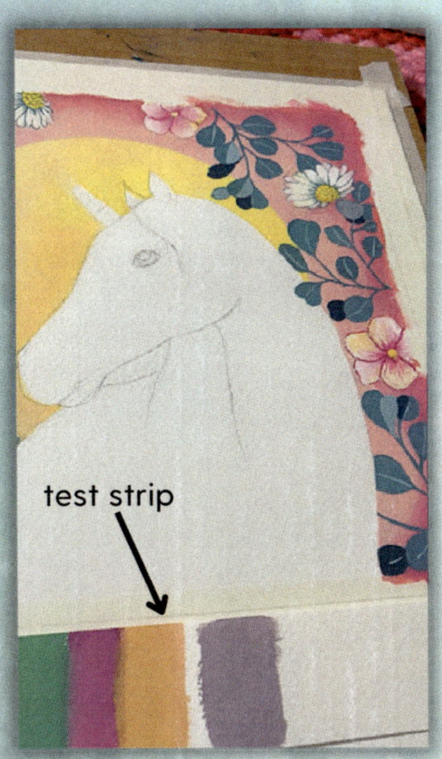

It is often useful to test out some colors for your subject before committing to painting it.

By painting a wee test strip, you can hold it against your painting to see which colors would work best.

This will save you a lot of potential upset later on if you begin painting and then decide you do not like your color choices!

You can also do this for all of the colors in your composition.

Take the time to play around and make decisions rather than jumping straight to painting! I love swatching colors!

I mixed up a greyish purple by adding some white and black into my purple paint.

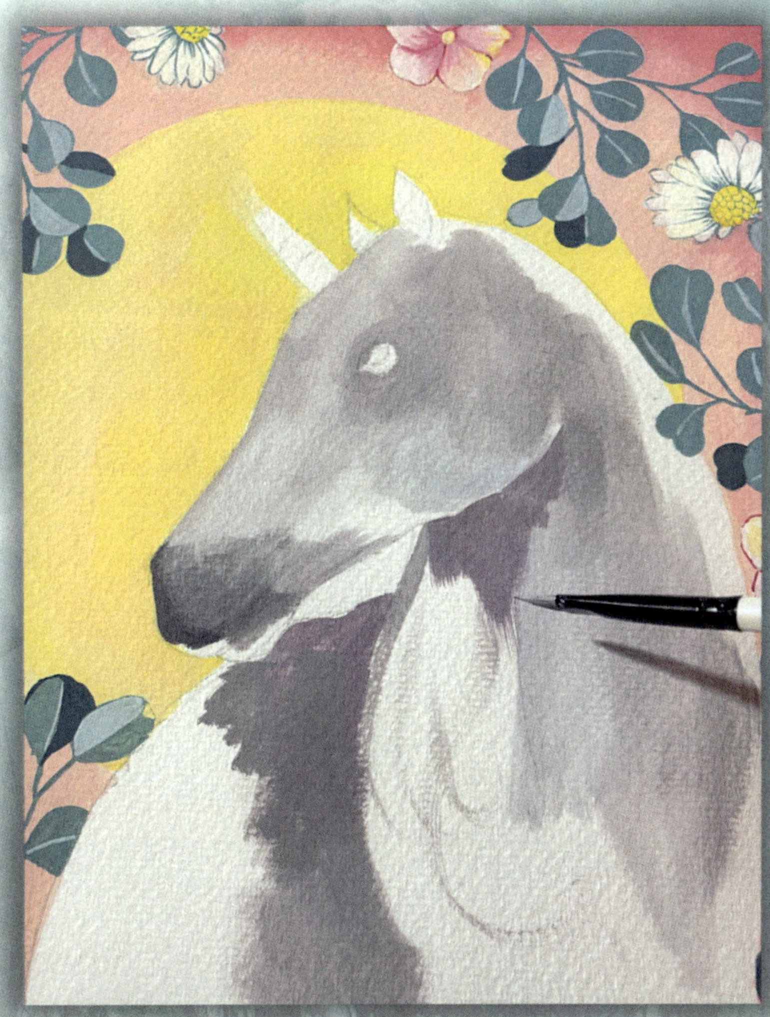

Add more white to make lighter tones and loosely paint in the first layers of the unicorn looking at your reference image to see what parts are lighter and darker.

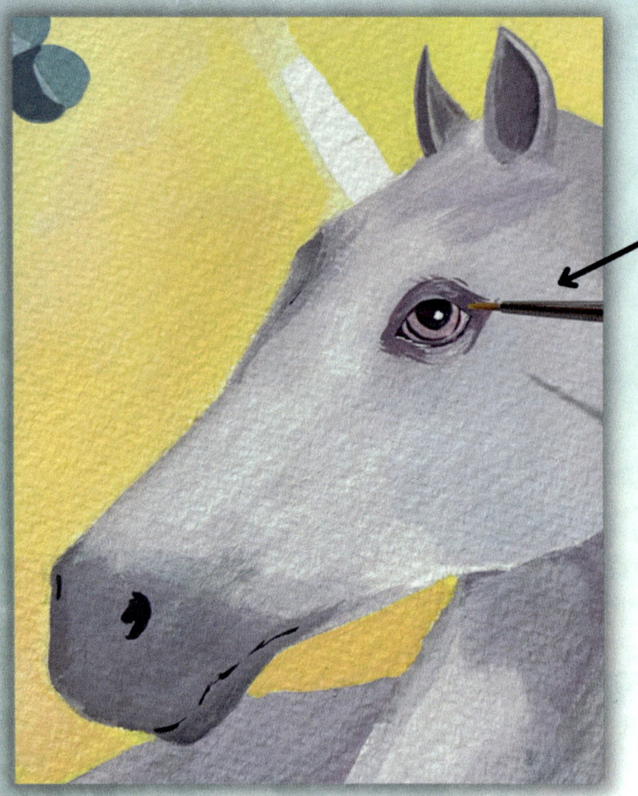

It's important and easier to paint when you pick the correct brush for each stage of the project.

Use a tiny brush to help you more easily paint the eye, nose, and ear details on your unicorn.

Rim the eye, nose and inner ear in a darker purple.

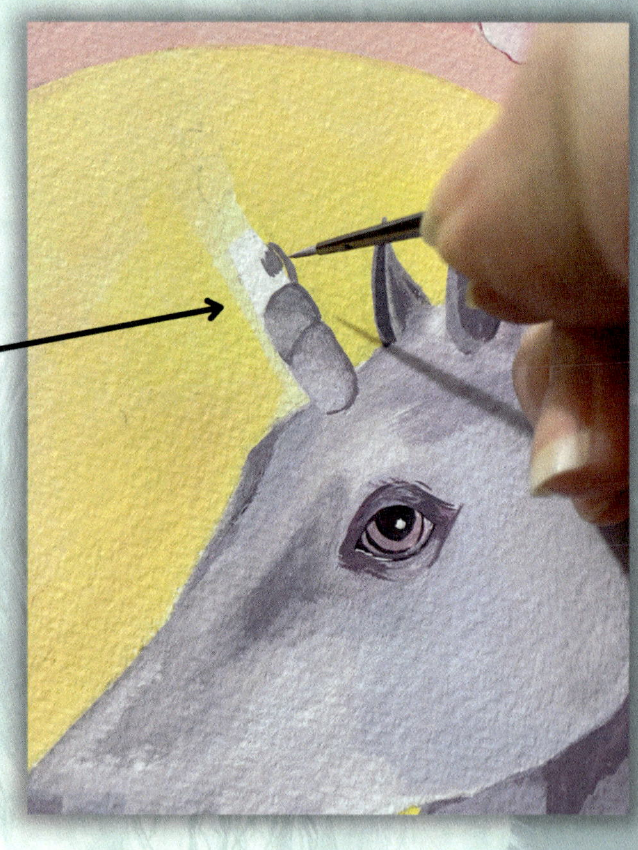

Paint in the horn by using the same colors too. I painted highlights and then used a darker tone to show the individual sections.

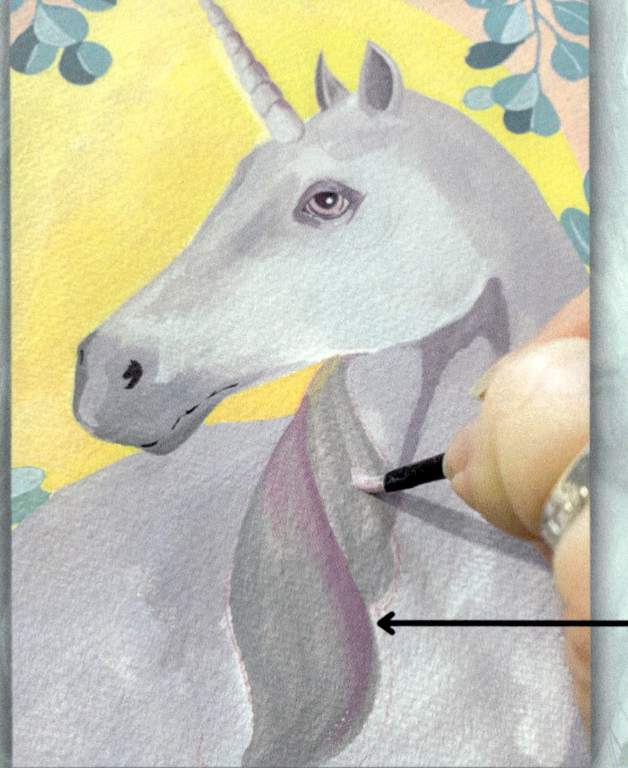

If you need to add more layers to correct your tones do so!

You can now begin to add in the background color of the mane. Alternate between grey and shades of purple. Gorgeous!

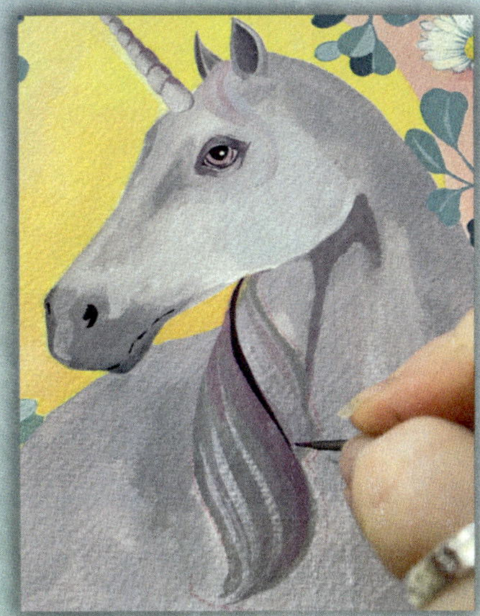

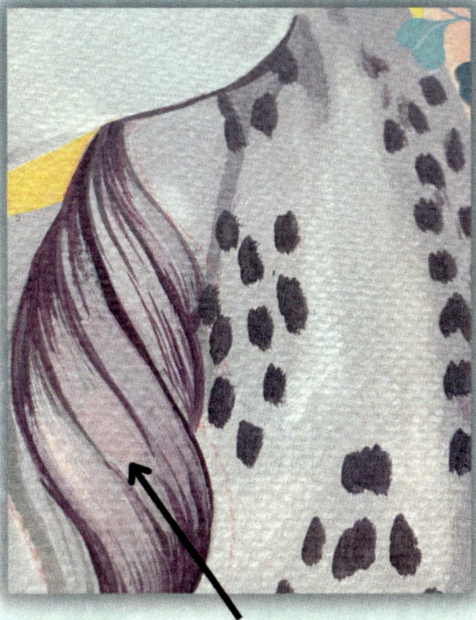

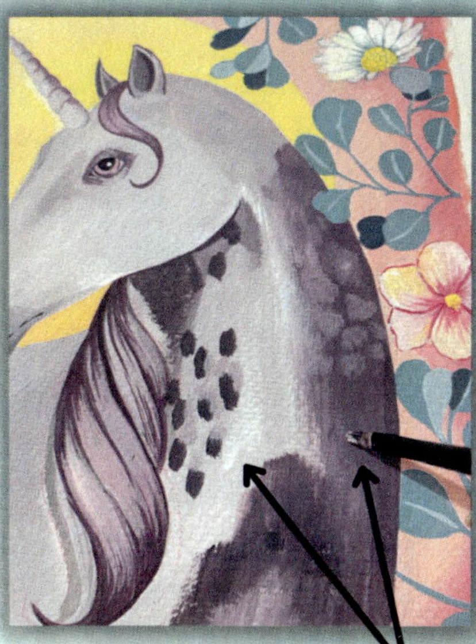

Once you have the main colors down for your unicorn's body, you can take a smaller detailer brush and begin to put in all of the tiny details.

To make the hair look "realistic" paint darker tones on either side where it curls under and lighter tones in the middle where the highlights would be.

To make your unicorn dappled, paint in darker and lighter spots along the neck.

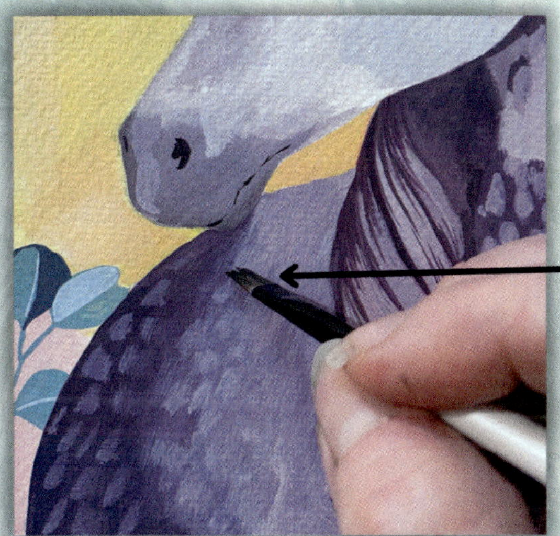

Paint some of the dapple spots on the back and rump of the unicorn, using a lighter tone against the darker paint there. Try not to paint the shapes too regularly!

Use a flat brush to make these "dapples" quickly and easily!

Then go in with a teeny tiny brush and some white or very pale purple and paint some highlights and fur strokes on top.

When searching for tiny brushes look for "detail brush" in the description! Luckily gouache brushes are very affordable! You don't need to shop for the most expensive ones; craft grade is perfect!

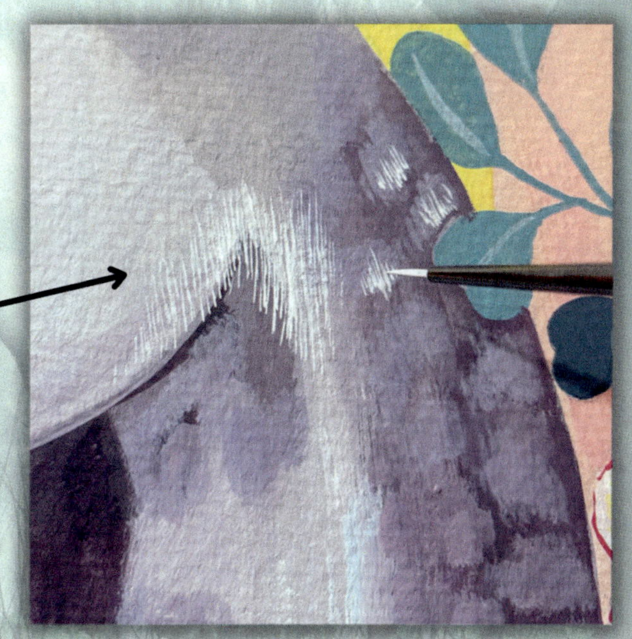

The finishing touches are the most fun! Here is where the painting really comes to life and starts to become magical! It is helpful to use a tiny little detailer brush. White gouache (or very pale purple) will make things like the hair strands really pop!

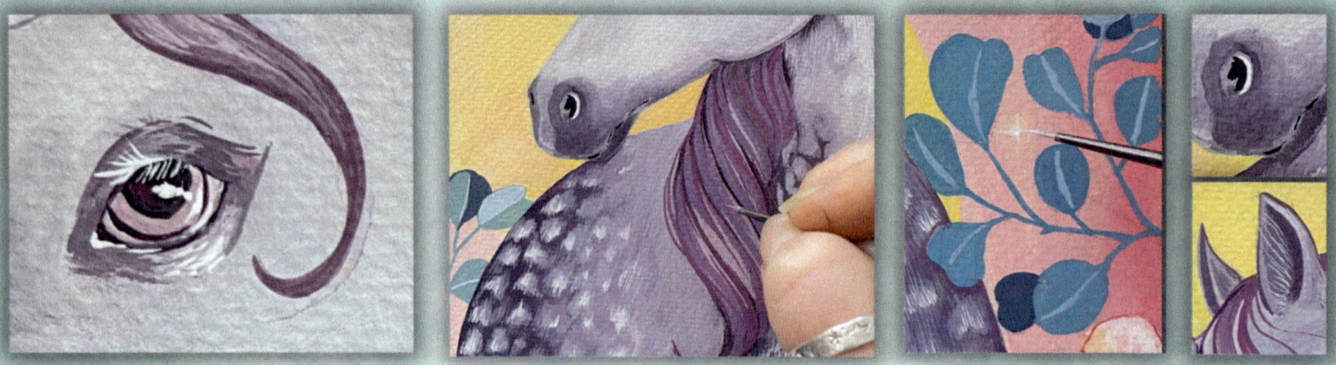

I added fine hair strokes to the face, around the eye as eyelashes, and in the ear too. Finally, use a pale yellow or white to paint some small glowing stars in the background of the painting. I make some of them as circles and some as shining star shapes. This is one of my favourite ways of finishing off a painting! You did a great job!!

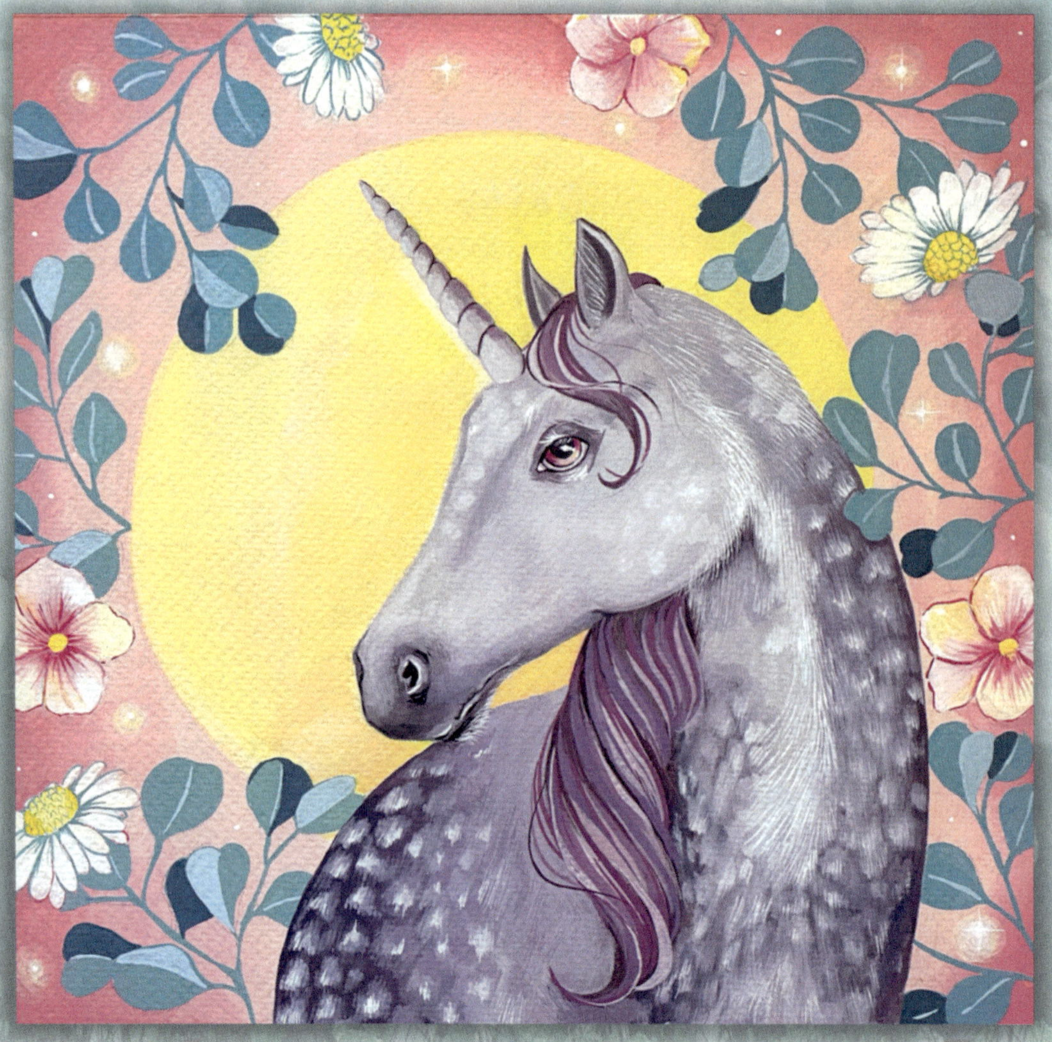

Galaxy Witch

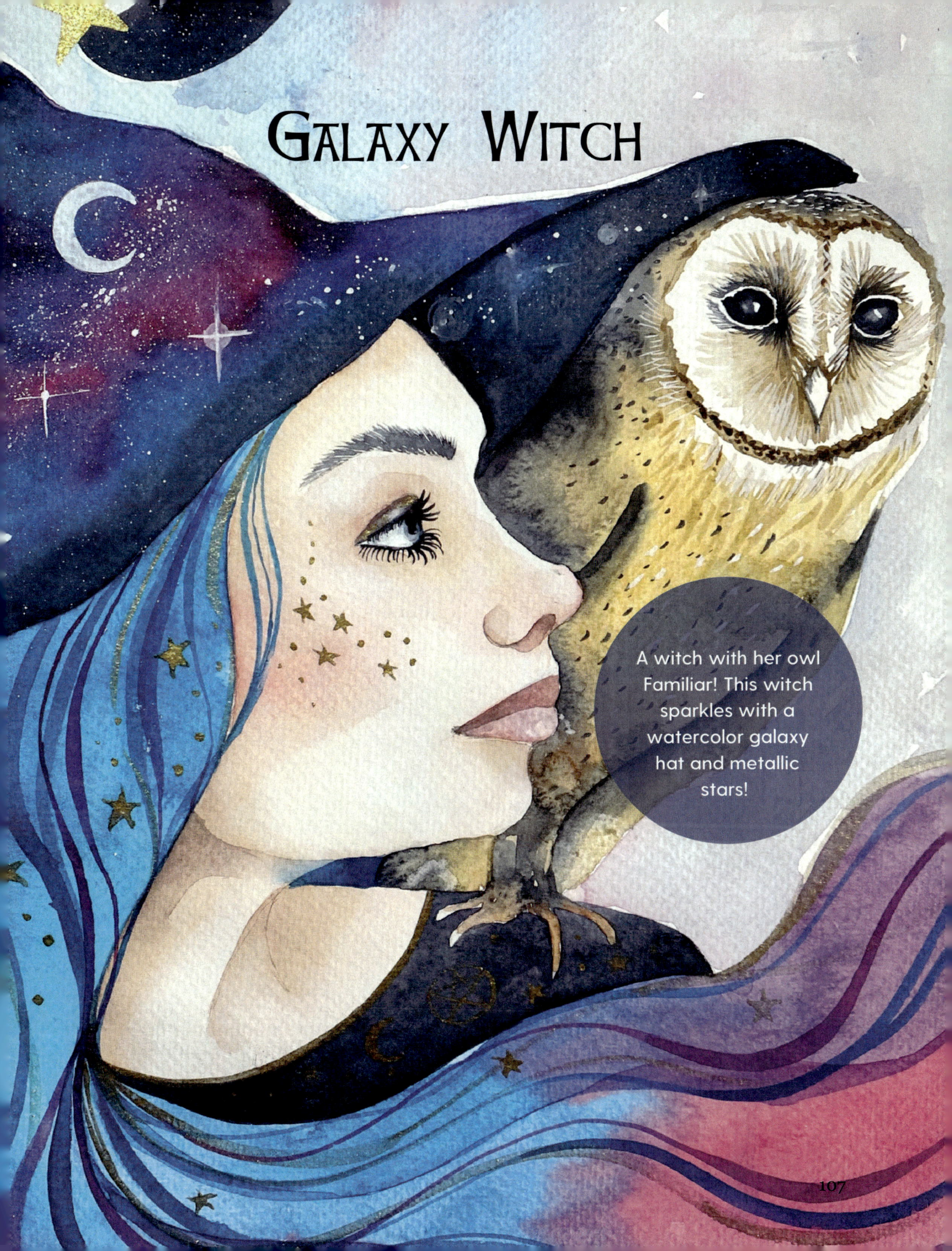

A witch with her owl Familiar! This witch sparkles with a watercolor galaxy hat and metallic stars!

Supplies

Watercolor paper 140lbs
Metallic watercolors
Water
Watercolors (any brand will do!)
Bleed Proof White (or white gouache)
Selection of paintbrushes
Lightbox for transferring your image (optional!)
Masking tape
DALER ◇ ROWNEY
Cold Pressed
300 g/m²
140 lb.
320 x 240 mm
12.6 x 9.4 inches
Dr Ph Martin's
BLEED PROOF WHITE

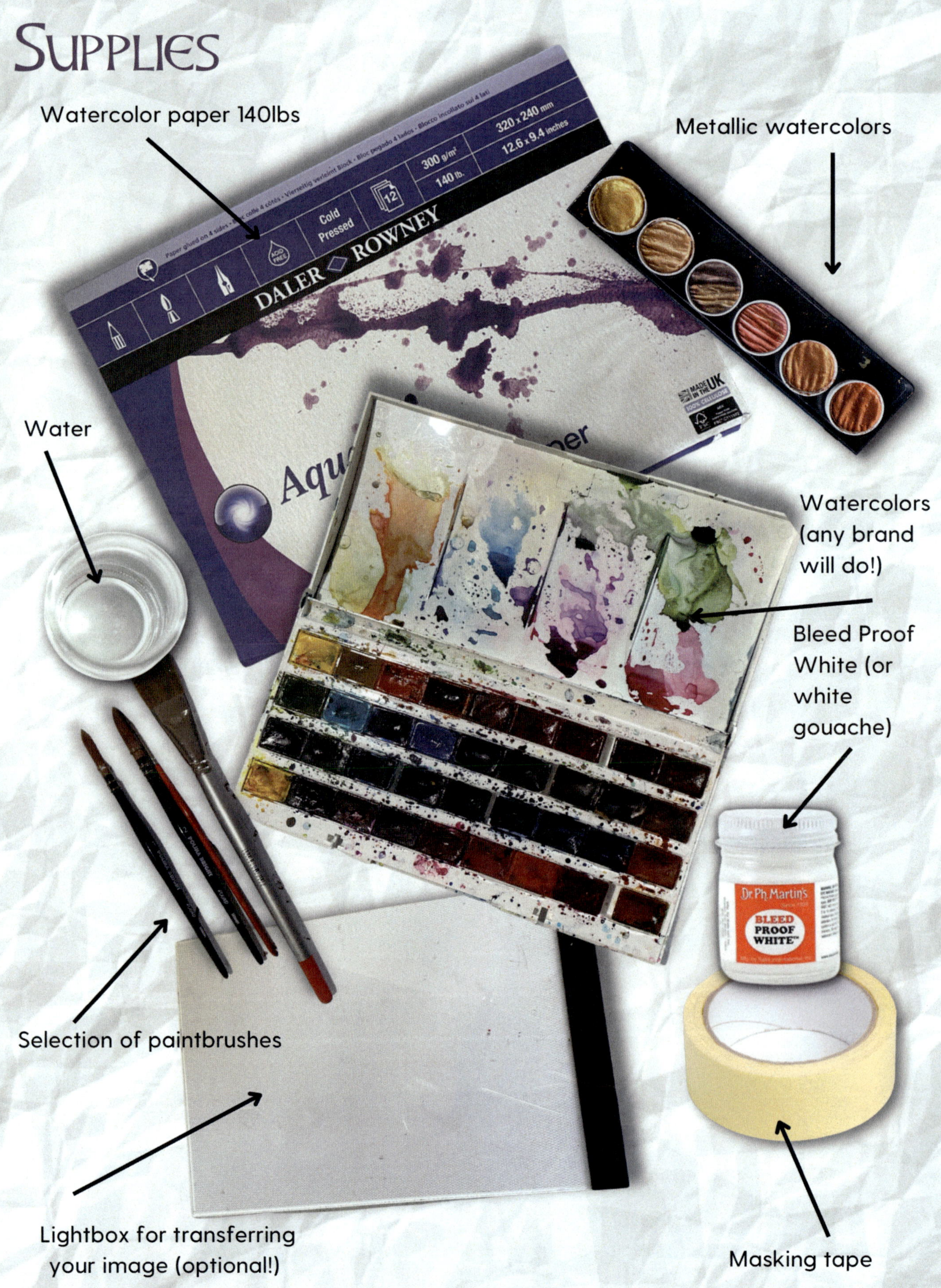

Gather your reference images for your galaxy witch. You can turn any reference photo of a woman into a witch by just changing her dress and hat, and painting extra "witchy elements" in the painting. I wanted to paint a galaxy sky in her hat so I also sourced a picture of that for inspiration.

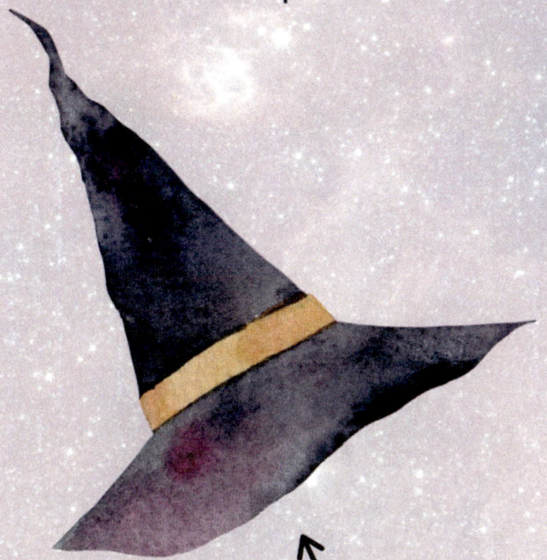

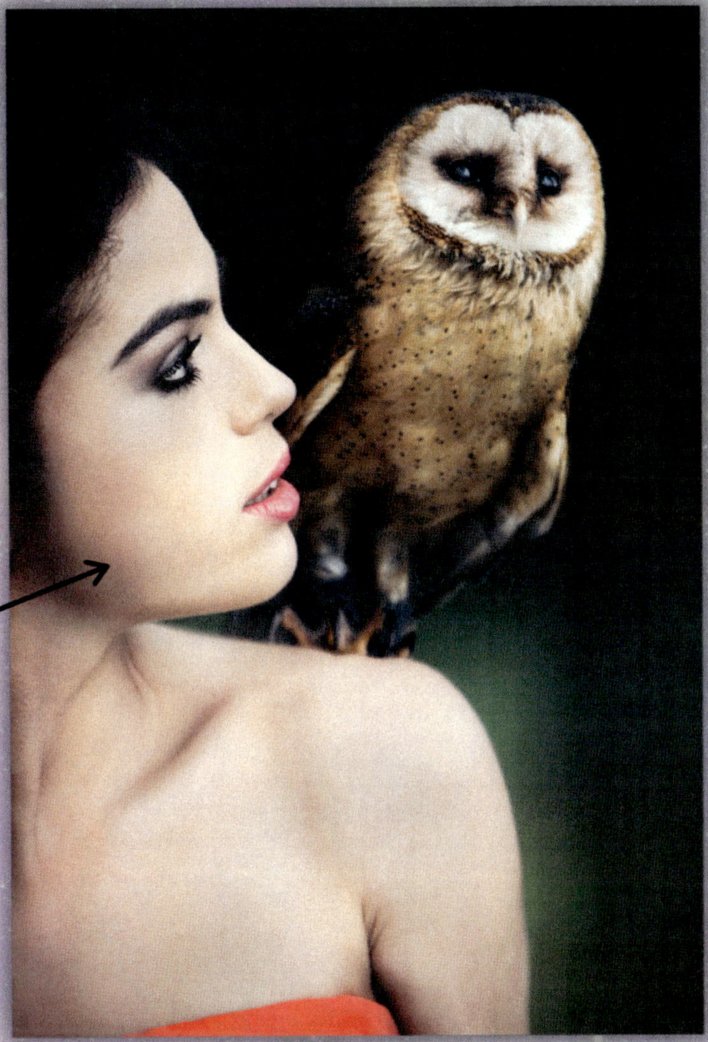

You don't need to have a complete reference photo to copy. You can find all the separate "elements" and piece them together.

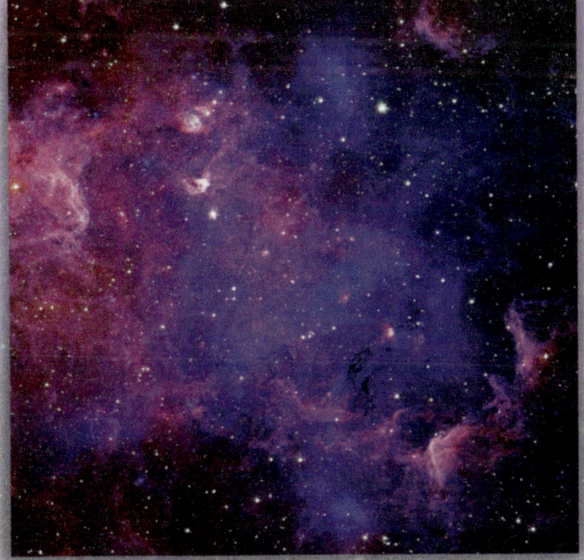

There are so many cool galaxy photos online to look at for inspiration. We are not concerned here with painting them exactly as we see them. Rather, we are going to use them as inspiration for the swirls you see, the stars and the color combinations!

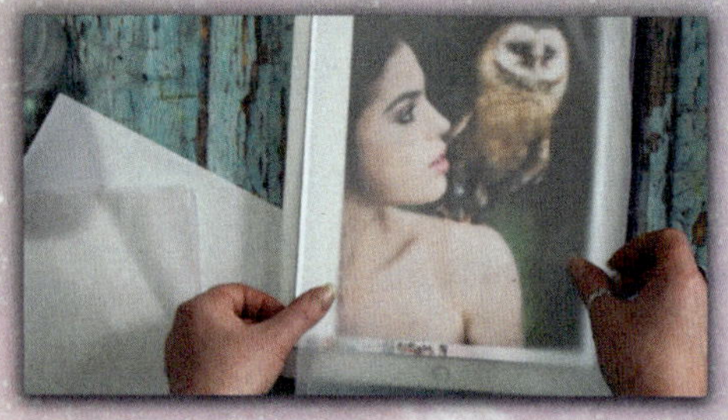

Start by either tracing the image directly from your iPad or transferring it from a print (if you do this, you can use carbon paper to transfer it to your watercolor paper). If you're drawing from scratch, follow the steps below.

To clarify, I traced the guidelines in black and features in red, over the reference.

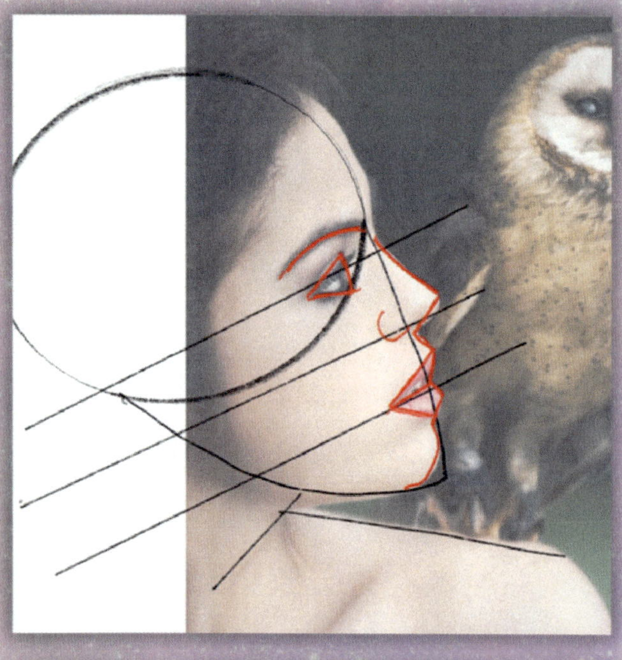

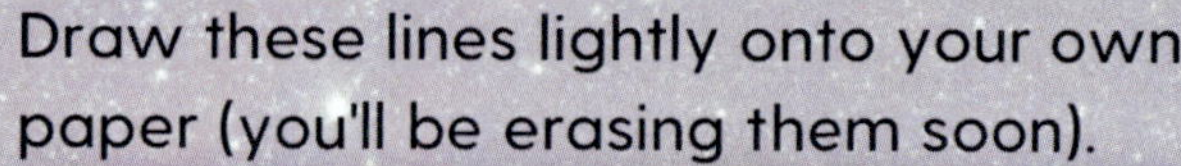

Draw these lines lightly onto your own paper (you'll be erasing them soon).

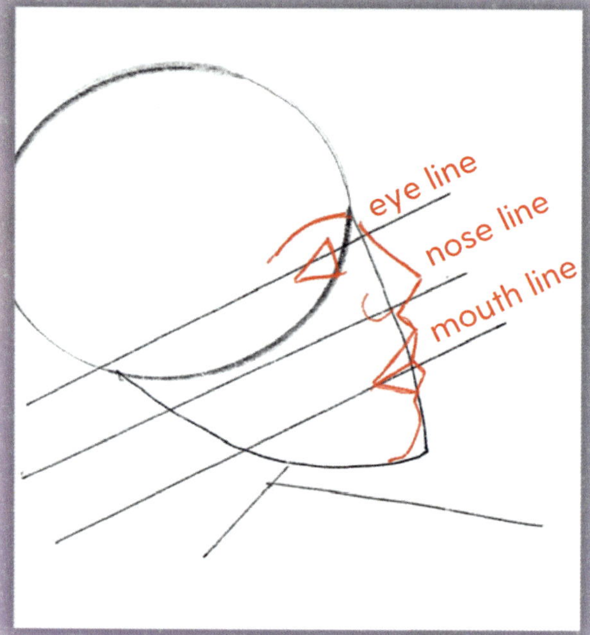

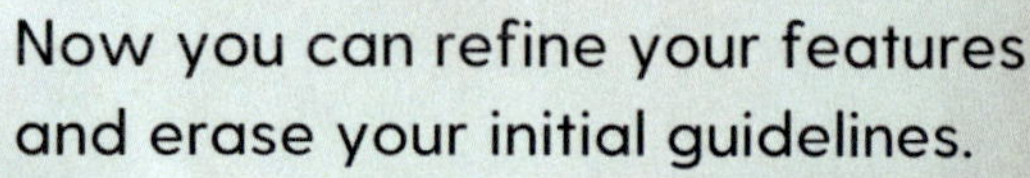

Now you can refine your features and erase your initial guidelines.

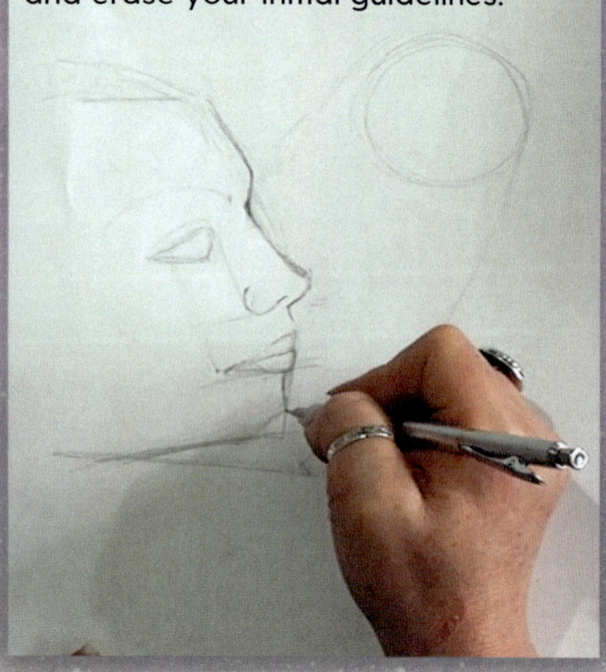

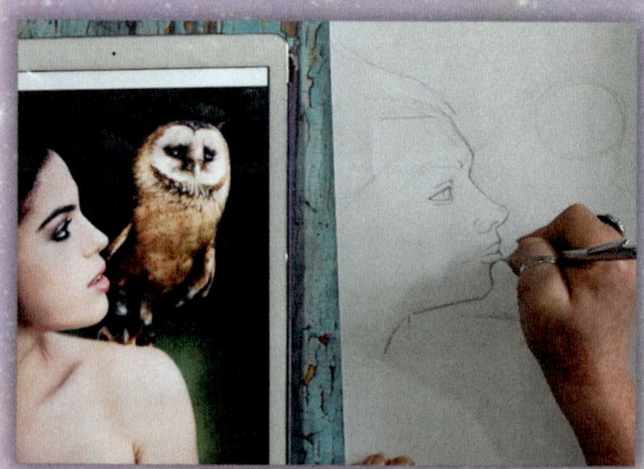

Continue refining. Make sure that her eyes are looking up at her Familiar!

Look at your reference photos continually while you work. This will help you capture all the important details!

Begin the owl by drawing a circle with a line down the middle for the beak. Then draw the two eyes on either side and a heart-shaped face in the middle. Draw a long oblong shape for the body. You can add in the claws at the bottom so they sit on the witch's shoulder.

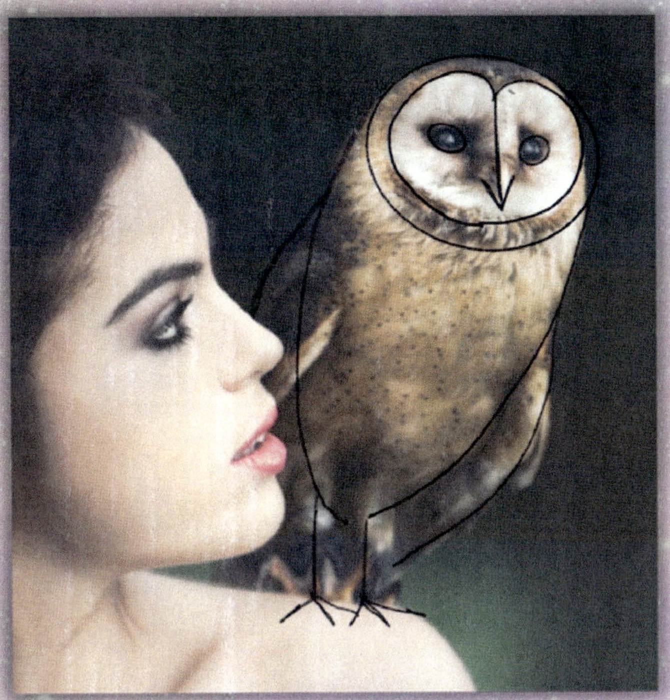

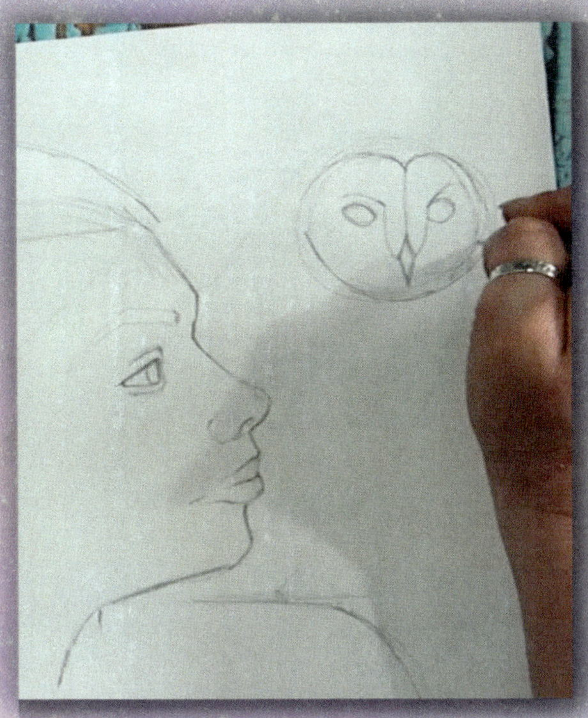

Now that the witch and owl are properly placed and sketched, add the hat and hair to the overall composition as shown. Get ready to add color. So fun!

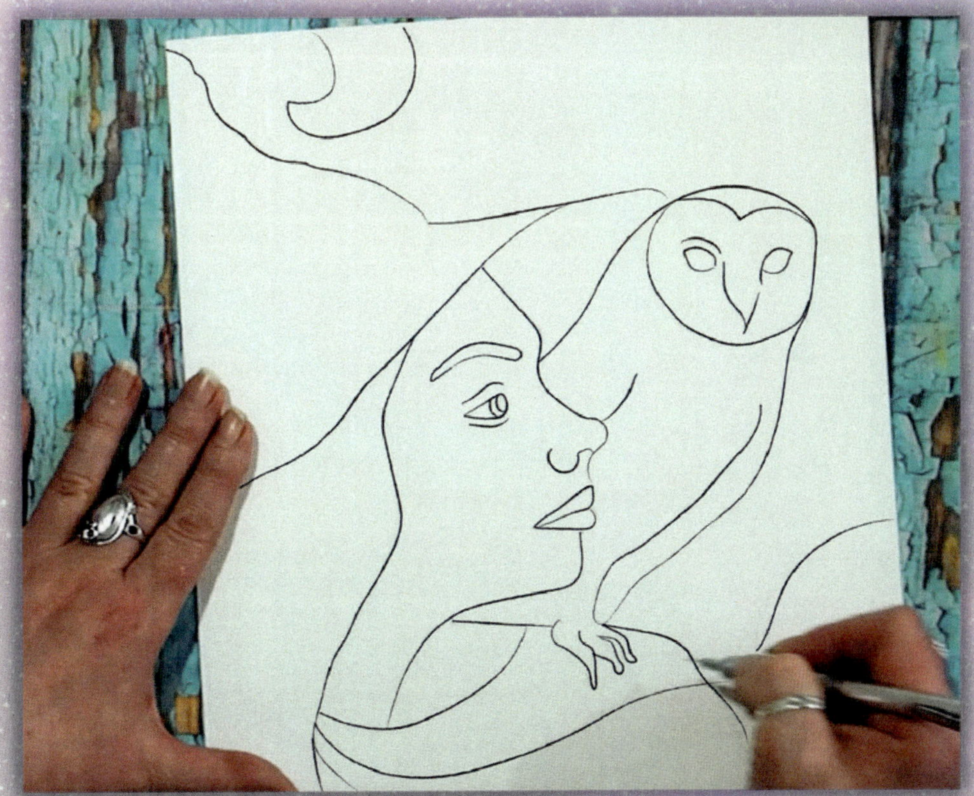

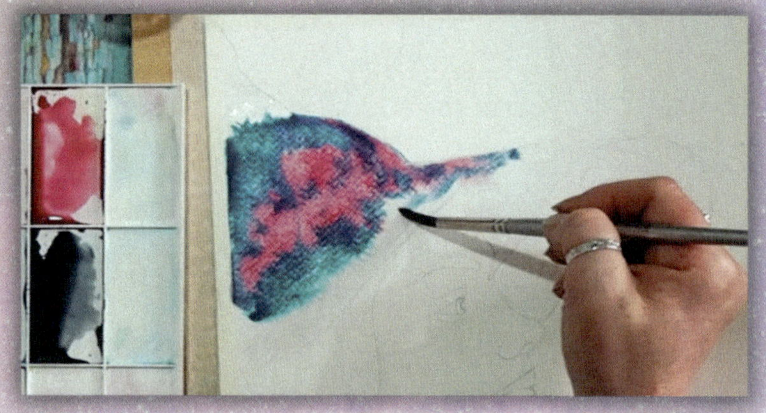

We will start with the galaxy hat. First, gather some of your favorite pinks and blues. Use a clean wet brush to dampen your paper all over the hat area and begin by dropping in the colors loosely, letting them blend naturally. Don't overwork it but let them do their magical watercolor thing!

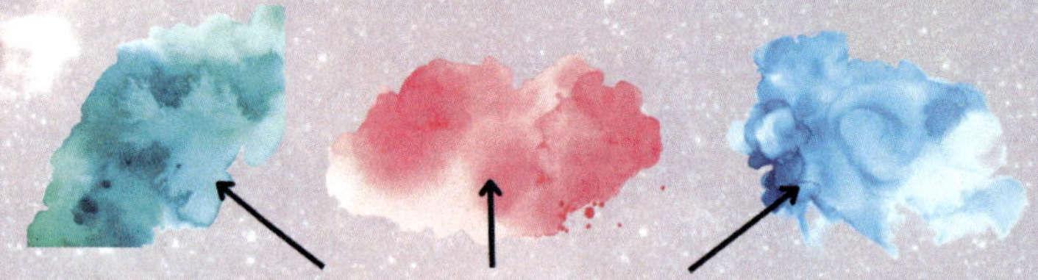

These colors go well together.
Be careful to keep them separate on your hat.
Mixing them will create a brown mud color!

Drop in darker tones of blue or even some Paynes grey or black along the rim. Work quickly while your paper is still damp. If your paper starts to dry, wait for it to dry completely, then add more water and begin again where you left off.

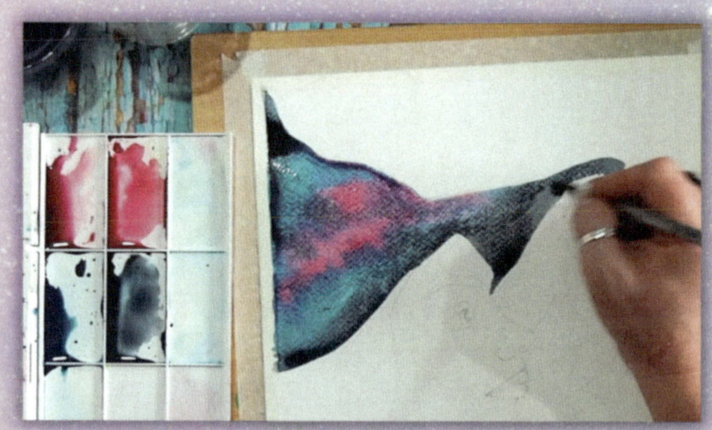

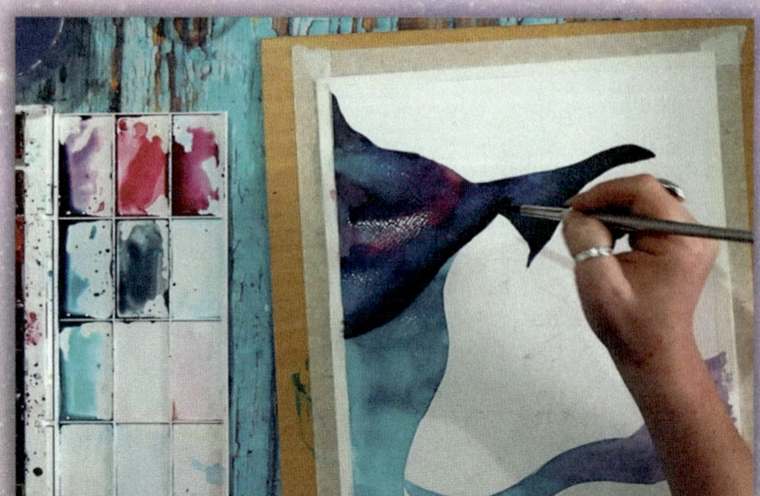

If your first layer is not dark enough, you can paint a second layer on top of the first ONCE the first layer is completely dry (you can use a heat gun or hair dryer to speed up this process).

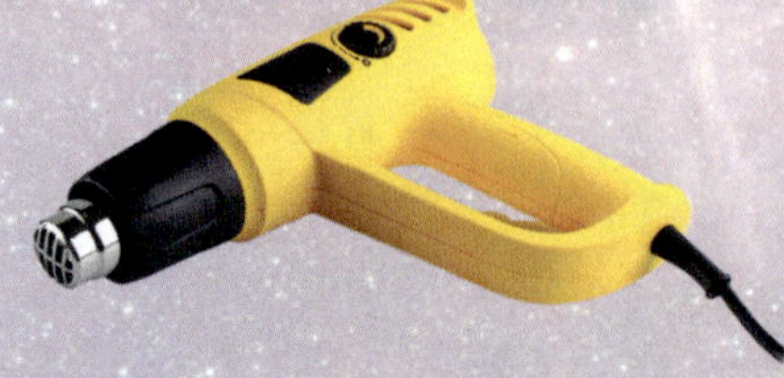

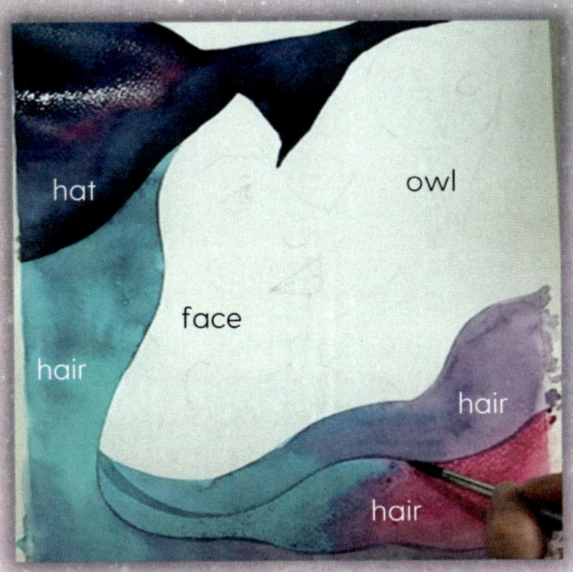

You don't need to wait until the whole hat is dry before painting the hair, but let the rim part dry so that it doesn't bleed down into the hair. Mix up some turquoise, purple and pink, and paint a flat wash for the hair.

Make sure you mix up enough paint so you don't need to make a new mix half way through!

Now we are going to start painting the face. You can either use a skin tone watercolor palette or make a mix with some Naples yellow/Alizarin crimson. Make it pale by adding a lot of water and begin to paint in the face, adding in more paint around the shadow areas (eyes, under the chin etc).

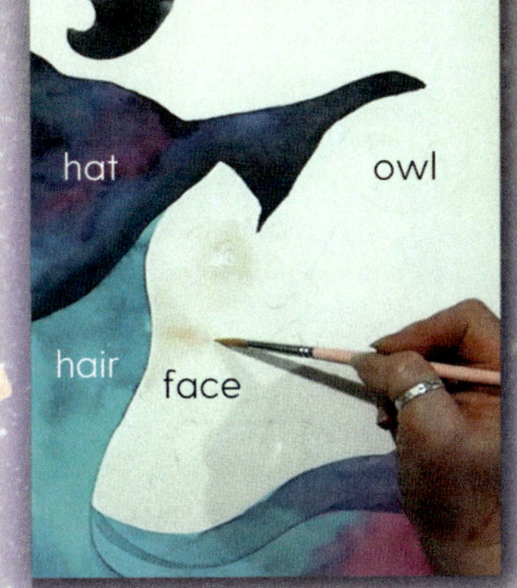

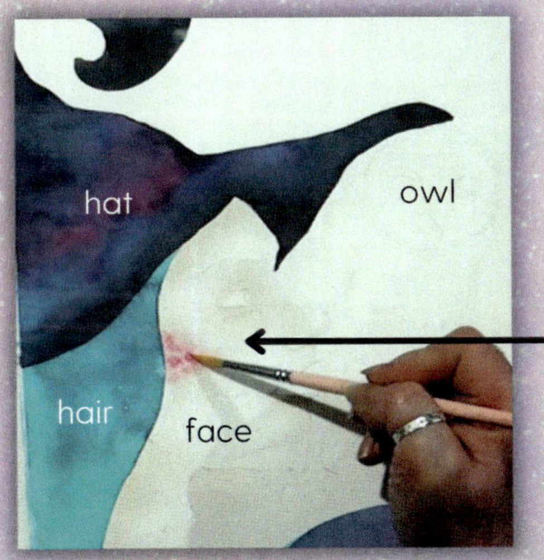

You can blend out your color by using a second, wet brush and blending it out to the lighter areas such as the cheekbones.

While your paper is still wet, drop in some pink tones in the hollow of the cheeks, and on the nose, around the eyes, and on the neck.

Once this first layer of the face is dry, you can begin to paint in the eyes and eyebrows. Use the same colors you used in the hat to paint in the darker line along the top and the iris/pupil. Remember: if your paint is still wet, anything you put next to it will bleed and mix. So if you want precise clear lines wait for your paint to dry before painting anything next to it!

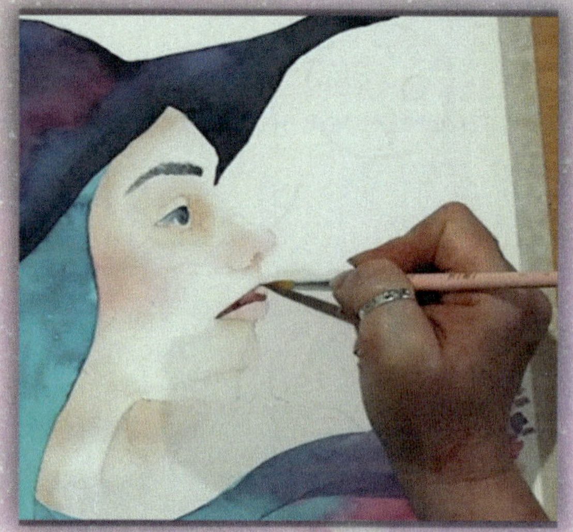

We will now start to build up the layers of paint on the face to create depth. You can work your way around the face so you don't have to wait for each part to dry before continuing. For the lips, mix up some pink and brown. Note: the top lip is always darker than the bottom one so use more brown to make a darker shade.

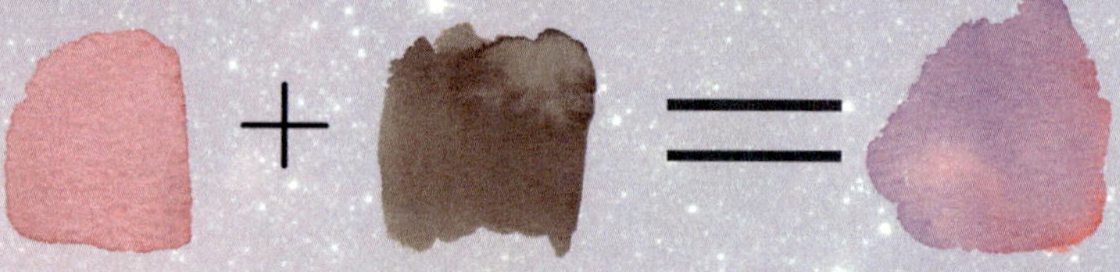

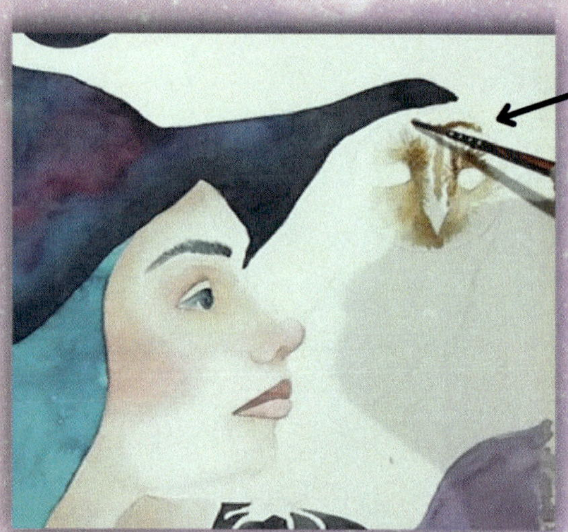

While we wait for the lips to dry, we will start painting the owl. Starting with the head, use a smaller paint brush to paint in some burnt umber and yellow ochre around the eyes and beak. Make brush strokes that go in the direction of the coat.

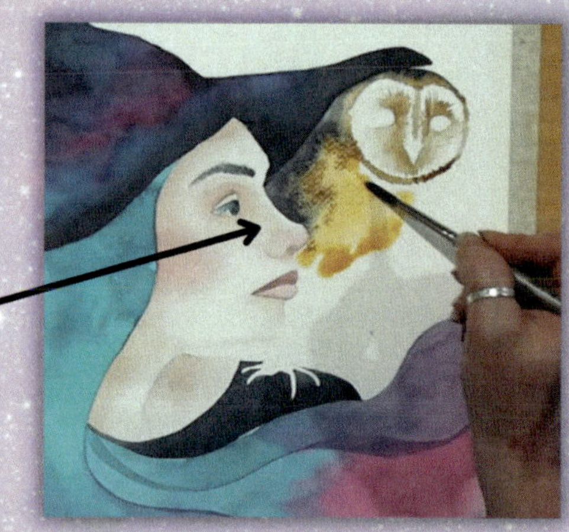

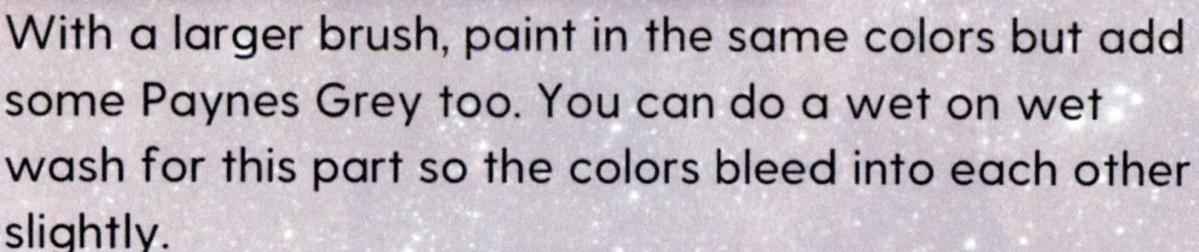

With a larger brush, paint in the same colors but add some Paynes Grey too. You can do a wet on wet wash for this part so the colors bleed into each other slightly.

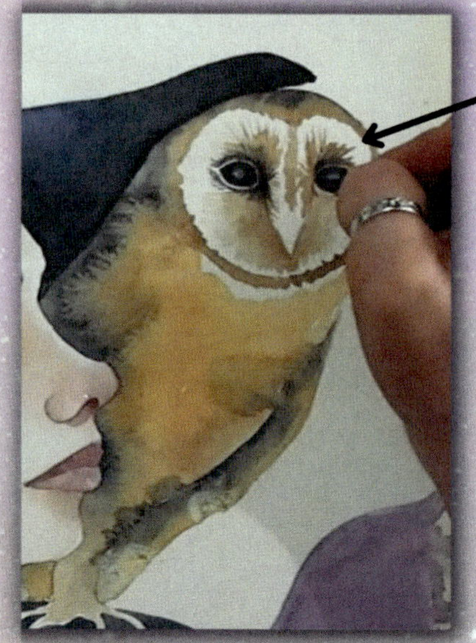

Let the first layer of the owl dry completely before moving on to the next layer. Be sure to capture the outline marks of the head (around the owl's face). This helps define the face and shows where it separates from the body area. Paint in some darker tones using Paynes Grey and some Burnt Umber.

Again, paint your brushstrokes in the same direction as the feathers grow. Don't worry about leaving lighter areas for the eye highlights. You can always add twinkles in later using white gouache or a paint pen.

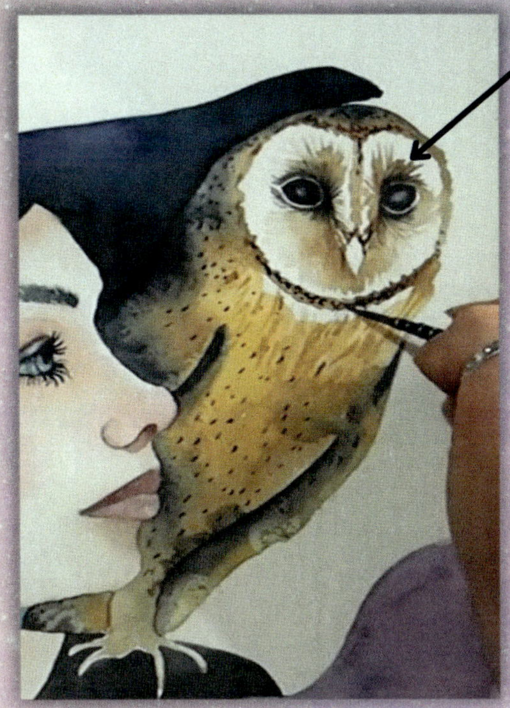

For the owl's body, use your brush to indicate the texture of the feathers, especially around the face area. This type of owl has little black spots on its body. Use Paynes Grey (rather than black) as it's a more subtle color. We will add in some white areas later! Paint some dots on the body - but don't make them too uniform!

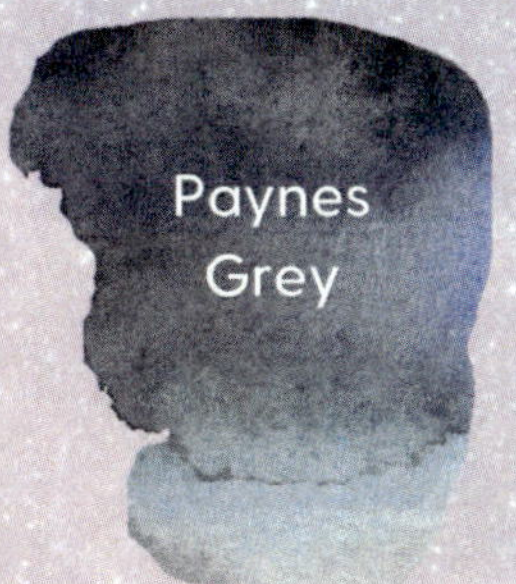

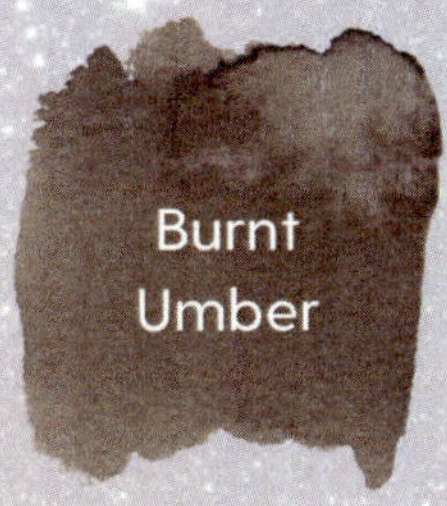

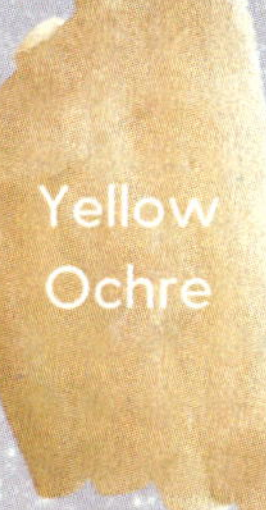

Paynes Grey, Burnt Umber and Yellow Ochre are perfect colors for the owl.

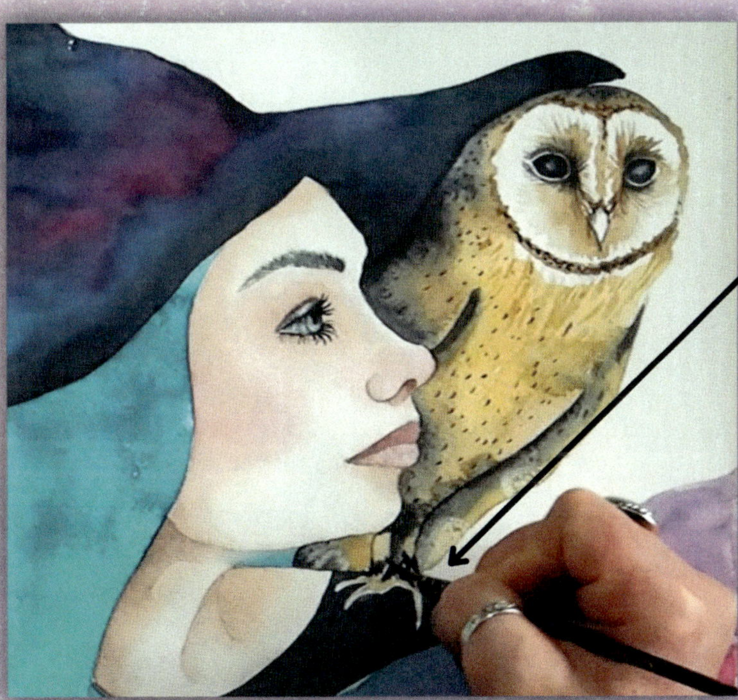

You can also paint in some texture marks around the feet! Just make little scribbly lines to mimic the look of the skin on this part of the owl's body.

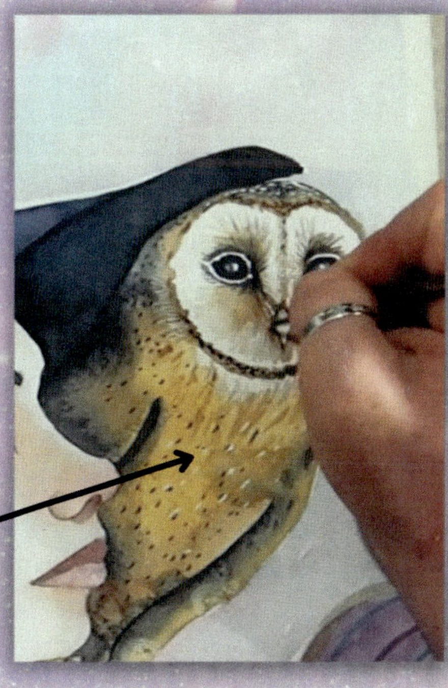

Finish the owl by using your Ph Martin Bleed Proof White or some white gouache.

Add white highlights to the eyes, some fine white feather strokes around the face and some white dots on the body.

Let's return to the face now that the owl is complete. It is always helpful to move to different areas when painting with watercolor. This gives each part a chance to dry while you work on the next area. This is especially helpful when you need to do several layers with your watercolors on your piece.

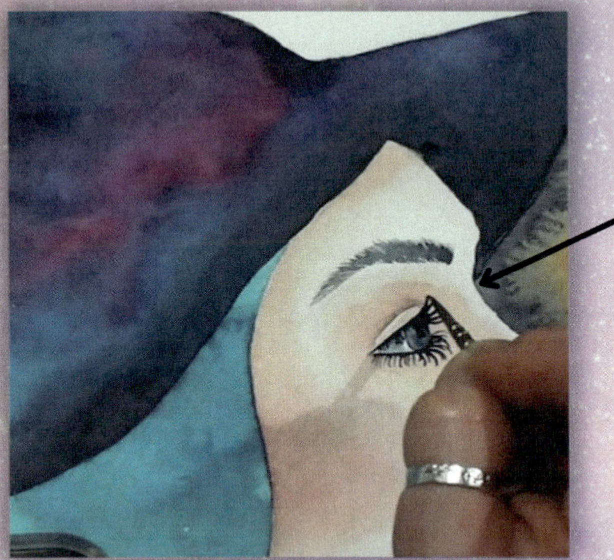

Use a detailer brush to paint in the eyelashes. I used the same Paynes Grey, but this time I added MORE pigment and LESS water so it was darker. Paint fine lines along the eyebrows to make them appear more realistic.

Next we will define the chin. Apply some Burnt Umber under and along the jawline and neck. Use a second brush with just clean water to blend it out.

Also use this technique to add a shadow. This will help define where the neck meets the shoulder.

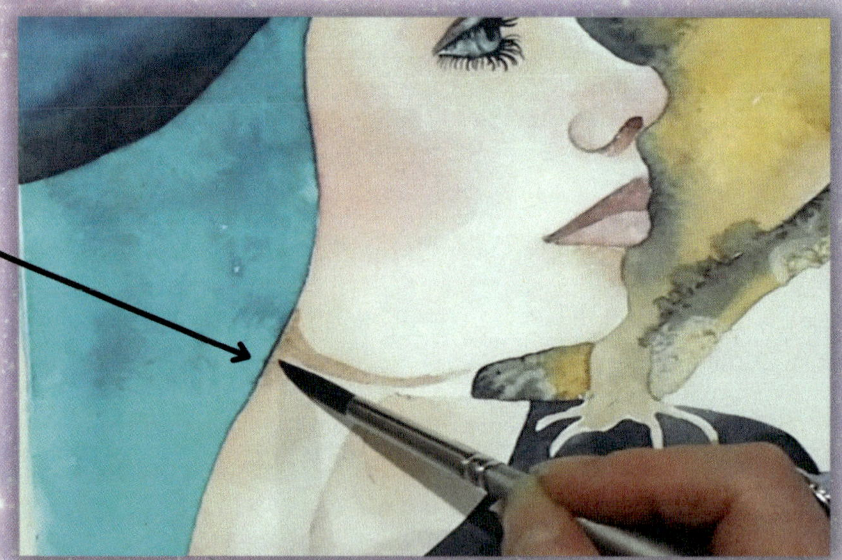

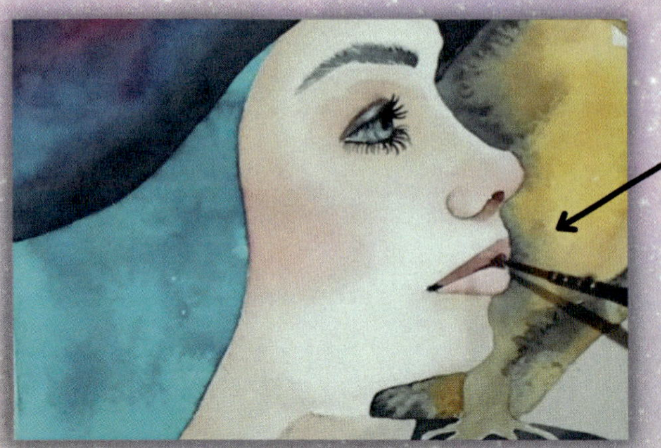

Add in another layer of dark brownish/pink to the upper lip. Watercolors dry lighter than when they first appear on paper, so sometimes you have to go back in and add a second layer.

Add in a second glaze on the hair to make it more interesting. We aren't trying to get "realistic" hair here. Adding some of the hair strands looks really lovely!

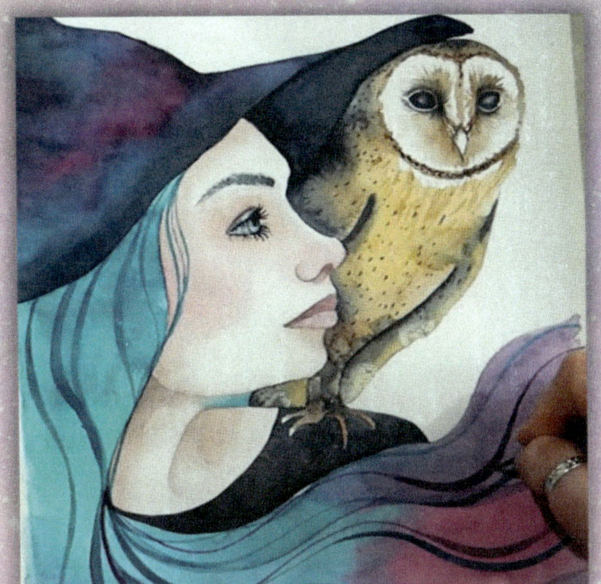

Using a darker mix of the purple and turquoise, and a thin brush (a rigger is good for this!) paint in some hair strokes on top of your original hair layers. It looks more interesting if you make the strokes thick and thin. You can do this by alternating how much pressure you apply to your brush as you create strands from root to tip!

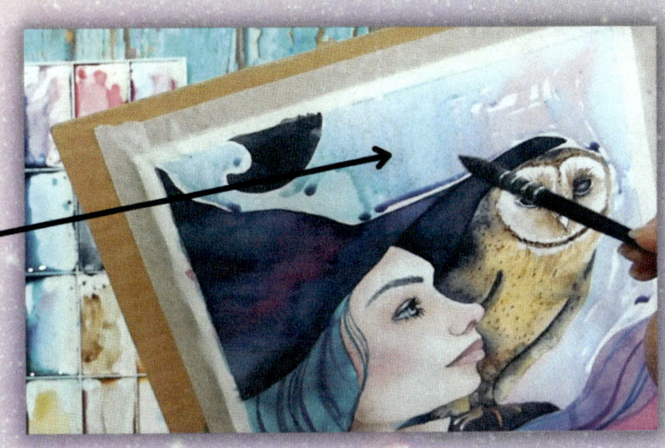

For the background, paint a pale wash of pinks and blues. You can tilt your board and let the colors run to create some interesting effects! If you do this, just make sure it doesn't run onto your witch or owl!

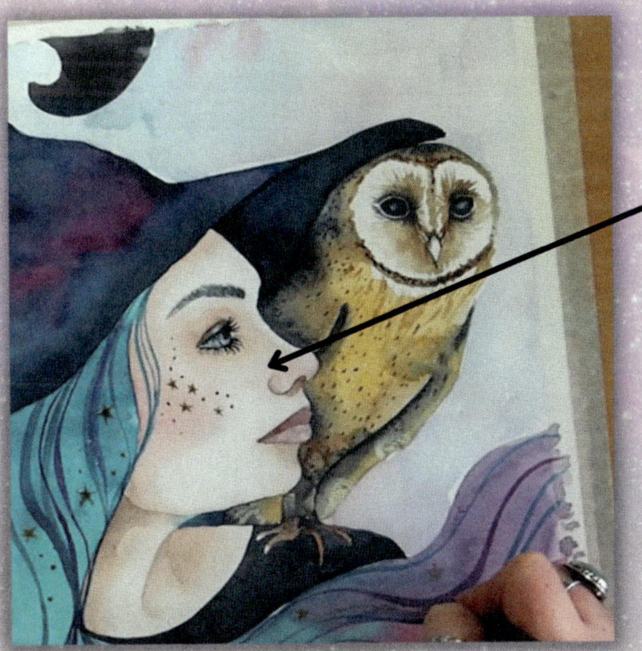

We are going to add some sparkle! With some gold watercolor (or acrylic ink/gouache) paint some stars to add some bling! Paint some witchy symbols on her dress and a star at the tip of her hat for more fun!

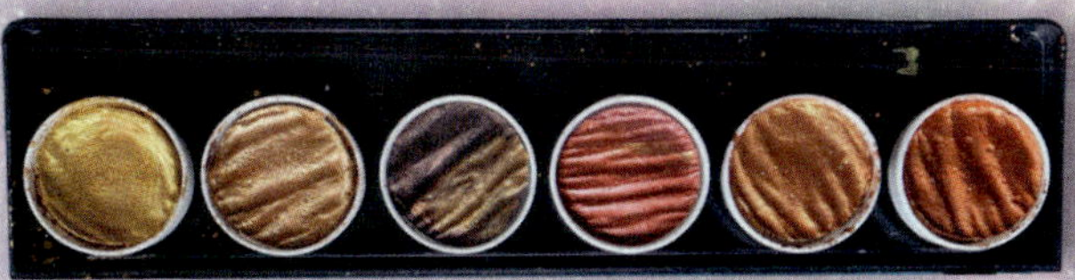

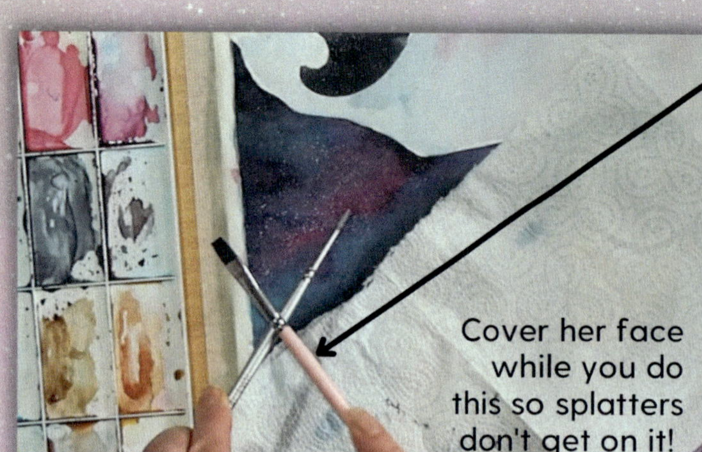

Add stars to your galaxy hat by gently tapping two paintbrushes together. Doing so will splatter small dots of white gouache to look like stars!

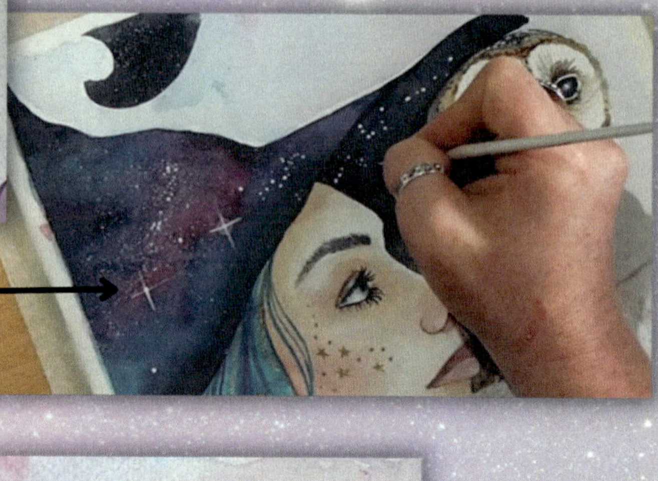

Finally, paint in some larger stars in random places to make it even more magical! And we are finally finished!!

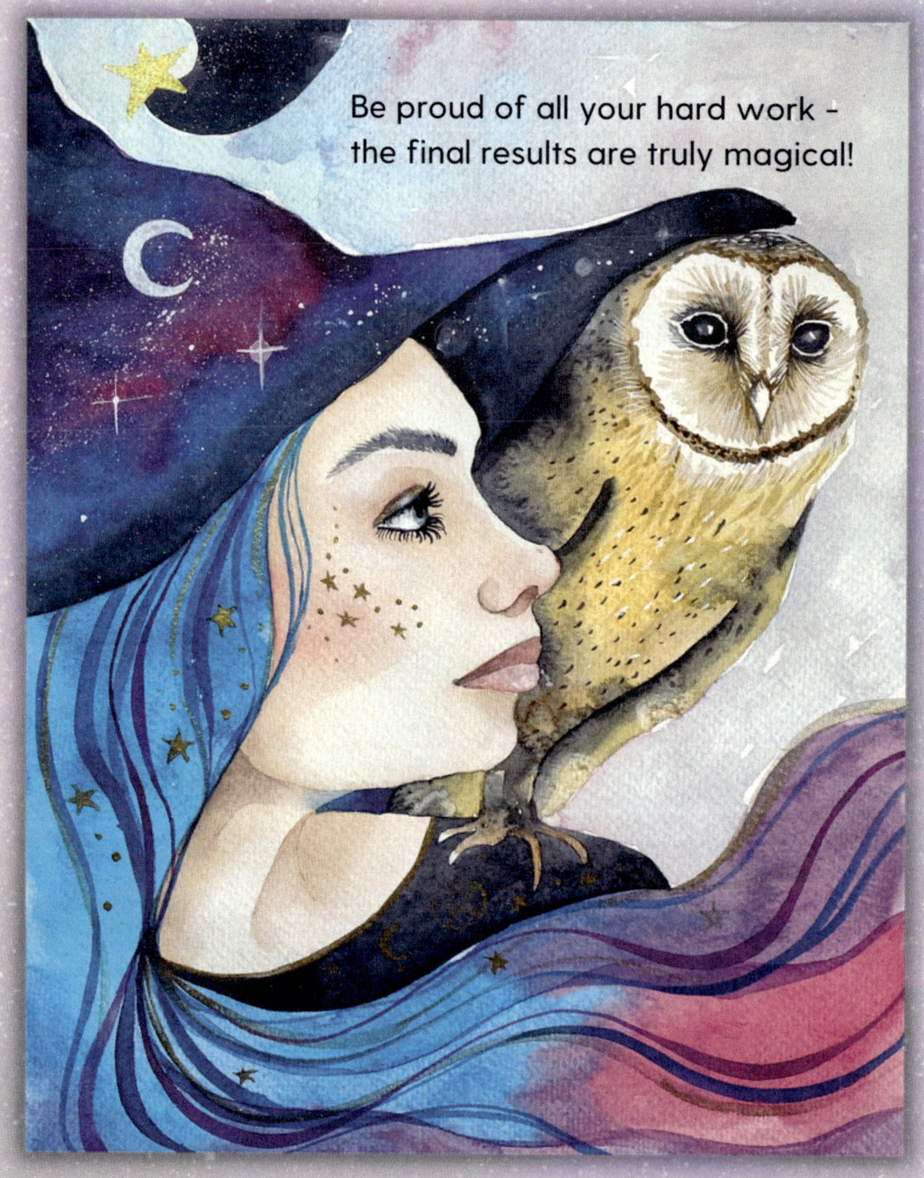

Snow Queen

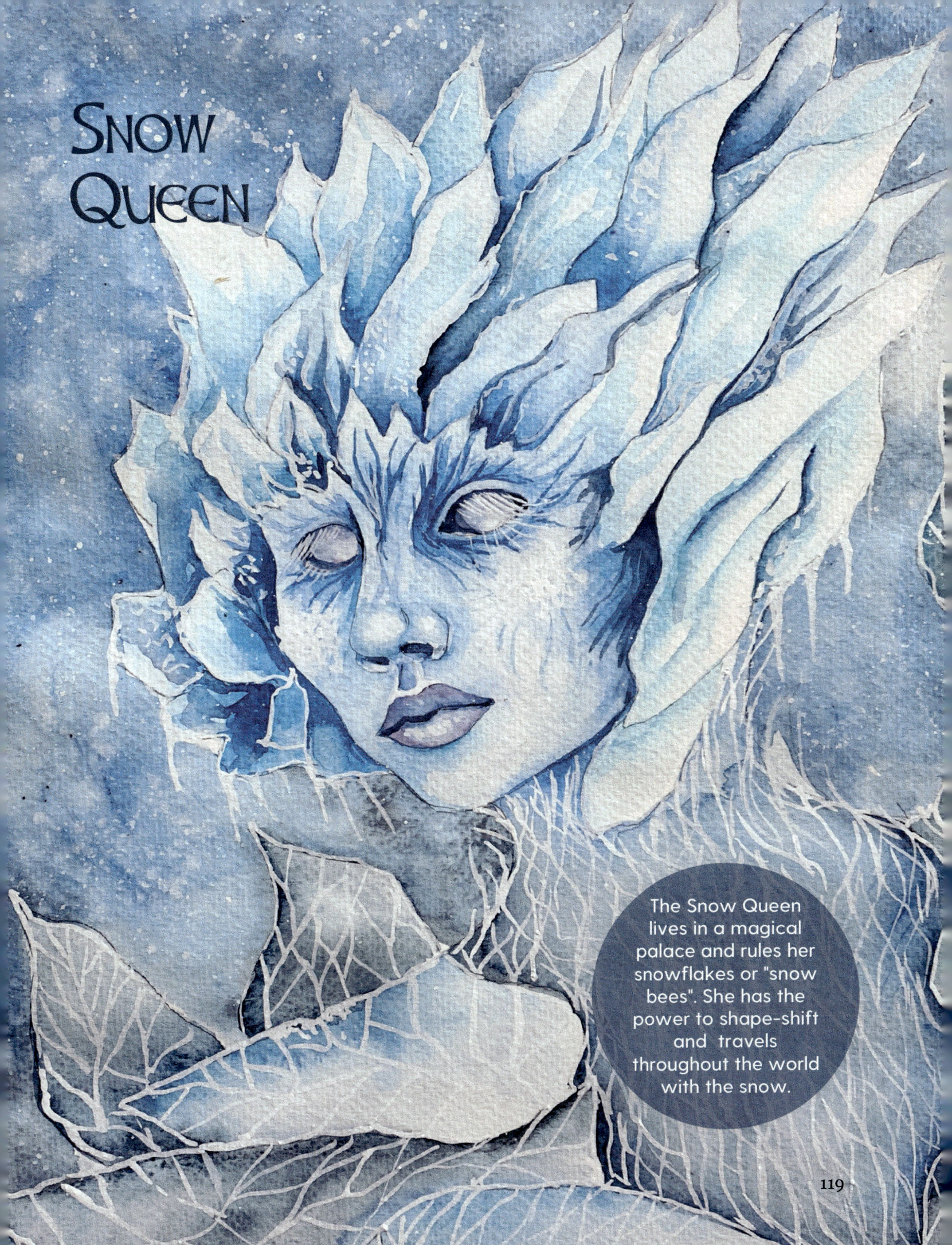

The Snow Queen lives in a magical palace and rules her snowflakes or "snow bees". She has the power to shape-shift and travels throughout the world with the snow.

Supplies

Watercolor paper 140lbs
Pencils
Masking tape
Lightbox for transferring your design
Water
Bleed Proof white or white gouache
Selection of paintbrushes
Gouache in various blues
CANSON
WINSOR & NEWTON
ARTEZA
GOUACHE COLORS
BLEED PROOF WHITE

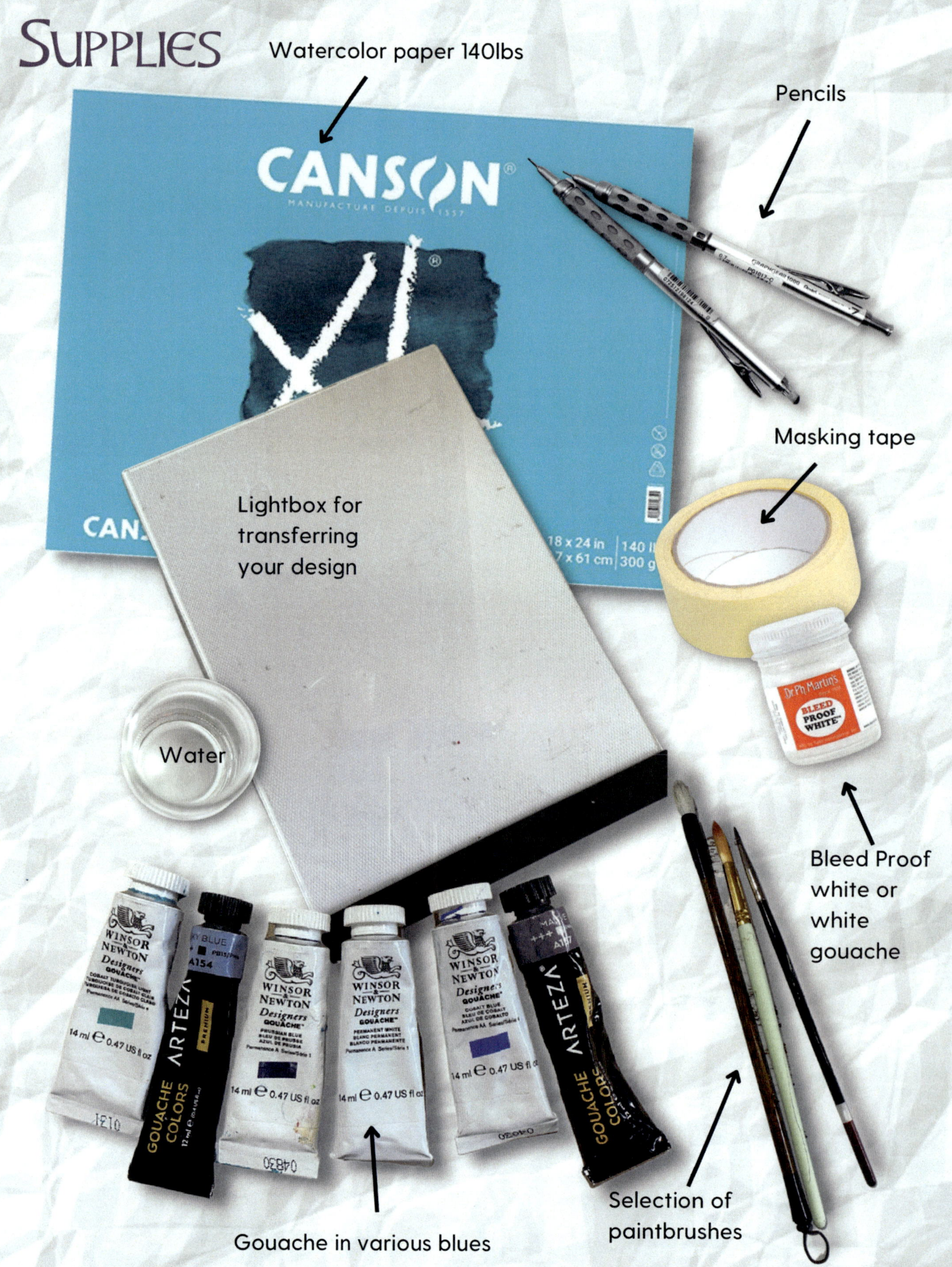

This is a royalty free reference from Canva! Isn't it just perfect for a snowy Fae Queen?! We will concentrate on her face so we don't have to worry about painting her hands (you're welcome!).

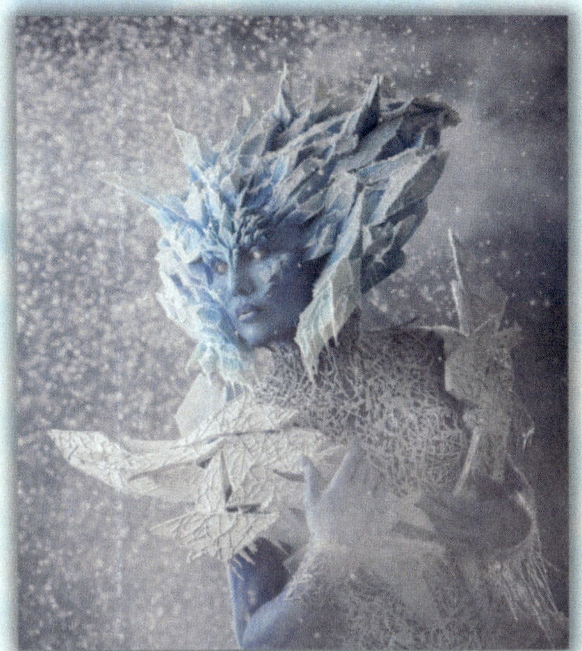

If you like, you can trace this image but it's always good fun to stretch your drawing skills by drawing freehand! It develops your drawing and observational skills and the more you do it the easier it gets. Plus, your finished painting does not need to look like an actual copy of this image - feel free to change it up a bit!

Just like you did with the witch, you can put some tracing paper over the original image and draw the guidelines if it helps you see where they should go.

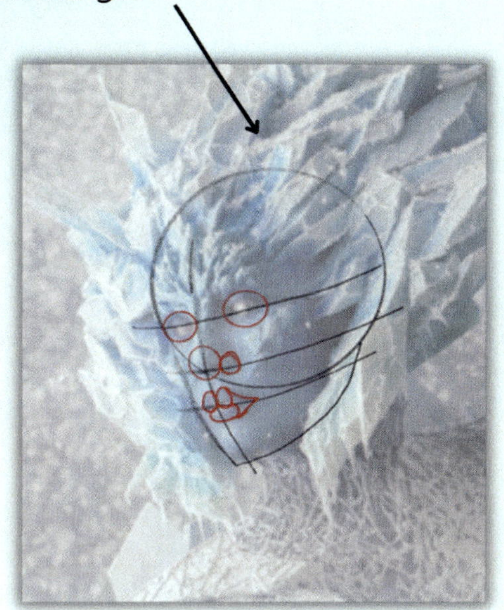

We are drawing a 3/4 face. Start with a large circle for the shape of the head and a loose triangle below it for the jaw. Then, draw the curved guidelines as shown. We will use these to help us place the eyes, nose and mouth!

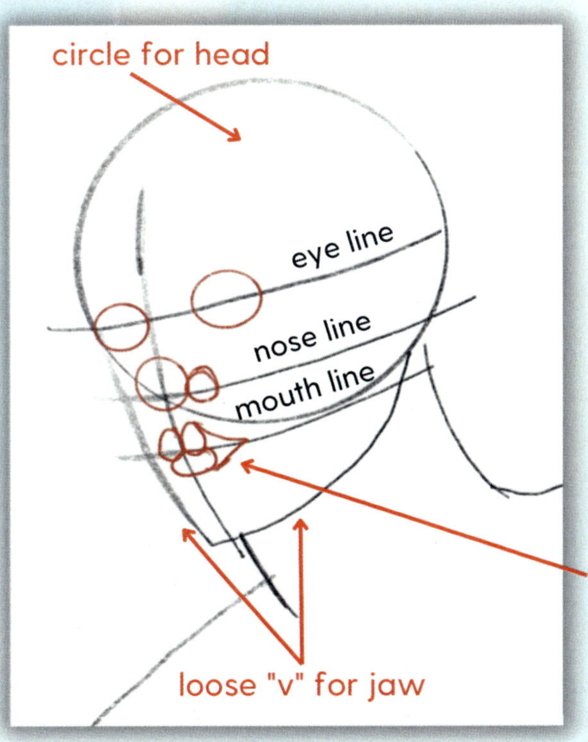

The red circles indicate where the eyes, nose, and mouth will be placed, based on the guidelines we just drew. Pay close attention to the placement of the features.

For the mouth, draw three ovals with and a sideways "v" shape to indicate the side of the mouth that's visible from this angle.

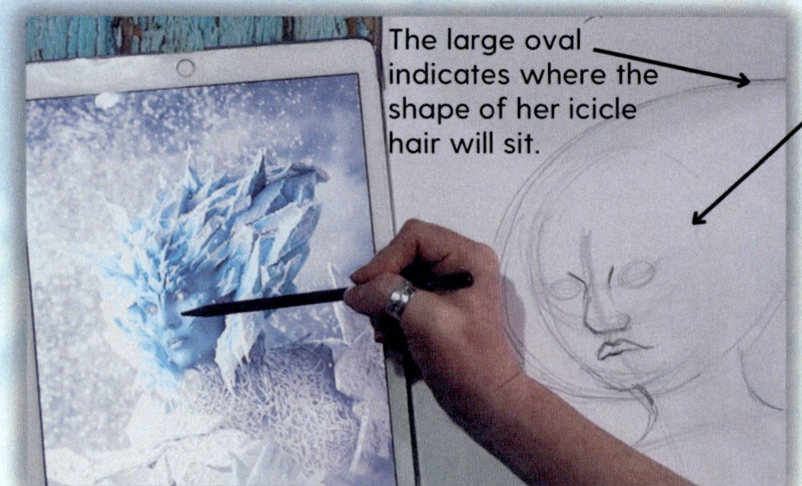

The large oval indicates where the shape of her icicle hair will sit.

Once you have sketched out the guidelines, you can begin to refine the features.

Sketch on scrap paper now, so you can transfer your drawing onto watercolor paper when you're ready to paint.

Sketch and refine the main shapes of the eyes, nose and mouth as necessary. Don't worry about putting in too much detail at this stage.

Refine the shape of the left side of the face. Notice how it bulges slightly where the cheekbones and lips are.

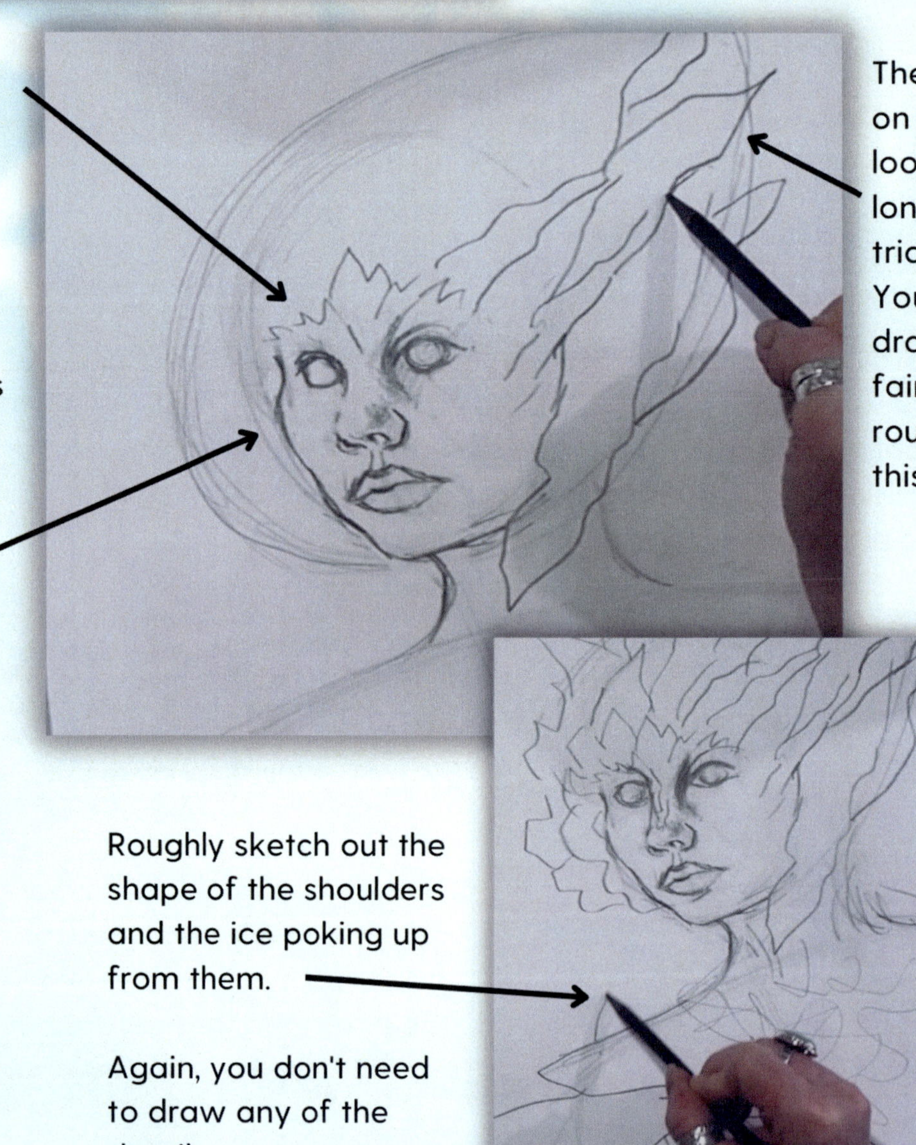

The icicles on the hair look like long wiggly triangles. You can draw them fairly roughly on this sketch.

Roughly sketch out the shape of the shoulders and the ice poking up from them.

Again, you don't need to draw any of the details.

Now you are ready to transfer your sketch to watercolor paper!

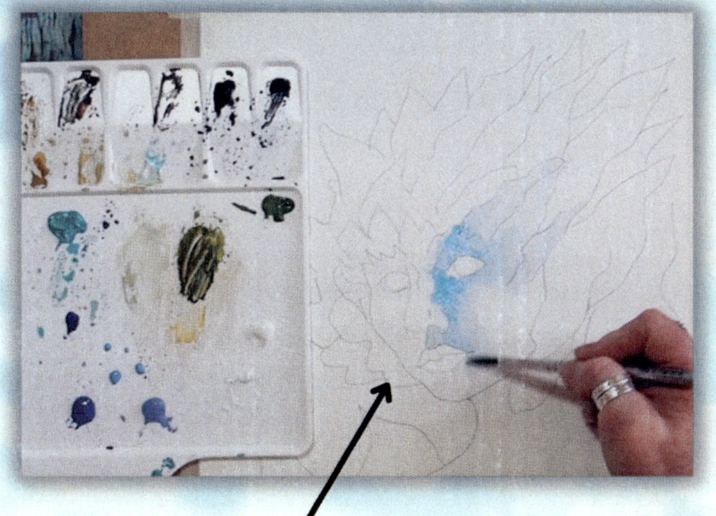

In this project, we will be using the gouache like watercolor, and adding a lot of water. This gives a different effect than using either watercolor or thick gouache. Begin with one shade of blue, I'm using a turquoise.

Use a large brush and a watery mix of the turquoise, begin painting it around the face.

You can use two paintbrushes to make your process a lot easier. Have paint on one brush, and clean water on the other. Apply the paint to the shadows of the face, around the eye sockets and down the side of the nose. Then use the clean brush to blend the color evenly to create the lighter areas.

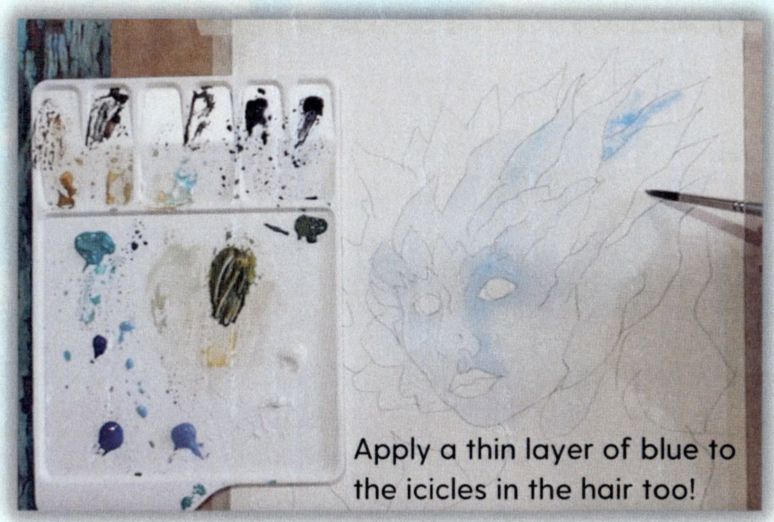

Apply a thin layer of blue to the icicles in the hair too!

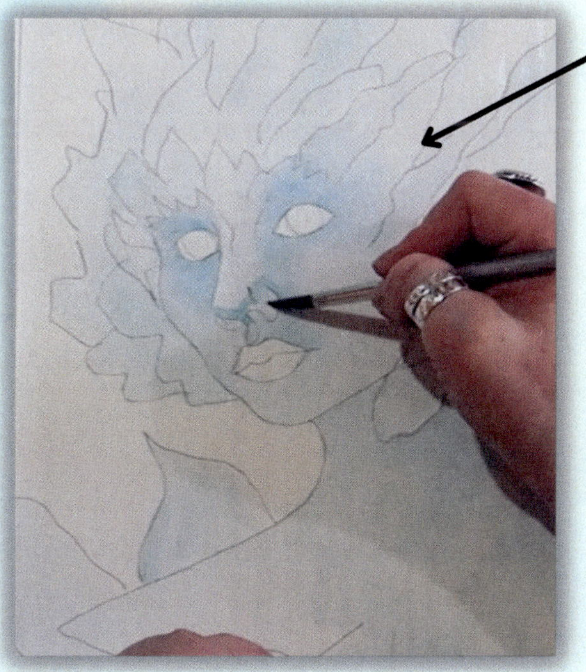

Continue to apply the turquiose blue around the face. Add a second layer if it isn't dark enough.

Add more blue around the nose area to show the shadows. Refer to the reference photo (or my finished piece) to determine where the dark regions are.

At this point, leave the eyes and the mouth free of color.

We will paint them in later!

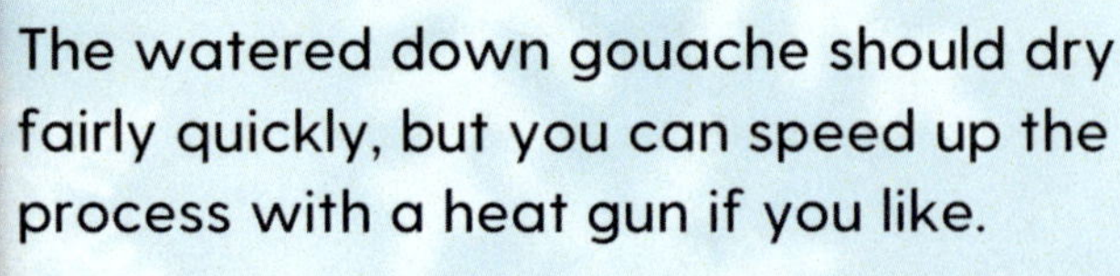

The watered down gouache should dry fairly quickly, but you can speed up the process with a heat gun if you like.

Paint the shades of turquoise over multiple layers. Keep adding layers to darken the shadows but let the previous layer dry first.

For the icicles in the hair, put the darker shadow in the overlapping parts. Using your second, clean, wet brush (loaded with water only) to blend the paint out towards the tip of each icicle. Alternate icicles so that your sections have a chance to dry and they won't bleed into each other.

As your layers get darker, start to add in some the other blues like Cobalt, if desired.

Now, you can paint in the first few layers of the eyes and lips.

The cool part? The eyes in this painting have no irises or pupils. Freaky!

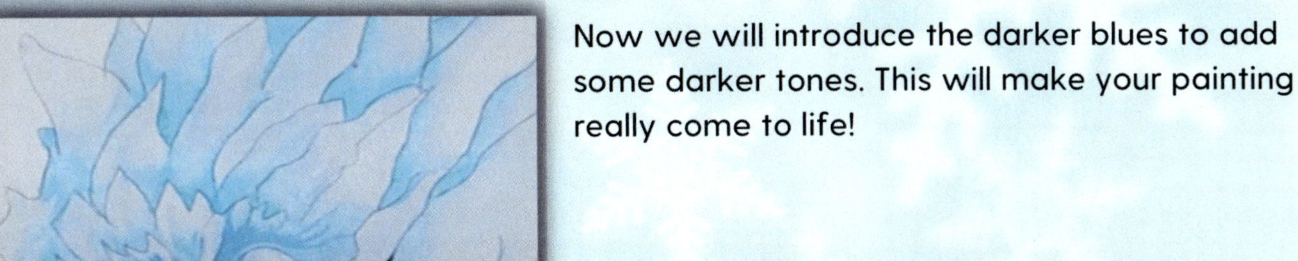

Now we will introduce the darker blues to add some darker tones. This will make your painting really come to life!

In addition to Cobalt, Prussian Blue is also a good choice. You can also experiment with mixing some colors together!

Use a fine brush to paint some darker blue streaks coming out from the eye areas.

Keep using the same dark blue and brush technique to blend the colors as you go around to each icicle section.

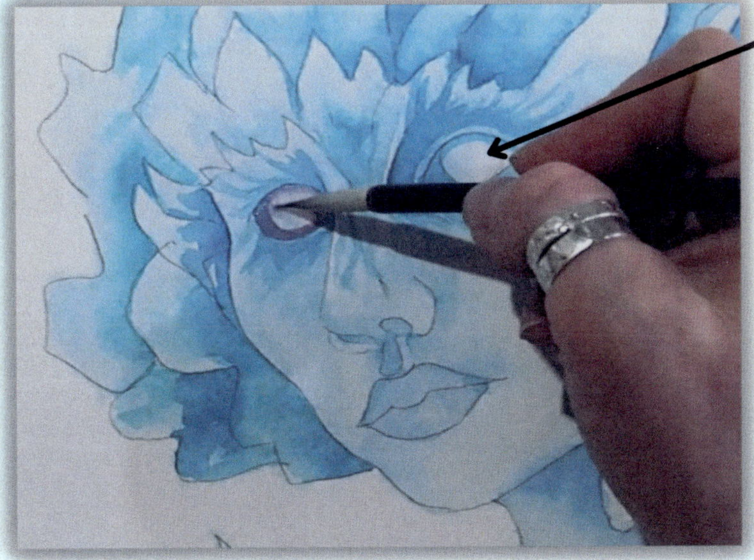

Using a darker blue, use a fine tipped brush to paint a darker in the white of the eyes. They are going to look really spooky!

Just like when you are working with watercolor, move around the page, adding in your layers to gives each part of the paper a chance to dry before you add more layers.

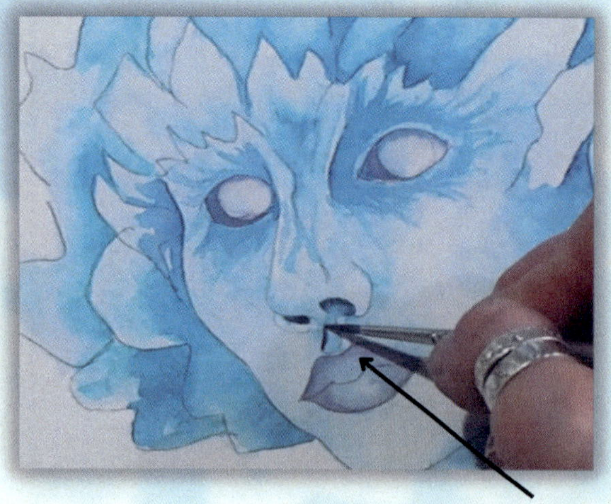

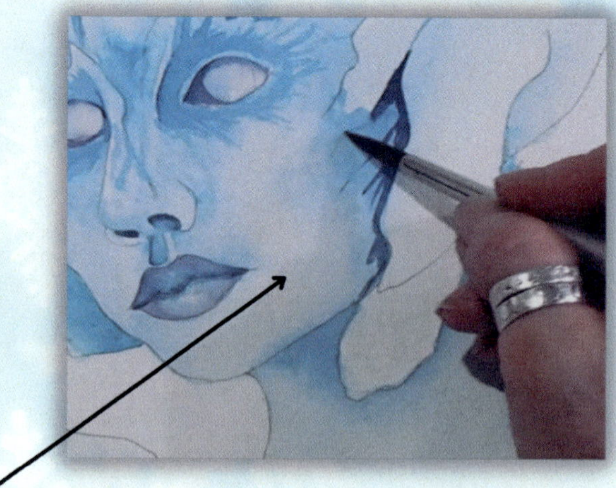

Continue to add in some darker shades around the mouth, nose and where the icicles meet the face. You can blend some of these out with a clean brush, and leave some as defined lines so they look like icy streaks spreading out around eyes and face.

Now we are going to do the background. Use a large brush and spread some clean water all over the paper. You will need to work quite quickly so the paper stays wet!

Then use a large brush and some watered-down turquoise gouache and paint in the background. Because the paper is wet, the color will blend out and cover the area very quickly.

Backgrounds like this are super fun to create because they come together so quickly! Be sure to keep your paper nice and wet and to apply the paint evenly as you go.

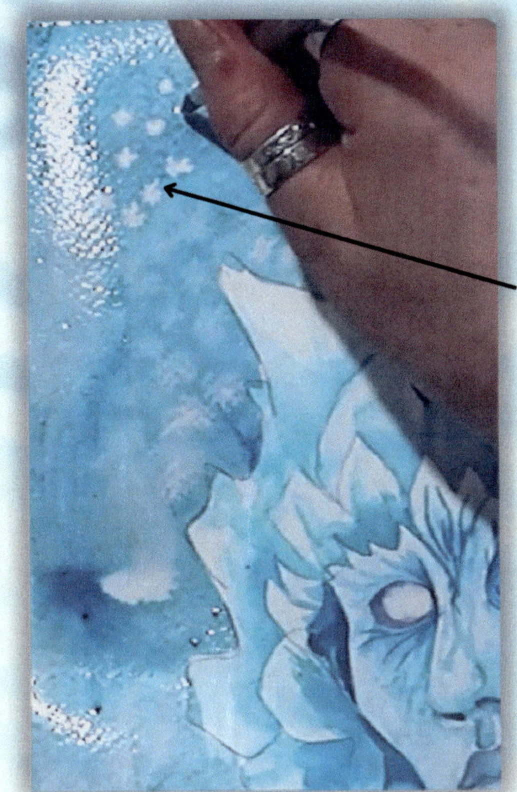

Continue keeping the paper wet for this section.

Take some white gouache and drop it onto the wet paper and into the wet paint. The white gouache will spread out and create lovely mottled patterns. The wetter the paper, the more the white will spread out. When the paper starts to dry, the white will appear even brighter. Like snow!

Paint the bottom part of the Snow Queen (the neck and shoulders) using the same methods as before (adding in watered down gouache and blending out with a clean brush).

An additional technique for applying the spots of gouache is to use two brushes (one loaded with white gouache) and tap them together over your paper.

The gouache will splatter into the background blue and look just like snow.

To create the finishing touches, add in lots of details using white gouache. This will really make it all "come together"! I recommend using Ph Martin Bleed Proof White because it is a super vibrant, opaque white, and perfect for the icy details.

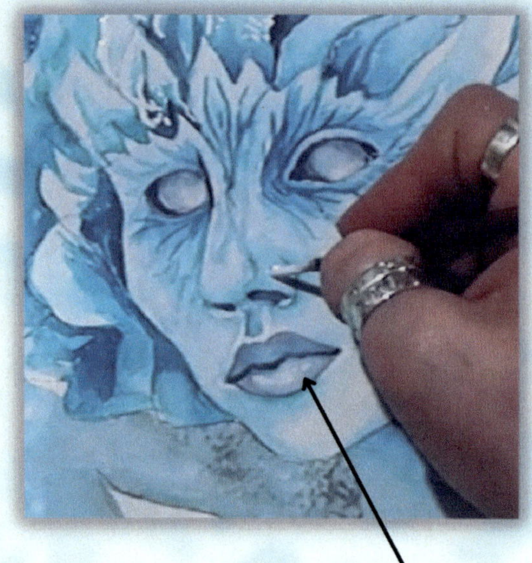

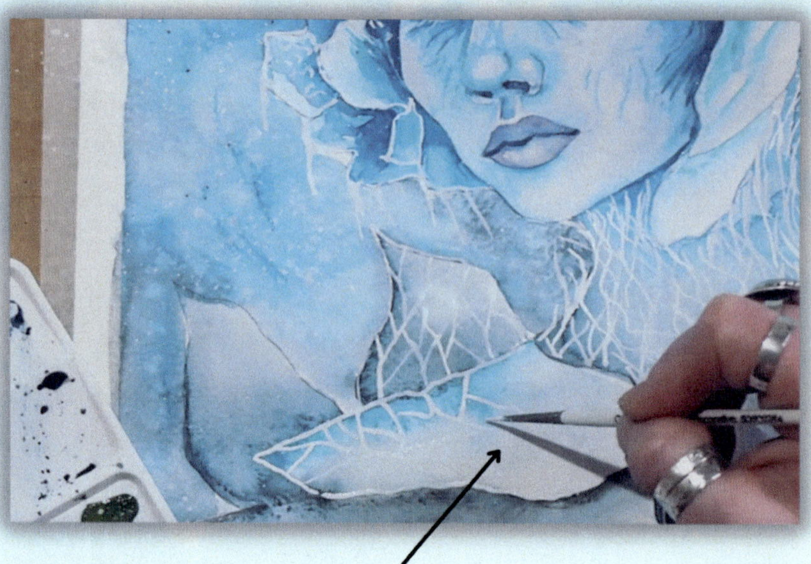

Add white to the parts of the face that have highlights like on the nose, above the lip, chin, and cheekbones. Add some white eyelashes too!

Paint lots of white frosty lines around the icicles of her dress to create the illusion of a loose weave lace.

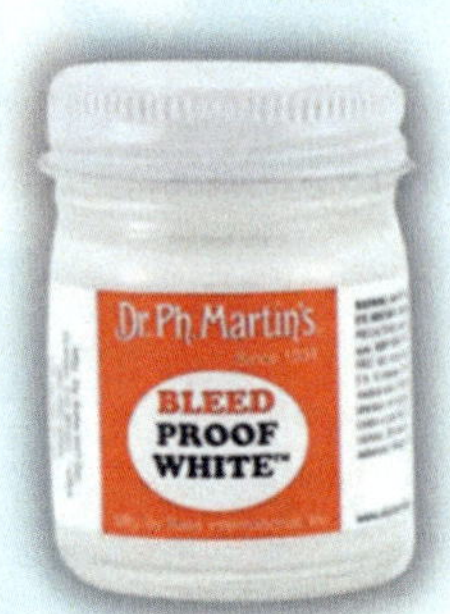

You can see that white has been added to the tips of the icicles, creating the effect that water is dripping down from them!

Do not be afraid to add lots of white drips and splatters and highlights to this painting. She is THE Snow Queen after all!

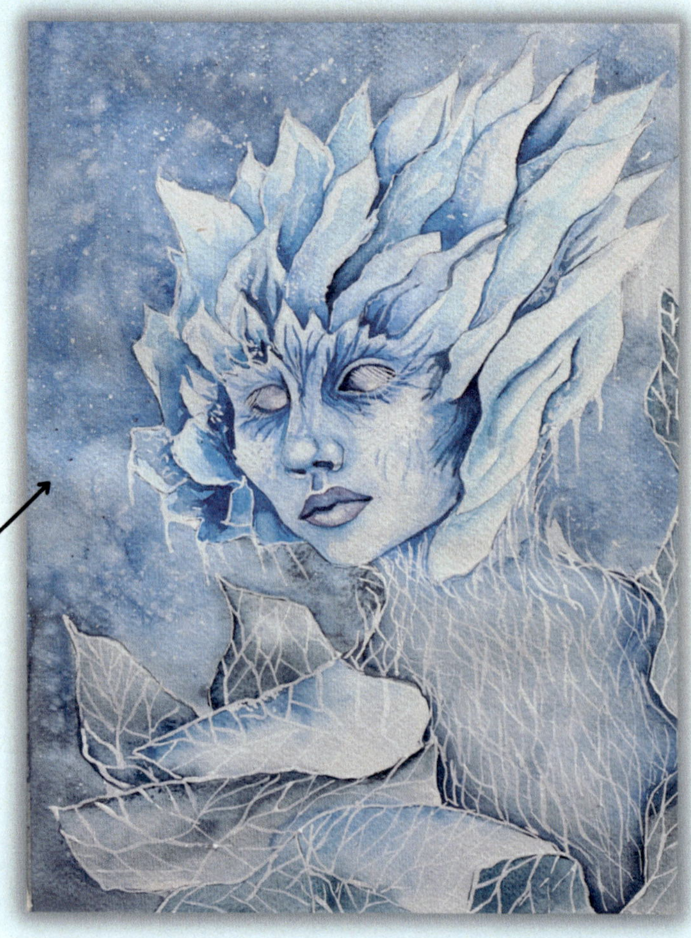

Help with Watercolors and Skin Tones!

We hope you've enjoyed learning to draw and paint with us! Of all the cool creatures we draw and paint, we know that rendering skin tones for humans can be the most challenging (darn humans)! If you'd like to grow your skills when it comes to using watercolors to create dreamy skin tones, Lucy created this 8 page packet for our Celtic Collective students.

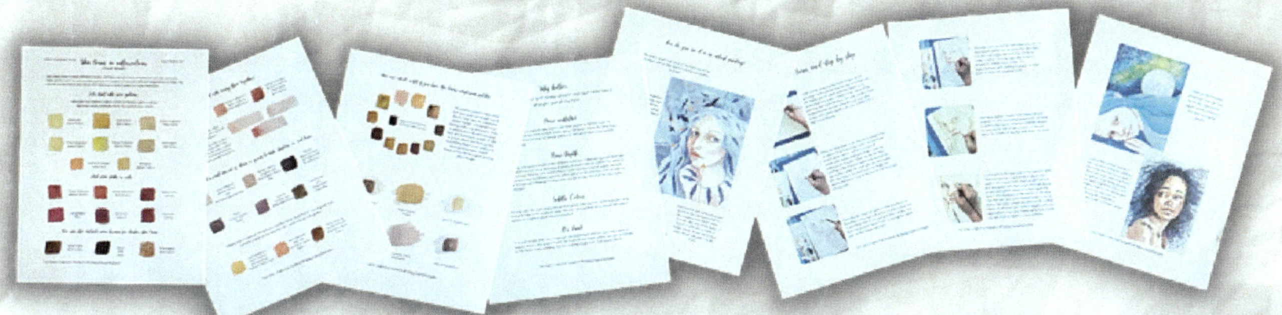

While it's easy and fun to use sets like the Prima Complexion Watercolor Skin Tone set mentioned in the book, it's GREAT to be able to create your own skin tones, from SCRATCH! Buuuuutt, it can be intimidating! Not only does Lucy list colors that work well together, but she also teaches how to add just one or two colors to your existing Prima Complexion set if you're feeling a bit shy about getting fancy :)

We set it up so that you can have it emailed right to your inbox! Simply visit:

https://bit.ly/watercolorskintones

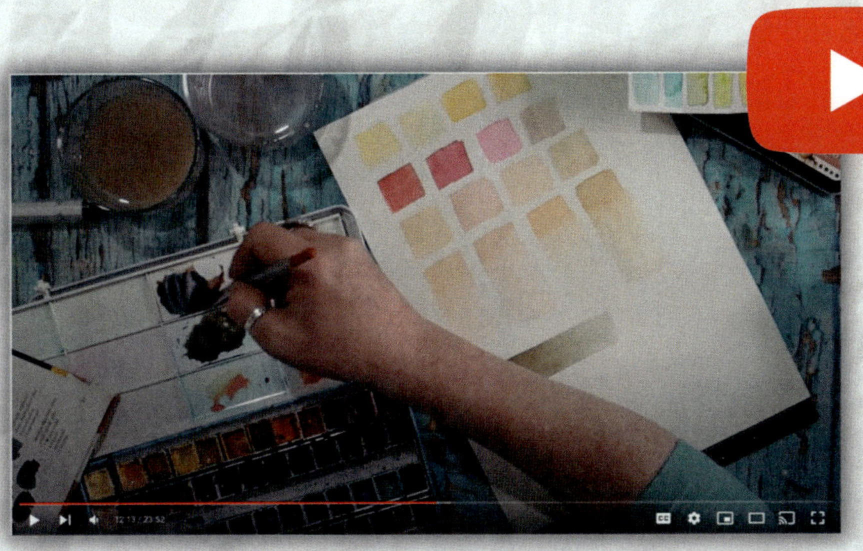

Lucy also created a 24 minute video skin-tone lesson to accompany the 8 page pdf.

We will send them to your inbox when you enter your email at the link above!

Let's connect!

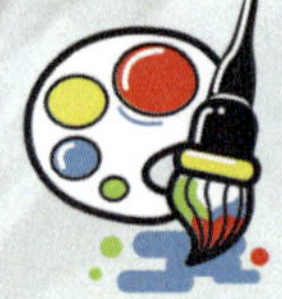

awesomeartschool.com (Karen's online art school website)
lucysartlab.com (Lucy's online art school website)

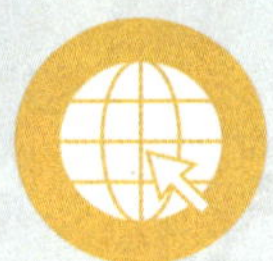

karencampbellartist.com
lucybrydonart.com

youtube.com/karencampbellartist
youtube.com/LucyBrydonArt
youtube.com/1Scot1Not (our joint one for the podcast)

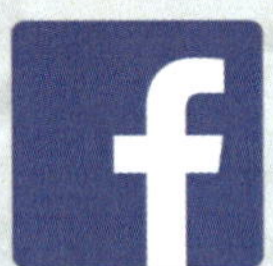

facebook.com/karencampbellartist
facebook.com/art.by.lucybrydon

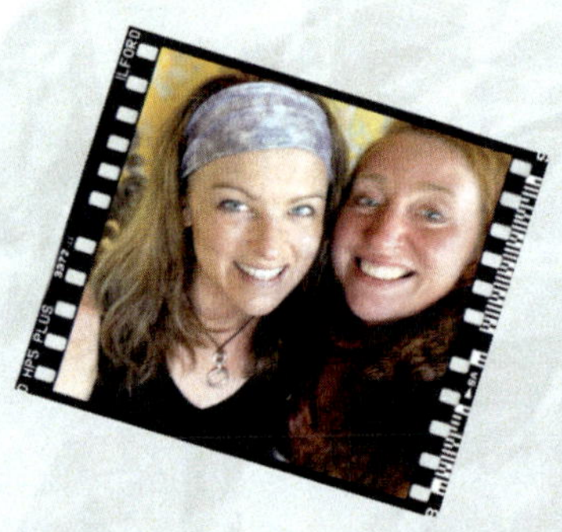

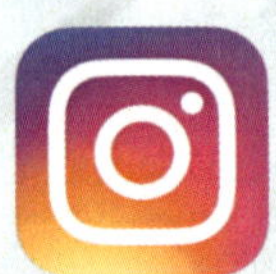

@karencampbellartist
@lucybrydonart

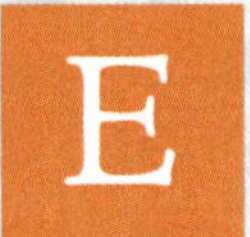

amazon.com/author/karencampbell (links to all art books)
amazon.com/shop/karencampbellartist (links to art supplies)

etsy.com/shop/karencampbellartist
etsy.com/uk/shop/LucyBrydonArt

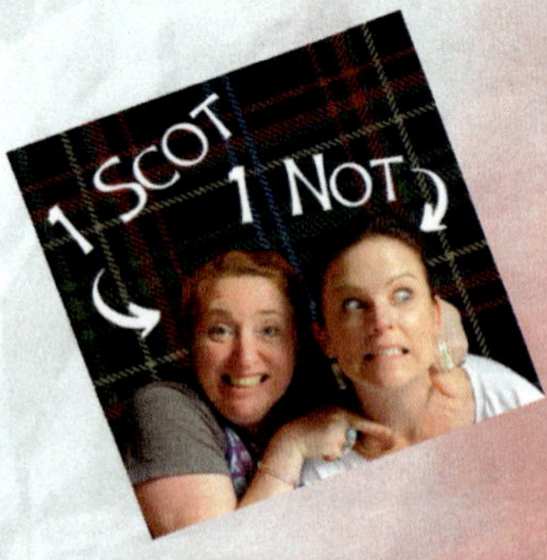

1 Scot 1 Not Podcast (wherever you listen)

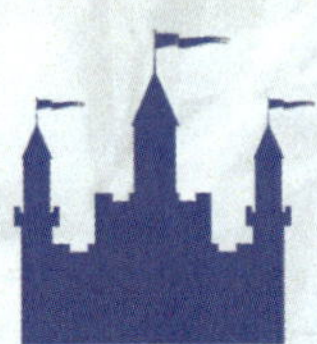

Celtic Collective Waitlist at awesomeartschool.com - add your name for FREE and we'll email you when a spot opens for the most fun fantasy art membership around!

Scottish Castle Art Retreat at awesomeartschool.com (add your name for FREE to the Interest Form and we'll email you when enrollment opens for this annual event. Celtic Collective members get first priority).

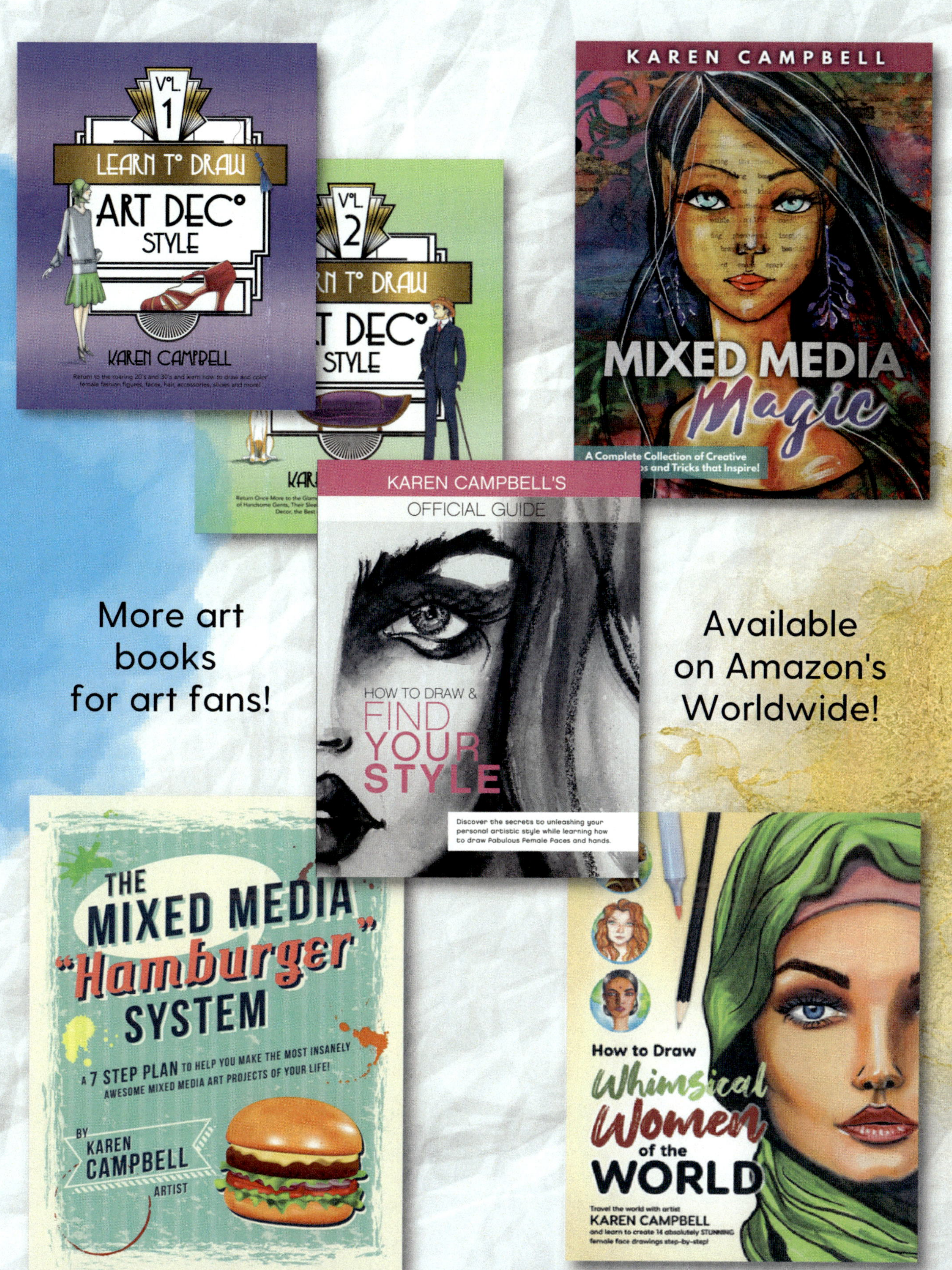
Vol. 1
LEARN TO DRAW
ART DECO
STYLE
KAREN CAMPBELL
Vol. 2
ART DECO
STYLE
KAREN CAMPBELL
MIXED MEDIA
Magic
KAREN CAMPBELL'S
OFFICIAL GUIDE
HOW TO DRAW &
FIND
YOUR
STYLE
Discover the secrets to unleashing your personal artistic style while learning how to draw Fabulous Female Faces and hands.
More art books for art fans!
Available on Amazon's Worldwide!
THE
MIXED MEDIA
"Hamburger"
SYSTEM
A 7 STEP PLAN TO HELP YOU MAKE THE MOST INSANELY AWESOME MIXED MEDIA ART PROJECTS OF YOUR LIFE!
BY
KAREN
CAMPBELL
ARTIST
How to Draw
Whimsical
Women
of the
WORLD
Travel the world with artist
KAREN CAMPBELL
and learn to create 14 absolutely STUNNING female face drawings step-by-step!

Made in the USA
Middletown, DE
16 December 2022